ALSO BY MARTHA GRIMES

RICHARD JURY SERIES

The Man with a Load of Mischief
The Old Fox Deceiv'd
The Anodyne Necklace
The Dirty Duck
Jerusalem Inn
Help the Poor Struggler
The Deer Leap
I Am the Only Running Footman
The Five Bells and Bladebone
The Old Silent
The Old Contemptibles
The Horse You Came In On
Rainbow's End
The Case Has Altered
The Stargazey
The Lamorna Wink
The Blue Last
The Grave Maurice
The Winds of Change
The Old Wine Shades
Dust
The Black Cat

ANDI OLIVER SERIES

Biting the Moon
Dakota

EMMA GRAHAM SERIES

Hotel Paradise
Cold Flat Junction
Belle Ruin
Fadeaway Girl

FEATURING MAUD CHADWICK

The End of the Pier

NOVELS, SHORT STORIES, AND POETRY

Send Bygraves
The Train Now Departing
Foul Matter

MEMOIR

Double Double

THE WAY OF ALL FISH

A Novel

Martha Grimes

Scribner

New York London Toronto Sydney New Delhi

Scribner
Division of Simon & Schuster, Inc.
1230 Avenue of the Americas
New York, NY 10020

First Scribner hardcover edition January 2014

SCRIBNER and design are registered trademarks of The Gale Group, Inc., used under license by Simon & Schuster, Inc., the publisher of this work.

For information about special discounts for bulk purchases, please contact Simon & Schuster Special Sales at 1-866-506-1949 or business@simonandschuster.com.

The Simon & Schuster Speakers Bureau can bring authors to your live event. For more information or to book an event contact the Simon & Schuster Speakers Bureau at 1-866-248-3049 or visit our website at www.simonspeakers.com.

Manufactured in the United States of America

1   3   5   7   9   10   8   6   4   2

Library of Congress Control Number: 2013016760

ISBN 978-1-4767-2395-2

ISBN 978-1-4767-2400-3 (ebook)

"The first thing we do, let's kill all the lawyers."

—*Henry the Sixth, Part Two*

Not quite. Here's to three of the good ones:
Kenneth Swezey, David Wolf, and Ellis Levine

"Reardon [is] behind his age; he sells a manuscript as if he lived in Sam Johnson's Grub Street. But our Grub Street of today is quite a different place . . . it knows what literary fare is in demand in every part of the world, its inhabitants are men of business, however seedy."

—George Gissing, *New Grub Street*

INCIDENT IN THE CLOWNFISH CAFÉ

1

They came in, hidden in coats, hats pulled over their eyes, two stubby hoods like refugees from a George Raft film, icy-eyed and tight-lipped. From under their overcoats, they swung up Uzis hanging from shoulder holsters and sprayed the room back and forth in watery arcs. There were twenty or so customers—several couples, two business-men in pinstripes, a few solo diners who had been sitting, some now standing, some screaming, some crawling crablike beneath their tables.

Oddly, given all that cordite misting the air like cheap champagne, the customers didn't get shot; it was the owner's aquarium, situated between the bar and the dining area, that exploded. Big glass panels slid and slipped more like icebergs calving than glass breaking, the thirty- or forty-odd fish within pouring forth on their little tsunami of water and flopping around in the puddles on the floor. A third of them were clown fish.

All of that took four seconds.

In the next four seconds, Candy and Karl had their weapons drawn—Karl from his shoulder holster, Candy from his belt—Candy down on one knee, Karl standing. Gunfire was exchanged before the two George Rafts backed toward the door and, still firing, turned and hoofed it fast through the dark.

Candy and Karl stared at each other. "Fuck was that?" exclaimed Candy, rising from his kneeling position.

They holstered their weapons as efficiently as they'd drawn them, like the cops they were not. They checked out the customers with their usual mercurial shrewdness, labeling them for future reference (if need be): a far table, the two suits with cells now clamped to their busy ears, calling 911 or their stockbrokers; an elderly couple, she weeping, he patting her; two tables shoved together that had been surrounded by a party of nuts probably from Brooklyn or Jersey, hyenalike in their braying laughter, all still under the table; a couple of other business types with Bluetooth devices stationed over their ears, talking to each other or their Tokyo counterparts; a blond woman, or girl, sitting alone eating spaghetti and reading something, book or magazine; a dark-haired woman with a LeSportsac bag slung over the back of her chair, who'd been talking on her Droid all the while she ate; and a party of four, girls' night out, though they'd never see girlhood again. Twenty tables, all in all, a few empty.

All of that ruin in under a minute.

The Clownfish Café was nothing special, a dark little place in a narrow street off Lexington, its cavelike look the effect of bad lighting. A few wall sconces were set in the stone walls, apparently meant to simulate a coral reef; candles, squat and fat, seeming to begrudge the room their light, were set in little iron cages with wire mesh over their tops, their flames hardly flickering, as if light were treasure they refused to give up. They might as well have been at the bottom of the sea.

Now the brightly colored fish, clown fish, tangs, angelfish of neon blue and sun-bright yellow, were drawing last breaths until the blonde who had been eating spaghetti tossed the remnants of red wine from her glass and scooped up some water and added one of the fish to the wineglass.

Seeing this, Candy grabbed up a water pitcher, dipped up what he could of water, and bullied a clown fish into the pitcher. The other customers watched, liked it, and with that camaraderie you see only in the face of life-threatening danger, were taking up their water glasses or flinging their wineglasses free of the cheap house plonk and refilling them from water pitchers sitting at the waiters' stations. The waiters themselves ran about unhelpfully; the bartender, though, catapulted over the bar with his bar hose to slosh water around the fish. Wading through glass shards at a lot of risk to their own skin, customers and staff collected the pulsing fish and dropped them in glasses and pitchers.

It was some sight when they finished.

On every table was an array of pitchers and glasses, one or two or three, tall or short, thin or thick, and in every glass swam a fish, its color brightened from beneath by a stubby candle that seemed at last to have found a purpose in life.

Even Frankie, the owner, was transfixed. Then he announced he had called the emergency aquarium people and that they were coming with a tank.

"So who the fuck you think they were?" Karl said as he and Candy made their way along the dark pavement of Lexington Avenue.

"I'm betting Joey G-C hired those guys because he didn't like the way we were taking our time."

"As we made clear as angel's piss to him, that's the way we work. So those two spot Hess in there, or they get the tip-off he's there and go in with fucking assault weapons thinkin' he's at that table the other side of the fish tank, and that's the reason they shoot up the tank?"

"Call him," said Candy, holding tight to his small water pitcher.

Karl pulled out his cell, tapped a number from his list of contacts, and was immediately answered, as if Joey G-C had expected a call. "Fuck's wrong with you, Joey? You hire us, and then you send your two goons to pull off a job in the middle of a crowded restaurant? No class, no style, these guys got. Walked in with Uzis and shot the place up. And did they get the mark? No, they did not; they just messed the place up, including a big aquarium the least you can do is pay for. Yeah . . ."

Candy was elbowing him in the ribs, saying, "Tell him all the fish suffocated and died."

"And there was all these endangered fish flopping on the floor, some of them you could say were nearly extinct, like you will be, Joey, you pull this shit on us again. Yeah. The job'll get done when the job gets done. Good-bye."

"We saw Hess leave through the side door. You'd think he knew they were coming."

"Jesus, I'm tellin' you, C., the book business is like rolling around fuckin' Afghanistan on skateboards. You could get killed."

"You got that right."

They walked on, Karl clapping Candy on the shoulder, jostling the water pitcher as they walked along Lexington. "Good thinking, C. I got to hand it to you, you got everyone in the place rushing to save the fishes."

The water was sliding down Candy's Boss-jacketed arm. "Don't give me the credit; it was that blond dame that did that. She was the first to ditch her wine. You see her?"

"The blonde? I guess. What'd she look like?"

Candy shrugged; a little wave of water spilled onto Lexington. "I couldn't see her face good. She had a barrette in her hair. Funny."

"You didn't see her face, but you saw a hair barrette?" Karl laughed. "Crazy, man."

They walked on.

There are those girls with golden hair whom you half notice in a crowd. You see one on the outer edges of vision, in the people flooding toward you along Lex or Park or Seventh Avenue, blond head uncovered, weaving through the dark ones, the caps and hats, your eye catching the blondness, but registering nothing else. Then you find, when she's passed, it's too late.

A girl you wish you'd paid attention to.

A girl you knew you should have seen head-on, not disappearing around a corner.

Such a girl was Cindy Sella.

Some of them would talk about it later and for a long time. The businessmen climbing into a cab, the girl with the LeSportsac bag, her Droid lost inside.

As if there'd been an eclipse of Apple, a sundering of Microsoft, a sirocco of swirling iPhones, BlackBerrys, Thunderbolts, Gravities, Galaxies, and all the other smartphones into the sweet hereafter; yes, as if all that had never been; nobody, nobody reached for his cell once the fish were saved and swimming. They were too taken up with watching the fish swimming, dizzy-like, in the wineglasses.

Nobody had e-mailed or texted.

Nobody had sent a tweet to Twitter.

Nobody had posted on Facebook.

Nobody had taken a picture.

They were shipwrecked on the shores of their own poor powers of description, a few of them actually getting out old diaries and writing the incident down.

Yes, they talked about that incident in the Clownfish Café the night they hadn't gotten shot, told their friends, coworkers, pastors, waiters at their clubs, their partners, wives, husbands, and kids.

Their kids.

—Way cool. So where're the photos?

—Remarkably, nobody took one.

—Wow. Neanderthal.

—But see, there were these neon-bright blue and orange and green and yellow fish, see, that we all scooped up and dropped in water glasses, and just imagine, imagine those colors, the water, the candlelight. Look, you can see it . . .

But the seer, seeing nothing, walked away.

NEW GRUB STREET

2

Cindy Sella walked along Grub Street in the West Village with a clown fish in a big Ziploc bag that Frankie had furnished when she'd asked whether she could keep her fish, the one she had saved, and take it home with her. Yes, he had told her, my pleasure.

As many times as she'd eaten at the Clownfish Café, she could not remember coming across Frankie. He must have been there, somewhere behind the bar or in the kitchen or watching the fish, but she hadn't been observant enough to see him.

That was the difference between today and yesterday.

She thought about the extraordinary episode at the Clownfish as she passed the stingy little trees set in their foot-square patches meant to beautify the streets of Manhattan. They were blooming thinly, their branches mere tendrils. She didn't know what kind of trees they were. This, she thought, was shameful. If someone threatened to beat her with a poker until she named ten trees, she'd be dead on the Grub Street pavement.

Cindy had decided she was one of the least knowledgeable people she knew. And she was a writer. How did she ever manage to create a book without the most rudimentary knowledge of basic facts, such as what this little tree was right outside the door of her building? What reader would want to place himself in the hands of a writer who didn't know that?

Didn't she really know the names of ten trees? Apple cherry lemon orange peach banana. For God's sake, if you were going to name fruit trees, any five-year-old could do it.

Speaking of which, there was one sitting on the stoop of the row house right next door to her building. A five-year-old named Stella something. What was she doing out here at ten at night without her mother?

"Stena!"

Oh, there she was.

"Stena!"

Mrs. Rosini yelling from the doorway. Stena, not Stella, because Mrs. Rosini was adenoidal or perhaps had a cleft palate. You see, Cindy told herself, you don't even know the difference between these physical maladies.

Stella stood up and gazed at Cindy, who said, "Hello."

Stella stuck out her tongue.

"Stena, get in here!"

When Stella turned her back, Cindy stuck out her tongue, too. Then she entered her building.

Cindy liked her apartment building. It was painted white and was only eight stories high. It was dwarfed by the new high-rise co-op across the avenue, which was all metal and glass, glass at odd angles so that the sun staggered around it, drunk with its own light, setting off knifelike reflections. The building ran unsteadily upward to thirty or forty stories. The higher it got, the more it became the sun's broken mirror.

The doorman, Mickey, caught the door as she pushed it. Mickey and his little mouse-brown terrier were standing guard. The dog was tiny enough to carry off in a spoon. With the light from one of the art deco–ish door sconces illuminating the dog, the little scene looked as if it were an illustration by Sempé. A *New Yorker* cover, surely. Sempé with his little cats and dogs.

Cindy said hello to the doorman and bent and patted the terrier. It barked once, and its stubby tail wagged frantically.

Mickey touched the worn shiny brim of his cap. His uniform jacket was not in the best of repair. "Miss. Was your evening full of laughter and music?"

He couldn't just say "hello." No, he seemed to feel he had to make up these things.

"Not unless you count gunfire in a restaurant music."

Naturally, he thought she was joking and snickered and held the door for her.

In Prague or Marienbad or wherever he'd come from in Czecho-slovakia, Mickey had been a dancing master—an improbably roman-tic occupation—and he missed it passionately, as he missed Prague (or Marienbad).

Cindy was from a small town near Topeka, Kansas, where she had been not a dancing mistress but a cashier in a Walmart, which she con-sidered the most soul-depleting job in the universe. At night, she took classes at a community college, among them creative writing. She had discovered she could write. Short stories, then a novel. Naively, she had brought her novel to New York. Then she went back to Kansas and wrote another one.

After Mickey's long good night that rivaled Raymond Chandler's good-bye, Cindy stepped inside the elevator. It was always waiting as if it, too, had a tale to tell, and she rode, listening to its story of who'd gone up or come down that day before she landed at her floor.

She walked on the generic beige carpeting, along the corridor painted in Calamity White (a person at Duron with a sense of humor) to her own rent-controlled—*we will all get hammers and kill you dead*—apartment. Having a rent-controlled apartment in Manhattan was far more danger-ous than owing huge sums of money to Visa or the Mafia.

Her cat, Gus, was sitting in the little entry hall, looking bored, wait-ing not for her but for some fresh hell. He blinked in his bored way, as if he'd been forced to listen to Justin Bieber all evening, until he saw what Cindy carried. He pounced.

"Not so fast!" She'd raised the Ziploc bag quickly out of reach. She went directly to her kitchen cupboard and took down a big glass bowl some flowers once were delivered in, filled it halfway with tepid water, and carefully slid the clown fish, together with the old water, into the new bowl.

Gus was up on the counter, his paw nearly in the bowl, until Cindy pushed him and he fell like a sack of grain.

Cindy removed an armful of books from a sturdy shelf on the living room wall that was isolated enough from the other furniture that Gus couldn't get to it. Tomorrow she would get a proper tank and maybe another fish; she could ask Frankie or someone at a fish supply place if a clown fish would be okay with a strange fish. She could always get a second clown fish, or the pink skunk was nice. Frankie had pointed it out in one of the glasses.

Only now did she take off her down vest and her shoes and sink into one of the armchairs that matched the small sofa. They were all covered in a cream twill with dark brown piping. They came as a group, together with the glass and wood coffee table around which they "grouped." ("Shame to split 'em up," the salesperson had said, as if the sofa and chairs were three lost kittens.)

Finally, Cindy looked around the room painted in Calamity White. Last year, when the halls were painted, she decided to paint her apartment and asked the jack-of-all-trades manager if there was a gallon left over, and could she buy it? He said he had two gallons that he'd let her have at a discount, or better, he'd throw the paint in for free if she gave him the job.

The only reason she wanted the paint was because it was called Calamity, and looking at it now, she didn't see what had invited the name. It was just another shade of white, "A Whiter Shade of Pale" was what she thought of, and she reached over to a little stack of CDs by her Bose unit. She sorted through them and put on that song, Joe Cocker's version. She'd listened to several different singers and still didn't understand some of the words, which she counted as a plus, for it made the whole song, mysterious enough as it was, even more mysterious. They were dancers dancing a fandango, then turning cartwheels. There was a story Cindy didn't understand, involving a woman who was listening to a miller tell a tale, and her face "till then just ghostly, turned a whiter shade of pale."

Cindy didn't think she had ever written a line, not a single line, that was as good as that line. It was a startling line, the way Emily Dickinson wrote startling lines, lines that hit you like a slap across the face.

Gus was sitting beside her on the sofa, both of them looking at the fish bowl (for widely different reasons). The clown fish was proof of the events of the night. It had really happened. She thought that if she woke in the morning without her fish there, she'd put the whole thing down to dreams.

The two dark-coated men who'd marched into the café must have been Mob guys. But they shot the fish tank, not the other two (probably Mob guys also) eating in the restaurant. The ones who'd pulled guns and probably saved the lives of the other diners. The first two hadn't been aiming at the customers, either.

"They tried to murder the fish," she said to Gus, who kept his eyes on the bowl.

Did anyone call the police? No cops came. Of course, no one was shot, and they were all busy saving the fish. There'd been around thirty fish and twenty diners; some had saved more than one.

Frankie was too busy calling the emergency fish service to call the police. And when the fish were safely swimming in their separate goblet seas, Frankie had hurried around the room hugging and shaking hands and talking so fast in Italian or Spanish that it should have crippled his tongue.

Then it struck Cindy that she hadn't the faintest notion, the least idea, nor did anyone else in the Clownfish Café, what had been happening. If they'd all started turning cartwheels on the floor while the ceiling flew away, it couldn't have been stranger. A calamitous evening: Like the paint, like the song, it had made no sense.

Only one fish had gone missing: an albino clown fish. "Ghost fish," Frankie called it. "My poor ghost fish."

Had it been swept away by the water into some dark corner where it had lain, flopping back and forth, suffocating, turning even ghostlier, turning a whiter shade of pale?

That night she dreamed she was Dorothy (without pigtails), and in place of the dog, Toto, stood Gus.

They were in their small house when the tornado came waltzing— literally—into Kansas, "Tales from the Vienna Woods" playing in the background.

Everything was blowing to kingdom come; the winds were sawing and sawing away on the reedy marsh. But where had there ever been a marsh in Kansas? Even in dreams, she couldn't stop editing. This marsh had ducks bobbing and rising and flying and guns going off, missing everything they aimed at. The little house pinwheeled, floor to ceiling, ceiling to floor, and they went head over heels with it, doing cartwheels in the sky.

Awake, Cindy smiled and watched the ceiling fly away.

Really awake this time, she saw the ceiling was (sadly) intact. Gus wasn't on the bed, so he was out there in—

She rolled out of bed and ran to the living room.

The bowl was still on its shelf, clown fish intact. Gus was lying below it with his paws encircling his chest, watching.

She went back to the bedroom and drew on her blue chenille bathrobe and trailed its sash into the kitchen.

On the white (well, white-ish, though no calamity) Formica counter lay yesterday's mail, topped by a letter from her lawyers telling her more about her crazy ex-agent's unfolding plot, the fifty-page complaint he had filed with the New York state court, his convoluted plan to get his commission out of her for a book he hadn't agented. She'd fired him years before.

She put water and Dunkin' Donuts regular coffee into her Mr. Coffee machine and switched it on. She shoved the letter aside, not wanting to know what act this was in L. Bass Hess's play, though really, it had never gotten beyond Act One, had it? It had never really gotten out of rehearsals. The same old stuff was sorted through and moved around and mulled, argued, intrigued over.

Finally, Mr. Coffee dispensed his brew, and she filled one of her thick white mugs. This she took into the living room to join Gus. She sat down on the sofa as she had the night before. But she found herself thinking about the L. Bass Hess charade, and she would have to short-circuit such thinking. How she dealt with things she didn't want to think about was either to get down Proust and read a few pages, or allow herself a definite, limited time period in which to think. This morning she decided on sixty—no, thirty—thirty seconds. She watched the second hand on her watch as she thought:

Awful person, awful agent control freak, sociopath—perhaps psychopath?—no, sociopath because (she struck "because," reminding herself not to use unnecessary words) cold as Alaska—thirty seconds! Stop!

She drank her coffee and wondered if what she'd just done was a kind of anti-obsession. Was it like, say, Lady Macbeth allowing herself only one hand-wash?

Finished thinking about L. Bass Hess, she rested her eyes on the clown fish, who was darting (as well as could be darted) back and forth in his little water world. She thought over the problem of getting him another fish or two for company. There shouldn't be a problem if it were another clown fish, surely? What would be nice would be to get Frankie to sell her another of his fish, but she was pretty sure he wouldn't do it. It would be nicer for her fish if the new fish were familiar to him.

She sat up. She knew how to get another fish from Frankie!

3

Am I gonna have to put up with you obsessing about that goddamn fish?" Karl was reading the arts section of the *Times*. He rattled the page just to get Candy away from C.F. That was the name Candy had settled on for his rescued fish—C.F. Karl had said helpfully that it was the dumbest name he'd ever heard. Candy had said, "No kidding. What fish names have you heard?"

They'd been arguing about the fish not being a clown fish, anyway. Karl had snapped open a colorful book he'd picked up that morning on tropical fish. "It's like one of these symphon-whatever. It's completely different."

Candy insisted it was striped, so what?

"For God's sake, it's red squiggles. It don't look anything like a clown fish."

The fish tank had been purchased at midnight from a "colleague" with a warehouse. The tank was big. The colleague had tossed in a bag of pinkish stones, some gravel, some coral, other junk like a miniature deep-sea diver. It had taken upward of an hour getting back to East Houston and their own warehouse; the upper spaces of this one, however, had been converted into two very large apartments. The makeover for each floor had been one and a half mill. The interior designer, Lenny Babbo, was awed by the space he had to work in and the money he had to work with.

"You're feeding it too much, anyway," said Karl. "Frankie would be horrified." Karl had given up on the fish book and was reading a review of a new book.

Candy was watching his fish, considering a new name. "You think maybe we ought to go to Frankie's, see how he's doing? After last night," he ended vaguely.

"Dunno. Listen to this: It's a review of a book by some asshole writer calls herself Angel. What is this one-name shit? Only ones deserve that are Elvis and Frank."

"Frank Giacomo?"

"Sinatra, fuck's sake."

"Yeah. Ol' Blue Eyes. So how about Madonna?"

Karl shook his head. "No. See, that's a different kind of thing. She was always Madonna. Who is she, Madonna Jones? No, always one name. She didn't *earn* the right to use just one name. Not like Elvis. He was Elvis Presley before he got famous. He earned that one-name treatment. Like Sinatra." He tossed the paper down. "What the hell. The book looks like a real freak job." He slid down on Candy's white leather sofa. "How in hell does this twat get a publisher?"

Barnes & Noble had become one of their main hangouts ever since Candy and Karl had a run-in with Mackenzie-Haack's publisher, Bobby Mackenzie, who'd come up with the novel scheme of getting rid of a writer named Ned Isaly by hiring a couple of contract killers. To do Bobby the little credit he deserved, the idea did not originate with him but with mega-bestselling author Paul Giverney, whom the avaricious Bobby Mackenzie wanted to publish, and who would agree only if Ned Isaly were terminated. Nobody knew why Paul wanted him gone, including the hit men. It was fortunate that Candy and Karl had "standards," the chief one being that they always got to know the mark before they offed him, insisting that they be the ones to decide whether the guy goes or stays. Two years ago the "guy" had been an award-winning writer named Ned Isaly. Now the guy was New York agent L. Bass Hess, whom they had been following around Manhattan for a couple of weeks.

Books had added a new dimension to their lives. Books were to die for. Literally. They were things you got killed over. Candy and Karl knew New York, licit and illicit, better than half the Metropolitan police and as well as the other half. How would they ever have guessed the publishing world was so shot through with acrimony that they'd just as soon kill you as publish you?

Their experience up to the time Danny Zito had thrown this job at them was Danny Zito himself. Danny had rushed headlong into hell by writing a tell-all ("meaning tell-some," Karl had said) book about the Bransoni family. ("Danny can write?" Leo Bransoni had snickered. "Danny can't even fucking spell." "Probably he had a ghost," Candy had said. "Probably he'll *be* a ghost inside forty-eight hours," Leo had answered.)

Danny had gone into the Witness Protection Program by hiding in Chelsea. WITSEC had strongly advised against it. "In plain sight," Danny had told them. He wrote books and painted. There were so many galleries in Chelsea now.

Joey Giancarlo, or Joey G-C, as people called him, had asked Candy and Karl, three weeks before, to do a hit on a guy named L. Bass Hess, of the Hess Literary Agency over on Broadway.

"My son, Fabio, he's got this book he wrote. It's a novel about Chicago in the thirties, a time with which he got no speakin' acquaintance, but it's fiction, so what the hey?" Joey shrugged shoulders so meaty that his neck disappeared into them. "So Fab, he talks to Danny Zito—"

"Danny's in WITSEC. How's Fabio get to talk to him?"

Another shrug. "Who cares. Danny got his book published—"

Karl laughed. "Which is why he's in Witness Protection."

Joey ignored this. "So Fab figures Danny can give him some pointers who to publish the book, but Danny says, 'No, first you get an agent.' 'What the hey?' says Fab, he's like, 'Agent?' 'The agent sells the book,' says Danny, 'the writer don't.' Danny gives him the name of this guy Hess. Well, Fabio goes all the way into Manhattan down to Broadway—"

The present conference was taking place behind the eight-foot stone wall surrounding a five-acre estate on the Jersey shore.

"—and the guy won't see him. Won't see him." Joey removed the Cuban cigar from his mouth and spat out a tiny piece of tobacco as if spitting in the eye of L. Bass Hess. He continued: "This bleach-head old ho that's sittin' in the outer office behind a counter says for him to leave his manuscript with her and they'd get back to him. Well, Fabio don't much like leavin' it, but he does. And does this asshole agent get back to him? A month, a friggin' month, goes by until the ho calls, says"—here Joey changed his voice, upping it several decibels—"'Mr. Hess says the manuscript is not marketable in its present form. Sorry.'" Joey shook his head slowly again and again. "Let me tell you, I never seen Fabio so down. You know the kid—"

They did, a real jerk.

"—always the smile, always the sunny side showin', Fabio. A regular sunset kinda guy."

Key West has sunsets, maybe Santa Fe, but not Fabio. Fabio dragged his bad mood around like a cart horse pulling life's bleak side.

His cigar gone cold, Joey struck a match on his thumbnail and said out of the corner of his mouth, "It's a personal insult to the family. Get him."

"You know the way we work, Joey: Follow the mark around, get to know him, see how he goes about things—"

"Christ sakes, Karl, I just told you how the sumbitch goes about things . . . Yeah, yeah, okay, I know you got conditions. But you're the best, so get on it." Joey removed a fat envelope from his inside pocket.

They refused it. "No money up front, Joey. Only if we take the job."

Joey G-C rolled his eyes. "You guys."

From his office promptly at twelve-thirty, L. Bass Hess ventured forth for lunch every day at 21 or the Gramercy Tavern; these were the restaurants where he took clients or met up with editors or other publishing people. During the week, he stayed at his pied-à-terre on the Upper East Side and ventured downtown for dinner at Bhojan on Lexington (which surprised Candy and Karl, Hess eating Indian food, but then it was cheap, too). But Bhojan was closed for a few days, and that was when he decided to go to the Clownfish Café. Again, much to Karl and Candy's surprise.

Beside the sofa where Karl sat was a stack of magazines, mostly trade, like *Publishers Weekly, Booklist, Kirkus*. They liked to keep up, but they got behind sometimes. Karl had picked up a several-weeks-old *Publishers Weekly* off the top of the pile and was leafing through it.

Candy had picked up a couple of *National Geographic*s early that morning in an ancient coffee shop that stashed them. Candy had been reading aloud from the one that had a photograph of coral reefs on its cover until Karl told him to shut up, just let him drink his coffee.

They both thought e-books were terrible. They thought the Kindle was cretinous; you read, you want to read a book, not a slab of hardware. Hardware was something that shot bullets.

Candy had managed to get out of P.S. 111 with body and brain intact, but with no books in it, as it were. Karl, on the other hand, had gone to college and read Hemingway and Scott Fitzgerald before that fracas with the dean of students. He was only a month short of graduating (a fact that stunned Candy, who had never known anyone within light-years of finishing any school) when he'd signed on to do a job on the dean. Nothing serious, no wet work, just a warning, a little shin-busting, when a couple of guys had stepped out of the shadows—another dean, a phys ed department head—*guys who were teaching our youths, can you believe it, stepped up with guns, teachers with guns!, and gave me no choice, right?*

Candy had never been clear on the details, like who was paying Karl or why. The dean of arts and sciences landed in a heap, and Karl had taken off from the college, from the town, with nothing but his .38, his bolt-action Browning, and a copy of *The Great Gatsby*.

"Hey, C," said Karl from the couch, "check this out: This friggin' agent we been following around. The asshole's suing one of his former clients for a commission on a book the writer says he had nothing to do with; says she had a new agent that worked on it." Karl put down the magazine, thinking. "Maybe it's time we did a face-to-face with Hess." They always did a face-to-face before they decided if the mark was worth the bullet. Karl swung his legs off the sofa.

"You mean, like, now?"

Karl was getting into his "I Am Not Available" Arfango loafers. "Yeah, now."

"Bass Hess," said Candy. "Sounds like a snake hiss."

They had tracked L. Bass Hess's comings and goings for two weeks, and a bigger tightass they had never come across. It was the first time they'd considered turning down a job because the mark was so boring, they didn't want to be around him.

They could have offed this guy in their sleep; he was as routinized as a day with Martha Stewart (in or out of jail). They could have stopped in front of Saks and fired over their shoulders at Fifty-first and Fifth and dropped Hess on the pavement in front of St. Patrick's as long as they did it at precisely 5:55 on a Wednesday, when, for some reason, he went to church. The same routine day after day, the only differences being in the people he met for lunch at the Gramercy Tavern or 21 or a new French place that had a lot of buzz going, named Arles, in SoHo. At these places, he'd meet up with clients or editors or fellow agents.

Since Candy and Karl knew in advance he'd be at one of those restaurants, they'd call and ask if he'd arrived yet. After finding out which one he was going to, they'd go there and get a table near his. They ordered whiskies and steaks, rare, and didn't bother with the menu. The stuff on it was hardly pronounceable, much less edible. They did not want the soup de mer, the baby-greens salad, the ahi tuna (which Karl said sounded like a fish sneezing), the charcuterie pâté. They liked to watch plates being served, the saucy designs, the bright colors, the small broccoli trees, the canoes of romaine lettuce—boats that should be out on a lake somewhere, the flutes, the volutes, the drifts, the sprinkles. What the fuck was this stuff doing on a fork? It should have been on a runway. They should make plates with little legs that could walk, turn, spin, hobble back to the kitchen.

They liked the Gramercy Tavern best. They liked its straightforward fish dishes (even though the chef did like to dress up the cod and halibut with superfluous bits of this and that). They liked to listen to Hess ordering the striped bass. That gave them a kick. Hess always ate a piece of some kind of fish with a boiled potato and green peas or beans. Never strayed into the fried or the sauced. But that was almost noneating. No dessert, no booze. Drank iced tea. No wonder he was skinny as a subway rail. Candy and Karl were always happy when Hess's writer or editor guest ordered up a double martini, rocks, three olives; this followed by food leaking butter and oil, designed back in the kitchen by some architect; then went for a bottle of Sancerre and several bolts of ice cream for dessert.

Hess really had to pay up the snout for that one. Candy and Karl enjoyed tuning in to the conversation behind them because they liked gossip about the publishing industry. As when an editor said, "The contract's lousy. If they can't up the payout, he'll walk." Or "I'm tired of being held up by these guys."

"Okay, so he doesn't do it. We can sign Bobby Three Winds." "Bobby Three Winds?" "Why not? Remember that Vegas job? Steve Wynn and the Bellagio?" "It was perfect." "Gorgeous. The guy never misses."

It sounded exactly like listening to Joey G-C putting out a contract. The shooter he mostly wanted was a short muscle-bound guy named Ralph Double-Shoes Bono. Ralph had his shoes specially made to add another inch or so. The other guys started calling him "Double-Shoes," and the name stuck.

"Who the hell is Bobby Three Winds?" Karl asked afterward.

"He's that writer that's part Sioux or Cherokee. Some Indian."

"Native American is what you say," said Karl.

"Okay, Native American Indian. He's some hotshot travel writer."

Karl snickered. "Such acrimony in publishing."

"Very hostile people."

So they knew their way around L. Bass Hess and the route to his office near Broadway and Twenty-third. They could have found it blindfolded.

That was where they went.

4

Cindy was standing on a street in Sunset Park in Brooklyn in front of a desiccated-looking building, more like a warehouse than any sort of residence, doubting her judgment in answering the ad on Craigslist for an albino clown fish. "A hundred," the seller had said.

She had agreed and said she'd be there in an hour or a little more. She wasn't sure how long it would take to get there. He'd told her to take the N train, so she'd walked over to Washington Square.

She was glad at least that it wasn't dark, although it was looking pretty dusky. Still, it was only midafternoon, probably a downtime for killers, drug drops, joyriders, carjackers, rapists, kid—

"Yeah?"

The single word seemed to explode through the opening of the door, and she was jolted from her fantasy. The heavy door had swung inward with a clatter as if nuts and bolts were falling out of its hinges.

She took in the flat face of the man, youngish, the ripped jeans, the T-shirt with lightning bolts and knives and other ephemera of death. This did nothing for her confidence.

When her response was slow in coming, he said it again—"Yeah?"— and looked her up and down, though in an oddly nonsexual way.

Her hand went to her throat. "Oh, I'm sorry, I must have the wrong—" She was backing off.

"Hey. You're the lady called about the fish. I'm Monty. Come on in, come in." He turned back into the hall and drew his arm in an arc like a discus thrower, gesturing for her to follow.

Too late now. She followed him down a narrow hall, dully carpeted, dully painted, the surface webbed in fine cracks.

He went into a room where there were three other men—or boys? they could have been anywhere from eighteen to thirty-eight—all looking glassy-eyed and vaguely smiling from smoking (she guessed) the same thing the fish owner, Monty, was. They, too, wore torn jeans, but less threatening T-shirts. One said "Now You See It." The other T-shirt sported a smiling alligator.

The three of them squinted and nodded and smoked, sitting on a couple of dilapidated daybeds. One had wrapped himself in an Indian blanket. The other two roused themselves a little, seeing a stranger, and one of them moved his genitals from one side to another with a look of profound accommodation that had nothing to do with her.

Monty introduced them: Molloy, Graeme, and Bub. Bub was the one in the blanket.

They seemed to regard her as just one of the guys, so she stopped thinking murder and rape; yet she felt a little hurt that no one seemed to give a damn that this young blond woman had stepped into a setup that couldn't have been more conducive to some sexual attack if it had been choreographed by Bob Fosse or whoever did *West Side Story*.

Her host had retreated into a darker region and was now back. "Here we go! Here's your fish. Albino clown fish." The little fish was in an oversize Ziploc bag. "Cute li'l fucker, ain't he?"

"Is it the same as a ghost clown fish?" She caught movement out of the corner of her eye, but nothing there seemed directed at her.

"You like fish?" One of them, Molloy, had spoken in a dreamy way, through a haze of smoke. Was it a real question? Was it a dream question? His T-shirt was the one with the friendly alligator. He wore a headband with *aquaria* printed on it in bouncy letters.

"Yes," she said to him. Then again to the owner, "But is it a ghost fish?"

"Well, yeah, I guess."

"It does look, well, not quite opaque."

They all looked at her with varying degrees of frown.

"Well, I mean, kind of transparent orange and not quite white." The ghost, the spirit of a clown fish, or a clown fish slowly leaving. She smiled.

He held up the bag and squinted as at a too bright sun. "Yeah, yeah." He didn't know anything about it.

Molloy of the alligator T-shirt said, "It's an albino, yeah, a ghost fish, all right. Albino clown fish." He spoke with some authority. Cindy wondered if Aquaria was a shop that sold fish and fish tanks and so forth. She wondered if he worked there.

"See?" Monty brushed his brown hair off his forehead and looked at her out of innocent eyes. He looked six years old.

That was what seemed familiar to her, what she recognized from childhood: her little brother in an old shed out back with three or four of his friends. It was their club. It could have been them transplanted from the Kansas fields right here and now in Brooklyn. It made her so sad, she was afraid she'd cry if she didn't get out.

She opened her bag and brought out the two fifties she'd folded into one of the little pockets inside. "A hundred, right?"

"A hundred? A hundred for that there little bitty fish? Monty, you cheatin' this gal?" This came from the one she thought was Graeme. The introductions had been hastily performed.

Cindy held up her hand. "No. He isn't. This kind of clown fish sells for even more some places." She didn't know whether it did or didn't. "It's a fair price."

Monty went back to smiling at the money she handed over. He set it on a table with a glass to hold it down, as if the winds were roaming.

Cindy adjusted her shoulder bag and smiled at them and said goodbye. She held up the bag as if giving the fish its chance to say good-bye.

They all nodded or grinned through the smoke scrim, held up their hands in a powwow fashion. Indians around a campfire.

Now she wished she'd brought a lot more, for she had a sudden yearning to enlist their help. *If I pay you five hundred, would you go to Manhattan and beat up some people for me? Or even a thousand? I'd really appreciate it.*

They would put their heads together. *Yeah, okay. Where we find this dude?*

Dudes. More than one dude. There are lawyers and a literary agent.

Hell, yeah. They'd high-five all around.

Then she would tell them how to find them—her lawyer, Wally Hale, and the Mackenzie-Haack counsel and L. Bass Hess—put the five hundred on the table with a glass to keep it down, and leave before the ceiling flew away.

———————

She did not want to walk to the Thirty-sixth Street station carrying a fish in water. She found a cab on the corner and, on the long drive back to Grub Street, sat in a peaceful frame of mind, wondering about the world Monty and his friends inhabited.

She sat thinking about them, riding back to Manhattan with the watery bag on her lap.

5

There was no one in the outer office of the Hess Literary Agency, so Candy and Karl just walked in unannounced (and uninvited).

Candy attested to surprise that the outer door wasn't dead-bolted and security-locked. This was, after all, New York.

There was a curved desk at the other end of the room for the secretary or receptionist, neither of whom was present. The two long walls held shelves of books—lots of books. Prominently displayed were big photographs, a couple almost poster-sized, the subjects presumably L. Bass Hess's clients. These big pictures appeared on tiers to the left and right of the door.

The most prominent was a famous High Desert writer named Creek Dawson, in a ten-gallon hat and neckerchief with a rope slung over his shoulder, a toothpick in his mouth, and a stable full of horses way behind him. He had a lined, weathered face and eyes squeezed tight to blue slits.

"Ever read him?"

"Hell, no. I like Louis L'Amour. He lived in a real place. Durango."

"This desert ain't a real place?"

"It's California, C. California's California. Hey, look." Karl indicated a photo of a dark-haired, youngish man posed with half-shut eyes and one arm wrapped like a scarf about his neck, a pose meant to look smoldering. "Dwight Staines. Remember, the guy was in Pittsburgh same time we were?"

"Mr. Idiot, yeah. Hess and old Dwight, that sounds like a good match. Pair of pricks."

Beside Creek Dawson was affixed a photo of Mia Pennyroyale, wearing gold hoop earrings you could have rolled down Seventh Avenue if you had a stick. She wrote things called romans à clef.

Then there was a bronzed-god-like guy with the snappy name of Harve Hanks who wrote a series about an L.A. private eye "in the great tradition of Raymond Chandler."

"Yeah, sure," said Karl. "Only guy that writes in the great tradition of Raymond Chandler is Raymond Chandler."

Candy snorted. Karl read a lot more, but Candy was catching up.

Fifth and last was a girl or woman, hard to say, with burnished-to-gold hair that looked like she'd cut it herself, raggedy as it was, and calm gray eyes and an unsmiling mouth. A kind of silent face.

Candy's mouth dropped. He punched Karl on the arm, saying, "Christ, K., it's her, the girl in the Clownfish."

"Huh?" Karl leaned closer. "She's kinda cute."

"It's her, one that started saving the fish. Same girl!"

Karl was reading the brief text. "Jesus." He turned to look at Candy. "This is Cindy Sella. This"—he flung his thumb over his shoulder at the photo—"is Cindy Sella, for fuck's sake!"

It was then that the receptionist/secretary breezed in from a side door and fitted herself behind her desk. "Oh!" she said. "So sorry. Yes, gentlemen, you're his three o'clock." She checked her watch. "You're twenty minutes early, but I think Mr. Hess can see you." Her smile was near beatific.

Karl was about to respond that they weren't his anything, they didn't have an appointment, but Candy said to him, "Gift horse. Mouth."

"Oh, right." Karl smiled broadly.

L. Bass Hess's receptionist raised a gentle hand, letting them know they needn't inconvenience themselves with a response. She pressed a button. A staticky reply came through, and she answered, "Mr. Hale and Mr. Reeves are here." More static.

Karl saw the nameplate as they passed her desk, which told them she was cutely called Stephie, although she was well into her sixties.

The office was leather, glass, and books, much the same as the reception room. It was inhabited by a couple of leather sofas face-to-face across another magazine-toting coffee table; a couple of chairs pulled up to Hess's desk; and the desk itself, holding neat stacks of books and folders and writing tablets.

And inhabited by Hess himself, a man with insanely red hair that looped and whirled around his head, untamable. His eyes were such a watery light brown that they looked washed away, and his face was haggard and hawklike. He wore a wide-striped shirt and a bow tie, and the jacket hitched on the back of his chair was a dark Donegal tweed that did not go with the tie, the shirt, or the hair. A man of many parts, and none of them fit.

He stood behind the desk as if he couldn't bear to waste a minute of his time by sitting down. Instead of greeting them with a handshake and hello, Hess darted a look from Candy to Karl and back. "Who's Hale and who's Reeves?"

Candy and Karl looked at each other, Candy making a gesture that said "you first." Karl said, "I'm Hale." Candy said with a wide smile, "That makes me Reeves, then."

Hess didn't wait for confirmation, nor did he invite them to have a seat. He bent over a folder on his desk, slowly fingering its pages. He wet his forefinger to help with this task.

Candy thought that was kind of cute—that is, for Hess being otherwise a perfect jerk. No manners at all, probably treated everybody but his high-flying clients like scumbags.

"I'm adding this to the complaint. She should certainly want to settle."

Since they had no idea what he was talking about, they simply looked thoughtfully at different fixtures in the room. They shrugged, then muttered versions of "yes," "maybe," and "who knows?"

Candy wondered where the Bass came from. On the wall beside the window that looked out over Broadway, there was a big stuffed fish that could have been a bass. Interesting name, wasted on this guy. And what did the L. stand for?

"Right. Now, about this complaint—"

Hess's eyes narrowed. "Duke Borax told you, didn't he?"

Duke Borax. Candy mentally sorted through the names of Joey G-C's outfit, but he didn't come up with anybody as insecure as a guy who would call himself Duke.

"Of course, of course," said Karl. "Only, you know, Borax, he ain—he isn't always a stickler for details."

"He's one of the partners at your law firm, for God's sake. Of *course* he's a stickler for details. Just what don't you understand?" The eyes nar-rowed to even thinner slits.

Candy heard the suspicion in his voice and said, "We understand. It's just that Mr. Hale here likes things straight from the horse's mouth." He smiled.

The horse's mouth didn't exactly smile back. It was more of a crumple of the lips, up and down in a wavy line, as if the mouth couldn't decide on a course of action. It was a Charlie Brown mouth without the Charlie Brown charm. Bass Hess hovered over the file, leaning on it as if it were about to come alive beneath his hands. "Let's be clear about one thing: I've got the papers on her. You should be urging her to settle."

As two circles flushed in Hess's cheeks, Karl said, "Understood." He reached out for the folder that Hess had clamped to his chest like a mother reluctant to give up her child to the baby minder. Then he unclenched and handed the folder over. "Otherwise, her career will be in ruins."

Candy was used to snakes, but the hiss actually made him retreat a step.

With a few more assurances of confidentiality, they left.

Just as they set foot outside the Hess Agency door, they glanced down the hall to see the elevator doors open and two guys in suits emerge. The suits looked as if they shopped together to make sure their clothes complemented one another. Both in pinstripes, one gray, one navy, they stood for a moment conferring. The taller and handsomer of the two reminded Candy of somebody, but he couldn't place him.

"If that's the three o'clock appointment, we better hit that exit." Karl nodded toward the red sign on their side of the elevators. "Hess is going to go bananas. He'll call security."

The two who had just exited the elevator were walking slowly, turned toward each other, hands moving. To Candy they looked, in their syn-chronized movements, like a couple of tap dancers. Then he realized who the tall one reminded him of: Richard Gere in *Chicago*.

They reached the exit before Hale and Reeves (if that was who they were) passed them. It was only four flights, and they were used to run-ning down stairs. They reached the lobby in two minutes flat and left the building.

6

A rent-a-cop was on his cell and beginning to move out from around the counter as they exited through the glass doors. He hadn't seen them. They stopped right in front of a coffee shop two doors down and pretended to be pondering the menu. Candy watched the guard out of the corner of his eye look left and right, then across at the park, probably thinking the two men had made a dash for it through the trees. He went back into the building.

"What the hell is this shit?" Candy was trying to read what was in the folder as Karl hailed a cab.

They went back to their East Houston warehouse, where they lived on the second and third levels. The first level was dead space. They wanted it that way. That empty floor was probably worth $2 million, but they didn't care; they liked the look of a warehouse. They believed in a low profile. And nobody who had a beef with them would be looking for them in Manhattan. Probably thought they were in South America, Venezuela or Guadalajara, or on some island off the map. Not that it made much difference, because anyone with a beef would rather give up the beef than go up against Candy and Karl.

Anyway, they didn't want anyone else living in their building. Despite their many superficial differences, they were much alike. They had no families; they bought their clothes in Façonnable; they mourned the passing of *The Sopranos* (and thought the weird ending heralded a return someday); they ate at good restaurants; they liked women but not too many and not too often; they killed people; they were solid.

They entered the building on Houston through its thick metal door and took the old cage elevator that ratcheted up to the second level and Candy's flat. He wanted to check on his fish.

Karl rolled his eyes as they went in through the bulletproof walnut door to cool white comfort. Except it was getting less and less cool, since Candy had been out all morning buying new stuff more "in synch" with a fish's environment.

Where before had stood a wooden butler who held out a small tray for keys and cards was now a sculpture of a boy on a shark or whale or dolphin, Karl couldn't say. Its head was flattened to serve as a tray. Candy had bought it at a secondhand place on Broome.

There was nice white butter-leather furniture all over and clean glass tables, including a dining table surrounded by Louis Ghost chairs. Now there were shell candlesticks on the handsome white fireplace mantel. On one wall was a hammered metal school of fish, all looking determined.

Candy said C.F. looked content.

Karl said he damned well ought to, look at the size of the tank he was hanging out in. "You know, that's what it mostly does: hang. I never saw any fish just hang there like that one. And that tank'd hold a fuckin' great white shark."

The tank was really big; it took up half a wall. And it was filled with the aquarium stuff Candy had gotten from their friend the night of the café incident. Candy had added what looked like a whole coral reef. "Fish ought to have room to swim in," said Candy. "And privacy. His own space." The clown fish had plenty of personal space. Candy had put a structure in the tank that Karl said looked like a W Hotel.

Karl went to the glass table on wheels where the whiskey and gin and Scotch sat and unstoppered the whiskey.

Candy sat down with the folder and an *omph!* as if he'd been on his Bruno Magli–loafered feet all day. He opened the folder again to the first page. "What is this shit, K?"

Karl was fizzing soda into two glasses. "How should I know?" He carried the drinks over to the fireplace where two leather chairs faced each other and handed one to Candy. He took a swig of his own while looking over Candy's shoulder. "It's some legal shit."

"Yeah, I know that. You know who the plaintiff and defendants are?"

Their legal vocabulary was stunted except when it came to matters with which they had grown familiar.

"Hess is the plaintiff, and the defendant's Cindy Sella."

"The only one in those photos in his waiting room who looks like she's got a life."

"He's suing her publisher, too. Some outfit called Harbor Books— Whoa! Listen to this: Harbor Books is part of Mackenzie-Haack." Candy slapped down the folder and stared at Karl.

"Our old buddy Bobby Mackenzie, the friggin' son of a bitch! Is he back from— Where'd we get him a ticket to?"

"Africa? Who knows. No, it was Australia, I think. Clive called me last month." Clive Esterhaus was the unfortunate senior editor at Mackenzie-Haack whom Bobby had assigned the dirty job of finding a hit man. Candy went for his glasses. The print seemed to be deteriorating before his eyes.

Karl was up and firing the soda from the syphon into his glass. It was more that he wanted exercise than soda water. "So what about Clive?"

"Clive's okay. Bobby gave him some reward, like his own book thing. What d'ya call it? Imprint? Like that."

"Good. Clive deserved it. I'm surprised Bobby Mackenzie can make a generous gesture. Maybe we taught him something." Since their foray into the shadowy halls of the publishing world the year before, Karl had become well acquainted with its language, some of it extremely peculiar. It was almost as bad as legal.

"Bobby really treated him like shit."

"Bobby treats everybody like shit. Except he's cool." Karl chuckled.

"So how does Bobby keep 'em in line?"

Karl snuffled a laugh. "Breaks legs. Y'know, if Bobby Mackenzie wasn't such a self-centered SOB, I think he coulda made a name for himself in our line of work."

"No, he ain't got our scruples, K."

"Yeah, I guess that's so. Come on, what else's in those papers?" Karl picked up his glass from the cocktail napkin that stuck to it. It had red coral printed against a turquoise background.

Candy said, turning a page, "As far as I can make out, Cindy Sella— defendant—is guilty of breach of contract and the tacit—tacit?"

Karl said, "It means unspoken but understood."

Candy nodded. "Okay. Tacit understanding of the irrevocability of the agency clause—"

"What the hell's that?"

Candy raised his hands in an "I surrender" gesture. "Don't ask me."

"Okay, so the bottom line here is what?"

"Can't find one."

"It's got to be money, maybe love. How many bottom lines are there? There's 'I love you dot dot dot'; or 'I owe you dot dot dot.' How much is he claiming she owes him?"

"I don't see it." Candy leafed through the sheaf of papers. "I can't read this stuff. I bet his own lawyers never read it. This looks like some sleight-of-hand guy at one of Trump's casinos did the writing. It's definitely in the 'now you see it now you don't' category." Candy got up and went over to the fish tank and tapped in a few flakes of something.

Shaved truffles, probably, thought Karl, who was staring up at the ceiling, thinking.

They were silent for some minutes. Candy contemplated renaming his fish.

"You know what?" said Karl.

"What?" Malcolm, maybe. Or Oscar.

"Is her address in there?"

"Yeah. West Village, on Grove. Why?"

"I think maybe we ought to pay a visit to our girl Cindy."

Already she was their girl.

Lucky Cindy.

7

Cindy was looking out of her Grub Street window at what she could see of midtown Manhattan. Not much. She wished it were dark and the Empire State Building would light up, because a corner of it was visible if she stretched her neck a little. The rest of what she saw was the building across the alley and up on the corner, Ray's coffee shop, where she spent a large part of her time. There was even a booth at the rear that they kind of kept for her, "kind of" meaning if somebody else got to the booth first, that was okay with them. New York, she had found almost immediately upon getting there, was a world of everyday small betrayals.

She thought she might have gotten along extremely well, albeit in her extremely minor key, with Dr. Johnson and Addison and Steele and the others (the "others," Cindy?), not in any way because of her writing (as if that fact needed saying even to herself) but because she loved coffee shops. When she imagined eighteenth-century London, it was so easy to insert herself into a chair at White's or the St. James or the Turk's Head, and there to sip coffee and smoke . . . did women smoke pipes? That was a really nice touch.

She had lived in this same apartment for nearly seven years, and she was happy knowing it wouldn't be turned into condos or a co-op, because then she'd have to buy the apartment or move. She'd remind herself she'd written three books in this place, and it might be ungrateful to kick it aside like an old shoe.

For God's sake. It was bad enough assigning feelings to every cat dog mouse roach that crossed her path, did she have to anthropomorphize the inanimate?

She pressed down a key on her typewriter. She still used her old IBM Selectric. She smiled at the stir it had created when her dad's secretary got one, her fulminating over the machine. Miss Duckworth (the secretary) liked to draw comparisons between the Selectric and her elderly Royal or Remington. Why she liked to discuss the IBM with the child, who was four or five, Cindy couldn't imagine. But she had the impression that she had known back then. How queer. She'd made her father promise that he would give her the typewriter.

If she told people this little chapter from her life, they would always say (in a smarmy tone, for how could it be otherwise said?), "Why, then, you always knew you were going to be a writer! Of course!"

She would shrug and say, "I never gave it a thought until I was thirty."

What she should do was go into hiding. She was getting less and less done. She thought of George Gissing. It had taken him only two months—*two months*—months, not years!—to write *New Grub Street*. Over five hundred pages and three volumes. And here she was after two years and not two hundred pages, less than half what Gissing had written, to say nothing of not being anywhere nearly as good as George Gissing.

The time that had gone into this absurd legal business with her agent and publisher was time she could have spent on her book. Then she told herself (as if she couldn't leave feeling bad alone; no, she had to go to feeling worse) that she hadn't had to take all of those calls from Wally Hale, those calls for no reason except "just to check, see how you're doing, Cindy," to which she'd say, "I'd be doing better, Wally, if you hadn't already racked up three minutes, which will come to around fifty dollars just to check on me. Now it's fifty-five. It will soon be seventy if I don't hang up. Good-bye."

She wasn't a Luddite; she did have an Apple computer and an HP printer. She just hated that booting-up sound first thing in the morning. The skittering of the IBM Selectric was comforting; it sounded like work; it sounded as if the rolling ball were keeping time with her mental processing, digging around in the twirl and pivot of the type ball. The computer received the print in silence, as if it had no stake in the operation, as if, in its fluid way, it was all taking place in another writing dimension. It rejected nothing; it kicked out nothing; it allowed all sorts of awful writing because it was so effortless.

If she'd stop slopping around in her chenille bathrobe and Acorn slippers half the day, she might get a grip. That morning, early, she had gone out to get some supplies for her clown fish bowl, then gotten back into the chenille bathrobe, as if it were some kind of writing uniform. The fish especially seemed to like the two green plastic leaves that stuck to the bowl. They liked to lounge on them.

Cindy sat back and looked around the room for the thousandth time, considering moving. If she could afford a New York lawyer, she could afford a New York row house.

Here it was noon already, and she hadn't written a word. She looked at the sheet of paper in her typewriter, at the words she had set down last night:

```
Whatever the cost, Helena would pay it.
```

Christ. Had she been into the second bottle of wine writing that? Helena. Yes, she would pay the cost, because she was an idiot. Cindy tried to remember why Helena was thinking this. She leafed through the last few pages she'd written, but there was no mention. It was like writing "I'll never be hungry again" and forgetting why Scarlett was standing on a hill with a carrot.

It was not a novel she was writing but a short story. How could you forget a character's dilemma in a short story?

Cindy went to the kitchen and got the coffee out of its airtight can; she shoved a filter into her Mr. Coffee machine, then a half-dozen tablespoons of coffee.

After she flicked on the coffeemaker, she leaned against the counter and thought about her novel. Then she went back to the desk and looked at the last page: 196 pages in two years (not 500 in two months). Cindy feared she was becoming like her main character, Lulu, in this novel she could not seem to make go forward.

Perhaps that was the point, or at least the trouble. Lulu could not move forward. She was stuck in the tragedy of the everyday.

```
    Lulu had gone no further than switching off the
ignition. Now she merely sat in the car, in the
dark, with no coherent thought. The streetlights
had flickered out or had not yet flickered on.
She had so little sense of time anymore.
    There had been a time when letters had been
written, envelopes addressed, stamped. Not
just cards; people now depended on the message
supplied by the cards. Some of the work done for
them, the artwork shouldering the rest of the
responsibility. Even the blank ones could fare as
letters with a bare minimum of original message.
When had she last seen a real letter? Lulu had
herself written them, if only to help stave off
their total loss, her own letters adding to that
small cache that a few people still kept going.
One day some horribly misguided person would
put together an organization of letter writers
because nothing could be left alone anymore. Not
even a letter on a mat. It would have to be put
together with another letter on another mat.
```

Cindy rose to get her coffee. She had no idea what Lulu was doing, sitting in her car where she'd been for nearly twenty pages. How long could a reader be expected to stay for that? Even though she should be getting Lulu out of that car, she drank her coffee and closed her eyes and saw—her mind's eye moving from house to house down the street—all of those letters lying on all of those mats, homeowners opening doors and looking down in surprise: A letter? A letter! They would bend down, a mother in a nightgown, a father in a business suit . . .

```
    Lulu put her head in her hands.
```

Cindy was afraid that Lulu might just quit cold.

There was a knock at the door. Who in God's name could be coming to see her? Twelve-thirty it was, and here she was in this old blue robe. She left the coffeemaker and went to the door.

Forgetting, as usual, to look through the security hole, she opened the door and saw two men standing there. Her eyes rounded, her mouth fell open. A perfect response for Helena, who never rejected a cliché.

"Somethin' wrong?" said the shorter of the two. "Did I spill somethin' on my tie?"

"Miss Sella?" said the taller one.

Cindy found words. "You're the ones in the Clownfish, the men with guns!" She stepped back and yanked the tie of her robe tighter, as if it were armor loosening.

The short one smiled wickedly, held up his palms. "We never started it, if you recall."

"Oh. Sorry. No, of course you didn't. Please, come on in." Cindy's smile was not wicked. It was one of those flame smiles. It lit up and warmed the place.

Candy and Karl walked in and felt immediately at home. For Karl it was the smile; for Candy it was the fishbowl on the shelf.

"Yo!" said Candy. "You got the fish! You got two of them." He was already over at the shelf that held the bowl. Gus the cat sat there, eyeing him.

"Don't let him get started," said Karl. Then "Oh, yeah. Let me introduce us. I'm Karl; he's Candy."

"How do you do. I'm Cindy."

"We know."

"Sit down, please." She nodded toward the sofa-and-club-chair suite (which was about the only thing to nod toward for sitting), and Karl thanked her and sat. Candy was stationed in front of the bowl. So was the cat. Both of them were looking at the fish.

"Hey, C., get over here, for God's sake." Karl turned to Cindy. "He took his fish home, too. It's taking up half his life, such as it is." He smoothed the crease in his pant leg. "Reason we're here is this agent of yours, Hess—"

Cindy took a step back. The crazy agent. She managed to forget him, and then his name bubbled up like the surface of the La Brea tar pits. "Did he send you?"

"You kidding?" said Karl, getting comfortable, resting his arm along the back of the sofa.

From his place by the fish, where he'd picked up the little tin of food, Candy said, "We work for that guy? Come *on*." He sprinkled a bit of food over the water. The cat watched.

"No, no. We're taking this on for you, pro bono, strictly. Call it our yearly donation to the National Arts Foundation or whatever." Karl let loose a hacking sort of laugh.

"You're working for *me*?" said Cindy, perched on the edge of the chair that faced the sofa with Karl on it. "What was all that at the restaurant? You guys had guns."

"True. Like the other guys had guns," said Karl.

Said Candy over his shoulder, "We always got guns."

"Come over and sit down, for God's sake, C. That ain't your fish."

"So what's this other one?" said Candy. "Kind of transparent?"

"A ghost clown fish."

"Wow. I like the leaves you stuck in here." He turned around. "They don't swim much, do they?"

Cindy smiled and shook her head.

Candy went on, "Now, I thought the one I saved was a clown fish, only turns out it—"

Karl yanked himself around. "Candy, for fuck's—excuse me"—this to Cindy—"sake! Cut it out with the fish."

Candy looked around, frowning. The cat looked around. He could have been frowning.

"Yeah. Okay."

"We got business here. You forget?"

Candy sat down on the sofa. Karl moved his arm. Candy said, as if he'd been talking about the incident in the Clownfish all along, "Personally, we thought it was pretty cold, them shooting up the aquarium, endangering all the fish."

Karl nodded. "I have to agree. If all they wanted was to pick off someone in the place—"

"Who?" said Cindy, feeling a chill. "Who were they after?"

"Hess—"

"Was he trying to kill me?" Her voice was anxious.

"Him? You gotta be kiddin'. You think he's up for that? You think he's got the balls?"

"I don't mean holding the gun; I mean he could have hired someone."

"Cindy, you watch too much TV. No, Karl means it was Hess they were trying to off."

Cindy's eyes widened again. *"What?"*

"You know, you probably ain't the only one he's tried to run over. We had a peculiar run-in with Hess earlier in his office—"

Cindy sat up even straighter. "Did you shoot him?" One could always hope.

Candy and Karl laughed. That was rich. "No," said Karl, "we didn't know what a miserable shit the guy was at that point. Excuse the language, except you being a writer, you can handle it, I imagine."

"No words are off limits if you're talking about L. Bass Hess. I think he's crazy."

"We know he's crazy." Karl held up the file. "The documents in the case."

"That's the name of a story by Dorothy L. Sayers." Now she stared at the folder. "He told my lawyer he was in possession of certain things that could ruin my career if they came out."

"You're a writer," said Karl, shoulders hunching up in a fuck's-sake shrug. "It'd be like broadcasting that Ernest Hemingway kept a case of Scotch in his cellar."

"Or Scott F. Fitzgerald," said Candy, not wanting to be found less conversant with the habits of some writers.

"F. Scott," said Karl.

Cindy remembered the Mr. Coffee and asked, "Do you want some coffee? Or a drink? I've got bourbon and vodka."

"Coffee would be great," said Karl.

She was trying to process the knowledge that the men in the restaurant who'd whipped out guns and shot at the ones who'd come in were sitting here, in her apartment, talking about L. Bass Hess. She went off to the kitchen. "Milk? Sugar?" she called.

"Black."

"Black, four sugars." That was Candy.

Cindy came in with two mugs of coffee, set Karl's on the table beside the sofa, and handed the other to Candy.

He was back with the fish tank. He said, "You got a nice arrangement in this, you got your ferns, coral, seaweed, leaf things—"

"Candy, shut up."

"I was just sayin'."

"Okay, what's in the folder?" Having brought their coffee, Cindy perched herself again on the chair with her own cup of black coffee. "That folder." She nodded toward the folder lying beside Karl. "And why did he give it to you two?"

"A problem of identity." Karl smiled.

Cindy didn't. "What identity?"

"He thought we were two other guys."

Cindy waited. He didn't elaborate. Heightening the suspense, she supposed. "*What* other guys."

"Lawyers. Hale and—" He looked toward Candy. "What was the other one?"

"Richard Gere?"

"Oh, come on, C., that wasn't the guy's name."

"Reed, no—"

"Reeves?" said Cindy. "You mean Wally Hale and Roderick Reeves? They're my attorneys."

"Yours? Well, what in hell were they doing in Hess's office?"

"I don't know. He's been trying to get me to settle, so maybe they went to talk about that."

"I thought lawyers talked to lawyers. I mean, the guy's got his own lawyer. Why aren't they all putting their heads together instead of him talking to this Hale and Reeves himself? That looks pretty sneaky to me."

"Probably because Hess wants to control everything. He's obsessed. What's in the folder? May I see it?"

Instead of handing it to her, he opened it. "Okay, he's saying he took you on as a client, and I quote, 'against my better judgment.'" Karl hooked his fingers in air quotes. "'When no other agent would represent her.'"

"What?"

"Continued quote: 'Since it was obvious she needed help.'"

"Help? Help?"

Karl nodded and wiggled his index fingers again for the quote. "'Not only for the business end; her writing, also, was in need of heavy editing, which I supplied.' Here he includes a chapter from your last book, *Mean Time,* that has a lot of penciled-in stuff in the margins."

Cindy held out her hand for these pages and leafed through them. "Oh, for God's sake! I was humoring him. He asked me, 'Could I just have a peek at the manuscript?' I had it with me to take to my publisher, and I just thought, Well, why not? After he riffled around in the pages, he paused on one, and with this tight little smile, he said, 'I think you need a semicolon here; shall I change it?' I shrugged and said, 'Go ahead.' Pretty soon he was off like the fire brigade, penciling in measly little changes as if it were one of his contracts."

"You didn't stop him? How come?"

"He was enjoying himself so much. I'd just tell my editor to ignore the markups. Which I did."

Karl shook his head and went back to the folder. "Next, there's all the editors you pissed off—"

"Like who?"

"There's a bunch of letters here from publishing people, editors, I guess: Adeline Larch, Maurice Dobbs, several others."

Cindy sighed. "Those are foreign editors. They didn't like what I said about the changes they wanted to make."

"What did you tell them?"

"Kind of 'fuck off.'"

"Yes!" cried Candy, pumping his fist in the air, congratulating Cindy on her candor.

"Then there's the drinking, the drugs—"

"What drugs? I take Aleve."

Finger hooking again: "'Reports from unimpeachable sources disclose use of marijuana, cocaine, other drugs.'"

"Where's he getting all this? How can this be any part of a lawsuit that's claiming I owe him commission money? The 'mutual trust'? There was never any trust. And we never worked on my books together—"

Karl held up the chapter pages and waved them. "I assume you're lawyered up?"

"Of course. Snelling and Snelling. It's a big firm."

Candy frowned. "You read that book by that lawyer called *The Firm*."

"John Grisham. Yes."

"That's the kind of stuff lawyers get up to."

Cindy smiled. "It's probably not that bad."

"Oh, you better believe it. We know a lotta attorneys."

"Handling intellectual property?"

"Not exactly," said Karl. "Other stuff. You wouldn't want one of them."

"What stuff?"

Karl ran his thumbnail across his forehead, thinking. "Graft, murder, like that."

"Oh." Cindy was looking dubious. "You never told me what it is you two do."

Karl studied the ceiling. Candy said, "We're consultants."

Karl brought his eyes down. "That's it. Consultancy."

"About what?"

Candy shrugged, said, "People who got problems."

Relentlessly, Cindy kept at it. "What kind of problems? Give me a for-instance."

"Well, for instance, whoever was the target at the restaurant. He'd want to solve that little problem."

Cindy frowned as Karl rose and said, "Another time, okay? We really gotta go."

"Aren't you going to give me the folder?"

"Let us keep it for a little, okay?"

Candy said, "So after you gave this Hess the heave-ho, you got another agent."

She nodded. "Jimmy McKinney."

"What agency's he with?" Karl was rather pleased with himself, being able to converse so smoothly about writing and publishing.

"Just him. He's his own agency."

Karl nodded, said, "You mind if we go see him?"

Cindy shrugged. "No. Why?"

"Background." Karl took a little notebook out of his shirt pocket and a stub of a pencil out of his inside jacket pocket. "What's his address?"

Cindy gave it to him. "It's really nice. An old brownstone."

"What's this agent guy doing about this?" He held up the folder.

"There's nothing much he can do." She smiled. "Except he did offer to kill him for me."

"That was nice of him," said Karl.

"Yeah. Our kind of guy," said Candy.

They grinned. They left.

8

J immy McKinney sat in his office, trying to plow through a manuscript submission from an aspiring writer about a moose who, together with some other moose(es), was taking over the town of Moosehart, Indiana, all of this a veiled satire of the writer's own hometown, Elkhart.

Jimmy was having a hard time bringing Coleridge's willing suspension of disbelief to this project. The mooselike proclivities of the characters, rendered as all too human, failed to gain empathy without any of the moose's redeeming features, such as its huge size and its ability to trample a person, such as the writer. He heaved the manuscript onto a stack beside his desk. He hated writing rejection letters. He had another stack of manuscripts that were bad, though not moose-bad. He had received this manuscript because the writer had managed an interview with some editor at Breadloaf or some other writing conference, and the editor had suggested Jimmy as an agent.

Jimmy was popular with publishers and editors because he was, in an old-fashioned way, more interested in a writer's ongoing career than a quick payoff. He knew he could have gotten much heftier advance money for some of his clients, including a couple of new writers who might be poised to make a big splash with their first novels—he hated the word "debut"—but Jimmy wasn't in favor of big advances.

Agents liked to impress writers with their ability to get a king's ransom up front. But it could turn into exactly that: ransom. And when the book didn't "earn out," when it sold many fewer copies than the advance warranted, the publisher might be a lot less eager to take the second book. Or down the road, just kick the writer back into the street. Huge advances were a bad idea unless you were already a megaseller like Paul Giverney or Stephen King or John Grisham.

Jimmy was careful to explain all of this to prospective writers. Some of them wanted the big bucks—not just the money but the rush, the ego pump-up of commanding six figures. He had a print on the wall behind his cluttered desk, a sketch of Margaret Drabble, with a quote: "Writing and money have nothing to do with each other."

He loved that. The writers he wanted to work with understood it.

Jimmy used to work for a high-powered agent named Mort Durban who laughed at the idea that money and writing weren't connected. As far as Mort was concerned, money was writing's *only* connection. Publishers were there to do battle with him about it. But Jimmy had to hand it to Mort if a publisher said, "Hell, I'm not paying that for a first novel! Don't be ridiculous!"

"Fine. I'll be ridiculous somewhere else. Bye." Down crashed the receiver. (Mort liked landlines precisely for the crashing-down feature.)

Within thirty seconds the phone would ring again, nearly jumping off the desk with ringing. Mort just sat with a big cigar stuck in his mouth like a cork, waiting for the final ring, picking it up, saying "Mort Durban" as if he had no notion of who would be on the other end. Accepting the offer.

Mort loved this kind of deal-making. He claimed he always operated in the interests of his clients, but Jimmy knew better. Mort operated in his own interests.

An author would think, and with perfect reason, if he were going to fork over 15 percent of his royalties to an agent, that this agent would be working for him, looking out for his career, looking forward, making the moves now that would advance that career. A writer didn't think of an agent having his own agenda.

Jimmy had only half a dozen clients, two successful enough to write for a living. The others had to hold down jobs and write in their spare time. Jimmy knew what that felt like, as he'd done it for years himself, writing poetry, holding down the job with the Durban Agency.

It was the writer Paul Giverney who had damned near saved Jimmy's life by talking him into going to one of the writing colonies where you could shut the door and turn to complete silence. For a long weekend he got away from his beautiful but shrill wife, who was seldom satisfied, and his teenage son, who never was.

At the colony were little cabins sprinkled throughout the woods. The setup was meant to give writers the freedom to turn their undivided attention to their work. The silence inside and out was so pure, it should have been distilled, as if it were a bottle of Château Lafite Rothschild. The irony of the weekend was that he was continually interrupted by drunk writers wanting him to go along and party. He had little of the Château Lafite silence. But it still worked its magic. The fact that he couldn't stand the interruptions, that he didn't want people around, that he wanted the silence, told him just as much as if no one had knocked on his door. He knew he'd have to leave his wife and son and get a place by himself.

The marriage had gone sour years before. In the less than a year he'd been separated from Lilith, he'd written enough poetry for the second half of his second book. It had taken him fifteen years of married life to write the first half.

Right now Jimmy pulled the manuscript from a drawer and looked over the last poem. He thought maybe he was trying too hard with it. It was a sestina, so it was hard not to try too hard. He crossed out a line.

The doorbell sounded its tearful little chimes. Sighing, he got up, went to the door. Two men, strangers, stood on his front stoop. "Jimmy McKenzie?"

"McKinney." A lot of people made that mistake. "What can I do for you?"

The taller of the two had a folder under his arm, a little too thin to be a manuscript, Jimmy hoped. And authors didn't show up like this; they called before they came.

"We just got done talking to Cindy Sella?" The man held up the folder.

Cindy sending a prospective client? No, that wasn't Cindy. "Come on in. And you are—?"

"Karl."

"Candy," offered the shorter one, who was giving the hall the once-over, looking appreciatively at the small bronze dolphin Mort Durban had given Jimmy when he signed the dreadful Myra Byington, prolific writer of romantic thrillers. The dreadful Myra had insisted on going with Jimmy when he left the agency. "Good riddance," Mort had said, though it was never good riddance to any commission in the six-figure zone. Myra was one of the ones who made a living from writing.

"Come into the office."

The tall one, Karl, was stretching his neck to take in the chandelier (came with the house) and the high ceilings and old moldings. "Real nice place you got here. Prime real estate, Chelsea. And you got a whole house."

"It's a pretty small house." Jimmy led them into the next room, Karl and Candy all the while scoping out the place as if they might come back to rob it. Their designer suits notwithstanding, Jimmy had the feeling that the crime rate on the block had just spiked. He waved his hand toward a crewel-work wingback chair and an upholstered easy chair that sat pretty much in tatters.

Karl said, "I guess you know about this agent, L. Bass Hess's, complaint against her."

"Yes, certainly. Trying to collect a commission on her last book, one Hess didn't even represent. It's been tried before, but either the writer paid or the agent gave up. It's never been carried this far for the simple reason that it's an absurd claim."

"So how come this Bass Hess thinks he's got a case against Cindy Sella?"

"Revenge."

"Jesus," said Karl. "Don't authors have the right to get rid of agents they don't like?"

"Of course they do, happens all the time. But Hess is so egotistical, he thinks nobody leaves him, nobody. Kind of like a Mafia boss, if you know what I mean."

Both of them nodded soberly. "Yeah, we know," said Karl.

Jimmy went on. "He also thinks Cindy Sella owes him, like he saved her career and other such shit. He's an egocentric, self-deluding, out-of-touch, self-absorbed son of a bitch."

"So, personally, what do you think of him?" asked Candy.

Jimmy grinned. "He could've been a good agent, maybe was at some time. He's hell on contract language. Which has him picking over contracts like a gibbon searching for fleas, and that's what makes him think he can twist the option clause to his advantage. It's in every contract, purely for the benefit of the publisher, a right of first refusal. There's absolutely no benefit for the writer, which is the irony about this situation. If an agent's doing something to help an author, he should try to take the damned clause out. If Hess really worked hard on it, he'd have gotten it taken out." He nodded toward the folder. "What's in there?"

"It's the documents in the case."

"That's a book by Dorothy L. Sayers."

"Hell, does everybody know that but us?" Karl handed Jimmy the folder. "Anyway, this is the Hess take on it. We happened to go to his office. What it is, is a lot of stuff about Miss Sella's personal conduct and behavior. He claims he's got the goods on her: drugs, drinking, et cetera. And of course how bad she acted, firing him out of the blue, forcing the publisher to keep back money owed him, twisting her foreign agents to do her bidding."

Jimmy was looking at the papers. "Not Cindy, definitely not Cindy. She's the most legit person I know. Sits in her little apartment in what she calls Grub Street and writes."

Candy frowned. "Lives on Grove. What's Grub Street?"

Jimmy looked up from the papers, smiling. "A novel by George Gissing called *New Grub Street*. Grub Street was a part of London inhabited by hack journalists, novelists willing to sell out for money—it was the turning up of commercialism in writing, a street dedicated not to art but to money. Cindy makes money, spends hardly any. Why am I telling you this?"

"Oh, kindred souls and shit like that." Karl flashed a smile. He had teeth that looked like an ad for Sonicare.

Jimmy's eyes narrowed. "What do you guys do, anyway? You're not writers." Then, thinking he sounded snobbily dismissive of them, he added, "*Are* you writers?"

Candy had just folded a stick of Doublemint into his mouth, so his tongue was a little clotted when he said, "We might be thinkin' of a book, yeah."

Karl yukked. "Oh, sure, with all our free time."

They seemed to have it. Jimmy asked again, "Why did you go to Bass Hess's office, anyway?"

Karl said, "A client-author had some questions he wanted answered." They both looked at Jimmy.

He looked back. "Client? You guys aren't in the publishing world, are you?"

They laughed. "Sometimes it sure feels like it," said Candy, his chewing gum under control.

"Why did Hess give you his papers?"

"He thought we were Hale and Reeves." Candy sat forward and picked up the brass paperweight that had been holding down some manuscript pages. "A case of mistaken identity."

"So Hess never saw you before and didn't ask you for ID?"

"He told us who we were," said Karl. "He thought we were the guys he was expecting. Thought we were his three o'clock."

Candy chortled. "Dumb prick. It's what you was saying before. Anyone that's so—" He twirled his hand in the air in a dancer's gesture. "Whatever you said, wouldn't that kinda person think everything's going according to plan because it's his plan?"

Jimmy rested his chin on his fist and looked at Candy. It wasn't a bad analysis of the incident, after all.

Karl said, "I'd be willing to bet he even believes all this crap he's put together. Me, just gimme an old-time crook any day. A fraud that knows he's a fraud. A pair of frauds like in *Dirty Rotten Scoundrels*. Michael Caine and Steve Martin. A couple of straight-up, old-time crooks. Guys that know damned well they're stealing the socks off their grannies. Like if I rob somebody at gunpoint, I don't say, 'Hey! It's what you owe me, scumbag.'"

Jimmy laughed. Then he held up the papers and said, "Can I keep this?"

"Yeah, sure. We stopped in at a copy place and had a couple made. So why can't she sue him for libel?"

Jimmy shrugged. "I don't know. Probably because it's in a legal document. He's already filed a complaint. I don't know how he's going to present this stuff."

"So this jerk can say whatever he damn pleases, and all she can do is sit on her hands?"

Jimmy nodded. "That's my guess."

"Man, that is cold."

"And it could drag on for a long time. That's what he wants. It makes her spend a zillion bucks in attorneys' fees." He smiled. "But Cindy says it's better than paying Hess another cent."

"Yeah, but doesn't he know he's gotta be hurting himself? What writer is going to hire an agent who sues his own clients, for God's sake?"

Jimmy spread his arms. "Bass Hess feels righteous. That's what I meant by out of touch with reality. He can't imagine anyone wouldn't see him in the same light that he sees himself. Maybe he actually thinks he'd appear heroic, the agent who'd go to the mat for you, who'd fight to the death, who'd never—"

"Hey. It's the wrong damned mat, ain't it? It's his client that he's trying to beat up and pin down."

"True."

"So, Jimmy," said Karl, "I think we should have a talk with her lawyers."

Jimmy pushed the file folder toward him. "I don't know where it'll get you. But go ahead. The firm is Snelling. Or, to be precise, Snelling, Snelling, Borax, and Snelling."

"I wonder how Borax got in there," said Candy.

"Duke Borax?" said Karl.

"I don't know. You know him?"

Karl shook his head. "Heard his name." He rose. "We gotta be going. Where is this firm?"

Jimmy rose, saying, "Spurling Building. It's on Twenty-third, near Fifth. Across from Madison Square Park. Hold on." He flicked through his Rolodex, where he still kept contact information. He gave them a number.

Candy had gotten up and was casing the room with grave deliberation.

"Looking for something?" said Jimmy.

"You don't have a fish tank?"

9

The Spurling Building was a black marble and glass monolith that reflected a blue-shadowed light onto its surroundings.

Candy and Karl pushed through its big revolving door to an outer lobby that served no purpose other than to announce it as spare Manhattan real estate. They passed through thick glass doors to an inner lobby that told them it was fifteen by fifty feet of the same. Black-suited security guards disguised to look like civilians, for some unfathomable reason, stood placidly and loosely at attention, their hands hooked in front of their groins, Bluetooth studs in their ears with tiny mikes near their lips. Hell, nobody'd ever guess they were security, would they? There were even two "guardesses," as Candy called them, gussied up by Tory Burch, a lot of meaningless gold on their dark suits, belt buckles, and pocket flaps.

"What does this place think it is, fuck's sake? They got more security than the Pentagon."

Candy and Karl stood before one of the banks of elevators. Karl had found Wallace Hale on the fancy name locator riveted to the black marble wall. "Fifteenth floor," he said.

"Low-rent district; this building must have fifty floors."

They got out five seconds after they got on, with the uncomfortable feeling that they'd been compressed and decompressed. "Even my hangnails curled up," said Candy.

Here was another set of heavy glass doors, with the name of the firm in gold: *Snelling, Snelling, Borax, and Snelling.*

The two receptionists, Karl Lagerfeld runway twins; makeup by Bobbi Brown, as natural as birch bark; hair long, straight; the other short, straight; both razor-cut by Sweeney Todd.

"Good afternoon, gentlemen. May I help you?" The one with long hair smiled as if honestly happy to see them.

"Yeah, we'd like to see Mr. Hale," said Candy. "And no, we do not have an appointment, we just—"

Karl gave his shoe a kick. "He was highly recommended." He smiled but couldn't compete with the long-haired receptionist.

She said, "If you'd just have a seat." She gestured toward a suite of chairs by Philippe Starck, Mies van der Rohe, and the Eameses (all of whom had probably just left), situated in a waiting room that no doubt had won the *Architectural Digest* award.

"Shit, and I thought our place was cool."

"Ours is cool. This one is full of fucking lawyers, C. They probably make three, four times what we do. Keep in mind, we're a lot more selective."

Candy picked up a magazine in some foreign language he'd never heard of and leafed through it until he came on a gorgeous palm tree–lined stretch of white beach peopled by muscled men and bikini-clad women, or rather half-clad, as most were topless.

"Where the fuck's this?" He showed Karl the photo.

"South of France," said Karl, sticking a piece of gum in his mouth and offering the pack to Candy, who slid out a stick.

"Are you just sayin' that, or do you really know?"

"Shit like that's always the South of France."

A slim, beautifully engineered woman with black hair and a red dress as dark as dried blood, almost as dark as her hair, bled her way across the carpet and told them she was Mr. Hale's secretary and that he could give them fifteen minutes. It was like Christmas, she seemed to be saying.

They followed her to a burled-wood door that turned out to be not a section of the paneled wall after all. She ushered them through it. "He'll be finished with his call in a minute." She left.

Wally Hale played with his blue silk tie and laughed into the phone. Wally Hale was one of the two who had stepped out of the elevator.

"Are we busted?" whispered Karl.

Wally put down the phone and stood up. "Gentlemen." He smiled. "Have a seat."

Side-of-his-mouth mutter, Candy said, "He don't recognize us."

"Mr. Karl, Mr. Candy, what can I do for you?"

They sat and tried to get their bearings. Since they spent a lot of their time shooting people, getting their bearings wasn't as hard for them as it might have been for your average citizen. They sat with well-trained, expressionless faces.

Karl shoved the folder between himself and the chair arm, cleared his throat and said, "We got a client—"

They always had a client. Candy waited. Karl was good at coming up with crap. They were both good at it.

"—a client who's in a world of trouble, you could say."

Wally nodded, smiling over a world of trouble. "And you—"

"Oh, incidental to that, it was one of your clients that recommended you. Cindy Sella."

"Cindy! Ah." The smile seemed to want to evaporate but hardened like lacquer.

Karl said, "Just to get it straight, you ain— Ah, you aren't an intellectual property attorney?"

"No. We handle contract law, mergers and acquisitions—"

"Yeah. We're in contracts, too."

"You're attorneys?" Wally looked a little doubtfully from one to the other. "Contract law?"

Karl nestled in his seat. "I mean book contracts, that kind of thing."

Candy, discreetly chewing his Doublemint, said, "It's how come we know Cindy. Well, I don't have to tell you she's having her share of trouble with her ex-agent."

Wally was apprehensive. "You know him?"

Candy and Karl looked at each other. "Us? No. Just heard about him. From her. So how come Cindy chose a lawyer in mergers and acquisitions?"

"That's not all I do. To answer why, well, family. Our parents were friends." Wally swiveled his chair, then he swiveled his thumbs.

What a crock, thought Karl, smiling. Interesting that the precious fifteen-minute allowance had walked out the door with the Duchess of Fuck-All. Wally must want something.

"So you're acting . . . as what for Cindy Sella?"

Karl said, "Just advisers, consultants. You know."

No, he didn't. Wally readjusted his smile and said, "Let's hear about this client of yours, the one that's in a world of trouble, as you said." To let them know he wasn't asleep.

Karl sorted through troubles, most having to do with bodily harm. Too bad Wally here wasn't a criminal lawyer. "Let's say he wasn't one of the smartest guys in the room." He looked at Candy. They sneaked a laugh. Neither one knew what he meant by that, but something would turn up.

"Hey, you're not telling me he worked for Enron?" Wally smiled and showed little paddles of very white teeth. "I thought that bird had flown."

That bird had flown. Jesus, this guy was a fucking disaster.

"Our client's in the import business."

"What does he import?" It couldn't, the tone said, be good.

Karl opened his mouth, but it was Candy who spoke. "Fish," he said, treading on Karl's answer.

"You mean exotic or tropical fish?"

"That is correct." Candy crossed his legs, regarded his well-polished Italian loafer with the tassel.

With a pristinely raised eyebrow, Wally Hale asked, "And the trouble is with, possibly, Fish and Wildlife and, possibly, some offense to CITES?"

Whatever that was. Karl was regarding Candy with a similarly raised eyebrow. Instead of verbally replying, Candy made an *o* of thumb and finger and winked.

"So where's he getting the fish from?"

"Mostly Indonesia and the Philippines. Some from Europe."

Karl sat, expressionless.

"Where you got your greatest coral reefs: the Philippines. Now." Warming even more to his subject, Candy leaned forward in his chair, crossed his arms on Wally Hale's desk. "Your coral reefs, as we all know, are endangered, an endangered species—"

Karl needed to know what he'd have found out if he'd ever listened to Candy reading to him from *National Geographic*. "What spec—"

Candy threw up his hands, cutting him off with a smile. "Yeah, I know what you're going to say. Why'd we ever take this client on in the first place?"

Karl raised his chin, ran his hand down his tie, smoothing it. "It was your call, C., if you remember."

"Family. He's family. First cousin, once removed."

Wally, growing either more interested or more perplexed by the second, said, "The firm doesn't really do much by way of environmental protection; we're not exactly hand in glove with the EPA." He half-laughed to see how it would play. It did and it didn't.

Karl gave the other half of the laugh and said, "Yeah, neither is our client."

Candy made a tsking noise and moved his finger like a metronome before Wally. "Come on, Wally. What about that clear-cutting thing in Kentucky. That Adirondack Dewitt deal?"

Wally was back to smiling. "Yeah. That wasn't me, exactly— Hey, Rod!" Wally was looking at the connecting door.

Richard Gere entered. The three o'clock appointment was all here now.

Wally introduced them. They shook hands; Richard smiled. His other name was Rod Reeves, even more of a movie name than Richard Gere.

Rod sat, or rather, flung himself down in one of the Eames (probably) chairs, white and with a kind of dripping Dali look, with underpinnings of crossed wood and narrow steel tubes. It looked made especially for Rod, he seemed so at home in it. "So?" Rod asked this as if to be updated on whatever had passed, be it their conversation or the latest report from the Warren Buffett newsletter, was his, Rod's, royal privilege.

"They're friends of Cindy Sella," said Wally.

Which, as far as Candy and Karl were concerned, gave it all away, what they were interested in.

Rod sat right up, hard to do if you'd been reclining in that chair. "Oh?" He and Wally exchanged a look.

Wally summed up the conversation thus far. "You want us to take on this client in trouble with customs or in violation of EPA statutes—"

"The Philippines?" Rod looked as if he knew every inch of them. "Coral reefs. Some of the best diving in the world."

"They take crowbars to the reefs to pry them apart," said Karl.

Candy was surprised that Karl had heard even a little of the article.

"Crowbars? What for?" said Wally.

"To get at the fish," Candy said. "After they've been stunned with cyanide."

"Cyanide?" Three pairs of eyes swiveled toward Candy until Karl caught himself and nodded, as if he'd forgotten for only a second about the cyanide.

"Cyanide fishing? You never heard of it? They spray cyanide into the water, stun the fish, then net them."

"The cyanide doesn't kill them?"

Candy chuckled. "I don't think there'd be much of a market for dead fish, do you?"

Rod asked, "What or who is the market?"

"You'd be surprised. We're talking high-up people, places. You didn't read about that shooting at the Clownfish Café off Lex the other night? Shot up this huge fish tank. Frankie, he had a fortune in fish—"

Rod laughed. "The shooters were looking for somebody, not for a fish." He laughed again.

"You're half right. And do you know who the target was?"

Rod and Wally looked blank.

"You didn't know your client Cindy Sella was at the Clownfish that night?"

They both jutted forward as if working opposite ends of a circular saw. "What? What the hell does Cindy Sella have to do with it?"

"You mean you didn't know she was writing this book about the fish cartel in New York? You never heard her talk about how much she hates fish being mistreated? You been to her place? You seen her aquarium? No?"

The answer was, obviously, no. They looked bug-eyed, which wasn't good for the hotshot-lawyer image.

"Those shooters? Probably one of the Bluefin Alliance. Sending another message. You don't mess with these guys, Wally. Rod. We're talking big, big, very big business. It's not your Mexican cartels, no, at least not yet—"

Karl broke in. "Come on, C., there's no way these two know about this." He tossed Wally and Rod a glance just this side of contemptuous. "This is the best-kept secret in New York." He turned to the lawyers. "Check it out with your colleagues. They won't know anything about it."

Candy said, "But my God, Wally! You're Cindy Sella's attorneys, and you didn't know she was into this?"

Karl was beset with pleased astonishment. They were so far away from option clauses they might as well have been on the moon. Or fishing in Indonesia.

Wally said, "How much are these fish going for?"

"'These fish'? Do some research before you bring this up with Cindy. If you're talking your platinum arowana. That'd set you back a hundred large. If you can find one."

Their jaws dropped, reminding Candy of the bass on Hess's wall. Hess. Fucking tree toad. "Maybe you should try and talk her out of it."

"What?"

Jesus. His fish, Oscar, had a longer attention span than these guys. "The book she's writing."

Wally flattened his palms against air. "Wait a minute. If this fish cartel, or whatever the hell it is, is so under the radar, then where's Cindy getting her information?"

Candy shrugged. "I don't know. You're her lawyers, not us."

"Hess never mentioned—" Rod shut his mouth like a doll. His teeth clicked.

Candy and Karl loved it. Karl said, "You mean Bass Hess? That half-assed ex-agent of hers? Why would he tell you anything?"

"He wouldn't," Wally snapped. "Nothing was mentioned in discovery."

Oh, shit, thought Candy. "You mean this frivolous lawsuit has gone to discovery?"

Wally was shuffling papers. Rod had gone to lean against the wainscot woodwork behind his desk as if he needed support from both the wall and Wally. He crossed his arms, hugging himself. Then he said, "Haven't I seen you before?" The look slid from Candy to Karl and back.

Without missing a beat, Karl said, "Probably. I'll bet it was that public defender's pro bono bash back in March. You know, nearly every attorney in town was there."

Candy's face nearly wrapped around itself, trying not to laugh. You listen, you learn. Woody Allen was right: 80 percent of life was just showing up. The other 20 percent was paying attention when you got there.

Wally and Rod exchanged a look. Wally drew a pad toward him, picked up his Mont Blanc. "We need your client's name if we're going to take this on."

So do we, thought Candy. "We got to talk to the client about this. We'll get back to you."

They rose. It had been clear for some time now that Wally and Rod didn't want Candy and Karl running loose. Cindy's so-called attorneys wanted to keep them as close to the vest as a poker hand.

Wally came around his desk, trying not to look hurried about it; Rod pushed off from the wall, and the two walked the other two to the door.

"We'll be in touch." Candy held out his hand, and Wally shook it. Karl and Rod did the same, and all the hands crisscrossed. It looked as if the four of them were about to make a tower of fists like kids on a playground, which, thought Candy, was essentially how it was. He smiled.

Wally said as he ushered them into the chilly area of the reception desk, "I'll give Cindy a call, talk her through it."

Talk her through it? You couldn't even talk yourself through it fifteen minutes ago. Candy merely shrugged. "Go ahead, but she'll probably play dumb. She won't tell you anything."

Wally looked offended. "She told you, didn't she?"

Connect the dots, asshole. "That's because we have this client that imports fish; because we were in the Clownfish when the shooting started; because—"

"Right, right," said Wally impatiently. "I still think Rod and I had better get in on this before it, you know, gets out of hand."

Karl and Candy looked at each other. Karl said, "By all means, Wally."

Out of no-man's-land and back on the rowdy Manhattan pavement where every passerby hugged close enough to pick your pocket, they both started laughing. The stony expressions they had used so well on attorneys, receptionists, and security guards cracked like ice crust on a pond.

"That was some tale, C. How'd you ever come up with that?"

"*National Geographic*. I read it to you."

"The cyanide, I remembered that. How much of that shit was true?"

"All of it. That's the great thing about truth. You don't have to make it up."

Karl stepped over the curb, looking for a cab, which was like finding an unlit star in the Milky Way, especially at six P.M., which it was.

Candy said, "But you sure nailed that party. Rod was beginning to look as if he'd seen us. 'Pro bono bash.' Righteous. As if they'd ever have anything to do with that shit."

"Yeah, only, where's this get us?"

"It got the foot in the door so good that even when we take it away, the door won't close. That's how curious they are; that's how nervous. Where the fuck's a cab?"

"In Jersey. Come on, let's walk." Karl was back on the sidewalk, walking.

"Oscar ain't eaten since this morning." Candy started tapping away at his cell phone as they walked.

"At least nobody fed him cyanide. Why don't you wait till we pass a Balducci's, pal? Call your fish from there, see what he wants."

Candy snorted. "So funny. I'm trying Cindy again." Long pause. He snapped the phone shut as they swaggered along, tails of Façonnable coats flapping behind them.

10

Cindy was out of her blue chenille bathrobe and into jeans with a tear on the knee made by Gus, not fashion; a gray cowl-neck sweater; and an old dark peacoat.

She was also out of her apartment and into Jimmy McKinney's office, her favorite place in Manhattan besides Ray's coffee shop. She liked the brownstone, although it was the same as the others on the block; she liked the stone steps worn in the center to the image of a shoe; she liked the cherrywood door to his office, the thin pale Oriental rug, the floor-to-ceiling bookcases, and every item of furniture, including the big desk, the swivel chair he sat in (and liked to skid around), but mostly him, Jimmy McKinney.

Jimmy was talking about this and that, but she wasn't really listening, only looking, her head cocked to the side, trying to recall who he reminded her of.

"I offered to shoot the bastard, but you turned me down."

"Who?"

He grinned. "How many have I offered to shoot?"

She looked around the room.

"Is that your cell?" said Jimmy.

The ringtone was the one that had come with the phone; it was barely audible. Jimmy was just used to listening to clients, excepting Cindy, to whom he talked more than he listened.

The bag she had slung over the chair was nearly the size of a brown grocery bag, and she started rooting through it without enthusiasm, as she'd rather listen to Jimmy than her cell phone. Still, she had to make a show of looking, so she took out papers, notebooks, a beat-up paperback copy of *The Aspern Papers,* pens, a lipstick. "I can't find it," she said rather happily.

"How many notebooks do you carry around?" He nodded at the stack.

She started putting everything back. "Several."

"But not a laptop."

Cindy frowned. Why was this turning dull? "No. Why?"

He sat back, locking his fingers behind his head. Smiled. "It's interesting."

"No, it isn't."

He had told her about the visit from her friends Candy and Karl and got back on that subject, still unsatisfied with Cindy's explanation. "These two—what is it they do, exactly?"

She sighed. "How would I know? They pulled out guns in the Clownfish Café. Maybe they're federal agents or something. They were pretty evasive."

The cell bleated.

"That's your cell again." Jimmy nodded toward the bag Cindy had dumped on the floor.

She pulled up the bag and went through the whole business again. The cell phone continued its silly tune, whining to be picked up. "I'll never find it." She sighed as if she cared.

Jimmy was enjoying the little show. He'd enjoyed it the first time, too. He said unhelpfully, "Why do you carry a cell phone around? If you can never answer it?"

"Usually, I don't. It's just when I have an appointment and maybe I'll be late and want to notify whoever. Like you."

She turned eyes on him so intensely sad that he had to look away. Jimmy sometimes felt there was something about Cindy Sella that could engulf him. He thought of his wife, soon to be his ex-wife, Lilith. He could not help but think, "Not even Lilith with her famous hair." Edwin Arlington Robinson. There was a poem to fit every occasion. It was why he loved poetry so much. It was why he wrote poetry. There was always a poem waiting just around the corner to explain a situation. "And Lilith was the devil, I have read."

"It stopped," Cindy said, jamming the junk back into her bag.

"You've got to unload Wally Hale. You can't stand him, and he's not an intellectual properties lawyer. Go to the guy I told you about, Sam Walsh. Did you even call him?" He was talking to the crown of her head. All of that pale hair was natural, apparently. There wasn't root number one showing. He sat back. "How did you ever hook up with Hale?"

"At a party," she said to her lap. "I just met him. Them." Finally, she raised her head, as if she'd skated to more solid ground. "He was with the other lawyer, Rod Reeves. They work together, they said. He looks like Richard Gere. Did you see *Chicago*?"

"No. But I know a con man when I see one."

"No, you don't."

He guessed he didn't. "So what did you do? Hire them on the spot? After some cocktail chitchat?" It really irritated him. "And you never go to parties." As if that were the larger problem. He just shook his head. "These guys who came to see me? Candy and Karl—"

Cindy smiled. "Aren't they a scream?"

"A scream they might be, but why are they working for you?"

"They aren't. I mean, they just seemed really interested. I didn't actually hire them. But I guess I didn't discourage them, either. Look, what were we talking about? And is the tea ready?"

This time the phone that rang was Jimmy's landline. He picked up. "McKinney." Stillness while he looked at her. "She's right here, yeah." He held the receiver toward her. "Speak of the devil. It's your pals."

Puzzled, she spoke: "Hello." She sat back, listened. "Thanks. Thank you." She handed the receiver back to Jimmy. He dropped it in place.

"What?" he asked.

"That was Candy. He and Karl went to see Wally Hale but didn't tell him the real reason for their visit."

"What *did* they tell him?"

She frowned. "Something about a fish alliance." Her frown deepened. "A *what*?"

"Maybe a fin alliance?"

"Well, that clears things up."

"If Wally or Rod get in touch with me, I'm to say I don't know what they're talking about. That won't be hard. Karl said I should fire them *tout de suite*." She smiled. "I'm going to anyway."

Jimmy was picking up the phone. "I'm calling the lawyer I told you to see. Sam Walsh."

"He'll say I have to drop my other lawyers before he can see me, won't he?" She was picking up her luggage-sized bag.

Jimmy tapped in numbers. "I don't think Sam stands upon such niceties." He glanced up as Cindy stood, looking forlorn, her bag slung over her shoulder.

Cindy just stood there a few moments. "What's a nicety?"

11

Candy fed Oscar his soupçon of dinner, which the fish attacked like a missile.

Karl barely looked up. "Why don't we take him on a Carnival cruise? The fish could eat whenever he wanted."

Candy ignored this comment. He picked up his drink and went back to the white leather sofa to continue, with Karl, their search for justice. "Why don't we just whack Hess and be done with it?"

Karl had set down his own glass to fire up a Monte Cristo. "Come on, C., you know why. That bastard, he'd fall right at the feet of Cindy Sella. Who's the person with the most motive to want him gone?" He puffed around, inhaled, let out a flat stream of smoke.

"Listen, there's probably a lot of people with a motive. So we make sure Cindy's alibied."

"You know that won't work. They'd say she just hired somebody to do the job."

"We know people; we could hire somebody for her."

"Candy, hel-lo—" Karl rocked his hand back and forth. "We're the guys that people hire."

Candy rose and revisited the fish tank as if Oscar might have some ideas. Then he paid another visit to the cocktail shaker, very retro, very art deco. Like the table lamp beside it, where once rested the brass figure of a girl holding the moon. This had been replaced by leaping fish on a frosted circle of glass that shaded the candle bulb. Candy filled his glass and reseated himself.

Karl stopped blowing smoke rings. "Remember, we need a client."

"For the illegal fish trade, yeah."

"I'm not exactly sure why we need one, since we don't know what the fuck we're goin' to do with this client." Karl tapped off ash with his little finger into a big Murano glass ashtray.

"Did you ever stop to think that we don't know all that many people, K.? Or at least most of them are dead?"

"Yeah, it's the downside of this business. Wait, how about Danny Zito? He's the one got us that job working for that asshole Mackenzie."

"Danny Zito? He's in WITSEC, remember? But you'd never know it, the way he's always around handing out advice."

"Anyway, we need someone who's good at getting information out of people."

"Danny can."

"So could Cheney's favorite people. I'm talking more like the PI line of work."

"A detective?" Candy made a face. "I dunno." It was his turn to get up and pace. He did so by the fish tank, with Oscar swimming slowly back and forth, in what Candy decided was fish pacing. "Listen, listen to this idea: Paul Giverney. Remember?"

"I'd have to be dead to forget. We told him, right? Told him to stop fucking up other people's lives."

"So he owes Ned Isaly—"

"What the hell's Ned Isaly got to do with this?"

"Nothing. I'm saying Paul Giverney owes writers, owes authors . . . you know, owes them something. So he should maybe pay that debt off to Cindy."

"I don't know what the hell you're talking about. That fish is gettin' to you, C."

"Yeah, yeah. Listen. One, we gotta get this someone inside the law offices of Dickheads, Esquires. And number two"—Candy held up two fingers to make his point—"we want to get someone inside the Hess Agency." He tapped the tank, making tiny waves that Oscar breasted and breached before dropping down to the Hotel W and hiding.

"So what the fuck you saying?"

"Paul Giverney." Candy smiled broadly and fleshed out the picture a bit more.

Karl sniggered. "I like it."

12

Paul Giverney had just about decided never to write another word when the intercom buzzer made its annoying insectlike sound.

"Who's that?" he called out to his wife from his study/office.

She called back: "Not being able to see through three floors below us to Clarence at the desk, I honestly don't know." She had begun saying this in the kitchen and finished up in the study doorway.

The intercom buzzed again. "Are you going to answer?"

She turned away, and her place was taken by his daughter, Hannah, who was holding another page from her book called *The Hunted Gardens*. In the last chapter, she had said, "the Draggonier will figure out what's going on." There were dragons in the garden. Hannah had come up with a Draggonier to do battle with them. But Hannah's crinkled brow, when Paul had questioned this development, seemed to imply there was a great deal of uncertainty.

Hannah said, "Why don't we live in the Dakota?"

"Why should we?" he said. He heard Molly's voice, apparently talking to Clarence on the phone. He wished people would go away.

"Well, this is a rent-controlled apartment, and we're taking up what a poor person could live in."

She was seven. When had she developed this humane view of things?

"Well, believe me, this apartment is not all that cheap, and we're not all that rich."

"Yes, we are. My friend James at school told me you were a billionaire and we could live in the Dakota."

Actually, James wasn't far off. Multimillionaire was closer. "Are you sure James didn't say Dakota-s, plural? Meaning North and South

Dakota? Maybe he said, 'You should live in the Dakotas.'" Paul smiled at that bit of cleverness. Chew on that, sweetheart.

She looked suspicious. "That would be a long way away from here, and you wouldn't be able to see your publisher."

In mock joy, Paul sat up. "What a great idea! I'll give the landlord notice tomorrow!" He drew a hand across his forehead, dramatically wiping away imaginary sweat. Then he returned to his former tone. "You mean you don't like this apartment?"

No reason why she should. No reason why anyone should like it or dislike it, for that matter. It was a two-largish-bedroom-plus-study with a big eat-in kitchen and a small dining room they seldom used. He himself loved it. It was so wonderfully ordinary. Molly liked it for the Dean and Deluca a short distance away. "If you want to move, I'll look into the Dakota and also the Carlyle. That's got a few really exclusive apartments. Neither one of those buildings is here in the East Village, they're more Central Park, and you might have to change schools . . ." That should stop her cold.

It didn't. After a short think, Hannah said, "It would be closer to the zoo. That would be good."

At that moment, Molly appeared behind Hannah. She smiled. "Your future is here, Paulie."

Paulie? What the hell did that mean? "What does that—"

She had turned away and said something to the visitor or visitors (for there seemed to be several voices). Candy and Karl appeared behind Hannah. "Hi!" "Hey, Paulie!"

"Hello," said Hannah. She turned away, too, but did not leave. Her head was covered with very fine pale brown hair, mostly curly. She was wearing a pale pink dress. Hannah loved dresses. Bloomie's should have snagged her ages ago as a model for their catalogs.

"Hey, kiddo. Wow! You are really cute from the back. Are you that pretty from the front?" said Karl.

Hannah actually giggled. These goons had a rapport with children? Paul couldn't believe it. Hannah wasn't a giggler. She turned around and presented herself.

"Hmm. Well . . ." said Candy, hand at chin, feigning concentration.

"I'm not?" Hannah sounded quite alarmed.

"Yeah, you are." Karl landed a pretend punch on Candy's shoulder. "Absolutely first-rate, four-star pretty."

That satisfied her. She drifted off like a petal.

"So, Paulie!" said Candy.

"What's this Paulie crap, you guys? Why are you here? What have I done now?" Paul checked out their jackets for telltale bulges. Nothing, but maybe they were wearing shoulder holsters.

"Mind if we sit?" said Karl, who then sat.

Candy took the third chair. There were two others, in addition to Paul's own creaky wooden desk chair.

"Nice suits," said Paul, noting that this would be his single foray into small talk. "I'm guessing Bruno Magli."

"You'd be guessing wrong. But we appreciate your attempt to be social, especially as you didn't expect us."

"You got that right." Paul leaned back in his chair, hands clasped behind his head as if he felt all relaxed and loose. Which he didn't. "What do you guys want?"

"A favor." Candy smiled and folded a stick of gum so dry in his mouth it felt splintered.

Paul raised his eyebrows. "I hope you don't think I owe you one."

Karl took out a dented silver cigarette case.

"That's nice," said Paul. "Antique?"

"No, just messed up. A couple bullets." Karl offered the cigarettes.

Paul shook his head. "Quit."

"Tough, man."

Candy held out his fresh pack of Doublemint.

Paul smiled and shook his head.

"Good choice," said Candy. "This stuff is dry as a bone."

"The favor?" Paul wasn't eager to hear it.

"We was just thinking: You might want to help out a fellow writer."

"Can't imagine why. But go on."

"You know Cindy Sella?"

Paul studied the ceiling molding for a moment. "Yeah. I mean, we have the same agent: Jimmy McKinney."

"We know. Do you know about Cindy's legal hassle with her ex-agent?"

"I heard something. Who is it?"

"L. Bass Hess. He's trying to hold her up for a commission on the last book she published, even though she fired him two years before. He thinks she owes him money for a book he never worked on."

"That's absurd." Paul frowned. "So what do you two have to do with it?"

"It's just we got sucked into it by accident."

"So now that you're into it, what's up?"

They told him: Karl, speaking of the identity mix-up; Candy, about the visit to the Spurling Building.

Paul laughed. He could not help but like the story about the cyanide fishing. "So you want someone to ooze into the law offices of these sleazeballs by posing as a fish importer?" Paul was as fascinated as a deer caught in a Hummer's headlights.

"Yeah. To see what information we can get about what in the hell they're doing playing footsie with Bass Hess."

"Where do I come in?"

"You and her are both published by Mackenzie-Haack."

"Me and her are?"

They both nodded.

Karl said, "All of this hugger-mugger with the agent and the lawyers trying to take down Cindy Sella almost sounds like what you did to Ned Isaly."

"It does not in any way, shape, or form resemble what I did." Paul was getting angry. "I had no intention of ruining Ned Isaly's life."

"But you almost did."

"Correction. Bobby Mackenzie 'almost did.' Could I help it if Mackenzie got the bright idea of hiring you, uh, guys?" He almost said "goons" but caught himself. "You're not going to suggest I be the fish importer?" Paul was slightly alarmed that, yes, that's what they were going to say.

"Nah. You're too well known. I mean, your face is plastered on the back of all your books."

Paul sighed, relieved.

"What we want is for you to take on Bass Hess as an agent."

The relief quickly dissipated. "Wait." Paul shot both arms out in front of him, waving this idea away. "I have an agent. You know that. Jimmy McKinney."

Candy said, "Oh, he'd be good with this. I mean, obviously, you're not firing the guy. We're talking about something temporary."

"How temporary?" Forgoing the larger question of "Why?"

Candy pursed his lips. "Not sure. However long it takes to get the job done."

Paul sighed. "What job?"

Candy shook his head slowly. "Not exactly sure about that, either."

Paul stared. It was like his books, trying to figure out what the characters were doing.

Karl said, "What we are sure about is we'll need someone who can make Hess do what we're going to want him to do, even though we don't know just what that is yet. And the someone, Paul, is most definitely you."

Paul looked from one to the other. He thought he knew just how the Draggonier felt, forced to wander indefinitely through the hunted gardens until Hannah figured things out.

13

I've seen a python eyeing a pig in a greater spirit of cooperation than you're getting from your publisher." This was Sam Walsh, the attorney Jimmy had recommended Cindy to. He was flipping over the papers she had brought the next morning in a folder. He went on, "No invoices, no explanations. You don't actually know what the billable hours reflect. Your attorney requested invoices. Mackenzie-Haack's lead attorney said he would take the request into consideration. That might be a client confidentiality issue."

Cindy clapped her hand to her head. "But I'm the client. I must be, if I'm the one paying."

"Not exactly. Hess is suing both you and Mackenzie-Haack—"

"He's suing us for exactly the same thing."

"Right."

"They build up all of these legal fees without telling me, without giving me a chance to settle. No one ever told me what firm Mackenzie was going to hire or what their billing rate was or said at the beginning, 'Look, this could get very costly, Cindy. Do you want to think about settling?' And now they won't let me see how all of these hours have been used; they won't let me see what I have to pay for." Cindy let her voice trail off. "Good-bye, Sam."

Sam dropped his feet from his desk and sat up. "Jesus, don't sound so final, girl."

"I've got to feed my cat. Then go back to Kafka, Sartre, and Celine for comfort. I wish David Foster Wallace were alive. He'd have this nailed."

———

There was more cooperation being displayed between Gus and her two clown fish. Her mind felt so friable, she couldn't come up with names for them.

She let a few specks of food drift across the water's surface. The first clown fish went on lying on his leaf; the ghost clown fish made a slow swim upward and snagged a bit of food. The fish tank looked so complete, so together, she almost wished she could dive in. She did a standing meditation for a minute. She emptied her mind and then let a few images drift in: waves, light, leaves. Whatever came, she labeled. If you labeled thoughts, you helped distance yourself from them. Gus had gone into the kitchen and was impatiently knocking his bowl about. Gus knocking bowl.

She tried saying her mantra, but it kept slipping away, and her life intruded. Maybe it was because it wasn't, strictly speaking, "her" mantra. She had bought it from her friend Benny Bennet for twenty dollars. He'd paid to take a course in Transcendental Meditation, and in the little ceremony at the end with the handkerchief and the flower, he had been assigned this mantra. "Nobody else has it; it's strictly yours," Benny had told her as he pocketed the cash. He'd stopped meditating because he said he'd rather spend his time drinking, smoking, doing lines of coke. What bothered her was that Benny knew the mantra. He could go back to meditating and using it, and that might throw everything off. What "everything" might be, she had no idea. Astral bodies. The Om community. She did not know the slightest thing about Transcendental Meditation except that David Lynch was really into it, and she thought anybody who could come up with *Mulholland Drive* was a man worth listening to.

She finished her standing meditation, thinking she hadn't meditated at all. All she had been doing was thinking the same things she'd be thinking if she were sitting down or walking along Grub Street. Gus was sitting at her feet, staring at her, trying to throw her off again. She gave up and followed him into the kitchen, giving him a little push with her foot, which he took the time to resent before he marched on as if he were a contractor bent on a complete renovation with easy access to his special food.

Cindy looked at the cans in the cupboard. Why did she keep thinking she could foist on him the Science Diet, the Blue, the Wellness, the Iams,

or any other food except Milky Empire, the one that cost about as much
as a trip to outer space? Once she had even tried packing Science Diet
into an empty Milky Empire can and then, with Gus watching, making a
big display of opening the can and shoveling some into his dish. He took
a sniff and looked at her, outraged. At least that was what she imagined
was swimming in his citrine (or peridot) eyes: How dare you. It was not
a question.

She fetched down a can of Milky Empire, pulled off the lid, spooned
half into the bowl. He set about eating and had no further use for her.

Cindy went back to the living room to write.

Lulu had her head in her hands.

Cindy found the story so sadly unsettling that she couldn't seem to
get on with it. Lulu was still sitting in her car. She had been thinking
(Cindy recalled from twenty pages ago) about Johnny. Lulu had just
taken him to the train station in the unidentified city where she lived.

This was what defined Lulu: Until the person left her—that is, left
for his or her own home; left to go across the country or to some foreign place; left, died—Lulu never knew how important that person was
to her. Like Johnny. Lulu seemed blinded to any sign of love until the
person was gone. Gone and irretrievable. No sudden realization on the
train station platform, just as the train was beginning to chug and pull
away, no "Johnny, Johnny! Come back oh please come back!" No. That
she truly loved Johnny was revealed to her only now, while she was sitting in her car.

This was the reason, thought Cindy, Lulu had been sitting there for
nearly twenty pages.

This was the reason the book was named *You Had Me at Good-bye*.

Cindy put her head in her hands.

14

Bobby Mackenzie, publisher of Mackenzie-Haack, had just poured himself a liberal measure of Talisker and was sitting at his desk, staring at the jacket art for a new book.

"Bobby!" said Candy and Karl simultaneously. They had bullied their way past Bobby's assistant.

Bobby gave them a sip's worth of silence before he held up his glass and said, "Scotch?"

Candy said, "I got to hand it to you, Bobby. We run you out of the country for six months, you come back, and all you say is 'Scotch?'"

The question hung in the air as they sat themselves down on the other side of Bobby's desk, which looked like a slab off a redwood tree. It could have been, Bobby not being the most green-thinking person in Manhattan.

He was wearing one of his half-dozen bespoke-tailored suits, which both Karl and Candy envied. They were not bought at Façonnable or Saks. Some wizened little tailor with a tape around his neck had run them up. All of the suits were the same cut, only different weaves and colors. They were woven of ethereally fine threads, merino wool and hummingbird's wings, who knew? Bobby was considered the best-dressed person in the publishing world. That he was amused many people, since it was so out of line with the rest of him.

The phone rang and Bobby picked up. He had a Droid; he had a Bluetooth. But he liked good old receivers he could slam down, and he was easily a match for that hell-on-wheels agent Mort Durban. He listened for about five seconds before saying, "This cover? Is this book about trolls? There's a troll on the jacket. Oh, a *child*? It's a little *girl*? So why am I puzzled? Do not show me shit like this. Ever." He hammered down the receiver and, looking from Karl to Candy and back, said, "I can hardly wait."

"For what?"

"To hear what you guys want. Like, who do you want me to punt onto the *Times* list this week and make sure he/she hangs out there for two months?"

Karl said in a meditative manner, "Bobby, here's what we fail to understand: Ned Isaly is your author. So when we 'made you' get him on the list and he stayed there for two months and got a lot of money, you, Mackenzie-Haack, made out, too. What we fail to understand is why you wouldn't have done it anyway." He thought this an obvious and excellent point.

Bobby didn't. He made a sound in his throat as if battling back a nasty reply and lost. "What you fail to understand is you are so full of shit, you rain turds all along Madison." He cocked his head toward the huge window overlooking Madison Avenue.

Tsk, tsk. "That's not helpful, Bobby."

"'That's not helpful, Bobby,'" he mimicked Karl in a high and nasal voice as he made a return visit to the crowded drinks table. "You guys think because Ned Isaly wound up on the *TBR* list, you've got a whole fuckarama going about publishing, like you could start your own house. I wish you would, and just shoot any writer walking through the door who doesn't sell one million copies of his 'debut' novel." He sat down. "There are some writers who, like Isaly, are so good, they'll succeed without making an armored car full of money, which is not success anyway, and he'd do it in spite of publishing."

Candy and Karl were taken aback that Bobby wasn't equating success with money. Karl held up his hand like a flag he'd bring down to start a race. "Whoa, Bobby! 'In spite of'? Man, Ned wouldn't have his books in print, much less selling like hell, if it wasn't for you and publishing."

Bobby's eyes turned to him, molten with something Karl thought was maybe real lava. "Ned's books shouldn't be bestsellers; the books are too good for that. Bestsellerdom can only get him off the track. He'll move from his cramped apartment, get a corner condo in Chelsea or someplace with fifteen fireplaces in TriBeCa, go out more, join something or other like the Groucho Club in London, get himself a wardrobe—"

"Excuse me, but this don't sound like Ned Isaly, this person you're describing."

Bobby got up and roamed the office as if looking for something, stopping now and then to stare at an expressionist German print or to kick at a stack of flashy-jacketed books. "It will be. Ned was doing all right." Here Bobby clapped a hand on each of their shoulders. "And then you two guys, you decide he should be a bestselling author. Oh, yes, you who know fuck-all about publishing, decide what's best."

"Hey, hey, *hey*," said Karl. "Yeah, Bobby, we decided it was best if the guy went on living for a while. It was you that paid for the hit. We just didn't do it; we told you our terms; you should be damned glad."

"Again, you don't know what I'm saying." Bobby dropped like a boulder into his chair. "What the hell do you guys want, anyway? Why are you here?"

"Yeah, we did get off the track there," said Karl. "You know an author named Cindy Sella?"

Bobby's frown looked locked in place. "Why?" Treading carefully.

"Well, you should. She's published by Mackenzie-Haack."

"No, it's Harbor Books, an imprint."

"What's that?"

"As I said, an imprint. One of many. I'm not the publisher of Harbor Books. That's Bella Bond."

"But you're all part of the same outfit?"

"You mean publishing conglomerate, as they say? Yes. Why?"

"You know an agent named L. Bass Hess?"

"Of course. He's a sociopath. In my opinion," Bobby added generously. He got up, snatched the bottle of Talisker and two stumpy glasses, and poured them each a couple of fingers. He handed them the glasses and said, "Whatever": Bobby's way of saying "Cheers." He set the bottle on his desk, where he would, ostensibly, have more control over it. "What's he got to do with anything?"

"You don't know about him and Cindy Sella?"

Bobby rolled his eyes and spun the cap back on the bottle. "Yes, I heard something come down the pipeline. I know our lawyers have been busy. Well, busy for them. I try and stay away from legal."

"You should keep better informed, Bobby."

"Better informed? Let me remind you goodfellas that some of my information went out the door when I was escorted to Australia. I just got back, guys. And if I kept informed of every scam, scheme, and shell game that goes on in this business, I'd be the fucking CIA and MI5 combined."

Candy filled in the blank spots on the Cindy Sella situation.

Bobby's laugh was a single-malt blubber. "Jesus! Why doesn't Hess just get up a poker game, mark all the cards, put a gun in his lap, and shoot them as they walk through the door? What's it got to do with me?"

"We found out Dwight Staines's agent is also L. Bass Hess."

"Don't I know it? He's always trying to claw more money out of me, not satisfied with the million or two Dwight gets for each one of his parapsychotic books. What a jerk."

"Yeah. We met him in Pittsburgh. The point being that Hess—"

Bobby interrupted. "Hess will move Dwight Staines to another publisher if we don't drop Cindy Sella."

"This is sounding familiar," said Candy, looking at Karl. "That really sucks." Candy cleared his throat of what sounded like major wreckage.

"It's like blackmail, right?" said Karl. "So is that what authors do? They do whatever some dumbass agent tells them?"

"Not always. But Dwight Staines is a dumbass author. So they're a lock." Bobby interwove his fingers. "Hess is going to have a hard time, since Staines's contract calls for two more books."

"You know that stuff right off the top of your head?"

"I'm the publisher; I'm supposed to know it." He yanked open a drawer, pulled a few pages out of a folder, held one up. "From Cindy Sella's last contract—"

Karl interrupted. "Then you know all this stuff. Why'd you let us go on about it?"

"I figured you'd give up and go away. So, here's the clause: 'The Author shall indemnify and hold the publisher harmless against any loss, liability, damage, cost or expense . . . arising out of any breach or alleged breach,' et cetera. And it continues, points a, b, c, d, e, f—you get the idea? It's pretty much standard in contracts, but how many times have I seen it invoked against an author? Never. Now, tell me, are you guys actually working for Cindy Sella?"

"If you mean 'employed by,' no. This is, you could say, pro bono."

"Then why the fuck don't you do what you do so well?" Bobby made a gun of his thumb and forefinger.

"Who'd be the first person the cops would put the hit down to? Stop and think."

Bobby sat back, hands tight behind his head. "Probably Cindy Sella, although with him, there could be other candidates."

"Yeah, Cindy Sella would be prime, seems to us."

"I still don't see what this has to do with me."

"Really?" Karl stopped chewing his gum and stared. It had the unnerving effect of a thumb slowly pulling back the hammer of a gun. Bobby wasn't about to give in to these two again. "Yeah, really." He switched his gaze from one to the other.

Candy said, "Cindy is one of your authors."

"I told you. She's Harbor Books." He got up, reached for the bottle of Talisker, and wheeled the cap off with the index finger of the hand that held it. Seeing the twinned lethal stares, he said, "So?"

"Harbor Books is run by Mackenzie-Haack. And you're missing the point here, Bobby. You owe us."

"I don't owe you two squat."

"I mean Cindy. Ned Isaly. Writers. Them, you owe."

"You two? Nobly standing up for the rights of authors? Don't make me larf." He took a sip of whiskey. "You guys think you own me, right? I'll do whatever you want, correct?"

Together, Candy and Karl lifted their hands, palms out. Karl said, "You'll do it, Bobby, but not because we want you to." He smiled. "You'll do it because you want to."

"Oh, sweet Christ, there's an elfin statement." Bobby plopped himself down. The chair's fine-grained leather really did go *pfffff.* "How do I interpret that? I join the Family? Get to be a made man? Become a capo?"

Candy tch-tched. "You take Francis Ford Coppola too serious, Bobby. Besides, you ain't Italian. You think we're mobbed up? No. We are independent contractors. You'll do it because you like it, because of the rush."

"The rush. I get no kick from this stuff"—he said, raising his glass—"so I have to turn to you guys?"

"Come on, Bobby. She's a Mackenzie-Haack author. That name is all over Hess's complaint. So come off it, stop winding us up."

Bobby leaned over the desk. "I'm telling you, it's Bella Bond you want to strong-arm, not yours truly." He smiled insincerely and drank.

Karl said, "Listen: You're sitting there bantering away, and you don't even know what the hell we want."

"I figure you'll tell me when the moment is ripe. Like a cataract."

"Cindy Sella—"

Bobby slid down in his chair, looked at the ceiling. "She's not one of mine." He slid up. "I do not own Mackenzie-Haack. I do not own the controlling stock in this house. As you work your way up the publishing ladder, don't you ever read the trades?"

"*Publishers Weekly*, yeah."

Bobby's eyes raked the ceiling as if searching for clouds. "You read *PW*?" He laughed.

"You just told us we should."

"If you were reading *PW* while I was vacationing in Australia—at your request—you'd know Mackenzie-Haack was taken over by two brothers from Dubai."

"Dubai? The fuck. I thought they put their money into racehorses and hotels. What conglomerate?"

"D and D."

"What's D and D?"

"Dubai and Dodge."

"Dodge who?"

"Dodge City."

Candy and Karl laughed and punched each other. "Dodge City! Who the hell's the CEO? Randolph Scott?"

Bobby smiled. "CEOs, plural. The Dubai brothers: Saad and Sahan bin Saeed."

"That sounds real Old West."

Bobby snickered. "The younger one's into Westerns. He wears ten-gallon hats, and his horse's bridle is studded with bullet casings from a

Remington. These two thought it would be a friendly gesture to the U.S. to call it after Dodge City."

"Dodge wasn't open to friendly gestures, last I heard. It had more gunfighters than anyplace. It had Wyatt Earp, too. So? You're solid with this arrangement?"

"Of course. As long as they keep their butts out of my business. Which they do because they're rarely here, the Dubai boys, they're always leaving for Dubai. I call them the Good-bye Boys."

Candy and Karl laughed. Karl said, "So you're still running the show."

"Up to a point." Bobby tried to be modest.

"Where's the point snap?"

"Probably here." Bobby held up the page with the catchy clause. He sank the Bluetooth around his ear, saying, "Dolly. Get me Jackson Sprague in legal— Legal? What? Legal meaning lawyer, Dolly. Sprague is Mackenzie-Haack's senior counsel. Get him down here!" Had he been holding a telephone receiver, he could have slammed it into the cradle, but that pleasure was denied him, this being Bluetooth technology. Slamming it into his eardrum to gut the voice of Dolly would have been something, at least. Not finished, he yelled, "Dolly!"

Dolly, whose name said it all, was blond, with bee-stung lips and a comely presence. In the open doorway, she kept her hand on the doorknob, in case she needed to slam it fast, and asked what he wanted. Now.

"I want you to get hold of Bella Bond—"

"Can't. She's gone to Block Island."

"Block Island? What in hell? Never mind. Get me her assistant, that Sandy something."

"Susie Archer. She's not here. She's gone to the Vineyard." The doorknob was getting a shellacking.

Bobby looked pained. "Then get me her other assistant. How many's she got? A hundred and six?"

"If you mean May Spinner, she's not here, either. She just left for Boston." With her free hand, Dolly held up a pink "While You Were Out" note as proof that she wasn't inventing it.

"Jesus. It's only Tuesday. Do these people think Tuesday's the new Friday?"

Leaning against the door, Dolly gave the knob a hand job. She was not good with rhetorical questions. "I don't know."

Bobby waved her away. "Just get Sprague, will you?"

She made her exit, and the three of them agreed it was time for topping up drinks. Bobby hauled the Scotch over to Candy and Karl and poured.

Two minutes into their drinks, Dolly reappeared. "Jackson Sprague says he's already late for drinks at the Algonquin with an editor from, uh, Des Moines?"

"Dubai, Dolly. They don't have editors in Des Moines. Tell him to get his ass in here pronto or he can park it permanently at the Round Table and hope Dorothy Parker shows."

Dolly disappeared.

Jackson Sprague was tall, reed-thin, and with a voice that was, in some weird way, reed-hollow, as if he were testing out flutes in his mind. His name was Jack, but how could a man of such unquenchable pretension live with just plain Jack?

He was a fashion plate in a Ralph Lauren way—quartz suit, tiny-striped shirt with a stiff white stand-up collar that looked as if it would prefer to get down and walk around on its own. His eyes were contact-lens green, his hair a silvery wheat field with a shimmer of cornhusks.

Jackson claimed to be English. He possessed just the sort of Britness that Monty Python was forever sending up. It was the Britness that takes generations to cultivate or a week at Wimbledon. Jackson was born in King of Prussia, PA, so there was at least that small bow to royalty.

Bobby said, "I'd offer you a drink, but I understand you'll be doing that two-fisted at the Algonquin."

Jackson curled a lip or two. "I would do, only you called me in here."

Without a further waste of words, Bobby said, "Jackson, what is this shit?"

"I beg your pardon?"

Bobby waggled the page like a dog's tail.

Jackson frowned. Frowning, he looked over the paper. "This is a standard indemnity clause."

"I know what it is. I've never seen one invoked against an author."

Jackson's laugh was idle, as if he were waiting by the curb for something worth a real laugh. "How often have you seen a situation like this arise?" He looked toward Karl and Candy as if they might weigh in on his side.

Tough luck. Faces of stone.

Jackson, who hadn't been invited to sit, stood, one hand in his jacket pocket, thumb on the outside. Nostrils quivering slightly, he said, "Let me walk you through this, Bobby—" They could have skied down the slope of Jackson's condescension.

Said Bobby, "Let you not. That would take a billable hour for which Cindy Sella would have to pay. Jackson, here's how I see this shitty deal: Cindy Sella wanted to continue being published by Mackenzie-Haack. The only way she could do this was to sign a contract that included this indemnity clause. Now, I would guess she saw very little danger in so doing, because she thought there wasn't a snowball's chance in hell that her ex-agent, with whom she's had no contact for two years, would try and collect a commission he never earned because he never worked on the book in question. But the son of a bitch does just that. In this country, you can go around suing anybody for anything, as you well know and no doubt approve of.

"Now, seeing that Cindy isn't willing to pay him, he goes after the publisher, us, and sues them for money he also hasn't earned. Or money he has earned and has received but claims he hasn't—"

Another bit of idle laughter from Jackson Sprague. "You're assuming, Bobby, that—"

Slam. Bobby's hand on his desk as he rose and leaned across it. "I'm assuming that here's a writer who finds herself surrounded by three sets of lawyers—hers, yours, and the ones you outsourced this to. Then there's Hess, probably demanding that she pay for his lawyers. That adds up to one writer and four sets of lawyers. Lawyers to the right of her, lawyers to the left, lawyers in front, lawyers behind." He came around his desk, directly up to Jackson Sprague. "Is there a vision of hell, even in Dante, that could possibly compete with that?"

Jackson Sprague stood his ground, or his remaining ground, having given over a couple of feet when Bobby advanced on him. A little anger flared up or, rather, spurted, the depth of Jackson's emotions strong enough only to light a cigarette. "Bobby, I don't report to you. I report to the Dubai brothers. I report to their man Tom Nix—"

It just popped out: "Tom Mix?" said Candy.

"Nix, Nix."

Oh, if only. Candy had never seen him or Hopalong Cassidy or Gene Autry, but he had seen YouTube. He felt he was back in the saddle again. "Totin' my old forty-four . . ."

He grinned when Jackson Sprague stared at him. Candy was solid with putting a bullet right between Jackson's contact-lensed green eyes.

Too bad nobody was hiring.

15

The Chelsea Piers, thought Karl, didn't have the right ambience anymore. "How noir is this? Look, it's a fuckin' park up there? Trees, grass, where the old tracks used to be? It's against the laws of gravity, forget nature, having a goddamned park overhead. Where's your fog? Your foghorns? Your miasma of all kinds of crap?"

"Your what?"

"Crap?"

"No, that other word."

"All kinds?"

"Forget it. Anyway, you can't see the park now, so just pretend it ain't there."

It was dead dark, eleven P.M. Pier 61 was the only place Danny Zito would "take a meet."

"That's what he said: 'take a meet,'" Candy had said with a snort once he was off the phone.

"Why in hell is it so easy to call up a guy in Witness Protection?"

"I got the number from Clive. He got it from Bobby Mackenzie. If it's Danny's publisher and editor, naturally, he'll keep in touch."

"'Take a meet,'" said Karl. "What is he? CEO of SnitchCO? Administrator of FannyFuckYourMortgage? President of GoldmanSachsofShit?"

Candy snickered. "Wall Street. Talk about crooks."

Karl shook his head, adamant on this point. "No, no way. Those people are not your old-time crooks. It's like I said. Those people are your retro crooks, your Night of the Undead crooks. Those people are mutants. They wouldn't know how to rob a bank if John Dillinger came back and led the way."

In the distance, if the Hudson River could be said to have a distance, a foghorn sounded.

"There you are. You got your foghorn."

Karl was not mollified. "Sounds fake. Look at this place. It's got a sports center, a golf center, a fitness center, a spa. The best thing to say for it is right now it's closed." Karl shook his head. "After that book Zito wrote that put away half the Bransoni family, including Papa B., this guy has the brass balls to go on living in New York?"

"Hiding in plain sight. Like that story about the what's-it letter."

"That one by Poe I told you to read?"

"Yeah." Candy slapped his gloved hands against his coat. It was cold out here, with the wind blowing off the river. "Only that story kind of cheats, don't it?"

Karl, in the act of relighting a cigar that had fizzled, said, "Cheats?"

"I mean that letter, it really wasn't in plain sight."

"Yeah, it was. It was right there with a bunch of calling cards."

"It looked completely different. It was the very opposite in looks than the one this guy heard about. I do not call that in plain sight. Look, I'll give you plain sight." Candy pulled out his wallet, yanked out a hundred-dollar bill, and dropped it on the ground. "There's plain sight."

As they argued for a fruitless moment the merits of Poe's plain-sight-edness against that of the bill lying at their feet, Danny Zito appeared out of the fog tendrils. He was dressed completely in black.

"I'll be damned," Danny said, grinning. "Is it really you guys? I thought maybe somebody was shittin' me." He thrust out his hand. "It's an honor. You guys, you're a legend. 'It was a righteous hit, but it wasn't Candy and Karl' is what Papa B. used to say whenever one of the mechanics he hired came around for their money. 'It wasn't Candy and Karl.' He never said it to them, given their propensity for violence. You guys are the gold standard."

"Hardly," said Karl. "We do okay. Listen, I thought *Fallguy* was a terrific book. We never wrote a book, right, C.? So you got it all over us, Danny."

Modestly, Danny shrugged off the compliment. "Thanks. My next one is nearly done. I need to take a meet with Clive Esterhaus. You guys know him; he's the one contacted you. You met Clive, didn't you? He was in Pittsburgh when you were. That job I linked you up with? How'd that work out for you?"

"We didn't take it. It wasn't good."

"The mark was a writer, *n'est-ce pas*?" Danny pressed his hands against his chest.

Christ, thought Karl. Zito was speaking French? He writes; he talks French. What was the life of a hit man coming to?

"So did Clive bring in somebody else?" Danny hiccupped a laugh as he lit a cigarette, tossed the match. "You gotta watch your back in this business."

Candy said, "No, they saw the error of their ways."

"So. What can I do for you?"

"We know you're in WITSEC, but you always had connections, and we figure you still got some. Us, well, what we do, we don't usually go looking for people; they usually come looking for us. We need somebody."

"Wet work?"

"No, that we take care of ourselves. We need someone in a law office to get information about what these lawyers got on our client."

"Ha!" Danny dropped his cigarette and scrubbed it. "Lawyers? People would probably line up at my door."

The three laughed, did a little shoulder pounding.

"So what's this person supposed to do?"

"The cover's an exotic fish importer. Ornamental fish for private aquariums. Also coral. From coral reefs. You know."

"Hell, yeah, I know what coral is, but why the fuck'd somebody want a reef of it?"

"Not a whole reef, Danny. Maybe for jewelry, or just pieces to display. There's some that collect it," said Candy. "Coral's your most endangered aquatic species. In the world."

Danny had folded a stick of gum in his mouth and stopped his strenuous chewing long enough to ask, "What kinda fish we talking?"

Candy searched his memory. "There's your walking catfish—"

Danny laughed. "You shittin' me?"

"No. There's other walking fish, too."

"Huh." He chewed more ferociously, then stopped and said, "This ain't easy, guys." He looked up. He looked down. He said, "Yeah. The Dragon Lady."

"Who the fuck's that?"

Danny looked all around the pier, then lowered his voice to a whisper. "Her name's Lena bint Musah. She's from Malaysia. Lampoor or something. Wait." Danny removed a tiny book from his pocket, thumbed through it, got out a ballpoint, and wrote on a scrap of paper from the book. He tore it out. "Here. She's good."

Karl looked at the note. "Lena bint—?"

Danny held out his hand, palm out. "The night has a thousand ears, man."

"That's 'eyes,' ain't it?" Candy frowned.

"Whatever."

"So what is it she does?"

Danny looked from Karl to Candy in exaggerated disbelief. "What is it? You pay her; she does it."

"What we mean is," said Karl, "does she know anything about fish?"

"It don't make no difference, she knows it; it's whether your mark knows she knows it. Good talking to you guys again."

Danny melted back into the fog.

16

L. Bass Hess was nearly wetting his pants.

Paul Giverney was coming to see him at noon, which was now. This must mean that Paul Giverney was looking for a new agent. L. Bass could taste the commissions coming his way from a Paul Giverney contract. Even for just one book, the commission would come in at, let's see, $225,000. Just one book. Any book by Giverney netted the writer $1.5 million. The thought of it was so heady that Bass Hess sank into his chair.

Noon would mean that he would be late for his luncheon date with Madeline Crow, an editor at Quagmire whom he was trying to persuade to take on one of his client's books, described by Bass as an "existential prizefighting novel" about two gay fighters having an affair who then find themselves in the ring together.

Madeline Crow had laughed uncontrollably and unforgivably. "Oh, fuck a duck, Bass; it's ridiculous."

L. Bass clenched at the gritty language; he had never been able to manage such scatological outbursts from women. "If it sounds unlikely, that's where the existential theme comes in."

"Tell me another. Anyway, he's already a Quagmire author. So what's wrong with Melody LaRue?" His present editor.

Her name, for one thing. It made him shudder. He could see her squirming around a pole. "To tell the truth, Madeline, she's just not up to a book this profound." To tell the truth, the author thinks you're hot. Naturally, he did not share this with her.

"'Up to' it? What, for shit's sake, is there to be 'up to' in this business?

Proust, Flaubert, Xing Ho Shit aren't around anymore. I can't just waltz in and take Melody's authors away from her. Get real."

Bass frowned. Who was Xing Ho Shit? He said, "I'm simply saying you have the intellect to handle this sort of multifaceted novel."

She sighed heavily. "Lunch, you said?"

He was relieved. He thought of himself as a persuasive man. "Wonderful. Gramercy Tavern, say one-thirty?"

"Okay. I have to tell them how to make dirty martinis, but the food's all right."

All of this lunchtime drinking. How did people manage to work?

It was fifteen past noon, and Paul Giverney still hadn't appeared. Bass was prowling his office. He stopped to realign magazines on his glass-topped coffee table. He stopped to straighten the stuffed bass. It was an eighth of an inch higher on the right end. Lack of alignment annoyed L. Bass Hess.

His father, Louis Hess, had been a first-rate bass fisherman and Bass had put the fish here in his memory. Bass fished himself when he went to the Everglades. He hated it, fishing; he hated the Everglades; but it was part of his annual visit to his aunt. Aunt Simone, whom he hated as well, and who made him shudder far more than Melody LaRue.

His intercom buzzed. He stiffened.

"Mr. Giverney is here," said Stephanie gaily.

He fairly ran for the door, composed himself, tried on a few different expressions, and went for the one suggesting curiosity but not excitement.

"Paul! So nice to see you."

"Bass." They shook hands.

"Come in, come in."

"You'll have had your tea."

Bass was confused. "What? Tea?"

"It's what they say in Glasgow. 'Come in, come in, you'll have had your tea.'"

A brief silence. Then Bass said, "Have you been to Glasgow?"

Paul sank down in one of the dark leather chairs on either side of the coffee table. "You don't get it?"

Bass assumed it was meant to be funny and laughed. The laugh was as thin as parchment.

Paul Giverney knew Hess didn't get it. "In other words, the Glaswegians are notoriously cheap."

Bass ran his hand over the back of his skull with its thinning red hair. "Right. Now, Paul, what can I do for you?"

"I'm thinking of changing agents."

L. Bass Hess could hardly sit still in his chair. He wanted to bounce like a baby. To control himself, he moved an ashtray, free of ashes, and coughed into his fist. "You need an agent who can handle everything for you, I'd say. So you can spend your time writing your wonderful books." He smiled, crookedly, charmingly, he thought.

Paul thought the smile merely looked fake, and the "wonderful books" sounded faker. Who the hell did Hess think he was patronizing?

Bass went on. "I believe your present agent is James McKinney? That isn't working for you?"

"Jimmy's a great agent. He just hasn't got the time."

The time? For Paul Giverney? Was McKinney insane? "I don't understand. How can he not?"

"Jimmy's more interested in representing good writers who haven't broken out yet, or haven't been published right, or need someone with vision." Vision. In the publishing industry? Oddly enough, one person who did have it was Bobby Mackenzie. If only he weren't such a bastard. "A writer like Joe Moss or—" He was dying to say Cindy Sella, but that might tip Hess off, even though he didn't seem to be operating on a fully charged battery.

"A noble calling for Jimmy." To avoid going along with nobility himself, Bass said, "I screen potential clients carefully. That's why I have only eight or nine." Actually, it was six or seven, and he badly needed more, screened or unscreened.

As if disturbed by Hess's apparent unpopularity, Paul looked at the door, giving the impression that he might make a break for it. He said, frowning deeply, "That's not very many."

Quickly, Bass said, "I want to be able to give my full attention to each one."

"You couldn't do that with twenty writers? What would you be giving them? Your half-attention?"

"No, that's not exactly what—"

"So what are your criteria?"

A blank look. "Criteria?"

"You said you screen carefully."

"Oh, yes. I would be looking for writers who were, say, on the same wavelength as myself."

As *I*. Or even *me*. People were always saying "myself" instead of "me" because they were so damned afraid of sounding like they hadn't graduated from high school. Why was Hess representing writers?

"I have no idea what that means, the same wavelength. You mean temperamentally twinned or something like that?"

"Beautifully put!"

Oh, Christ. This guy would be chewing his cuffs in a minute.

Hess went on, without the chew: "A suitable temperament, nonmercurial, you know what I'm saying . . ."

As Hess droned on, Paul rose and walked over to the bookshelves against the wall, stuck his hands in his pockets, and studied the titles, not listening. There was a framed photo between two Don DeLillo novels of Hess lounging against a Mustang. How un-Hess-like, thought Paul. He could not imagine Hess in a Mustang. He noticed one of the quarter panels was deeply dented.

". . . but what I mean about temperament is, I really don't want, you know, any of your highly volatile, easily upset writers."

Paul turned reluctantly from the books. "Bass—" He held up his hands, pushing back this absurdity, and said with as much condescension as he could muster, "This is the publishing world we're talking about. These are writers. Volatility is the order of the day all around. Level-headedness is not what you get unless you're looking for an astronaut or Obi-Wan Kenobi or Michael Jordan. Or—" It was fun, trying to think of guys who had it so together that even taking an ax to them wouldn't separate flesh and bone, but he guessed he should stop. Hess was looking pretty limp. He nodded toward the photo of the Mustang. "That your car? Nice." Cars bored Paul.

"It's a '64. It was in a small accident. Needs a new partial panel. But you know how hard it is to find parts for a '64 Mustang. Naturally, I park it in Connecticut."

Naturally. I park mine in front of 30 Rock. "I don't have a car." Paul sat down again, leaned his head back to stare at the ceiling. "Maybe I should just handle my own books."

That got a quick response. With a look of near-wild desperation, Bass inched forward in his chair. "Paul, that could spell disaster. There are too many different things to handle. You've got subsidiary rights, which grow more complicated almost daily. Then there are the foreign rights and spin-offs from them. Film, TV, not to mention electronic . . ."

He went on to pile right after right, searching for as many as he could come up with. He was stepping all over squishy ground in moorland rumored to be full of quicksand. Oh, for the hound of the Baskervilles! L. Bass on his back, throat ripped open. Paul's imagination was hotfooting it all over Dartmoor when he decided to break the subrights spell. "What sort of agency clause is written into the contract?" he asked suddenly.

"Agency? It's merely the standard—"

"Show me."

"Now?"

"Of course."

There was no spring in L. Bass's step as he rose and went to his desk. He shuttled drawers in and out, found a contract, and handed it to Paul.

Paul zipped to the last page, read it. "This right to see the next manuscript is going to have to come out."

"That? Oh, but that's just routine, a matter of form. Means nothing."

"If it means nothing, why is it in here? Standard? Routine? Matter of form? You know as well as I do the other guy's lawyers are just waiting for the defendant to invoke 'standard' and 'routine.' No way." Paul got up with the air of one about to leave.

Bass got up like a shot, wild-eyed, as if he had just viewed the hound coming over the hill. "Paul, I'm sure that clause could be reworded to your satisfaction."

Paul smiled. "Then reword it and call me."

He thanked Stephanie and walked to the door, which he would have continued walking through, except he saw the big photos of writers lined up on screens.

Cindy Sella. The bastard was suing her and using her to advertise at the same time.

17

The provenance of the woman who answered the door was not the Bronx or South Jersey.

They were expecting a small woman, wrinkled and nutlike. This one was tall, onyx-eyed, dark-haired, the hair pulled back so tightly it had the finish of mahogany. She wore a jade-green dress of some damask-like silk whose small covered buttons went up to the neck.

Very Asian, thought Karl. Well, that's what she was—Malaysian, wasn't she?

Candy stuck out his hand, then withdrew it, unsure. She gave no sign that she'd noticed the withdrawal or that she did or didn't mind the appearance of two strangers at her door who were probably neither CIA nor FBI operatives.

"Miss—" said Candy.

"Madam bin Musah—" said Karl.

"That would be 'bint' for a female," she said. "'Bin' is the male form."

Before Karl could step on his foot, Candy said, "Like bin Laden."

Her smile was ironic. "An unfortunate example, but that is correct. And you are?" She made a very small sweep of her hand to take them in.

What surprised Karl was the excessive politeness in her tone and in the little gesture. They introduced themselves, Candy adding, "Danny Zito, uh, recommended you."

"Ah. Mr. Zito."

They could not remember ever hearing Danny referred to as "Mr."

Another sweep of her hand, somewhat broader, gesturing them in. Her fingers were long and slim and ended in tapered nails with colorless polish. "Then I infer you're in the same line of work?"

"As Danny? You could say that," said Karl.

She smiled. They entered. The elaborate formality made Karl feel like he was walking on stilts.

They moved from a dimly lit foyer into a dimly lit living room that would have served well as a stage set for *Miss Saigon,* or what he imagined it must have been like, never having seen it. It was all dark reds, dark golds, and browns, and the whole of it seemed to shimmer in the lowered lights beneath silky-looking shades and in the glow of the even silkier fire.

"Please sit. Would you care for a little espresso? I was just having some."

They both nodded, Candy thinking she could have offered a cup of poison and he'd have accepted. Some dame. As she poured into two little cups that had appeared miraculously from a drawer-like enclosure in the coffee table, he said, his memory tumbling over something that ended in "-pore" that Danny had mentioned, "You're from Singapore, right?"

"No, not quite. I believe you mean Kuala Lumpur. Singapore has always been in China, very close to Malaysia's border. Many people make that mistake."

Jesus, thought Karl, this dame should be secretary of state. She knows fucking well "many people" didn't make that mistake, because "many people" knew where Singapore was but didn't trot out Kuala Lumpur at a moment's notice. Until he'd looked in the Eyewitness guide, he hadn't even known where the hell Malaysia was.

A thin brown cigarette, smoke pleasantly pungent, burned in a bronze ashtray beside a small soapstone Buddha. She picked up the cigarette, tapped off the ash, and lifted a silver-plated box from the table. This she passed to them. "Smoke? These are quite good, much more interesting than the usual."

They each took one, and she closed the lid and replaced it. "Now, what can I do for you?"

"We need someone to pose as an importer of exotic fish," said Karl. He lit his cigarette and sat back, slightly light-headed.

"An illegal," Candy added.

"Illegal fish?" she said, her black eyes moving from one to the other.

"No, wait," said Karl. "What we're looking for, see, is information. The 'importer' pose, that's just a cover to get you into their offices."

"Or their good graces," she said. "Interesting. What lies behind this?"

Candy and Karl took turns telling the story.

"Good heavens," she said, and exhaled a stream of pungent smoke. "How banal."

Candy wondered about banal. That was a new take on the situation. Anyway, the cigarette was getting into his bloodstream, and the effect was not unpleasant. He was melting into his chair. He studied the soapstone Buddha and wondered if he was becoming One with the universe. He preferred to remain Two. Hadn't Woody Allen said something like that?

Fortunately, Karl was still on the SoHo side of enlightenment, and he carried on. "This agent is nuts; he wants revenge; he wants to ruin Ms. Sella."

"I don't doubt it for a moment," said Lena bint Musah. "The lawyers, the publisher, the agent—sound like a convention of dunces." She paused. "No, actually, the lawyers sound like lawyers. But is the publishing world fraught with idiots? It's quite extraordinary. So. You need information, you say." She inhaled deeply but went on smoking with no visible sign of departing this earth's ether.

"Okay." Candy was back. "Okay. What we need is some kind of proof these shit-faced lawyers—pardon the language—" He waved his cigarette by way of explaining such verbal freedom.

She smiled. "I took it merely literally."

Candy laughed and tried to repeat "merely literally" and wound up almost swallowing his tongue. "Yeah. What we need is evidence these guys are working both sides of the street. Hess was giving them stuff about Cindy Sella."

"We can't be sure who's the guilty party, correct?" said Lena. "It could be the lawyers, it could be the agent, it could be all of them. What was in the documents that the agent mistakenly handed over to you?"

"Stuff about her character. He said he was making it part of the complaint. But there's no way to prove a connection with Hale and this Reeves guy. The name of the firm—Snelling, Snelling, Borax, and Snelling—isn't in these papers. Now that we've told this story about the fish importer, and a lot of stuff about illegal imports, we have to go along with it."

An old dog wandered into the room, a hound of some sort who very delicately sniffed around their pants legs then left them in order to sit quietly by her. The dog was probably smoking these fun cigarettes, thought Candy, dropping ash, sorry to see the ash go.

"What about the fish? I know very little. I do know cyanide fishing is carried out in Malaysia. What about coral reefs? It's illegal to import coral." She paused and stubbed out her cigarette. "There is a fish native to Malaysia and Indochina, the Asian arowana, which is much sought after by aquarists. I understand such a fish can bring in ten thousand dollars."

Karl whistled. Candy got himself another cigarette. "There's a platinum one worth a shitload more." He laughed, and smoke blew out of his nose.

"Really? How astonishing. May I suggest we find two or three others of similar value for export-import?"

"And similarly illegal," offered Candy. The "similarly" came out bristling with more L's than necessary.

She nodded, pretending not to notice the cigarette behind his ear. "And research those and become, or at least manage to sound, expert."

"Candy'll research it. He's really into fish."

"Well, then," said Lena, concluding the discussion by rising. "We should be able to go forward in a few days."

"You can do it that soon?"

"Oh, I think so."

"Hey," said Candy. "Listen, thanks for the coffee and smokes."

As she walked them to the door, Karl said, "Wait. We didn't ask you, how much do you charge for a gig like this?"

"I've never taken on a gig like this. Usually, my fee is five thousand. If I get the results the client wants, of course. If I don't"—she shrugged—"you don't pay."

It had the ring of the sort of operation the two of them handled. Karl liked it.

She went on, "But in this case, it would be expenses only."

Karl's eyes widened in surprise.

Candy felt to see if the cigarette was there and said, "You're kiddin'. How come?"

"I find it such an interesting situation. Here is a young woman who has done nothing at all and is then beset by a dozen people insisting she pay hundreds of thousands of dollars. Lawyers, agents, publishers. And who is it who's 'got her back'? A couple of contract killers." She smiled. "I like it. Call me."

18

Paul Giverney was plucking the mussels out of their shells and, at the same time, feeling sorry for them, wondering if he'd read "Jabberwocky" one too many times to Hannah. "'The time has come, the Walrus said, to talk of many things,'" he said aloud, and then fell silent.

Bobby Mackenzie noted the silence and filled it in. "'Of shoes—and ships—and sealing wax—Of cabbages and kings.'"

"'And why the sea is boiling hot—and whether pigs have wings.'" Paul smiled.

"Is that why we're here? Well, damn." While Paul ate mussels, Bobby drank his single-malt whiskey and ignored his Caesar salad. "How come this place?"

They were having lunch at the Clownfish Café. Bobby was already there when Paul walked in and interrupted Bobby's Bluetooth conversation about another book jacket.

Paul looked around and smiled. "Friend of mine told me about it. There was a little fracas in here last week."

"Ah. What kind of fracas?"

"It seems a couple of killers walked in and shot up the fish tank."

Bobby looked across the room at the huge aquarium. "A Hemingway moment." He drank his whiskey. "Why did they do it?"

"What I heard was Bass Hess was sitting on the other side of it."

"That works for me." Bobby pounded his glass on the table. A few of the other customers looked their way. Through the tank, they could see the watery outline of the two present diners seated on the other side.

"Why are we having this lunch, Paul? Not that I'm complaining, only I know you don't 'do lunch.'"

"Just to talk."

"I know you don't do talk, either."

"Cindy Sella."

Bobby took a long look at Paul and a long slug of his Scotch. "My God. Her again? I was recently paid a visit by two goons who wanted me to do something about Cindy Sella."

"Two goons who were not strangers to you, Bobby."

Bobby cut him a thin smile. "What I had a hard time making them understand is that I am not Ms. Sella's publisher, hence I could hardly step in on her behalf."

"What a dodge."

"You've got that right. Dubai and Dodge. Heh heh. What do you mean, a dodge?"

"That you can't stick your mug into Harbor Books." Paul pushed his mussel bowl out of the way and leaned across the table. "Before this D and D conglomerate came along, Bella was eating out of your hand, like everybody else at your goddamned place."

"Hey! The goddamned place publishes you well, doesn't it?"

"No, but that's not the point. You could at least get Harbor to stand behind her. And what the hell's wrong with her editor? He hasn't as much as said, 'Gee, tough luck, Cindy.' These people maintain an arctic silence."

"Of course they do. They're all scared shitless. You know how houses are closing, how people are being laid off."

"You're not scared."

"Me? Don't make me laugh. I'm too good at what I do. Everything's changed, Paul. Remember when there used to be the greatest publishing houses in Boston? In old brownstones where the wooden stairwells creaked and the Oriental carpeting was as thin as vapor? Beacon Hill? The Back Bay?"

"You're making me tired, Bobby, pedaling that bike down memory lane. You of all people, the most cynical man I've ever known and a brilliant publisher. You are not averse to the use of force. I've seen evidence of that."

"You have, since you were the instigator, my friend."

Paul shook his head. "I set you a problem. You chose the way to solve it."

"The problem was pretty damned cold-blooded."

"I agree. Are we two of a kind? No, we are not. We're one of two kinds."

"With witty repartee like that, no wonder you sell books." Bobby gave a whiskeyed-up laugh.

"You're really claiming you can't get Bella Bond or anyone else to intercede on Cindy Sella's behalf?"

Bobby shrugged. "I'll say it again. Harbor Books. I don't tell Bella what to do." He didn't add that she was on Block Island, or he would have.

"Then I'll tell you why we're having this lunch. It's a farewell lunch."

Bobby sat back. "Oh, come on! You're not serious!"

"All you've got is a one-book contract. After that, we're done."

It was hard to outmaneuver Bobby Mackenzie, but this had done it. Bobby hated a cliché far more than the next man, but with his back to the wall, he used one. "This is blackmail."

"Makes no difference to me who publishes my books."

"That's absurd." Bobby drank, took in an ice cube, and started gnawing it.

"Given the way I chose you, I'd think it would be obvious that I don't much care."

Bobby signaled the waiter with his upraised glass. "When my— our—friends Candy and Karl came calling, they were saying some of the same things." He seemed unable to decide upon the romaine leaf he had picked up from his Caesar salad. "It occurs to me that instead of all these late-night visits and secret lunches—"

"They came at night?"

"No, no, of course not. But I'd like something like that for your new title instead of the one you have. *Slow Motion*. How thrilling is that? You are a thriller writer, after all."

"No, I'm not, after all."

"Jimmy McKinney has been hard at work trying to get this book marketed as a straight literary novel."

"That is your job, Bobby; that's why I said you're not publishing me right."

"True. But I'm not a magician." He thought that over. "Well, not all the time."

"We're off the subject. You were saying—"

"I wasn't, but I will. Maybe we all should 'take a meet' at my office. Say tomorrow afternoon—no, evening. I've got a sales meeting at five. Say sixish? We'll consider our options. You, me, Clive Esterhaus, and the two goons." Bobby picked up the glass the waiter had just set down and smiled a sly smile.

Paul smiled, his own sly smile. "Make that the five goons."

19

Cindy Sella was watching her clown fish and wondering if they felt the limitations of their lives or were content to swim around the curves of their small bowl. She was going to get them a bigger one; she had furnished the present one with little plastic ferns and a rock with holes in it that they could swim through. But they did a lot of resting, she thought, for they seemed happiest reclining on the two plastic leaves she had attached to the tank.

Gus had carefully monitored the fitting of these items in the bowl, perhaps thinking they would give him greater access, but that dream was thwarted. He had joined Cindy on the bench, which would sit here probably forever.

What had caused this concern for life limitation, she knew, was her own wintry, thinly coated, brackish one. She wasn't doing anything about it but piling up adjectives, and the wrong ones, at that.

She had only two friends, besides people in publishing, and she'd hardly call them friends, not even her editor, whom she saw seldom and who, she sometimes thought, wasn't sure he recognized her. Her only real publishing-world friend was Jimmy McKinney. Her two regular friends were Sammy Tooley and Rosa Parchment. A lesser friend was Benny Bennet, who, when she'd last seen him, had sold her his mantra; then he'd gone back to drugs. She was afraid he'd also gone back to using the mantra he'd sold her, and she wondered how much that diluted it.

What she was thinking about was drugs: One of her characters was in danger of becoming addicted, and she knew nothing about heroin or crack cocaine or other hard drugs. Sammy didn't do drugs, not like

Benny; that wasn't surprising, as Sammy was so hyper already that any drug would have him flying above her instead of walking beside her.

Cindy knew Rosa was a user; she'd been in rehab twice and picked up once in Washington Square for dealing. Rosa wasn't routinely a dealer, but she was friends with Benny, and Cindy suspected that Benny did deal. Rosa had a boutique in the Village called Nevermore, where she sold "antique" clothing that she got mostly from Goodwill. When Rosa saw Cindy looking at the track marks on her arm, Rosa said her cat had done it; Renée (the cat) was always raking her claws over everything. Clearly, if Rosa had relapsed and gone back to sticking needles in her arm, she didn't want to talk about it. So she would be no source of information.

Cindy had been living in Manhattan for seven years and still had no group of friends—a group who hung out together, went to movies, Broadway shows, museums, and Central Park together. She spent her hanging-out time in Ray's coffee shop, writing. That wasn't really hanging out.

She watched the ghost clown fish and thought of Monty and his three friends in the room where marijuana and cigarette smoke hung like curtains at the window. Now, there was a group. A gang. Stoned was definitely togetherness. Four of them, yet they seemed as one. She thought for a moment. What she could do was buy another clown fish. The phone rang just as she was thinking about picking it up.

It was Sammy. "Cin, hi, want to get some chow?"

For a writer, he came up with awfully old, used words. Did people really call food "chow" anymore? She agreed to go with him. "Listen, do you know anything about drugs? I mean from personal experience?"

"I smoked some weed in ninth grade."

"That doesn't really count."

"No? Excuse me, but it counted to me. I'd've got the shit beat out of me if I didn't go along."

"Well, I'm sorry. But I need to know about the big ones: heroin, crack cocaine—"

"Cindy, don't even think about it. It'll fuck you over good."

"Sammy, I don't want to use anything. It's because of one of my characters."

Sammy sniggered. "Sure, they all say that."

She frowned. "They?"

"Writers."

"Sammy, we're writers. We're the they."

"Okay, we all say that. We get out of admitting we want to know about A.A. or we're going into rehab by blaming it on the characters."

Oh, for God's sake. There was no way to talk to Sammy sometimes. "Is Rosa using again? I think maybe she is."

"Rosa? Oh, you mean because you've seen what look like needle marks, you think she's shooting up? Nah. Those are claw marks. Her cat did that."

Cindy had slung one strap of her bag over her shoulder and opened the door to see Edward Bishop just coming through the exit door. He liked to use the stairs.

He stopped. "Cindy!"

She had to admit one reason she liked him was that he made her feel she was a real treat—a sight for sore eyes, a port in a storm, a harbor. That's enough, she told herself. "Edward! Come on in and have a drink."

He walked toward her, smiling. "Thanks. I could use one." He was wearing the same suit he always wore in the colder months. He had a high forehead, thinning brown hair, brown eyes, a mustache, wire-framed glasses, and no money. "You look to be going out."

"Not right this minute. In a while. I'm just going to meet Sammy at Ray's. Why don't you come?"

A couple of times he had. He fitted right in. Even Ray thought he was a "good guy," though he looked for all the world out of another decade. That suit, that mustache. Edward was a respected poet. Jimmy McKinney thought he was wonderful, that he might just be another Edwin Arlington Robinson. He had published two books of poetry, refreshing for Cindy, since the poems seemed out of an earlier era, too, one that made use of form and rhyme. Petrarchan sonnets, terza rima, sestinas.

"I can't manage that tonight, but I'd like to come in and talk for a minute. Anything to put off the writing."

"You mean you feel that way sometimes."

Edward sat down in one of the armchairs. "I feel that way most of the time. It's a kind of agony. Pardon the drama."

The idea of Edward Bishop being dramatic made her pour more Jack Daniel's into the glass than she'd intended. He drank bourbon, but very little. He tasted bourbon.

"Thank you. Mind?" He'd taken a pipe from his pocket, knowing she wouldn't, and now unrolled some tobacco, stuffed it in, used his lighter.

She handed him the glass. "But how do you manage to do it for hours on end, Edward, if it's so hard?"

"I don't have much choice, since I do nothing else."

"Oh, of course you do. Even Edwin Reardon—you know, the impoverished writer in *New Grub Street*—goes out walking for long periods of time."

"Ah, but poor Reardon had the weight of the world on his shoulders. Or at least the weight of a wife and child. An unsympathetic wife, at that."

"I hated her. I don't think it's fair that Edwin died and she wound up happily married to that writing-for-money Milvain at the end."

"Perhaps that was Gissing's final irony."

She thought about it. "I don't have the weight of the world on my shoulders, and I fool around most of the time."

"You don't carry a weight? Are you joking? I don't see how you manage to concentrate at all with this damned agent and his godforsaken lawsuit. Yet you stay right with it." He looked at the notebook on the side table, the pen atop it. "Today?"

"Yes, but I keep getting stuck. I don't know enough."

"Nobody knows enough."

"I've been working on this book for two years, and I'm barely halfway through, if even this half is half. Did you know George Gissing wrote this"—she picked up *New Grub Street*—"in two months? There were three volumes; he wrote one every two or three weeks. And all of it in two months!"

"Weren't there a lot of false starts and torn-up pages for a year before those two months?"

"Maybe, but—"

"Very probably he'd already done most of the work. I'd say Gissing's two months were more like two years."

For some reason, she preferred the two months. Maybe because it was something to hope for, to aim for, to admire.

Edward seemed to sense this. "You might very well be right. Perhaps he had tremendous focus and wrote for ten or twelve hours a day."

"I think that's it."

The tiny movements of the fish must have caught at the corner of his eye, for he looked over there. "You've got a clown fish." He rose and walked to the shelf that held the bowl, drink in hand.

Gus quickly uncurled from what had seemed a drugged sleep by the fireplace and hopped on the bench, as if he feared an interaction that he would miss out on.

"An albino clown fish, too," said Edward. He talked for a good five minutes about clown fish, a detailed commentary on the various kinds.

"Edward," she said, struck by his great store of knowledge. "Did you ever do drugs?"

20

They were gathered in Bobby Mackenzie's office—Bobby, Paul Giverney, Candy and Karl, and Clive Esterhaus. Clive had been a senior editor who was handed the plum job of publisher when Bobby went off (much against his will) to Australia, with a side trip to Dubai. He'd been gone for half the year and come back with a different view of things. Now Bobby Mackenzie liked to say, "To paraphrase Red Sanders, 'Mackenzie isn't everything; he's the only thing.' Just kidding." Which he wasn't.

They were all ranged around the office: Bobby was sitting with his feet up on his desk, smoking a Cuban cigar. Paul was lying on the big downy sofa against the far wall, his drink balanced on his chest. Candy and Karl were sitting in the same chairs they had last occupied, taking advantage of Bobby's Cubans. Clive was leaning against the sill of the big window that overlooked Madison and half of Manhattan.

Clive had been rewarded with his own imprint when Bobby returned. The gesture was uncharacteristically generous. Clive wasn't Bobby's fall guy any longer.

They were gathered in perfect companionable silence, which had to set a record, given what they were: publisher, writer, editor, and two hit men.

Bobby had been talking about publishing—self-publishing, Amazon, e-books, unsolicited manuscripts, over-the-transom. ". . . an antique phrase. The stuff that used to get read by editorial assistants, the old slush-pile stuff. No more. Now the reading public, they're the keepers of the slush pile, because practically anyone who can string three words together can get published on the Internet. Or Amazon-assisted. Or actually published by Amazon. Writers, take heart! The world is your slush pile."

Clive grunted. "Oh, shut up, Bobby."

"No." To the other three, he said, "Listen. Down the hall I have a little room. It was a small office that I've converted into a kind of library. Except there are no books, only unsolicited manuscripts. Shelves and shelves of them, ones that were never returned to the writers for one reason or another. I've been collecting them for years. Hundreds of them, maybe thousands, I don't know. I even got friends at other houses to donate them." Bobby leaned back in his chair again and swirled the Scotch in his glass. "Whenever I hear some writer whining about how he can't write, how he's lost it all, I boot him in there for an hour so he can leaf through a few. It's quite a tonic." He raised his glass. "Or whatever."

They were all drinking Talisker except for Clive, who was a Grey Goose guy. He had been in publishing for twenty-three years, long enough to be convinced that he was dumb when he was actually pretty smart. He had known L. Bass Hess for years as a conniving, litigious agent with an ego the size and shape of the Flatiron Building.

And a cheapskate, Clive had said. You wouldn't catch Bass Hess placing pieces of gold on the eyes of the corpse of an Egyptian king. He'd put them in his pocket.

"So what now?" said Candy.

They had all decided that running Hess out of town would be a temporary fix (and not punishment enough). They wanted something permanent.

"If Joey G-C's guys get to him again, that'll be permanent," Candy said.

Karl thought for a moment. "You know, we can maybe stop that hit if we show Joey we got something worse in store for Hess, and also maybe we can get Clive here to read Fabio's manuscript—"

"Whoa!" Clive shoved out the hand not holding his vodka, palm out. "I've already got Danny Zito breathing down my neck with his new book. Not another goodfella, thanks."

Karl shrugged. "Just a thought."

"It's not a bad one," said Paul, who was tapping a Scripto pen against a small notebook resting on his chest beside his drink. Every now and then he made a note. "Fabio might appear to L. Bass in a new and dangerous light."

"Meaning?" said Clive.

"I don't know. I'm just mulling. One thing leads to another. What do we know about Hess? What does the guy do? You said"—Paul looked over his shoulder at Clive—"the guy goes to Florida every year."

"To the Everglades."

"The 'Glades?" Paul wrote something down. "Sweet!"

"Visits his uncle. His uncle or his aunt."

Bobby took the cigar out of his mouth. "He can't tell the difference?"

"Uncle that went through a sex change, much to Bass's disgust," said Clive, knocking back his vodka, helping himself to more.

"You're shitting us. Hess visiting a transvestite aunt?"

"Not the same thing, Bobby. You should read your own Dunces series: *Sex Change for Dunces*."

"My God, that's not mine. That's E-Z Books, another imprint. That was started up after some birdbrainstorming by the Dubai brothers."

Clive said, "Whatever else the aunt is, she's rich. She's his father's brother-sister, and Bass is the only remaining relative. In other words, heir. But she's big on the Everglades, a real alligator guy-girl, and she likes to threaten him with leaving her fortune to Friends of the Everglades. So he really sucks up to her."

"The father," said Bobby. "Someone told me—you? him?—his father was a champion bass fisherman."

"No, not really. He cheated," said Clive. "He'd net some four- or five-foot bass, keep them trapped overnight, then go out and reel them in the next day. He, too, was an asshole."

"Does Hess fish when he's there?"

Clive nodded. "Pretends to like it. The uncle-aunt adored the father, so Bass has to imitate him."

Paul said from his prone position, with notebook, to Candy and Karl, "You guys have been tracking him for how long?"

"Three weeks," said Candy. "Guy's like a zombie. Ought to be down at the mall with the rest of the Undead, shopping. He meets up with clients or editors or whatever at the stroke of one at the Gramercy Tavern or 21 or that French place, Arles. He doesn't drink, doesn't smoke, doesn't eat nothing but fish and peas and a boiled potato. We could tell you where he'll be every damn minute. Once we got to Gramercy Park three minutes early, checked our watches, said 'Now!,' and here he comes around the corner."

"He lives where?" said Bobby.

"Upper East Side, during the week. But his home's in Connecticut. Wife and daughter live there. Second wife. I think the daughter's hers, not his. They live in Darien—no, Wilton. Wilton, Connecticut."

Bobby gave a small whistle. "You can't even look at a house there for under a million. He must be getting a helluva lot in commissions."

Clive shook his head. "His wife has money. I think she sank some of it in the agency when it wasn't doing so well."

Karl got up to top up his drink, said, "Every Wednesday on the way home, he stops off at St. Patrick's."

Paul looked up. "Yeah. Is he actually a Catholic, though? Or does he just like the cathedral?"

Karl shrugged, sat down again. "Dunno."

"But you followed him in."

"Sure. It's only been the three times. We just sort of case the joint. Pretend we're tourists."

"What's he do? I mean, does he genuflect? Do a little knee dip?"

Candy said, "No. He sits in a pew for maybe ten minutes, trying to work out another way to screw Cindy Sella."

Paul said, "Fabulous. You guys are good." He made another note.

Through air that was bluing over with smoke from cigarettes and cigars, Karl frowned at Paul. "You got an idea? I'm not so sure I like your ideas."

Paul just smiled.

So did Clive. "What we need," he said, "is another Pittsburgh."

Candy and Karl exchanged glances. "You mean like another situation where nobody knows what the fuck's going on."

"'Men with guns,'" said Paul. "That's what my wife said when she saw it on the news. Or 'goons with guns.'" He sat up. "Clive's right. What we need is another Pittsburgh."

"He's from there. Sewickley, I think."

"Hess is?" said Paul. Clive nodded.

"What the hell happened in Pittsburgh?" Bobby hadn't been there and was feeling the lack of less than utter control.

"Stuff," said Karl.

"Of course," said Clive, "we could just try to give L. Bass a hell of a scare."

Candy shook his head. "That's what we were just saying would only be temporary."

"With him, it might not be; I think Bass scares pretty easily."

"It's not very original," said Paul, getting up and going to the table where Bobby kept his excellent selection of liquors. Paul picked up the nearly empty bottle of Talisker, poured a mite for himself.

"Original? Who the fuck cares it's original?" said Candy.

Paul ignored that as he looked out at the swiftly coming darkness. "Unless you use the scare tactic to soften him up."

"What do you mean?" Clive joined him to look out at the funky geometry of the BOA building, its turquoise spear rising in a sky turning quickly to boot-black.

"You know. You beat somebody up awhile, and it's easier to get him to accept whatever you've got in mind."

Candy and then Karl wandered over to the window. Bobby was the only one still seated. Feeling left behind, he got up, too. "So," he said around his cigar, "what have we got in mind?"

"I'm thinking," said Karl, "Joe Blythe."

Candy looked at him. "Joe? He don't still work."

"Depends, I guess," said Karl.

"Who the hell's Joe Blythe?" said Bobby.

Karl picked a bit of tobacco from his tongue. "A guy."

The five of them stood there looking out the wide window at the Chrysler Building's silver-scaled heights, the gilded pyramid of New York Life, the neon greens and blues of the Empire State. They watched silver and gold and sapphire lights swimming in the enormous New York City sky, careless as a bunch of old-time crooks with nothing in mind but to steal Manhattan blind.

OLD-TIME CROOKS

21

"You don't remember me, I guess? Cindy Sella?" She was on the phone, holding the bit of paper on which she'd written the number from Craigslist.

"Cindy! Sure. How's the fish?"

"Oh, just great." She was speaking to Monty. "I was just wondering— do you have another one? A friend of mine, he lost his the other night when his aquarium broke." Why all the explaining? "And I thought I'd get him another one, I mean—"

"A ghost clown fish?"

"Yes. Are they hard to find?" Was she making an unreasonable request?

There was a pause as Monty turned away, perhaps to check his fish tank but more likely to check with his Aquaria buddy, Molloy, to see if he could get him one. Either way, he said, "Yeah, no problem, sure."

"Good. Same price?"

"Uh. I s'pose."

"A hundred?"

In a brighter tone, he said, "Hey. Hundred's good."

"When can I come pick it up?"

Pause. "Hold on." Another mumbled conference. "I can have it ready this afternoon, say, like sometime after three?"

"Okay. Three or four this afternoon?"

"Absitively. Hey, this time stay awhile, have a beer. Guys thought you were cool."

Cool? Herself, Cindy Sella? When she'd done nothing but stand there and speak when spoken to? Cool?

She must have said the word aloud, for Monty said, "Yeah. You comin' by yourself on the N train? All the way to get a fish? Fuck, yeah. Cool. See ya."

Cindy stood there, dead receiver in hand, feeling cool.

As Cindy put down the receiver in the West Village, Paul Giverney was saying, in the East Village, "Maybe we should save the scare-him-shitless tactic for the end."

It was the day following the evening meeting in Bobby Mackenzie's office. Paul had invited Candy and Karl to lunch, or rather, Dean and Deluca had invited them. Super-sandwiches had been smilingly brought into the small office by Paul's wife, who, for some reason all her own, got a big kick out of Paul's acquaintance with two contract killers. He got on well with anyone Mob-related. Molly once told him he should have been a cat thief.

"You wouldn't mean 'cat burglar,' would you?"

"Right. I can see you shimmying down a drainpipe with the swag."

Swag. "You've been reading Hannah's British comic books again. *Beano*." Hannah had insisted upon getting a dog so she could name it Gnasher. They simply waited for Hannah to dissuade herself, which she did by saying she was much too busy with her book to take Gnasher for walks.

Karl was chewing his mahimahi sandwich. He frowned. "End of what?"

"Yeah," said Candy, "of what?" Both of them were suspicious of, not to say intimidated by, Paul Giverney's imagination.

"Whatever we come up with to drive Bass Hess either completely mad or out of our field of vision. Out of Cindy Sella's, that is."

Candy had a bite of his croque-monsieur with prosciutto and washed it down with a swig of ale. He said, "We didn't come up with much last night, did we?"

"Of course we did. Weren't you paying attention?"

"Yeah, yeah," said Candy defensively. "I was."

Karl went on eating his grilled fish on sourdough contentedly.

"First thing," said Paul as he balled up his paper napkin and shot it toward the wastebasket and missed, "would be Florida. I'll find out if he's going soon, and if he isn't, we'll see that he does." He smiled. "This was a brilliant idea you guys had, that I take him on as an agent. We've got him in the crosshairs."

"Wait, wait, Paulie," said Candy. "Fuck, we do. We decided not to whack him."

Paul laughed. "Sorry. All I meant is to keep me as a client, L. Bass Hess will do whatever I want."

22

The Richard Geres were falling all over their tap-dancing feet offering chairs, coffee, a bowl of fruit, and imported biscuits to Lena bint Musah.

Not only was she herself as exotic as any Malaysian fish, there was something about her that oozed money. It wasn't just the ring she wore, which on its own would have accounted for the rape of the Congo; it was that one felt one could delicately strip thousand-dollar bills from her person.

"My license, I believe you'll find in order," she said, wasting no time. From her slim black bag that served as a new mark in briefcase elegance, she drew a letter-sized folder, and from that a document with fancy writing on old crushed-looking paper that might have been the Magna Carta and supposedly was signed by some Malaysian official.

From what Karl could squint up, the name was Tim-Tan X-something, and it was clear the Richard Geres didn't make much more of it than he could. But they looked at it and nodded as if they'd just had a beer with Tim-Tan.

Wally, wanting to appear one step ahead but was a league behind, said, "This gives you the right to import, but not to import a fish that's protected by either the FWS, the ESA, or the DOE."

Karl noticed he glanced at the cuff of his shirt with each new set of initials. It was the way guys in his American lit class used to claw out the answers to multiple-choice questions.

Lena nodded. "The fish in question is the wild Asian arowana. There are breeding facilities whose fish CITES has allowed can be exported. But the exportation of the wild arowana is illegal."

Wally pasted his palms together and leaned his chin on his fingertips. Rod tried to do the same thing, but as he was standing, he had no surface on which to rest his elbows, so he washed his hands over his cheeks and made his fingers meet behind his neck as if this were the gesture he'd intended from the outset. He lost his balance and had to sit down clumsily on the deep sill of the window. Candy wondered how he ever made it into the cast of *Chicago.*

"The Asian arowana . . ."

Lena and Wally said it more or less simultaneously, but the pronunciation varied.

"I was met," Lena went on, "at Chelsea Piers, Pier 61—"

Christ, thought Candy, but that place was busy.

"—by a supposed aquarist calling himself Miles Mutton, obviously not his real name."

Candy could tell "how did you know it wasn't?" was on the tip of Wally's tongue, but Wally outwitted himself for once and kept quiet.

Accepting a light from Wally for her brown cigarette, Lena went on, "He had done everything he could to disguise himself short of sending someone else. He'd chosen Pier 61 because it was the darkest. He wore a black Burberry and hat pulled down so I couldn't see his face. And he was armed, possibly with a Uzi—"

"Same shit-ass gun used at the Clown—" Candy burst out before Karl gave his ankle a kick that could have broken every little bone in it, at the same time giving him a look that a great horned owl might turn on a field mouse.

"Sorry, sorry," said Candy, who had pulled out his handkerchief and was doing a little drama of wiping his brow. "Thing is, I had two uncles gunned down on Mott Street with one of them—those—bastards, and every time I hear—"

Another kick from Karl, but Lena placed a delicate hand over Candy's knee and patted it, saying something that no one understood and everyone assumed to be Malaysian. At this point, they had forgotten where they were, that is, everyone except Lena. "His collection, he said, included the rarest of fish from every country in Europe and the East, including the *P. boylei,* the peppermint angelfish—which I seriously doubt because there are only one or two in captivity. It's a deep-water fish, as you may know."

(The lawyers' expressions, or at least Wally's—since he did what thinking was done—were fashioned to tell them that, yes, they did know.)

"But for some reason, the arowana escaped him. He's been trying to find one for years—surprising, since, although they are illegally traded, they are still traded. He would pay any price I required, he said, but were I to attempt to discover his true identity . . . I asked him why on earth I'd want to do that. I believe he was offended. He made a few casual threats, such as putting me on ice, to which I said my veins were full of it. I then told him I would be in touch through Mr. Zito. That the price would be between fifteen and twenty thousand." She stopped and smoked her cigarette.

Wally frowned. Rod selected a pear from the fruit bowl. Wally said, "Lena, what is it you want us to do?"

Her artfully plucked eyebrows rose fractionally. "I beg your pardon? I assumed, as you are the attorneys who handle environmental issues, you would not be asking me . . ." She sighed deeply and stubbed out her cigarette in the blue Murano ashtray. "I understand you have a client who happens to be an authority on the illegal trade in exotic fish."

From Wally came a sharp intake of breath. Rod ate his pear. Again, the eyebrows rose as Lena said, "You mean this is not true? It was my—our"—here a nod toward Candy and Karl—"reason for choosing you."

"Cindy Sella, you mean. Yes. We've been advising her every step of the way."

"Ah. Good. I would suggest we all meet."

"You mean with Miss Sella?"

Rod made a choking noise.

"Of course. She would be your expert witness regarding the trade."

Wally had resteepled his hands but now dropped them. "Witness? For what?"

Candy wondered, could this firm produce any dumber lawyers? Didn't these guys know how to fake anything?

Lena looked a tad surprised. "Against the U.S. government. The EPA. The Fish and Wildlife Service. For harassment. Entrapment. The usual laundry list of offenses." She put her hand to her shoulder and disengaged the silver brooch there. She clicked a tiny button, and a thin switchblade sprang forth. It was hardly bigger than one of the plastic dental picks one buys by the dozen.

Candy loved the musical little click that released the switchblade. With the other hand, she picked an apple out of the bowl and proceeded to cut a paper-thin slice, which she offered with her knife hand to Wally.

Rod tap-danced backward to the window. "Where'd you get that?"

Lena smiled slightly. "A silversmith. I had it made. Security in most places is rather sloppy." Holding the apple, she went on: "You do understand that this Miles Mutton was some sort of government agent? One does sue the government in this country, doesn't one? One sues everyone else."

Karl made a throaty noise that Candy recognized as trying to hold the laughs in.

23

This time when she knocked on the door, Cindy was armed with a six-pack of cold Amstel. There seemed to be a liquor store on every street corner.

This time Monty opened the door without the chain on and without his eyeballs showing in the crack between frame and door.

"Cindy!" He flung the door back and arm-waved her in. "Yes! Is this a fuckin' pack of beer I see? Guys! You can leave off the Ouija. Beer's been delivered."

Bunched over the board, Molloy and Graeme looked up and smiled. So did Bub, lying prone on the sofa with a striped blanket tucked around him.

"Thank God we don't have to go out!" said Molloy.

Cindy felt like the heroine of her own story—or was that the way David Copperfield had started out? They all looked grateful as Monty started tossing out the big cans, which they caught with the agility of outfielders. He handed one to Cindy, who said, "Just half, okay? They're so big."

Monty went for a glass and returned with one less than spotless, so he gave it a rub with the tail of his T-shirt.

"Thanks," she said after he'd frothed the Amstel into a glass. She moved over to the Ouija board. "Who was going to have to get the beer?"

Seated now on the other sofa, Graeme and Molloy pointed gun fingers at each other. The air was fogged the way London must have been in the days when they called it the Smoke. Cindy sighed.

Graeme raised his beer. "Real nice of you, girl."

"Saved the day," said Monty. His Adam's apple moved feverishly as he drank what looked like half the can. "Man." He wiped his hand over his mouth and shook a cigarette out of a pack of Camels and lit it. The others weren't smoking Camels, for sure. Graeme rose and pulled over an old wooden rocking chair for her, and she thanked him and sat down.

Cindy said to Molloy (the only one she knew had an actual job), "But you go out to work."

"It's different," he said.

Graeme wiped a few droplets from his T-shirt, the one that said *Now You See It* on the front. "Me, I work at home."

"Like, some people wish he didn't," said Monty. "Me. For example. We almost had a Chernobyl moment yesterday."

"Oh, come on. It wasn't hardly anything."

"I just don't like the sound of bang."

"You're such a pussy," said Molloy. "You wouldn't go one round with an alligator."

"You got that right, buddy. Can I have that joint?" He stubbed out his Camel, took the clip Molloy passed.

Suddenly, Monty was outlined in what looked like flame but obviously wasn't. "What the fuck?" He spurted up and beat at his chest and upper arms, or rather, at the zigzagging lights, which, in another five seconds, stopped. He glared at Graeme. "Asshole."

Graeme smiled his overtaxed face and shrugged.

"How did you do that?" asked Cindy.

Graeme slid down so that his chest was nearly in the seat. "Just fiber-optic crap."

Molloy said, "He worked in Vegas, if you can believe that."

"You did?" Cindy was delighted. "Doing what?"

Monty said, "Cirque du Soleil." He smothered a laugh in smoke.

Graeme sat up. "There was this magician—'illusionist,' he called himself. *Transfixed* is what he called his crappy show. It was in the moldy lower level of the Mirage. The Mirage, you remember, that's where Roy's pet tiger took a couple bites out of his face. You know how they did that, don't you?"

Cindy frowned. "The tigers?"

"No, the show. With mirrors. Most of the stuff they did with the tigers, it was illusion. Mirrors tilted up at the edge of the stage toward mirrors along the sides. It's amazing what you can do with mirrors." He took a long swig of beer and went on. "You think you're watching something in front of you, but you're not."

"Las Vegas," said Cindy wonderingly. The trouble with growing up in Kansas was that a person hardly ever got to Vegas. "What did you do in the act?"

"Set things on fire. Like Monty here. It's all illusion, like I said. People would be really disappointed if they knew how these famous tricks worked. How they're done isn't even interesting; it's boring." Graeme took a little flashlight, or what looked like one, from his tool belt. He flicked it on and aimed for Monty's foot, which was suddenly engulfed in flames, or looked it.

Monty jumped off the cot, stomping his foot, even though he knew there was no need to. "Christ, Graeme."

"Thing is," said Graeme, returning the torch to his tool belt, "people see what they're told they see. Most things are tricks of the light." He sat back and maneuvered a toke into a clip.

In her mind, Cindy saw the evening at the Clownfish Café. She saw the stubby candles lighting glasses brimming with water, in each a bright fish. It was the sort of thing Alice might have seen when she dropped into Wonderland. It should have been an illusion; it had ILLUSION written all over it.

Cindy started when Molloy handed her the clip they were passing around. "I never . . . I don't—you know—do drugs."

Molloy laughed. "I wouldn't insult this product by classifying it as 'drugs.' This is your primo weed, your quantum mechanics of marijuana, the best. Believe me, the worst it could do to you is make you sleepy."

She was researching drugs, wasn't she? And she wanted a gang of her own, didn't she? They were all looking at her encouragingly. "Okay." She sucked in and held the smoke in her mouth, wondering what to do. It had a pleasant, minty taste, with a licorice undertone.

Molloy said, "Don't drag it down deep, just a little at a time, slow."

Cindy did so. It was much like drawing on a cigarette. Nothing happened for a few moments, and she was about to tell them it was without effect when she began to feel as if a very fine piece of chamois or cashmere were buffing her skin. She was completely aware—hyper-aware—of everything going on around her, but smoothly. The slat-back rocking chair that had been pinching her before was now seamless wood.

"Really good stuff," she said, as if she had some basis for comparison.

"You bet," said Monty. "He gets it straight from the grower. None of your Mexican-cartel bullshit at all."

Cindy, unfamiliar with sources of marijuana, especially Mexican sources, could say only "Wow."

There was a chorus of "Wows" in response. Monty jumped up again as if his foot were on fire. "Wanna see your fish? I'll get him."

For the half minute Monty was gone, there was a silence like the shared toke.

The clown fish arrived like a baby bundled in water.

"It's beautiful," said Cindy. "Thanks."

"Don't thank me. Thank Molloy," said Monty, carrying the little fish carefully before him. "He's the one gets 'em."

Molloy raised two fingers to an invisible hat. "We got several of them at Aquaria."

She did not want to ask if he'd purchased this particular fish for her and would take the hundred to the store. "You must know a lot about fish," she said.

"I would have to say yes to that. We've got every kind imaginable."

Cindy turned to the one they called Bub, who'd been silent, albeit blissfully, throughout this exchange. "Bub, what do you do?"

"Barter in used-car parts." He smiled. "I live in wreckage."

"He works in an auto salvage yard." Monty snuffed a laugh. "Junk."

"You mean the kind of place where they lift cars on some hydraulic thing and then dump them in a heap?"

Bub nodded. "Or they take apart the really bad ones for the parts."

Cindy was wide-eyed. "Sounds like a horror movie."

Bub thought about that, taking her analogy quite seriously. "More science fiction, I'd say. More Philip K. Dick. I can imagine Philip K. Dick in a junkyard."

"Bub reads a lot," said Monty.

"Yeah. I can wrap up a book a day as long as it's not Proust. You'd be surprised how conducive my junkyard is to reading and writing."

Said Monty, "He writes a lot, too."

The others, Graeme and Molloy, just lounged and passed a fresh toke between them and listened or didn't.

Bub unfolded himself from the brightly striped blanket and reached for his beer. "I wrote a novel about pieces of metal, you know, fenders, grilles, trunks—that stuff all flying off—"

The ceiling flew away—

"—then coming together in a new shape. The title's *Robot Redux,* but I'm thinking maybe I should change that. It's, you know, too Updike."

Continuing his editorializing, Monty said, "Bub got an MS from Crankton U."

Cindy frowned. "Where's that?"

"Online. It's a great idea, lets you get your degree without leaving the junkyard."

Cindy was intrigued. "What's the MS in?"

Bub had pulled the blanket back around him. "Physics," he said.

She blinked. "Physics?"

"Yeah. You have no idea how much quantum mechanics has to do with a junkyard. It's where I got my idea for *Robot Redux.*"

"You actually wrote this book?"

"Yeah. Five hundred and twenty-three pages of it."

"How long did it take you?"

"Long time. Over a year. I couldn't do it full-time, seeing as how I had to take care of the junkyard."

Monty was popping the last can of beer and handing it around. Everybody took a swig except Cindy. She had some of her first one left. The can went around again. Monty said, "See, Bub's really into this bullshit string theory."

Bub took umbrage, but not overmuch. "It ain't bullshit, man. It's the explanation of every fucking thing in the universe. It's what Einstein was looking for and never found."

"If this shit is as small as you say it is, how does it have anything to do with our lives?" said Molloy, ending with a loud belch.

"Strings, he means," said Bub to Cindy. "They're smaller than even neutrons. They're small as hell. They explain the theory of many other dimensions. There's more than three, you know. We just can't see the other ones. They vibrate. The strings, I mean. Vibrate all over the place."

Cindy accepted the toke the next time it came around and filled up her lungs.

Molloy said, "So how would this affect me wrestling an alligator?"

Hearing the question, Cindy thought maybe she'd taken in too much smoke and was becoming delusional.

"It wouldn't, would it? You'd just go on in your normal way."

"That's me. But what about the alligator?"

"Aren't you taking this awful literal? As if strings were things you could take hold of. They're invisible, man. The gator, he'd still be the same."

"Then I don't get it. If it doesn't have any effect, and it's invisible, why the hell bother with it as a theory?"

Cindy thought they were going around in circles, or she was. She said, "You've done that? Wrestled alligators?"

Molloy nodded as he sucked in some smoke. "Still do. It's my winter job."

"Florida."

Cindy would have looked surprised if she'd been able to widen her eyes. They wanted to shut.

"It's not as unusual as it sounds," said Molloy. "One I usually work at, it's a kind of roadside attraction. One of those mom-and-pop operations. They call it Gator Garden. It's not far off the Tamiami Trail, near Everglades City. It's real popular. The owners try and make it appear a kind of animal refuge and an educational experience for the youngsters." He snickered. "You know the kind of shit. There's a big tank of water and a gator. I get in. We pretend to wrestle. All we're doing is having a little fun. Play-fighting."

"How do you know play-fighting is what the alligator's doing?"

Molloy laughed, threw his arms wide, stuck out his legs. "Still got all my limbs intact."

"Maybe you're a lot better alligator wrestler than you're making out you are."

Molloy looked pleased with himself but spoke modestly. "Nah. See, unlike this ugly couple that owns the place and their awful kids that tease them, toss things at them, I'm nice to the gators."

"Is this operation legal?"

"Probably. Though it shouldn't be, you ask me."

Monty put in, "Molloy here just has a way with alligators. We go out in a kayak."

"You, too?"

"Fight alligators? Hell, no. I just go down to visit. We go out on the river in a kayak or rowboat and row around. I'm deft with a boat."

"Deft." Molloy seemed to like that.

Monty went on. "Even the gators we see along the way seem to get on with Molloy."

Cindy frowned and wondered how he could tell, but she didn't ask.

Monty said, "I told him he's a gator whisperer."

They all laughed beery, smoky laughs.

24

Paul Giverney knew when writing his mysteries how trumped up they were, how artificial, manipulative, and everything else Raymond Chandler said of the Golden Age of crime writing and all of the mysteries that followed from it.

Paul was adept at pulling down pieces of sky from different heavens and pressing them all together to form a new heaven. All it took was a little imagination.

In this case, a few pieces of sky had been supplied:

1) Fishing
2) Florida
3) Uncle/aunt
4) Cathedral
5) Joe Blight? Blythe?

He looked at number three. A tight-ass like L. Bass Hess would not want the uncle-aunt sex-change broadcast. But it would hardly be enough to drive him permanently from Manhattan.

Number five: Dark horse, since Paul didn't know him. But he intuited bodily harm.

Paul rocked in his swivel chair. Fatal *accidents* were not ruled out. Push him off the 138th Street platform? That always went rather well in movies. A hand comes out of the crowd just at the moment the Pelham 123 bears down? Paul's mind was steeped in cinema. He had really liked the original version of *The Taking of Pelham 123*. He made a note. Pushing L. Bass in front of a cab might involve the driver in criminal negligence, reckless driving, something like that. Who was he kidding? As if yellow cabs ever drove any other way.

Besides, violent death would be momentarily unpleasant for Hess, but his legal team might simply carry on as before, or Hess's wife might continue the lawsuit though probably not, as she didn't sound like a big L. Bass supporter.

What Paul and the others wanted was restitution. L. Bass Hess had to make up for all the worry and strife he had caused, not to say all the money that Cindy had been forced to spend on lawyers. Just being ironed flat on the rails of the 138th Street station wouldn't do it.

Number two: Fishing. Some infringement of a fish-and-game law? Hess doing jail time would be fun, but he wouldn't get any. Probably the most he'd get would be a stiff fine and community work, or maybe confined to his house like Martha Stewart. So they wouldn't be rid of him.

"What're you doing?" He'd been studying number four, Cathedral, when Molly's voice came from the doorway. She stood there in her apron, holding a wooden spoon. A patch of late-afternoon sunlight made her hair glow.

Paul shook his head, clearing it of celestial visitations. "Just making a list."

"Oh, God, I hope not. Not after that last one."

"One what?" He aped ignorance.

"List."

He waved that away. "That was a list of publishers. I was trying to decide on my next one. What's for dinner?"

"I don't know. I'm trying to decide between coq au vin and duck à l'orange."

Two Dean and Deluca specialties. Molly hardly ever cooked except to make salads. Her salads were superb.

Another voice chimed in. "I want crepes Susan from the pancake house," said Hannah.

"Suzette," said Paul.

"No," said Molly, "they actually are crepes Susan."

"What's the difference?"

"They don't dump a quart of Cointreau on them and flame them."

"What's Cointreau?" said Hannah.

"Strong stuff that'll knock your ears off."

Hannah cupped her hands over her ears.

"What do you want, then?" asked Molly.

"Duck and crepes Susan with a quart of Cointreau," Paul said.

"Okay." Molly removed her apron and took Hannah's coat from a hook in the hall. "Here. You can go with me."

Hannah paused in the doorway to comment as she buttoned her coat, "Maybe that's what happened to Vango."

Paul frowned. "To what?"

"That man. Vango. You said he lost his ear."

"Ah, yes, the artist. The great painter."

"Whatever" said Hannah's shrug. She wasn't interested in his art, only in his ear.

They left for Dean and Deluca, and Paul went back to number four, Cathedral.

Interesting that Hess stopped by St. Patrick's every Wednesday. He did nothing unusual, just sat in a pew. The performance of this ritual probably sprang from the same well as did eating lunch at the Gramercy Tavern at one o'clock and going home at exactly five. Take it a step further: This guy was a slave to compulsion. Rack it up to obsessive-compulsive behavior, and a lot would be explained. People like that were much more subject to cracking than the ones who spent their lives in free fall, buffeted by any passing breeze.

Paul stuck his pencil in his mouth and got up and paced around his twelve-by-twenty study. The pencil was pretty chewed up, for he spent a lot of time pacing when he was writing.

What L. Bass Hess thought he possessed was control: control over his daily schedule, over his visits to his uncle-aunt, over his clients. What he had was no control at all, given that he wasn't able to shift around times and people. So when one of his clients jumped ship, it might as well be the *Lusitania* going down. For Hess, it was complete disaster unless he could somehow undo it. He wasn't interested in salvage. He wanted the whole creaking hulk set to rights, seaworthy once again.

The first thing he did was harpoon the cause of the disaster—in this case, Cindy Sella.

For L. Bass Hess, it was all down to her. Every misfortune he was suffering was the fault of Cindy Sella.

St. Pat's Cathedral brought to mind an old school chum Paul hadn't seen in years. Hadn't he heard that Johnny got religion while he was in prison (out on good behavior in three) and completely jettisoned his old life, got up from that table of money, booze, and women, and sat down at the table of faith? A poker table, more likely, thought Paul with a laugh. Where was he now?

Paul went to his computer and brought up Facebook. He entered the name of Johnny del Santos, and there he was, looking in his little picture as crafty as ever. Now he appeared to be in charge of something called the Abbey, which looked like a monastery, done in some Southwestern-Mediterranean sort of architecture. It was near Sewickley, PA, which was outside of Pittsburgh. (Hadn't Clive said Bass Hess was from Sewickley?) Paul was from Pittsburgh, but with his parents and his sister all dead, he rarely returned to that city. He shut his eyes for a moment, remembering his little sister, Jenny.

Pittsburgh was also Johnny's hometown; they had attended the same high school in Shadyside. Yes, Johnny looked the same as when he was knocking over 7-Elevens and terrifying cashiers.

Paul shut down Facebook and thought about the Abbey. He looked at his list again. Cathedral. A connection? He shrugged and turned his attention to fishing, uncle/aunt, and Florida. The three obviously went together. A fishing accident, maybe? What kind of fish? Fish fish fish fish . . . a shark? Did Hess fish in shark-infested waters? A shark attack was no good, because it would be over in seconds and consequently lacked the retribution criterion.

What about a *near* accident? A godawful situation in which you find yourself almost drowned, harpooned, or otherwise dead? Florida. Lake Okeechobee, Big Cypress Swamp. Alligators. Snakes. Pity he didn't know a snake charmer.

Wait a minute. Jimmy McKinney. Paul was up and thrusting his arms into his Burberry and writing a note to Molly that he'd be back in an hour or so.

———

When Paul Giverney walked unannounced into Jimmy McKinney's office, the agent was talking to one of his clients, a blond woman who looked vaguely familiar.

"Paul! Good to see you! How are you?"

"Great. But I'm interrupting?"

"No," said Jimmy.

"No, no," said the woman.

Jimmy introduced her. "Cindy Sella."

Paul's jaw dropped. "You're *Cindy Sella*? My Lord, haven't I ever heard a lot about you!"

Cindy blushed and asked him what. The what got lost in his questions to Jimmy. "Listen, you've got this author, the guy who writes those Swamp something books?"

"Swamp Heart. Yeah, it's a series. His name's Colin Whitt."

It struck Paul that it was odd Jimmy would have someone like that as a client. "Is there some way I can get in touch with him?"

Jimmy frowned. "I've got his details, but the guy's in South Africa."

"Shit." Paul said this under his breath.

"What do you want Colin for?"

"I need someone who knows about alligators. No, someone who can handle alligators."

Jimmy laughed. "What? You're working on a new book? Where's it set?"

"Big Cypress Swamp. Somewhere in the Everglades. I haven't got a title yet. I've just—"

Cindy was holding up her hand like a kid waiting for the teacher to call on her. "I know somebody."

25

L et me get this straight," said Paul. "You went out to Sunset Park on the N train just to buy a clown fish? You tramped its potholed pavements and engaged in repartee with four druggies you'd never seen before—"

"I wouldn't call them—"

"—just to buy a fish?"

"A ghost clown fish. Frankie lost his when the goons shot up the fish tank."

They had left Jimmy's office and were now sitting in Ray's coffee shop, he with coffee, she with a Diet Pepsi. It wasn't far from Paul's apartment in the East Village. She would have liked to point out they were almost neighbors, West Village and East Village, but thought that would be pushy.

"So one of these guys has experience with alligators?"

"He's really good with them. He works with them when he goes to Florida. Those roadside attractions you mentioned—that's where he does it. He says the place is awful. Not just cheap and tawdry but callous toward the animals."

"What exactly does he do?"

Cindy told him about Molloy's act.

Paul's smile grew broader. "I'd like to meet him. You have his number?"

She shook her head. "Only the number of the house we met in. I got it from Craigslist."

Paul rolled his eyes.

"That's where they all hang out."

"What about the others?"

Cindy thought as she sucked up her soda. "Monty. He's the one who advertised on Craigslist. Monty goes to Florida, too, sometimes. He's good with boats. Then there's Bub. He works in a junkyard. I think he lives there. He's writing a book that he says is in the Philip K. Dick vein. *Robot Redux* is the title. The idea is that all these pieces of metal somehow fly together—"

"And make a robot." Paul smiled and drank his coffee.

"He's into physics. Especially string theory, if you understand that."

"Enough to know I don't understand it."

"Then there's Graeme. He used to be part of a magic act at the Mirage."

"You mean Vegas?" When she nodded, he said, "What kind of act?"

She was making noise sucking froth through her straw. "He throws light around, for one thing."

"There doesn't have to be another. This is some gang you hang out with."

Gang you hang out with! Could he have said anything more pleasing? No.

"I wonder . . ." He was looking in his empty coffee cup.

Cindy waited for him to finish the statement of wonder. Finally, she leaned over the table and said, "You wonder what?"

He looked up. "Besides the junkyard guy—"

"Bub."

"Bub. Do these others have actual jobs?"

"Molloy does. He works in a place called Aquaria. It doesn't sound like a full-time job, though."

"Selling aquariums."

"That's right. I don't know whether Monty has a job. It's his place they all go to. He doesn't act like he has a job right now. Why?" She frowned and turned her straw in her empty glass. "And why do you want to talk to someone who's experienced with alligators?"

"My book. The one I'm researching."

She continued to frown. "The one you told Jimmy about doesn't sound anything like your usual books."

"You've read them?"

"Of course I've read them. Like half the rest of the world."

"Thanks. Anyway, can you fix it so I can meet these guys?"

She nodded, smiling. The notion that she was a fixer pleased her inordinately. "I can fix it. When?"

"How about tomorrow?"

"Okay. I'll give Monty a call. I don't think their calendars are full."

26

Candy and Karl agreed that meeting a contract killer in a crepe restaurant would cast serious doubt on his credentials if it hadn't been Arthur Mordred they were meeting. Anyway, they weren't looking for a hit; they just wanted him to fill in the rest of the action in Lena bint Musah's story.

They found him in a booth eating lemon and lavender crepes. "House specialty," he added. "Meyer lemons only."

"Oh, well," said Karl, seeing the smoking sign with the X'd-out red circle and taking out one of his thin cigars.

They had met Arthur Mordred in Pittsburgh. Arthur had been hired by Paul Giverney to protect Ned Isaly. If Paul Giverney hadn't put his dumb idea in motion in the first place, Ned wouldn't have needed protection. Thank God for scruples, they had said many a time since then; if they hadn't had scruples, Ned Isaly wouldn't be around to write another book.

"So, guys. Somebody need protection from the likes of you?" Arthur stuffed a slice of sleek lemon crepe in his mouth.

"Funny, ha-ha. No, Arthur, we want you to do a job for us."

"Something you two can't handle? Oh, dear, I feel like Elvis, with you guys as audience." He wiped his fork, loaded with a section of crepe in lemony-lavender sauce, across his plate. "Sure you won't join me? The champagne chai is to die for."

"We probably would. No, we're not talking about a hit."

"Not protection, I hope. That's such a bore."

"If you'd shut up and let us finish," said Karl. "How much do you know about endangered species?"

"About as much as I do a warm and loving home life."

"We're thinkin' fish. To be more precise, exotic fish. Say like the Andean catfish or the Lost River sucker, or the—"

Karl cut in on this showing off. "If we feed you some info about the subject, you got a good enough memory to spit it back?"

"The Lost River sucker, *sic.* You sure that's not some old geezer panning for gold back in Oklahoma a century ago?"

Karl shrugged. "Arthur, you can't take us serious, we're outta here." He was denied a dramatic rise from the booth because he was on the inside, pressed against the wall.

"Don't be so prickly. You haven't told me anything to *take* serious. You haven't said whatever the hell you want or as much as given a flying kiss re money. 'Re' goes with '*sic.*'"

Candy frowned. "You stoned? You on something?"

"Stoned? I'm just eating my lemon crepe. I may have a maple *crème fraîche* for dessert. I haven't had a drink since Pittsburgh. That was my single brief relapse. I'm back to my A.A. meetings. My sponsor thinks I was trying for a geographic cure by going to Pittsburgh."

"Which is shit. You got paid by Paul to go to Pittsburgh and protect Ned Isaly."

"Yes, well, of course I couldn't tell that to my sponsor."

"Tell him Pittsburgh never cured nothing, baby, except boredom."

They all laughed.

"Now, for this job, we've got in mind this organization called the Bluefin Alliance, a name someone would think up to make themselves sound like an insurance firm. Or maybe even sound like they're into Greenpeace shit. This bunch is definitely operating under the radar. What they do is, they bring illegal fish, exotic endangered fish, into the country. They do know the Bluefin Alliance is as bad as your Mexican cartels."

"How? How do they know that?"

"They know because we told them, Arthur."

"I never heard of this Bluefin bunch."

"That's because it doesn't exist."

Arthur forked up a bite of crepe. "So who is they?"

"Couple of lawyers."

Arthur Mordred actually put down his fork. "What are you guys looking for?"

"Well, not the *Law Review.*" Karl sniggered. "What we want is everything they have on Cindy Sella."

This meant filling Arthur in on who she was and telling him about the papers passed between L. Bass Hess and the Richard Geres, Wally and Rod, and the Snelling legal outfit.

"We got some of those documents by mistake. But there's nothing in them to prove anything came from the Snelling firm."

Mordred squinted. "So I go in armed and make this turd open his files."

"No," said Karl, "although that's a brilliant and really original plan."

"I detect sarcasm. So, what *is* the plan?"

"We need you to come to a meeting at this address." Karl scribbled it on the back of a coaster, pushed it toward Arthur. "She hasn't given us a time yet."

"Who's she?"

"Lena bint Musah. You'll like her." Karl nodded toward Arthur's cup. "Her espresso is terrific. So are her cigarettes."

"I don't smoke."

"You will."

27

Paul Giverney had his plan outlined, albeit sketchily, for it depended upon the availability of talent.

He'd been working on this all morning when he should have been writing the next chapter of *The Drowning Man* (a title he disliked but liked more than *Like a Drowned Rat,* from Hannah, and who refused to be dissuaded despite there being no rats in the book). The new book was not yet under contract, nor would it be while L. Bass Hess was on the horizon; Hess was ignorant of the fact. He didn't know it and was hard at work negotiating with Bobby Mackenzie, who had been prepped to offer terms either outrageously complex or merely outrageous. Or both.

L. Bass had not yet suggested shopping the book to other publishers. "Any publisher in New York would die for a book by you. Is Mackenzie insane?"

"You only just noticed?" Paul had said.

Hess blubbered. "I know he can be irrational sometimes, but he's a brilliant publisher."

"You can always try somebody else."

Hess wanted to keep on with Mackenzie-Haack because Bobby had made an (insane) offer of $3 million. For a single book. A 15 percent commission would earn Hess $450,000. It was the kind of deal an agent would jump off the Seagram Building to collect.

Paul's mobile, which he had left on vibrate, was quivering across his desk. He grabbed it up. "Yes?"

"Bass here. Listen to Mackenzie's latest demand. After I thought things were pretty well settled. He wants the advance paid out in twelfths. T-W-E-L-T-H-S." Hess spelled it out. "Can you imagine?"

"Is that how you spell it? T-W-E-L-T—isn't there an F in there somewhere?"

Paul could nearly smell the fumes coming off Hess across the wire.

"Paul, that's—ha-ha-ha—immaterial. He wants to divide up the three mill into twelve payments."

"I'll be damned. Well, I guess that's what they do with baseball players." Paul was studying the outline of his plan. He was looking at "magician." Beside his notebook on the desk was a copy of *The Magic Mountain,* which he fingered. It had nothing to do with the word "magician," or at least not consciously. He crossed out "magician" and penciled in "bush." The plan was organic; it was on the way to becoming a whole. It was like at a certain point when he was writing a book, he saw it. It. The whole picture. It really was like creating a tiny world. Maybe Wallace Stevens was right: God was the imagination.

Then again, it was like connecting the dots on those place mats they put down for children in some restaurants. Dot . . . dot . . . dot . . . until the picture came clear.

"One twelfth on signing, one twelfth on delivery of initial manuscript, one twelfth on final manuscript—that's after copyediting—one twelfth . . ."

Paul let him ramble on. He wasn't listening; he was leafing through Mann's book and thinking of the idea of sanctuary.

". . . and I'm going to demand he change this to six payouts. Six."

"You do that, Bass."

"And if he won't agree?"

"That's your job, Bass. That's what I pay you fifteen percent for. Gotta go, dude (and if ever a dude was not, it was L. Bass Hess); someone's at my door. Bye."

Cindy sat watching her fish and thinking about the talk with Paul Giverney in the coffee shop.

Maybe he was going to pay Monty and the others to lure Hess into a dark alley and club him. Or maybe, when Hess was on his way to Connecticut some weekend, the four of them would wait by the side of the road and flag him down, drag him out of the car, and leave him in a wheat field. Hess was allergic to wheat. Cindy pictured him, bleeding and staggering through the high wheat, arms out like a scarecrow, choking and sneezing . . .

She added several more not unpleasant images to this montage and hoped Paul Giverney would find the place in Sunset Park from her meager directions.

The building looked, as Cindy had said, like a warehouse, probably because it was. Paul braked, switched off the engine, and popped the trunk. He got out and went around to get the beer.

He schlepped it to the door, which opened on Monty as if he'd been waiting his whole life. He probably saw the beer and probably was.

Bub and Molloy nearly erupted off the low-slung sofa. "Whoa! What have we here?"

"Just what it looks like. Beck's, Sam Adams. Wasn't sure what you liked."

"All of it, man. Come on in." He introduced Paul to the other three.

"You're the *writer*? Paul Giverney the *writer*?" said Bub. "Man, let me shake your hand. I got all your books down at the yard."

"You're wondering why I'm here. I have a reason."

"Hey, man, you don't need a reason."

"I've got one nonetheless. For the moment, I'll just see in what way you—each of you—fit my plan."

"What plan?"

They had already opened beers and were settling back.

"Getting rid of Cindy Sella's insane ex-agent. When I say 'get rid of,' I don't mean bump him off. I know a couple guys who do that kind of work. No, I mean drive him crazy and out of New York."

"Didn't know she had an agent. She doesn't talk much about herself. That's cool," said Molloy.

Paul told them about L. Bass Hess.

"Jesus!" said Bub. "Maybe I shouldn't bother with my book, if that's what publishing is like."

"Cindy said you'd written one."

"Yeah. *Robot Redux*. It's about things falling apart. I work in a car junk yard. Auto parts, crushed cars, and like that."

"Okay. I won't give you details because I don't know all of them myself. But . . . remember Scrooge?"

They all nodded. "Dickens? That Scrooge?"

"It's kind of like that."

"He gets visited by ghosts. You want us to play ghosts?"

"No. Anybody could do that. No. I want you to use your various fields of expertise. And since I'll be taking up a lot of your time, I'll be paying you a lot of money. I'm thinking in the neighborhood of five thousand." Their eyes rounded. "Each."

Monty dropped his beer; Bub choked on a toke he'd just inhaled. The other two simply stared.

"Let's start with the Everglades." Paul looked at Monty. "You're good with boats." He turned to Molloy and grinned. "And you're good with alligators."

28

W e want to get him to Everglades City," said Paul. "Into the swamp."

"Why? And the next 'why?' is 'why me?'"

"Because you're a friend of Hess's."

"I'm not a friend," said Clive. "I only know him through books he's agented."

"Is that really a verb?"

"Isn't everything these days? We're in constant motion. What's your point?"

"You're an acquisitions editor. And you're interested in the story of his/her life." What Clive was to be had not occurred to Paul before just that moment.

"Lives."

"Okay. All I want is for you to get L. Bass to the 'Glades. You can be very persuasive, Clive."

"I hate Florida."

"Come on, Clive. Florida isn't a state anyone can hate."

"Why don't you go yourself? It would make more sense. It's your idea, after all."

"Bear with me, Clive. I've got a plan I'm working on."

"Your plans make me nervous, Paul. My mind keeps returning to your plan for Ned Isaly."

Paul sighed. "That was not *my* plan. That was Bobby's plan. I'm not responsible for what he does."

"He couldn't have done it if you hadn't made your contract contingent on getting rid of Ned. So it might just as well have been your plan."

"Clive, only Bobby Mackenzie is nutty enough to hire a hit man."

"And only you are nutty enough to give him a reason to do so. Okay, I'll get the address in Everglades City. I'll be your goon. I'll go to Florida."

29

Angelfish," said Lena bint Musah. "The Clipperton isn't illegal to import, but one has to have special permission to do so. There was a dealer who smuggled about fifty Clippertons into the U.S., claiming they were blue passer fish. They resemble Clippertons, but not so much that anyone with knowledge would mistake one for the other. The USFWS certainly knew the difference."

"So how much is this fish worth?" asked Karl.

"You could sell one for ten thousand dollars."

"What? That means this guy had half a million worth of these fish?"

They were all sitting in Lena's living room—Karl, Candy, and Arthur Mordred—having a little of Lena's coffee and a lot of Lena's cigarettes. The dog lay quietly, this time at Arthur's feet.

"Jesus, these are something," said Arthur. "It's as good as a couple shots of Glenfiddich." He inhaled, slowly exhaled. "Make that three shots."

"You're in A.A.," said Candy.

Arthur shrugged and inhaled. "For the most part."

"A.A.'s not in parts. You either are or you aren't."

Lena continued, "There's the peppermint angelfish. There are only two in captivity. One would cost you up to twenty thousand dollars."

"My God," said Arthur, leaning down to rub the old dog's neck. The dog did not respond.

"A further obstacle to owning one is that they are extremely difficult to take care of. They refuse food."

"What? They don't eat, they die," said Arthur. "Why in hell would someone shell out twenty large for a fish that's likely to die on him?"

"Serious collectors are often obsessed, hugely competitive, and egoistic. Such a fish would be worth that amount just to say you have one. What do we do with these elegant fish?" She looked from Candy to Karl.

Karl, who'd been lounging in his chair with his legs stretched out, said, "These are the fish the U.S. government is after you about. I mean, that's what you say."

"If there are only two of these peppermints in the world—"

"Not in the world, Arthur, in *captivity*. Do you think these ridiculous lawyers have ever heard of such fish?" Lena gave a small feminine snort.

"Right, you are right," said Arthur, helping himself to another fantasy cigarette. "What I'm wondering is what happens to Cindy Sella if this book of hers gets around? I mean, wouldn't the Bluefish Alliance put her on their dead-even-as-we-speak list?"

Both Candy and Karl swerved off course in lighting up fresh cigarettes. Candy said, "Arthur, there ain't a Blue*fin* Alliance. That is a made-up fiction."

"Meaning you don't really exist," said Karl, laughing through smoke.

"Yeah. Right. But neither does the fucking book."

Lena asked, "And does Miss Sella know that?"

"Know what?"

"That she's not writing this book."

"What would she have to know about a book she's not writing?"

"It's not impossible—indeed, not improbable—that these lawyers would call her and ask about it."

That was too many "nots" for Candy. He had to translate. "You're saying the Richard Geres might call her up and ask about it."

Lena nodded and sipped her coffee.

"What about this?" Arthur said, getting back into the swing of things. "What if, say, Herbie Fosdick, who's a big-time—"

"Who the hell's Herbie Fosdick?"

"No one. I just made him up to try and make a point."

"Arthur, just call him John Smith, will you?"

"What difference does it make if it's a made-up name?"

Candy exhaled a bale of smoke through his nostrils. "Because it gets us off track; because if you'd just said John Smith, I'd of known it was not a real person." Candy opened his arms wide. "Capice?"

"Stop with the 'capice' crap. That's the only Italian you know."

Lena sighed. "Gentlemen, you keep on getting sidetracked. Continue, Arthur, with your question about this Fosdick person."

Arthur scratched his neck "I forgot."

Candy and Karl inhaled simultaneously some more forget-everything smoke and laughed.

Lena ignored them and said to Arthur, "You were saying that he is a big-time something before you were interrupted." She gave Candy and Karl a veiled look with knives behind it.

Arthur thought. "A big-time exotic fish collector, that's what I was going to say. So here's Cindy Sella writing an exposé of the illegal importing of fish. What if Fosdick thinks he's in danger? Would he come after her? There doesn't have to be a book, just the rumor of a book." He sat back, rather proud of the way he'd put that.

Candy said, "I see what you mean. Like the Richard Geres could leak it."

Karl slapped his forehead. "Look, this is not exactly the Mob going after this book. Fosdick is not some made man and not one of those jerks that sprayed the Clownfish Café. We are talking about fish, guys and gals. F-I-S-H."

Candy said, "Hey, hold it, K. You're the one talked about this Bluefish—"

"Blue*fin*," Karl said, correcting him.

"—being as bad as the Mob."

Karl sat back. "Yeah, that's true."

Arthur said, "Look, don't we need some illegals instead of just a failure to get legal permission to import these fish?"

Lena answered, "We've got the arowana and some corals." Here she took some glossy pictures from the folder and placed them on the table. "In addition, the Clipperton angelfish can only be found in one place: an atoll not far from Hawaii."

"Seems to me it should be illegal to import them. And that peppermint angelfish? What the fuck—excuse my French," said Karl. "You're saying there's only two of those little fellas in captivity, and the U.S. government says go ahead and plunder them?"

Lena reached the small coffeepot across the cocktail table and refilled their cups. "The question yet to be answered is what story I tell these attorneys in order to gain access to what they have on Cindy Sella. They know the documents are out there and that the wrong people picked them up. Your testimony would be that Mr. Hess handed the papers to you, assuming you were Wally Hale and Rod Reeves."

"It doesn't prove Wally and Rod are in league with Hess. Or vice versa."

"Wait. The secretary. The two of them had an appointment with Hess."

"Yeah, but so what? They were Cindy's attorneys until a few days ago. So they could say they were there to discuss a settlement."

"All right. What exactly do you need?" said Arthur.

"Anything. A letter, a memo from the lawyers to the agent or vice versa, that shows they were, uh, collaborating."

"There's nothing in the papers you got that suggests they were working for Hess?"

"No cover letter, nothing. Not even a letterhead of Snelling and Botox," said Karl.

"Borax," said Candy.

"Tell me. Why would such information in the hands of these lawyers be a threat to Cindy Sella if they were allegedly her lawyers?"

"Get her to do what they wanted, maybe to hand over the commission to Hess, or all this stuff gets aired."

Karl said, "It doesn't make much difference what was in the papers. Just that Wally and Rod and Bass were in collusion. These lawyers were working for both the plaintiff and the defendant."

"You lie and I'll swear to it. Ain't nothing shows where that information was headed. So those papers we got don't prove collusion."

There was a silence.

"Blackmail," said Lena as if the word were always right on the tip of her tongue, waiting to be spoken. She lifted the Lalique lighter and was about to ignite it when three hands thrust themselves toward her with struck matches. "Thank you, gentlemen." Her exhalation was like breath blowing out candles. She repeated it: "Blackmail." It was as if the word were wedded to stars in the dark, merely waiting to illuminate their minds. "That's what we want. What do we have that these lawyers want?"

"Nothing," said Candy.

"What could we have that they would want? Think."

They settled down with their cigarettes to cloud-think. It was Karl's eye that first fell on the glossy photo of the peppermint angelfish. He picked it up, looked at it, and said, "They got a fish tank." A slightly abstruse comment, but Karl continued, "You know they wouldn't have the papers on it. I mean, if they had one of these." He floated the photo past them and looked at Candy. Karl said while Candy shook his head, "Candy's got a fish looks just like this."

"You're crazy. Oscar don't look like that."

"He does. He's striped. Red and white."

"Stripes? You said yourself it was squiggles. No." He had quickly come out of his cigarette trance, clear-eyed, clear-minded. "No way. No fucking way."

"Oh, come on, C. Nothing bad's going to happen to him. It'd only be for a few hours." He turned to Lena. "Candy's fish, I saw a picture of one, can't remember the name. The stripes are kind of zigzag, but—"

Lena intervened. "It could be an angelfish. Or a discus fish. They're carnivores, though. Discus fish. What do you feed it?"

Sullenly, Candy shrugged. "Fish food."

"You should check on that." Lena paused. "Hm. Perhaps something as elaborate as blackmail won't be needed. All we need is for them to be absent long enough to get at their files."

"Yeah, that's right."

"They've never seen Arthur, have they?" She looked at him.

Arthur shook his head. "No."

Lena thought for a bit longer. "Anyone else you could get?"

"How about Blaze Pascal?" said Karl.

Lena looked slightly astonished. "Blaise Pascal is a philosopher."

"Not this one." Karl chortled. "She's a PI."

"A woman, then?"

"Oh, yeah."

"For this particular job, I believe you'd want another man," said Lena. "The woman might be useful later."

"Danny Zito?" said Candy.

"He's in WITSEC," said Arthur.

"Ha! Makes no difference to Danny, the way he hangs around galleries and bookstores. Loves to sign copies of his book."

"Good. Two people would be better than one, I think."

"For what?" said Karl.

She told them. Everyone laughed but Candy.

"Just look at him; Oscar don't know what fate has up its sleeve." Candy tapped a little food onto the water's surface.

Karl looked up from *Publishers Weekly*. "If that fish is a carnivore, like Lena said, you should be grilling a steak." He snapped the magazine. Trouble with magazines, they didn't snap like newspapers.

Candy reflected on that. "Those other fish in Frankie's tank, they were ones Oscar knew, right? He was used to them."

Karl's tone was understandably edgy. "They were not frat brothers. They were not all members of the Sigma Chi chapter of the Clownfish Café. Trust me." He paused. "Who are you calling?"

Candy had the cell phone in hand and was tapping in numbers. "The Clownfish. Check with Frankie. What say we go over there for dinner?"

Karl actually liked the Clownfish. He wasn't sure why. The food was only average. It must be, he thought, what people liked to call ambience. Karl didn't like words such as "ambience"; he thought they were mirages. But the Clownfish Cafe was like being underwater. The fish were soothing, he had to admit.

He worked a lot of impatience into his tone when he answered, "Yeah. Well. Okay, I guess. But I'm not going to sit around while you confer with Frankie all night long."

"Nah. He can just maybe give me a few pointers." Candy snapped his cell shut. "I'll bet Frankie thinks Oscar looks nothin' like a peppermint whatever."

"Peppermint *angelfish*," said Karl, snapping *Publishers Weekly* as best he could.

30

Never one to put off the unpleasant errand, Clive had packed and departed for Miami the day after his call from Paul Giverney.

Again, never one to avoid the unpleasant, he had tossed the manuscript he'd barely looked at into his bag. It was titled *How (Very) Happy We (Never) Were*.

Titles had become not titles but undigested notes or shreds of conversation. He tried to recall what long title it was that had started this trend, because that's what had done it: bestseller with a talky title had spawned titles such as this one by Shirley Murphy. Pardon me, thought Clive, Shir-*lee* Mur-*phee*.

Shirlee's title (with its parenthetical stuffing) was as dreadful as the punning titles that seemed to turn up on slews of mystery series, such as knitting, *A Bitch in Time*; cooking, as in *Another Man's Poisson*; and handymen and woodcutters, as in *The Axman Cometh*. He could not imagine how anyone who believed in writing could jump on the boat and start trawling through the water for anything at all they could net.

Clive cast his eye over the page, Page One. He leafed through and found that, yes, each page was a spelled-out number. Page Two, Page Sixteen. All in some hideously medieval typeface about as easy to read as an income tax form. Could Shirlee Murphee possibly believe that this lent some artificial gravitas to her work? Written-out words, top-right-hand corner.

One could tell with such manuscripts, just from a look at the format and the font, the litter of exclamation points and troughs of italics, the way in which all of the technical stuff had been handled—one could tell such a book as straightaway bad.

Why was he sitting here with this book, leaning out into the aisle, watching the molasses-slow movement of the drinks cart that seemed to be stalled by an extremely loud passenger, either free of or bound for an A.A. meeting?

The only reason Clive was giving time to *How (Very) Happy* was Tom Kidd. Of all the senior editors at Mackenzie-Haack, this turd had landed somehow on the desk of the legendary Tom Kidd. As Clive remembered it, there had been some sort of family relationship involved, and Tom had agreed to "have a look." So Clive was doing this as a personal favor because he wanted Tom Kidd in his debt. The story began for some reason with a character spouting Shakespeare, the bit in *Hamlet* where Hamlet is instructing the players on how to perform. Shirlee's opening made no sense; it was another story that began in the middle of something, which would have been all right had Shirlee been Shakespeare. Clive flipped through the manuscript and found more people spouting Shakespeare or perhaps he should say respouting. "Get thee to Barneys New York" and "The rest is almost silence." Clive hung parentheses around "almost," feeling that was more in keeping with Ms. Murphee's style.

He stuffed the manuscript in his carry-on and settled back to think about the onerous task before him. He would have to spend the night at a motel smelling of air freshener and with a couple of cans of Raid under the sink. They were all pretty much alike, but he had chosen the Sawgrass, which advertised "Free Wi-Fi!!!" "Full Kitchen!!!" "'Glades at Your Doorstep!!!" He decided, as the cart pulled to a stop beside him and he ordered ("vodka rocks") (and *there*, Shirlee, is the correct use of the parenthetical), that Shirlee Murphee was writing copy for the Sawgrass Motel; that was her day job. He veritably snatched the drink from the flight attendant's hand and downed nearly half of it at once.

The 'Glades at your door. Anyone would want to open his door and find an alligator, a crocodile, a selection of invasive snakes (boa? python?), and one of the all-but-extinct Florida panthers left. Well, he guessed he preferred the Everglades at his door rather than a Shirlee Murphee manuscript lying there.

He was sipping the second half of his drink when he decided the plane was losing altitude, by way of either landing or crashing. He didn't care as long as the cart had time to come his way again and as long as Shirlee Murphee's manuscript was incinerated.

The only car the rental agency had available was an SUV that drank up gas as fast as Clive had downed his vodka. A full tank of gas dropped to under half not far from Everglades City. He stopped at a wreck of a gas station, fascinating because it looked straight out of the forties, where the gas was a few cents cheaper than the others'. It had to be, or nobody would have stopped there except Clive, who liked the thirties and forties.

The station had two pumps, neither equipped with a credit card mechanism. *Pump gas, Pay inside* was the instruction. Clive thought that amazingly trusting for South Florida, but he went ahead and pulled out the pump. He topped up the tank as he looked through the dirt-speckled window of an office where a seated figure hunched over his account books, or whatever he appeared to be reading.

He replaced the pump and walked inside. The man he had seen through the flyblown window was at a desk, peering at pictures—snapshots or photos, it looked like—with a magnifying glass. He didn't look up. A small sign on the counter said *Donny Lugz, prop.* Leaning against the wall behind him was a rifle, a Winchester or a Remington; Clive didn't know the difference. There were racks of chips and pretzels on the counter and, in the glass case beneath, candy bars lined up in boxes: Mars, Milky Way, Almond Joy, Hershey. It was strange to Clive how these had lasted for decades in their same old clothes, while everything else—people, cars, soft drinks, refrigerators—had donned new ones.

Clive assumed that the man scouring his pictures was Donny Lugz. He cleared his throat to get attention.

"Yeah." It appeared to be a response to the picture, not to his customer. Then the man slapped the desk, explaining, "Got the bugger right here!" Donny (if this were he), more sturdy than stout, wore a canvas cap beneath which gray curls sprouted around the edge.

"What bugger is that?" Clive had his money out. "I'm paying for gas."

"Just you look here," said Donny Lugz, who didn't seem to care about the gas as he held up the photo.

Clive looked. What he saw appeared to be a wide field of wheat or sawgrass; given that this wasn't Kansas, Clive went for sawgrass. In the middle of this field was a small dark blob. "What is it?" Clive felt a response was demanded of him.

"Skunk Ape. It's the damned Skunk Ape. Dead to rights, I got him!" Donny pinched the picture closer to Clive's face. "Clear as winter light on the Kissimmee."

Clive did not want to be saddled with metaphors involving Indian names.

"Yeah, when I take this over to Dave, he'll flip."

Clive, used to Dante and Shirlee Murphee, was no stranger to beginnings in medias res, but, unlike *The Divine Comedy*, which gave the reader some toeholds, the Skunk Ape story left Clive dangling.

Donny continued: "Dave, now, he's the expert on him over at Skunk Ape HQ."

Him, referring to the Skunk Ape, Clive concluded. He let Skunk Ape HQ alone.

"Yeah, he's written him up in a factual way. He gives you chapter and verse. Now, me, I ain't no expert, so I'm doin' it like fiction."

Fiction being completely irresponsible. "If I could just pay for the gas—"

Donny couldn't care less. He had grabbed up the big magnifying glass. "Now you see him better." What Clive saw through the glass was a bigger blob. "Ah. This is your Skunk Ape."

"Right."

"Well . . ." It could have been a moose, an ape, or a man, as far as Clive was concerned. "I can't really make out any features."

"Yeah, you can. You heard the Skunk Ape story, ain't you?"

Clive did not want to open up any channel that would lead to a complete rundown of Skunk Ape history, habits, and habitat, so he said, "Certainly, yes." Anyway, the word "story" was a dead giveaway. "Like Big Foot or Sasquatch."

Waving his hand, Donny fanned that similarity away. "Are they real? That's the question."

That was the question for about 50 percent of everything. "Many people believe they are."

Donny tapped the picture. "Here's your proof this one *does*. And Dave, he's got him on video. Vid-e-o. Can't argue with that! Now, there's but six or seven Skunk Apes in the Everglades—"

Donny was winding up. Clive knew he was never going to get out of this filling station unless he did something dramatic, like picking up that rifle and pumping a bullet into Mr. Lugz or maybe even himself, so he slid one of his cards out of a cramped slot in his billfold and handed it over. "This is my card. If you have some notion of getting your work published, let me know."

Donny Lugz looked at first astonished, then absolutely heaven-bound, then just plain as pleased as if the Skunk Ape had stepped through the door to buy a Milky Way. "My God! You publish *books* and stuff?"

"I'm just an editor. Mackenzie-Haack is the publisher."

Donny took off his cap and scratched his gray head. "Jesus! Just wait till I tell Dave."

Please don't. That would mean both fiction and nonfiction landing on his desk simultaneously. But having established some street cred with Donny Lugz, Clive could now break away. He handed over a fifty and said, "For the gas."

Donny was still gazing at the card. "Clive Ester—"

"Esterhaus. If you could just give me the change, I've got to get going. Got an appointment."

"New York. My God. Oh, the gas. Here, just forget it and pay me next time you drop by. Ain't got no change anyway."

"I'll do that. Nice meeting you, Mr. Lugz."

Clive banged out the door and into his gas-guzzling SUV.

The Sawgrass Motel was as he'd imagined it: like all of the other small motels lined up the Tamiami Trail or Route 29.

He tossed his overnight bag on the double bed (fast becoming a relic), switched on the palm-frond fan, which circled raspingly, and looked over the galley kitchen. The cups and mugs appeared to be various cast-offs from garage sales; the pots and pans had been hammered out back in the Industrial Revolution. He checked out the bathroom, just large enough for him to stand in the doorway and take aim at the toilet.

He glanced at his watch, saw it was approximately the time he'd told Simone Simmons he'd be calling on her, and opened the door. He was thankful that the 'Glades was not at his doorstep, waiting and panting.

31

After he'd rung the surly-sounding bell, Clive stood outside her door, observing a large tree entwined—or one might say embraced (though he wouldn't)—by some sort of ropelike smaller tree. How strange, he thought. But it was the land of the strange, and one had to get used to it.

Clive frankly thought it remarkable that Aunt Simone had ever been Uncle Simon. Even with the advantage of foreknowledge, he couldn't really see it. She was shoed in Louboutin (ah, those red soles!) and layered in L'Heure Bleu (a scent recalled from a former lady friend). Yes, Simone had taken a hike away from Simon.

She wore her dark hair in a thirties bob, had unusually white skin and high cheekbones, and except for being reminded of the Addams family, he found her quite attractive.

"Mr. Esterhaus? How nice. Do come in."

"Mrs. Simmons." He smiled and did as he was bade. The cottage was large but not ostentatious. The furniture was typical Floridian, Tommy Bahama strewn with near-reckless abandon, white wicker and bamboo. What surprised Clive was the color that drenched the room, including Simone herself: She wore a drapery of silk on which great swirls of yellow vied with deep blue, as across one shoulder a random trail of marquisette looked like a trail of distant stars. Well, van Gogh's signature had to be somewhere on that dress. The curtains and chair cushions were so jazzy with color that they had to be Jackson Pollock. Most surprising was the big Mark Rothko parrot, deep red and dead black, and squawking at him from its stand in a huge gilt cage.

"His name is Jasper," said Simone.

Clive canvassed the room quickly. Jasper Johns hadn't made the cut.

"Would you care for something? I make excellent martinis."

"And I drink them."

She drifted off to a dining room and a bamboo sideboard where bottles were clustered. He helped himself to a seat in a white basket-weave chair with a tall, deeply rounded back, more of a hut than a chair. He liked the privacy as he listened to the rattle of ice against glass and the gurgle of bottles. And Jasper punctuating this harmony with a squawk.

Back she came, carrying two very large fan-shaped chilled glasses with a lemon shaving floating on each surface. They were triples, at least, and icy-cold.

"I believe in chilling glasses and warming dinner plates. One shouldn't compromise heat and cold."

Clive gave some thought as to whether Sartre or Santayana might find some moral point to argue. He raised his glass to her, then sipped.

"Now, you wanted to see me about my nephew, Bass. You're in publishing, you said on the phone."

"Right. Mackenzie-Haack." Clive was damned if he was going to say D and D. "Senior editor." He also wasn't going to bother with his imprint, since people outside of publishing didn't know what that meant: "A Clive Esterhaus book." Big deal to him, but not to many others. "I've known Bass for a long time. I know he visits you from time to time."

"Every November. Thanksgiving. He stays for one week. He hates Florida."

Clive feigned surprise.

"Loathes it." She drew the word out to such lengths that it sounded multisyllabic.

Clive smiled. "Indeed."

"As he's the last of the family, I insist he come. He pretends to enjoy it, but he can't unwind. It's not New York that has him that way, it's that Bass is such a tight-ass."

Clive had just taken a drink of the martini and almost choked. He cleared his throat. "Really?"

"Oh, come, now. You know him." She sipped her martini, placed it on the Tommy Bahama coffee table.

Clive considered dispensing with the ruse but decided against that line of action. "I agree, he does seem hyper-controlled. Maybe that's the trouble. He's been acting very strangely."

"Spare me. How much stranger can he get?"

Clive was having a hard time striking a tone. He doubted that Simone had been apprised of the Cindy Sella case. "I think Bass might be having an emotional crisis."

"Bass? A nervous breakdown?" She laughed and then cut the laugh so short she might have taken scissors to it. "He doesn't have nerves."

She was hardly the doting aunt. Clive said, "Right now he's caught up in a legal battle."

"He's very litigious." She studied her flame-painted nails. "That's because he always thinks he's right."

"I honestly believe a change of scene would help him. If you could get him to come here—"

"If my nephew is truly in a state of nervous collapse, this is the last place he'd want to be."

"Hm. Well, he seems to have fallen out with the wrong people."

Her heavily green-shadowed eyes widened. "He has?" She seemed more hopeful than distressed by this news.

"There was a shooting in a café. Police are quite certain it was a Mob hit. The shooters appeared to be after Bass. He was in the restaurant."

"Good Lord, someone took a contract out on Bass? How intriguing." She sipped her drink. "Whatever did he do?" Her brown eyes sparked.

Clive sidelined the truth. Turning down Fabio's novel seemed a weight that the truth couldn't bear. "Insulted one of the capos."

All she could do was laugh. "You're saying the spineless wonder actually stood up on his hind legs and told off the Mob? Well!" She polished off the rest of her martini, rose, and collected Clive's half-empty glass. That Bass had no idea who he was dealing with when he refused to take on Fabio as a client was beside the point.

Simone said, as she made her way to the drinks table, "He won't, of course, tell me who it was."

Ice rattling in a shaker. Lovely sound. She continued talking over her shoulder from the dining room: "And he'll say coming here is inconvenient. No, I don't see how I'd ever persuade him." She came back and placed Clive's fresh drink on the table.

Clive was slightly buzzed already. If he drank this one off, he'd have had the equivalent of four martinis. Not bad. Made daring by vodka, he said, "I see a way. Tell him you're changing your will."

She looked twice surprised. "He told you he was the sole heir?"

Clive just smiled and drank.

She also smiled and drank. Then she said with a swish of a leg as she crossed them, "The thing is, Mr. Esterhaus—"

"Clive."

"Clive. You see, Bass isn't getting all he thinks he is. At least half of the money is going to the Everglades. I feel very strongly about the Everglades and its depredation over the last two centuries. Oddly enough, I was doing just that, changing my will. Changing it to favor the Friends of the Everglades. Bass will be speechless with fury." She laughed and drank.

"Have you told him that?"

"No. Why is it you want me to?"

"It would get him down here." Clive thought for a moment. "Or you could tell him you're dying. And you want to talk over several points in your will. That this simply can't wait until November. Is he the executor?"

"God, no. You think I'm barmy? No. My bank is the executor, together with my houseboy." When she saw Clive look around, she added, "Oh, he's not here. He watches over things when I'm away. He's really quite clever."

A houseboy as executor? "You trust him?"

"No, but he'll get a salary, you see, while he's taking care of things. I'm thinking that might keep him from trying to rummage around in the trust fund. Quite a lot of the estate will go to the Everglades Foundation. The houseboy will get enough. The rest will go to Bass. He'll be unsatisfied, but it will be hard for him to contest the will."

"You think he'll contest it, then?"

"Of course he will." She picked up her glass. "Dear me, I'm empty. You, too." She rose and collected his glass and went to the drinks table.

With a furious flapping of wings, the Mark Rothko parrot vented its irritation at always being left out.

"Where did you get Jasper?" He was hoping she'd say at the Museum of Modern Art.

"I got him at one of those turn-in-your-exotic-pet things. It's a way of keeping people from releasing their pythons into the swamp." She was back, handing Clive his third—meaning seventh—martini before she sat down with hers.

"What will happen to Jasper when you die?"

"He'll be well taken care of. I've arranged for a friend to take him in. This, too, is in the will. Now, are you sticking with the wrong sort of people?"

Clive frowned. "I beg your pardon?"

She sighed. "That's the trouble when you're less than truthful. You can't recall the details. The reason you want Bass to come to Florida: that he's in danger. I don't believe this for a minute. And we've jettisoned his having a breakdown, so what's left? What's the real reason for your coming here? Not that I mind your coming, understand."

Clive stretched out his legs and didn't answer immediately because he could think of nothing inventive enough. He decided he might as well let the truth in. "Let's just say we want to get your nephew off somebody's back, and forgive me if I don't say who or why."

She plugged a cigarette into her long holder, saying, "That's quite all right, only how would his spending a week here accomplish that? Wouldn't he just return to New York and get right on this person's back again?" She held out her cigarette for a light and then said, "Or were you going to ask me to kill him?"

Clive guffawed and picked up the ornate cigarette lighter. "We have a small plan which includes the Everglades."

"And who is we?"

"Several acquaintances."

"So Bass has ticked off a number of people, and they're out to get him. Is his wife among them?"

Surprised, Clive raised his eyebrows. "No."

"She can't stand him, either. Poor woman. Her name's Helen. It should be Joan of Arc. Now, shall we have dinner? I know a fabulous little restaurant in Naples. It's a drive, but it's worth it." She rose from the sofa.

"By all means." Clive was almost glad to leave the rest of his drink undrunk. Perhaps only the first one had been the equivalent of three. So it was only really four or five. He wasn't sure he could lift himself out of the chair, but he made it.

She returned to find him looking into the glassed-in room full of plants: orchids and succulents. "That's my orchid room. I guess that's obvious. Would you like to go in?"

Not really, but he did.

They passed between cluttered tables of bromeliads and birds of paradise, plants that Clive had never admired. Succulents had always given him the creeps. The very name conjured images of plants smacking their lips over food he would rather not think about. They looked tough, as if they meant business. Simone pointed out a creeping fig terra, then a walking iris, which made him shudder all the more. He had never gotten over *The Day of the Triffids*.

"Do you like orchids?"

He nodded. Depends, is what he wanted to say, as they stood by a table on which orchids stood in their customary histrionic postures and theatrical colors. "They require a lot of attention, don't they?"

"Not really. The temperature is important, of course. One I've always wanted is the ghost orchid. It grows in the Everglades. It's quite rare. I actually went out on an expedition with a guide, but I hate walking through sucking mud, don't you? Anyway, I would never take one; it's illegal in the Everglades. I just wanted to see them."

Clive thought for a moment and said, "What you ought to do is send your nephew. Send Bass to search for this ghost orchid."

She considered, smiled broadly, and clapped her hands. "What a *magnificent* idea! He'd go mad at the thought of it. Except I wouldn't want him to get one."

"He wouldn't, would he? I doubt he'd give it much of a try, beyond having you think he did. Certainly not if they're so difficult to find. Anyway, that's not the object; the object is simply to get him into the swamp."

"I can't imagine what you have in mind. It sounds awfully amusing."

"Um. Perhaps we're being too hard on him." As if.

"No, we're not. Shall we go to dinner?"

"Lead on. I'm starving."

They went back into the living room, where she donned a lightweight coat. Pale pink and white and yellow flowers on a pale blue background.

Manet?

Jasper screeched.

Outside, Clive inquired about the tree held fast by the thin entwining arms of some paler tree. "Oh, that? That's a strangler fig."

"Strangler fig?"

She nodded.

This place would have him for dinner if they weren't quick about it.

Clive hurried Simone up the walk.

32

At about the same time Clive was on his way back, L. Bass Hess was talking about Florida.

"Florida?" said Paul Giverney, feigning surprise. "Why in hell would you go to Florida?" He knew why. Because Hess's aunt Simone had demanded that he come. Given Clive's description in the call from Miami International, Simone sounded like quite a gal/guy.

Paul and Bass sat on opposite sides of Hess's coffee table with tiny little cups of espresso. His secretary had ground the beans.

"I go every year to see my aunt. In November, for Thanksgiving. It's her kind of ritual, you could say. This time it appears she's quite ill. Dying, she claims."

"God, I'm sorry. You two are close, I guess." No, he wasn't, and no, they weren't. It was all going according to plan. Paul felt quite proud of himself as he plunked another sugar cube into his cup of bitter-as-hell coffee. The cubes were tiny, too. He could have been taking his coffee with Munchkins.

"Quite close, yes. Peas in a pod, really. Regrettable." Bass tented his fingers.

Given L. Bass's perky little smile, it was clear that regret had gone south, to be followed by Bass the next day.

Paul drank his sugared-up, sludgy coffee. "You're flying to—?"

"Miami. I'll rent a car and drive to Everglades City."

Everglades City was a point on the map that Bass would happily drive a stake through. But if the damned woman *were* dying, and Bass suspected he—or rather she—was telling the truth, then Everglades City would soon be a thing of the past.

All that money! He could leave the big, drafty house in Wilton, along with Helen and his incorrigible stepdaughter, Esme; he could pay back the money he'd had to beg Helen to invest in the agency; he would never have to see another writer again; and he could go to the South of France. He could kiss all of these ego-driven writers good-bye. Oddly, given his phenomenal success and all his money, Giverney was not beset by the monstrous ego that Bass found in so many writers, but he was being impossible when it came to negotiating this contract that Bass himself had been slaving over. Giverney and Mackenzie deserved each other, both with their impossible demands and their idiotic terms.

"Exactly what do you want, Paul? We've got three million, e-book rights, bonuses if the book stays on the list longer than twelve weeks, again if it's on the list for five months, cover approval—and did I ever have to fight for that!—what else to you want?"

"More," Paul said. "I want interior design approval."

"What? *What?* You mean the way the words appear on the page?"

"I believe that would be the design of the interior, yes."

"God! Nobody asks for that!"

"I do."

"You mean you've had design approval before?"

"No. But I regretted it. You have no idea how they can fuck up a page."

"All right, all right. I'll discuss it with Mackenzie."

Paul took his feet off the coffee table. "I want it in the contract, not just a verbal agreement. Bobby Mackenzie's a thief and a liar—"

Which was exactly what Bobby Mackenzie had said about Paul.

"—and he'll fuck me over just because he can. He can if it's not in the contract."

"Why do you want him to publish you, then? Do you want another publisher?"

Paul snorted. "Don't be ridiculous. The industry is not a world of nuance. Better the devil."

A world of nuance? Better the devil? The man spoke in tongues.

But the money!

A four-hundred-and-fifty-thousand-dollar commission for one book, and since Paul Giverney regularly produced a book a year, Bass was looking at a fortune. He could drop every other client and deal exclusively with Paul. He'd be making four or five times what he was pulling in now. He could do it, dear God!, from the South of France!

And he could say good-bye forever to Simon/Simone. Either way, L. Bass Hess was looking at a windfall.

"Florida?" This was Bobby Mackenzie speaking.

"He's leaving tomorrow," said Paul.

They were sitting that evening in Bobby's office. Bobby had his feet on his desk, tumbler of Scotch in one hand, Cuban cigar in the other. Same as always.

Paul sat opposite him, mirror image on the other side of the desk. "He'll come back a changed man. Well, 'changed man' for any normal person. For Hess, he'll come back at least off-center."

"What in hell did you cook up this time?"

"Not as good as what *you* cooked up, Bobby, last time."

"Come on. You were the engineer. I was just chugging along behind."

"Yeah. The Little Engine That Could. That's why you do things, Bobby. You don't have any motive; you don't have any reason. You do things because you can."

Bobby blew a smoke ring, then another went gliding through the first. "Yeah." He grinned as he pressed down on the intercom and spoke: "Bunny, can you come in here for a moment?"

The woman who must have been Bunny stuck her head in the door. Paul thought, What wondrous hair. It was such a pale blond that it looked almost white. White hair with lowlights. When the rest of herself followed her head, he was even more struck, not so much by the shape but by the shape being dressed in what some would call winter white.

Bobby was holding the ill-fated book-jacket mockup in his hand.

"Take this up to art, will you, and ask them if anyone there's ever actually seen Venice? Or at least pictures, photos of Venice? Or could this art have more to do with the Venetian in Vegas?"

Bunny came up to the desk and took the artwork and smiled at Paul on her way out.

"Who's that?" asked Paul.

"Bunny? Bunny Fogg. She's the best steno in the whole building. She more or less free-floats around."

Paul smiled as he imagined Bunny Fogg free-floating.

33

B ass Hess was writing marginalia on the document he had placed on the tray table. He and his lawyer had rehashed the various causes of action that comprised the complaint against Cindy Sella.

That ungrateful little bitch. Bass could not understand why she hadn't folded the moment the complaint was served. Buckled under and just paid him his commission on the last book. True, he hadn't been the agent who *sold* the book, but the option clause was in the old contract for books he *had* been agent for, so he figured she owed him.

There was nothing new in this argument, the one he was making marginal notes on, his answer to the answer served up by Cindy Sella's new lawyer. No, this was merely a reworded thicket of the sixty-nine causes of action in the original complaint, all of which were described in rococo detail, a rechurning of the first complaint, hoping it would turn it to butter. He had spent many hours working on this with his lawyer, Phil Ffizz. Ffizz was no attorney for anything as straightforward as, say, divorce. No, Ffizz was a havoc lawyer, the sort who enjoyed chaos so that he could then chime in with irrelevancies and leave judges negotiating the flotsam in the stream. Yes, Ffizz fit beautifully.

Hess enjoyed reading such long-winded documents; he belonged to the school holding that you could and should bolster your argument by using twenty words where ten (or even five) would make the point. He believed in hiding things under cotton batting, wearying the opponent to the point where she would throw up her hands and say, The hell with it.

The only thing Hess enjoyed reading more than a long-winded legal document was a book contract. The minutiae of a book contract made writers give up reading after they'd checked the payout. Yes, the fine print that would drive any ordinary man mad was ambrosia to L. Bass Hess. He was like a surgeon; he could build up tissue with ever thinner layers until the underlying structure was barely recognizable. At times he felt the scalpel he used to slice through the standard contract was more sword than knife, was Excalibur rising from the water and he himself King Arthur. He knew he was a legend in the world of publishing. He made publishers want to run as if from burning buildings. It was exhilarating to have that kind of control.

Control! That was always Bass's aim: control the publishing world as if it were made up of enemy U-boats and he were Alan Turing, clicking away, decrypting the Germans' Enigma codes. He could feel it right down to his fingertips: control.

And the reason he loathed Simone (in addition to the awful sex change) was that she was controlling *him*. Blood suffused his face just thinking about her. How could anyone be controlled by so ludicrous a person? Simone, she who was once Simon. He shuddered.

Off the American Airlines flight, into the mini-nation that was the Miami International airport, and into a Chevrolet Impala, the typical rental car that acted like no owner-driven car on the road—that was where Hess finally landed. The roads swirled around like a soft ice-cream cone, seeming to go nowhere, but finally spitting him out onto the Tamiami Trail and thence at a steady sixty miles per hour due west for some eighty miles to Everglades City.

34

And here she was, Aunt Simone and Uncle Simon rolled into one, an untidy cigar that left bits of tobacco on his tongue. At one point after her "change," she had married a man named Simmons. Simon Simone Simmons. What a name.

"Bass, dear, how good of you to come! And so quickly!"

As if I had a choice. He was enfolded in swirls of colored silk, as that goddamned bloodred and coal-black parrot was hurling at him what Bass was sure were obscenities.

"Simone, but you're looking very well," which, unfortunately, was true. Her hair was lustrous as a crown of black pearls, her skin as translucent as white ones. Simone was quite good-looking. For a man. He went on, "You don't look at all ill."

"Oh, it comes, it goes. Have a drink, dear." She sashayed back to the dining room sideboard and her vast selection of bottles.

He was miffed. Raising his voice, which was too thin-timbered to reach very far, he said, "You said on the phone I must come at once, that the doctors had given you a gloomy prognosis."

"Whiskey and water, as usual?" Why ask when she was already dumping shots of it into a tall glass and picking ice cubes from the silver bucket.

"So what is it, Simone?" He did not try to keep the edge of annoyance from his tone.

"You sound almost sorry that I'm not dead at your feet."

Bass tried out a disbelieving laugh as he moved to the dining room door. "Really, Simone. I came right away, didn't I? I'm deeply concerned." His eye fell on a thick document which lay by the jug in which she was twirling vodka and vermouth. She poured herself a drink, put down the pitcher, and held up this sheaf of papers. Her smile was lively as could be. "My will."

He tried to temper his frown. "You're making changes again?"

She didn't bother answering as she walked their drinks—and her will—back to the Tommy Bahama room. She took her usual seat on the sofa. "Now, as you know, I'm leaving Bolly—my houseboy—something, and now I've decided to leave him another hundred thousand."

Bass blanched as he sat down in an uncomfortable wicker chair. That worthless son of a bitch of a houseboy was already getting a sizable amount. But how could he object? "Do you think that's wise, Simone?"

"What has wisdom to do with it? I'm fond of Bolly."

Bass crossed his legs and sipped his whiskey. "You'll leave him so well off he won't have a motive to shift for himself."

"Well, he doesn't do that now. I don't see how he could be more shiftless. But he is fun to have around, and he watches the house like a hawk when I'm away. Then there's the half million to the Everglades Foundation; I'm increasing by another million." She smiled broadly.

He didn't. He was horrified. "Another *million*. Why?" He checked his sharpish tone. "I mean, Simone, well, the Everglades have been here forever. It's unlikely the place will get run-down." He gave a little laugh.

"'Run-down'? Good god! It's not a housing development. Although there've certainly been enough attempts to turn it into one. That shows how little you know about Florida ecology, not to mention politics. The Everglades has been a political football for years. Development, builders, just waiting for the legislature to pass a bill that lets them in. Can you see the land being subdivided into all sorts of faux-Flagler, Mediterranean houses?"

In his mind's eye, Bass saw and applauded. Why on earth people would want to preserve this swampy, mangrove-treed, alligator-holed, marled and hammocked, snake-laced, mosquito-swarmed land, he had never understood. Better a few Meisner-inspired houses, surely. Better a flood of Flagler hotels. Better anything else.

She was off like the front-runner at Hialeah. He slipped down in his chair.

". . . and have you the slightest idea what this was like in the nineteenth century before one millionaire after another, including Flagler, and their harebrained schemes to drain the swamp? What a paradise for birds this was!"

Jasper let out a great series of squawks.

"Roseate spoonbills, green herons, carpets—*carpets* of egrets—"

As she went on with this, L. Bass sat reflecting on his shrinking inheritance: There went another million-plus right out the window. How much did she have, anyway? All he knew or had known when Simone was still Simon was that her-his-their father had been worth millions back in the days when a million was a real million and a millionaire somebody. The father had been what Simone was presently disdaining: a developer. He had bought up more and more land encroaching on the Everglades and might have successfully sliced off a few thousand acres for a mess of high-rise condominiums had he not dropped dead from a stroke.

". . . and as to your own inheritance—"

He sat up straight, ears alert.

"Oh, do get me a refill; my throat is dry as a bone."

Dammit! She would stop motormouthing right there! He quickly rose, took her glass, and all but ran to the bamboo sideboard, filled hers from the glass pitcher, and fairly flew it back to her, trying not to appear too eager.

"Thank you, dear. Now, where was I?"

Bass pretended to try to recall, knotting his eyebrows over his nose. "I believe you were talking about my own inheritance?"

"Oh, yes. Yours. Now, you will of course get the house; I know you always enjoyed coming here."

Sold! To the first snowbirds who dropped from the sky!

"And Daddy's famous collection of fossils, and the antiques. There's the dining room sideboard; that's extremely rare bamboo—"

And vodka, he didn't add. Why in hell didn't she leave some of her money to Absolut instead of Bolly? Denmark had done more for her than he had.

"All of this"—she swung her arm in an arc to take in the living room—"is largely Tommy Bahama."

God! Was she going to enumerate every last piece of furniture?

"As for other things, I'm leaving Bolly the silver service, the candle-sticks, and the rest of it."

Bass's financial antennae quivered upward. "All of the silver? That's a small fortune in itself."

"He's always said how much he'd like to have a silver service just like it."

"Let him buy one like it—ha-ha-ha—with that extra hundred thousand. He can afford to."

"I'm sorry. I never found you interested in the tea service or the silver."

Bass gave this a bit of thought. Rarely did he invoke his wife's wishes, but now he said, smoothly, "That's true, not I, but Helen admires it so much . . ."

"How is dear Helen? I haven't seen her in ages."

Oh, Christ, why had he dragged Helen into it? He could be sitting here until doomsday talking about her, since Simone clearly thought he mistreated her.

"She's good. She's fine."

"Why do you never bring her with you?"

It was not a question, but a judgment. He wanted to say, Because it's hard enough coming myself. "It's always something—you know, appointments, obligations. Her family always wants to have her over the holidays."

"Quite selfish." She laughed and reached across the coffee table and slapped Bass's leg with the rolled-up will.

"Before you tear that to smithereens"—he choked out a laugh— "carry on with the contents, why don't you?"

Simone looked at the document with little interest. "You know you get the bulk of the estate."

But what is the bulk? he wanted to ask. He totted up what had been subtracted from it in the last fifteen minutes—well over a million, so the bulk must be vastly more. "Ah. That's kind of you, Simone."

She sipped her martini and held the glass up to the late-afternoon light swimming through the slatted blind and said, "There are one or two little conditions."

Alert, Bass sat up. "Conditions?" Good Lord, condition as in the inheritance is null and void if you divorce Helen, or become a Mormon, or sell this cottage, or refuse to keep Bolly on as houseboy? The list could go on and on.

Just then, the parrot squawked.

"Ah," she said with a rueful look, "right there is one." She rose, glass in hand, to step over to the cage, about the size of a small tugboat, and stick in her finger, which the parrot sniped at. "Jasper. That's one condition. You will take care of Jasper."

God in heaven! He'd almost rather have Bolly in his spare room than this damned painted bird anywhere within a hundred miles of him. "You must understand, Simone, I've little experience with birds."

"Oh, there's nothing to it." She rose, moved over to Jasper's cage. "A little food, clean the cage, fresh newspapers. And, of course, his meds. But you'll manage."

What he'd manage would be to get rid of Jasper at the same place she'd found him: one of the exotic pet dumps. "Meds?"

"He needs his pill every day. And medication from a syringe. You give that orally."

Bass wanted to double up with laughter at the very notion that he'd be medicating Jasper. Fat chance. He stopped laughing when he heard her tack on "Bolly will stop by every so often to make sure Jasper is all right." With a sigh, she reseated herself.

"What? What?" He coughed behind his hand and lowered his voice. "Bolly will stop by the Wilton house to check on the parrot?" Was he going crazy?

On cue, Jasper yelled. It couldn't even be called a squawk this time; it was either a yell of derision or an SOS, DANGER!

Simone raised her superbly etched eyebrows. "Connecticut? Don't be silly. You'll be living here in the cottage. Remember, I'm leaving it to you."

In his quick rise from the chair, he knocked over his glass. Fortunately, he had drained it when she'd informed him that he would be Jasper's caregiver. A couple of ice cubes bounced on the grass carpet, and he retrieved them. "Sorry, uh, I don't see how I could relocate, Simone. My work is in New York."

"Oh, but it's the sort of thing you could carry on from here. Like those cold callers who solicit things over the telephone."

He could scream. "It's a bit more complicated than that, running a literary agency. Wait, Bolly could continue to live here and take care of Jasper, couldn't he?"

Simone looked crestfallen. "Really, Bass, if you're going to throw up obstacles at every little turn. . . You won't need to work at all after you get my money. There's quite a lot of it, you know."

He went to her and patted her arm and took her empty glass. "I'll give this some more thought. In the meantime, let me freshen these drinks." He carried both glasses to the sideboard like a water boy. He felt like bloody Gunga Din. Better Simone should set up a pulley between sideboard and sofa.

"Any other conditions?" he called over his shoulder in what he hoped was a smiley voice.

Jasper screeched.

Jesus, imagine having that thing around all day!

"Yes, there is one more. Thank you." She took the proffered drink.

"What's that?" He was wary, to say the least.

"As you know, I've my orchids."

"You wanted me to take them on also?" The next thing to be plowed under once she was gone.

"Heavens, no. I'm giving them to the Museum of the Everglades."

Wonderful. One less onerous chore for him. "That sounds like a good idea." He took another tug at his whiskey.

"What I want you to do is get me a ghost orchid."

"Oh? Is there an orchid dealer in Everglades City? Marco Island, more likely. Or could I get it by Googling some florist who deals in exotic flowers?"

Simone made an excellent play at a "how naive" tone. "Bass, it isn't that easy. If anyone had one for sale, he wouldn't advertise on Craigslist. No, you have to find one in its own habitat."

He didn't like the sound of that. "What? You mean actively search for one of these orchids? Where?"

"In the Everglades. The Corkscrew Swamp or Big Cypress National Preserve or the Fakahatchee. It's an epiphyte. I mean, the orchid is. It anchors to trees such as the bald cypress—"

Bass held up his hand. "Just a minute, just a minute. Are you saying one has to go into a *swamp* to find this thing?"

"Don't be so anxious. You've gone through the Corkscrew preserve before. On a fishing expedition."

"That's different." He hated fishing, but she insisted he live up to his father's name.

She ignored that. "I've arranged for a guide, a very good canoeist."

"Canoe? I'm supposed to *canoe* through the Fakahatchee or the others?" Bass couldn't believe what he was hearing. "If you've found a guide, why not let *him* get the goddamn— I mean, get the orchid?"

Simone smoothed her painted silk skirt and said, "That's the thing, dear. It's illegal. He makes his living here; he won't jeopardize that for—"

"Poaching? That's what I'm supposed to do? And what if I should run into some Fish and Game person?"

"That's highly unlikely. And Monty knows the swamp like the back of his hand."

"Monty?"

"That's the guide. He's very dependable."

"Really, Simone."

She sighed. "If you don't want to, I suppose I could get Bolly . . ." She picked up the will. "If I increase his part of the inheritance. Then I'd have to get my attorney to rewrite whole sections, given the complications of stocks, mutual funds . . ." She plucked a cigarette from a parrot-shaped holder that resembled a small vase and was the image of Jasper.

Bass went for his cell phone. "I must make a call. Will you pardon me?" He moved into the dining room and speed-dialed his office. When Stephanie answered, he said, "Has Mackenzie returned that contract?"

"Yes. He had it messengered over just an hour ago."

"Look at pages seventeen and twenty. See if he accepted those terms."

A pause. "No. Those paragraphs are X'd out."

Damn Bobby! If he'd given the go-ahead, Bass was going to tell Simone to stuff her orchid. He said good-bye and slowly made his way back to the living room.

"Bad news? You look like death, dear."

"No. No more than usual. You'd be surprised at all the bucking up and handholding one has to do in this business. Writers are such whiners; when they're not making impossible demands, they're crying on your shoulder. One might as well be a psychiatrist—"

Simone interrupted. "Now, Bass, what about this little excursion to find my orchid?"

"My secretary just told me of a pressing matter I need to attend to. I really should go back to Manhattan tomorrow." Seeing her expression, he quickly added, "And then come back here in another week or two."

Coldly, she said, "You were to stay for several days."

"I know, I know. But this just came up."

"Let me call Monty and see if he can take you out tonight." Before he could say anything, she was up and reaching for her cordless phone and punching in the number. She ignored his protests and his look of terror. "Monty, dear. Simone Simmons here. Yes. I was wondering if you'd be able to take my nephew out this evening— You would? Marvelous!"

Bass dropped his head in his hands.

"The poor boy needs a bit of distraction. A little canoe trip is just what he needs. Yes, I do understand you can't witness it. Yes, I know . . ."

Bass's head came up. Witness it? What in God's name did she mean? When she finally hung up from the accommodating Monty, he asked.

"Oh, that. Simply that he couldn't be there when you cut the orchid from the tree. And there's a procedure you must follow, for these orchids are fragile—"

"Yes, yes, but where will Monty be if he can't see me doing this?" Bass's high-pitched voice was almost as stringent as Jasper's, who chose that moment to echo him.

Simone picked up her burning cigarette and inhaled. "Oh, just paddling about, I expect." She checked her nail varnish. And then her will.

Bass nearly fell down into his Tommy Bahama chair. "He paddles off and leaves me on *my very own* in the *swamp*?"

Jasper shrieked.

Simone was paging through her will. "Or he'll just sit and wait. He doesn't want to be"—here she whispered, with her will-free hand poised to the right of her mouth in that exaggerated way people do—"an accessory."

Bass drained his drink. My God, *my God*. Then, craftily, he thought: I can just buy him off. Hell, just give him a few hundred to say we made the trip. He relaxed.

I can just buy him off.

35

No, he couldn't.

When they drove away, Simone waving at them from her little porch, Bass suggested five hundred dollars to Monty, "and mum's the word." He even put his finger to his lips.

Monty—a tall, spindly fellow wearing Ray-Bans and a baseball cap and brown hair in a ponytail—said that would not be honorable of him, and anyway, Simone was paying him five times that to take Bass out. "I guess you don't like the idea of getting caught poaching, right?"

Bass fumed. "Obviously, I don't. Neither do you."

Monty shifted down. On a trailer behind his dilapidated Ford Bronco sat a canoe that looked as if it had been in business before the Seminoles came.

"You got that right, Bass, ol'boy."

They pulled into a small touristy business called Captain Jerry's, now closed for the day.

"What's this?" said Bass. It was obvious what it was: another place offering airboat rides, alligator sightings, bird-watching.

"Belongs to a pal of mine." Monty parked his truck in the deserted lot.

"You keep your canoe here?"

"We're not taking the canoe out."

Bass heaved a sigh of relief.

"We're using the dory. Come on." They walked down to the marina, where two air-boats, a half-dozen rowboats and several aged motorboats were tied up at two long docks. The dory sat in among the row-boats.

Bass's relief was quick-lived. The dory looked no bigger than a canoe. He looked doubtful as Monty climbed into it, a small boat with two bench seats. Oars were locked in their sockets. There was also an outboard motor.

Monty waved him in. "Just settle in. I got me a nice little Honda 5 horsepower here. It ain't a speedboat, but it'll get us where we're going. Sun's going down." Monty squinted into the light. "Some sunset."

Bass didn't respond. He climbed in and took one of the bench seats, dreading the boat's lack of sturdiness. Monty got the motor going and they were slicing through the vast sheet of darkening water.

Up ahead, lights on the shore. One of the far shores. There were entirely too many shores, too many islands, for Bass's taste. "What's over there?" he shouted into a wave of cold spray.

"Chokoloskee."

"Where are we going?" Earth's end would be the answer.

"Over there." Monty pointed not toward the lights of Chokoloskee, but toward more dark mangroves, more hardwood hammocks.

Then they were at the mouth of an inlet, and Monty cut the motor. "Okay, this boat's got an electric motor, so we don't make noise." He nosed into the narrow opening.

Fear sprouted in Bass Hess. "What are you talking about? What in here has ears?"

Monty didn't bother answering but switched on a very dim light attached to the boat's side. It did not serve to illuminate as much as it served to heighten the general eeriness.

It might have been—this mangrove and cypress-crowded inlet, in deep silence and missing out on any sign of life beyond sudden birdcall—it might have been considered wonderful and mysterious by naive and senti-mental tourists with their cameras and binoculars slung around their necks.

To Bass Hess, it was just the opposite. Pools of water, sun gone down. Sawgrass not grass at all but a river of thin knives. When night fell in the Everglades, it fell like a banyan crashing. He thought he saw movement along the bank, something rising, something falling back. The boat was large enough for a dozen more, and Bass almost wished the dozen had come along.

"How long have you been doing this?"

"Years."

"Then you must know these inlets pretty well."

"Back of my hand."

"Are there alligators?"

"Oh, there's always alligators, right?" Monty gave a heh-heh-heh and shifted the light a bit, unbothered by the scream of a bird that sounded hideously like Jasper.

Monty kept telling Bass to peer straight ahead. That way, Monty alone would see the signal. He looked to his left as they passed an even narrower band of water . . . and God almighty, there it was! Molloy right on time and right on target. The light winked on and off through a tangle of branches. Molloy had a big, shuttered spotlight much brighter than a flashlight.

"Okay, we can pull in right up there. Right around there's where I saw trees full of dozens of ghost orchids. You see that movie?"

Bass was busy monitoring the gnarly fallen logs lying half in water to see if they were actually logs. "What movie?"

"Had Meryl Streep in it. She goes out looking for orchids."

"The movie was based on a book. Do you see that log over there?"

Monty squinted and looked hard, or pretended to. The temptation was strong to say, Yeah, it moved! And then watch old Bass react. But he quelled it. He could mess up Molloy's and Sammy's gig if he veered off the plan, a plan he made no sense of, but hey, ten grand? He'd lay a mindfuck on anybody for ten large.

"Yeah, I see it. Why?"

"I think it moved." Bass's voice was so tight, it squeaked.

"Nah." Monty laughed. "You got the heebie-jeebies, man." He pulled the boat up to a crowd of mangrove roots and said they were there. "Here's the spot. You got the clippers? Just go on in. It won't be far off to the right."

"In *there*? Are you insane? That's impossible! Look at those mangrove roots." Tall, exposed roots, intertwined, layered thick as the rippling locks of a Medusa, if Medusa had wooden hair. "A person can't walk through *there*, man!"

"Walk, no. You pretty much have to crouch a little, maybe crawl a little. But plenty's made it through there. You only have to go maybe fifteen, twenty feet. So let's go. I'll be right behind you."

"You're coming?"

"Sure." Like hell.

Bass stumbled out of the boat and immediately collapsed over a set of roots like knees. He cursed, dragged himself up, and more or less crawled forward.

Monty, still in the boat, wouldn't have made out the black shape near a mangrove had he not expected the black shape to be there. Nor would he have noticed the movement of the battered, weather-beaten log that lay right by the black shape had he not known the log could move.

"Bass," whispered Monty. "Bass."

"What?"

Bass's voice was way above a whisper, and Monty made a movement down with his hands, a pantomime to warn Bass not to speak above a whisper. "Don't take another step," whispered Monty.

"Why?"

This guy actually told people how to write books? And couldn't understand simple directions? In a show of frenzy, Monty motioned for Bass. "Just come toward me and the boat real slow. No, no, don't turn around, don't make any sudden moves."

As soon as Bass heard that, his face went moon-white, and he broke into a stumbling run, if one could be said to run in such circumstances.

Monty steadied the boat and helped Bass to clamber in. "Fuckin' alligator, man!"

The black log slid into the water behind him. Monty paddled, but not as fast as he might have.

And then it happened. Bass was halfway up from his seat when Monty yelled, "Sit down! For fuck's sake, you'll—"

The boat tilted to windward and sent Bass Hess over the side. Bass went under the black water and came back up, flailing and yelling that he couldn't swim. Monty stuck out an oar, shouting, "Grab this!"

Bass tried and failed. Bass's head went under, then popped back up, under, up, Bass yelling again he couldn't goddamned swim!

There was a sudden lurch. Then the log rose up with Bass on its back. "Alligator," yelled Bass. "Alligator got me!"

Only the gator didn't seem to want him, for what it did was move toward the boat and, once there, bump and deposit Bass back into it.

Bass was choking and puking up water as Monty tossed him a towel from his pack.

"Shit, I never saw nothing like that, Bass. Gator saved your fuckin' life!"

Bass stared back, slack-jawed, speechless.

Monty started the motor again and talked about this Good Samaritan gator all the way back to shore, shouting over the engine noise, then all the while he helped his charge back to the truck, and all the way back to Everglades City.

"I can't get over that, man. That fuckin' gator, it just got under you, lifted you up, and popped you back in the boat like some goddamned tour guide! Yeah, that was one triple-A fuckin' miracle, Bass. Gator musta had help."

God, maybe?

Molloy, definitely.

"What in heaven's name happened?" said Simone upon seeing Bass's soaking, muddy person. Had Monty not been there to confirm it, Simone would have questioned her nephew's sanity. She already had called that into question.

"I'm going to turn in," he said after giving her some of the story.

"What about my orchid?"

"Orchid? Orchid? Haven't you been listening? I was almost killed because of your bloody orchid! Good night!"

He turned in. He relived the scene again and again. He had embellished the incident, seeing himself as some lesser ocean god (in other words, not Neptune) rising out of the sea. Finally, he went to sleep. In his dream, he held a trident. Two tridents. One in each hand as he frolicked on the back of a dolphin in the small waves.

In the cold light of morning, drinking coffee and eating toast, with Simone still trying to get more details from him, he ramped his vision down from god of the Gulf to one for whom God was quite possibly on the lookout.

On the United flight back to New York, he tried to rid the event of any hint of the miraculous. The alligator rising up with him on its back was probably some odd reaction of its cretinous mental faculties or a reflex to something in the water other than L. Bass Hess. He gave a sour little snort. He had always considered himself as cynical as the next man. Ridiculous, of course. Still, it would be interesting to talk to an expert on alligators.

He vowed not to mention the incident to a living soul.

36

Alligator expert?" said Paul Giverney. "I dunno. Is there such a thing?" He was sitting on one of the black and chrome love seats with his feet on the coffee table. He knew this drove Bass to distraction. Tented on his stomach was the newest unacceptable version of the contract.

"There's an expert in every walk of life, Paul."

"Why? Is one of your clients writing something about alligators?"

"No. I had a very strange experience in the Everglades. Very strange." He gave Paul not a brief description but a moment-by-moment account of the entire episode. He even included the ghost orchid search, since he felt that bolstered his image as fearless and adventurous, even though he'd gotten nowhere near a ghost orchid.

"Ghost orchid? Did you see that movie?"

"That's got nothing to do with this."

"It does. It was based on *The Orchid Thief*. It's—"

"I mean the alligator, Paul. It's got nothing to do with the alligator!"

"So you think this alligator literally saved your life?" Paul's smile was broad and gathering itself for a laugh.

"It certainly seemed that way, yes."

Paul was laughing heartily. "Come on, Bass. You were scared shitless because you were drowning. You were hyper, so naturally the mind invents—the wishful thinking of the mind takes concrete form." He had no idea where that bit of psychobabble came from. "And plays out in an hallucinatory montage." Boy, he was on fire with this crap. He could have gone on all day.

"It was no hallucination!"

Paul gave it a moment, then said, "Maybe it was just a log caught on the mangrove roots."

Bass was close to springing from his chair. "Logs do not have teeth!"

No, but neither did Sammy. Molloy had described Sammy in meticulous detail. No teeth was a plus, since they were not trying to tear Hess limb from limb, just trying to organize an experience that would leave him in his current state of mind. Paul was going to give Molloy and Monty another thousand. He went on, "Listen, are you sure it wasn't just some guy dressed up in an alligator suit?"

L. Bass rose and slammed his fist on his desk. It was more emotion than he'd shown since Paul had known him. "Don't you think I'd know the difference between an alligator and an alligator suit?" He paused, breathed deeply, trying to calm himself. "Anyway, why in the name of God would someone be swimming around the swamp dressed as an alligator?"

"This is South Florida you're talking about. All sorts of weird things go on there."

Bass dropped with a thud into his swivel chair. "All right, all right. Let's just drop the subject and go back to the contract."

Which was why Paul was there. Ostensibly. "So what's Mackenzie want this go-round?"

"Page seventeen: He's struck out the twelve weeks and penciled in six months."

"That's ridiculous. Six months on the *Times* list? Did even Harry Potter hang on the list that long?"

"Yes." With a pale sigh, Bass said, "You want me to pencil it back in?"

Paul shook his head. "I'll compromise. Make it three months."

"Paul, that's no compromise. Three months *is* twelve weeks. That's what you already had."

"Oh yeah. You're right. Okay, let's say four months, and I get a bonus."

Bass made a note, saying, "It would be more politic to let Mackenzie have a smallish victory, I think."

"Such as?"

Bass had left his seat at the desk and wandered over to sit opposite Paul. He had loosened his tie and was sitting there like one of the boys in the locker room. He said, lowering his voice as if in confidence, or as if imparting the L. Bass secret for success, "The thing is this, Paul. I like to save my fights for the big issues. We don't want to waste energy on the small ones."

"I haven't seen any battles going on over any *big* ones. The advance? I guess three million is a big issue, but you didn't have to fight for it. The e-book split? Subrights? What fights did you wage over those issues?" Paul folded his arms across his chest.

"Mackenzie seemed to have no problems there."

"Then you haven't waged any battles except for this stupid payout scheme of Bobby's. So wage some." Paul looked at the contract, humming. He could find all sorts of snippy little things to keep this contract floating in the ether.

"Will you compromise with, say, a four-month bestseller list as opposed to the three-month?"

"Sure." Paul yawned, checked his watch. "It's after seven. You going home?" It would be dark soon.

"Yes, in a minute. I'd like to get this settled."

"Nah, leave it. Don't you live somewhere off Central Park?"

Bass nodded. "East Seventies."

"Listen, I'm going to meet a friend at the Boathouse. Why don't you join us?"

"No, but thank you. I've a very tight schedule. I do like to take my constitutional before going home. I never have a heavy meal in the evening."

"Let's take a cab to the park and walk through it. I've always liked the Ramble." Which was the path that Hess took every evening, like clockwork, according to Karl and Candy. "Maybe we can hammer out a few of the details." He held up the contract.

Bass rose, adjusted his tie, and said, "I'll be with you in a minute. I just have to give Stephanie a few instructions."

"Fine. I need to call this fellow to let him know I'll be there around eight o'clock."

When Bass left the office, Paul made his call. "Graeme. It's Paul. Listen, how much time do you need to set up? We're leaving Hess's office probably in ten minutes. The ride'll take maybe twenty minutes, depending on the cabbie's mood. Then there's the walk. Is that enough time?"

"Sure. We're completely ready. We've been here for an hour. It's keeping people away for that one minute that's tricky. But Monty and Molloy and me, we figured that out. Anyway, it doesn't work the first time, we just do it again. You go through the Ramble, then there's a path off to the right with a great hedge that might work."

"No, a hedge doesn't send the right message, Graeme. The road to Damascus wasn't lined with hedges."

"Yeah? How do you know?"

"I don't. It's just a guess."

"Whatever you say, Saint Paul." Graeme sniggered. "Okay, there's a bush, a holly bush." Graeme gave him several landmarks—bench, fountain, statue, oak tree—asked him had he got that right? When Paul said he had, Graeme rang off.

37

The cab stopped and shoveled them out at the entrance on Seventy-second Street, dumped them in the way New York City taxis almost literally do, seeming to begrudge the ride to every fare they pick up.

"I always take this route," said Bass, turning to his right. "It'll take us across the bridge and around the lake. So you can get to the Boathouse."

The route was imprinted upon Paul's mind. He'd found out more about Central Park in the last three days than he had in his whole New York lifetime. The next time he took Hannah to the Central Park Zoo, she'd be happy that he wasn't wandering around like a blind man.

"Let me just walk you through this," said Bass. He was talking not about the walk they were on but about the pending contract with Mackenzie.

If there was anywhere Paul didn't want to walk, it was in and out of the boring contract. Besides, the condescension and the suggestion that Paul needed a guide gave him the urge to shove L. Bass Hess off Bow Bridge and into the water. He paid no attention to Hess ticking off contract points; he himself was ticking off landmarks along the way. Massive oak. Stone bench. Water fountain, stone base. Two oaks. Statue. Holly bush (wrong one). Park bench, wood and iron. This grew more difficult in the descending darkness.

L. Bass's voice kept grinding on. ". . . and the point of this clause is . . ."

Nothing. Birdbath. Maple. Bench. They'd been walking for fifteen minutes when they came upon the half-moon curve. This bend was manned on the near end by Molloy, with his NYC park-works-like orange reflecting jacket; and twenty-some feet on by Monty, same gear. Both had furnished themselves with sawhorses. Fortunately, Hess's route wasn't as much used by city folk as the one that looped around on the other side of the Boathouse.

Third bench, regular park bench.

". . . and the payout, Mackenzie's agreed to ten instead of twelve, which I still think is . . ."

Molloy walking toward them with his sawhorse, passing, winking at Paul.

Okay, don't be so damned obvious with your thumbs-up sign. Had Hess noticed? Of course not. Molloy disappearing around the bend. Monty up ahead, the other end of the bend. Graeme? Who knew? Concealed somewhere.

And there was the bush at last, and . . . *Woooosh!*

It was all Paul could do to keep from jumping, and he knew it was coming, so it was hardly surprising that L. Bass Hess yelled, "My God!" and fell back, breathing hard.

"Bass, what's wrong?" Paul moved quickly toward him. "What is it?"

"Wrong? You saw it! That bush went up in flames!"

Paul looked along the length of Bass's outthrust arm, hand, finger. He squinted. "What bush?"

White-faced, Bass stared at the holly bush. One of its little berries plopped to the ground. "You didn't see the *fire*? You must have. *You didn't see the flames?*"

A couple strolled by and looked at the bush that Bass's eyes and index finger were trained on. They looked at Paul, then Bass, then each other. They obviously could not understand why Bass was looking at them in that beseeching manner. "You saw it, didn't you? You must have! You were just walking past it." A voice like weeping. The couple picked up their pace and walked on.

Paul marveled at the fact that after the barriers came down (the temporarily placed sawhorses and park attendants now removed), all of Manhattan appeared to have chosen this elusive little route for their evening ramble.

An old guy bent nearly in half with two canes plied the path beneath his feet, shouting, "End of days!" as he passed or didn't pass. He was sharing his message with whomever he saw, but he must have thought Hess, given his pale face and frightened look, was the person most likely to listen with an ear cocked. *"End of days!"* the old man yelled smack into Hess's face.

As Paul moved to intervene, two youngish men, their fingers intertwined, shoveled by with what looked like one wolfhound each—dogs almost as big as ponies—greeting everyone as if the party were in full swing. Hess shouted at them, "Have you seen it?"

"Practically everything, dear." They looked, they laughed, they walked on.

Hess had a handkerchief pressed to his face and seemed frozen in place.

Paul yanked at his arm. "Come on, Bass. The Boathouse is right up there. I see the lights."

Indeed it was, and indeed Paul had chosen it because it would be. Paul bet his timing was up there with Jay-Z or Chris Rock or Stephen Strasburg.

He manhandled Hess into the restaurant's bar and sat him down at a table. He ordered two double whiskies, and to the waiter's question about brand, he said, "Hundred proof." He went on, "Now Bass—"

L. Bass was mopping his sweatless face with the immaculately, precisely squared handkerchief, murmuring, "I don't understand, I don't understand. You had your back to it, that must be it."

"The bush?"

"That's why you didn't see the conflagration; it must be."

"I was kind of angled away, but I think I'd've seen, well, something go up in flames, Bass." Paul snorted.

"The vagrant! The tramp must have seen it. That's why he was shouting 'End of days!'"

"Yeah, but wait: Something on fire has to die out. You're saying you saw it in flames for two or three seconds, and then it just—stopped."

"It did."

The waiter set down the drinks.

Bass tossed back half of his whiskey and still looked sober-white. He ran his finger around inside a collar that looked too big for his throat.

Paul could swear Bass Hess was shrinking. The collar stood out around his neck, his jacket sleeves looked too long for his arms. Shrinking before Paul's very eyes. Henry James could have done wonders with the subject, better than Jules Verne. "You've been working too hard—"

"Every day of my life! I've always worked hard; hard work is a point of pride. Frankly, I'm sick of listening to whining writers tell me how hard it is to write a book!" He slammed his glass on the table. The couple sitting near them turned. "I'm sick of writers like Cindy Sella." It came out like a cat's hiss. Once he got started on Cindy Sella, Hess might even manage to set aside the burning bush.

"That's very stressful," said Paul. "That and all of your other work, like this contract of mine. Dealing with Mackenzie is no picnic. You need some sleep, Bass. Then we'll talk. Are you okay with going home?"

Bass nodded and clutched his drink with all the fervor of someone who was going to shout "End of days!" He finished his drink. "Something strange is happening. First the alligator. Now the burning bush."

That's about the size of it, Paul didn't say.

"I've got to go to my séance group."

Paul quickly checked the level of whiskey in his glass and wondered if he was totally smashed. "Your, ah, *what*?"

"Séance." Bass drained his glass, looked for a waiter. "I attend a bimonthly séance."

Paul stuck out his foot and nearly tripped the waiter without taking his eyes off Hess. He circled the two glasses in a "refill" signal, and the waiter walked briskly away. Only L. Bass Hess could combine "séance" and the time parsing of "bimonthly."

All Paul knew about séances was one on a wet afternoon with Richard Attenborough. The psychic, his medium-wife, was crazy as a bedbug. Good starting point. "That's . . . interesting. Now, is there, you know, someone you're trying to, well, get in touch with?" It was hard to ask the question.

The waiter was back, God bless him, with fresh drinks.

Bass drank. Glug. "My father. I've been trying for some time now. I get . . . soundings."

Paul chewed his lip. He wondered why in hell just not use a cell phone. They seemed to be good for everything else. Paul was not a believer in the cell phone culture.

L. Bass was moving on. "The thing is—Simone, my aunt. You know, the one I just visited. She's been baiting me for years about my father and her will and her money. Changing her will. She's been forcing me to go there and see her, to listen to her chatter about the ruination of the Everglades by men like Flagler and developers and politicians back in the twenties and thirties. On and on and on. Endless talk from her and that goddamned parrot!" The voice, rising, settled into a whisper. "My father disliked him—her—intensely. Hated her. And I know, I *know*"—the fist came down on the table—"that he can tell me something I can use, something that she wouldn't want known."

Aunt Simone didn't strike Paul as in any danger of further revelations. But Hess's line of talk was interesting.

"I could shut her up, just get the damned will revised in my favor."

Paul sat back. There were times he thought (along with Molly) that he himself was kind of crazy; but hell, he was a writer. And nothing he had done, nothing he had thought of, not alligators nor burning bushes nor junkyard antics (coming up), nor horsemen (maybe) could outperform this new wrinkle in the mind's fabric: L. Bass Hess at a séance, trying to get in touch with his dead dad, not to tell him how much he missed him but to get blackmail material from the astral body.

Leverage from a dead man.

Life was just too fucking thrilling to be believed.

It went down on the mental list.

38

Paul sat in his office, staring once again at the Facebook page of Johnny del Santos. Hard to believe. Handsome Johnny, the most popular kid in high school, the great mugger of local 7-Elevens, rip-off artist, and darling of juvie detention, this guy was now in a monastery somewhere near Sewickley, PA. He rocked in his swivel chair. He picked up Mann's *The Magic Mountain*. Well, well, well.

The only other pieces of furniture besides his desk and chair were a beat-up armchair and a rococo wing chair that resembled a dragon, with its cobalt blue and green upholstery, its scrolled arms and legs. Paul wouldn't have been surprised to see the Draggonier sitting there some evening.

He set the book aside. He studied his revised list, smiled at "Cathedral." Everglades, check; Central Park bush, check. He had been about to add "#7: Séance," when he heard, "Is that one of your lists?"

He jumped a bit at Molly's voice. "This? No. Just some notes. I guess you could say the notes are listed, if you want."

"What are you up to?"

"I'm not up to anything."

"You were two hours late for dinner last night."

"I know. I got to talking to Bass Hess about this damned contract with Mackenzie."

As if she hadn't heard, she said, "I don't like your lists. The last one was a list of publishers and writers. And we know what happened there."

Paul tossed his pencil on the desk. "Am I never to be allowed to forget that?"

"No."

"No."

The second "no" came from Hannah, who was standing by her mother. Sometimes the two of them together made a gang.

"How often," asked Paul, "do I have to remind people that it was Bobby Mackenzie who hired the hit men? That was never my idea."

Hannah glanced up at her mom for guidance.

Molly said, "But it was you who set the wheels in motion."

Paul was sick of that phrase.

"Yes," said Hannah. "You put the wheels—" She frowned and looked up at Molly.

"In motion."

"The wheels in motion," said Hannah.

Oh, it was a playlet they'd rehearsed.

"Life isn't a book where you can do whatever you want with your characters." Molly liked this analogy, so she repeated it. "Life is not a novel."

Hannah chewed that over. "Except maybe *The Hunted Gardens*. That's real life."

Paul crossed his arms and sat back. "That's real life, is it? With the dragons and the Dragonnier?"

Hannah nodded but seemed puzzled by his pronouncement. "Most of the time." She was covering her bases.

Molly said, "I hope that's not a list."

"Oh, for God's sake, Molly. Here, have a look." He held the page out to her.

Molly took it and looked it over and lowered it for Hannah to read. Then she said, "Everglades? I thought your new book was set in New York. Here." She pointed down as if the floor were New York.

"People do travel. And it *is* set in New York. See points two and three." Smugly, he smiled.

"Cathedral and Central Park bush."

"Yeah. Last I heard, New York had a St. Patrick's Cathedral *and* a Central Park."

"What's the bush?"

Paul shrugged. "Just a detail. Maybe someone's hiding behind it."

Hannah looked suspicious. "Like the Dragonnier?"

"Good grief, no." Seeing that Hannah seemed to be taking this disclaimer as a criticism of the Dragonnier, he added, "The Dragonnier is a hero; he's brave and smart. And young. The person in my book will be old and shambling and in the last stages of dementia. He'll be yelling, 'End of days! End of days!'"

"What's 'end of day'? You mean, like, sunset?"

"'Days,' plural. It's an expression that means end of the evil and the world. Like the apocalypse."

Came Molly's relentless voice: "Who are the horsemen?"

Shit. "What?"

"The sixth thing on your not-list: horsemen."

Paul's brain rattled away and came up with "No, no, no. Not 'horsemen.' 'Norsemen.' You know, Vikings."

Molly frowned. "Why would they be in New York?"

"I'm not about to sit here and tell you the plot of this book."

"Who's Joe Blight?"

"Blythe. Just a character I may or may not use; hence the question mark." Paul drew one in air. "Molly, you know how I hate talking about what I'm writing."

"All right. What about 'car parts, junkyard'?"

"It's just a setting. Junkyard at night. Full moon." Paul raised both hands, rounding the fingers in case they didn't know what a moon looked like, full. This was to kill time. "Now, the fella who takes care of the junkyard finds this big diamond kind of hammered in the hubcap of a tire from an Alfa Romeo. The diamond used to be in the head of a sacred statue—"

"Wait," said Molly, her tone suspicious. "That sounds like *The Moonstone*."

"What, you think I'm *plagiarizing* Wilkie Collins now?"

"What's that mean?" said Hannah, her forehead puckering.

"Stealing another writer's work," said Paul.

"A moonstone?" said Hannah.

"It's the title of a book by Wilkie Collins: *The Moonstone*," Paul said helpfully. "It was probably the first psychological suspense novel. Very influential, very famous."

"The Moonstone." Hannah was thoughtful. She drew her latest chapter of *The Hunted Gardens* close to her chest, as if plagiarism were rampant in the room.

"I just don't like you getting up to stuff and targeting some poor soul for one of your 'experiments,'" said Molly.

"You make me sound like Dr. Frankenstein. My Lord, Molly, I'm not targeting anybody. It's my new book." He looked from one to the other. "Now, are both of you quite through? Might I get on with my work?" he added self-righteously.

"All right. But I still think you're up to something." Molly turned and walked back to the kitchen.

Hannah hovered. "Are you sure you didn't steal from Willy Collins?"

"I do not steal other writers' stuff, Hannah."

Hannah left.

But I could, heh-heh. He wrote, "#8: The Woman in White."

39

Jackson Sprague, Mackenzie-Haack's chief counsel, was having a pickup lunch with Robson Jolt and Barry Weiss, lawyers from the firm representing Mackenzie-Haack in the matter of Cindy Sella; and the D and D attorney next in standing to Jackson, Bryce Reams. Jackson rose from the conference table where they were eating their deli sandwiches and went to the aquarium installed against one wall.

"What the hell do you care? She's the one who has to pay your fees." This reference was to Cindy Sella. Robson had been talking about their eight-hundred-dollar-per-hour fee. Bryce Reams was not a fan of eight-hundred-dollar-per-hour fees. Neither was he a fan of the complaint against Cindy Sella. He thought the whole thing was a complete cock-up. He did not say this; he merely listened.

Jackson, wanting to project the image of a caring man, dropped a feather of fish food into the water, and both a blue tang and a discus fish went for it; the discus, a bully, won. The tank had been professionally installed and was professionally maintained. Rarely did Jackson pay any attention to it; it just hung there like a painting on the wall.

Jackson returned to the table and his panini. Lunch had come from a small place called Gourmet Gourmand and meaning neither, hence a good place for lawyers to get their takeaway food. Gourmet Gourmand was an overrated deli that specialized in sandwiches. But its paninis were quite good. Jackson was eating one made of mozzarella cheese, prosciutto, avocado, and various add-on condiments. Robson Jolt and Barry Weiss were carefully munching chicken salad. Bryce Reams was eating an Eskimo pie.

The sandwiches and ice cream had been procured by Bunny Fogg. Bunny was the sure-fingered stenographer who made the fifth person at the table; she had no sandwich. Barry Weiss, Jolt's partner, said nothing but spent a lot of time adjusting the knot in his tie and taking notes in a handsome leather notebook.

Robson Jolt, a man no one would be tempted to call Robby or Rob, finished his sandwich. He then went on about post-discharged commissions and L. Bass Hess's alleged right to said commissions.

"Why would that be the case, Robson, given the concomitant committal of both parties only insofar as the contract states that the Hess Agency would receive commissions on extensions of all agreements going forward?"

Bunny's fingers hummed across her pad. She enjoyed taking dictation because she had to listen only to sounds, not meanings. She didn't ask for words to be repeated, as she knew they wouldn't make any more sense the second time around. She wrote what she heard, and her ear was a tuning fork.

"And don't overlook," said Robson Jolt, "the claim for promissory estoppel—"

"Which meets none of the criteria, including unambiguous promises," Jackson Sprague went on as Bunny whisked her pencil across the page. If the word "estoppel" was a word in the English language, Bunny didn't know, but she got it down right. These guys could vacuum up words better than any Hoover. She wondered if a bunch of lawyers talking was the source of the expression "bite the dust."

Bunny would have loved to tell poor Cindy Sella that she was making a mistake in trying to understand the legal terminology. The words were never meant to be understood, only to intimidate. You could make out good plain words, such as "works" or "agency" or "time," but they would immediately be set swimming in the torrent of legal babble that would sweep you downstream.

Bunny played a little piano, and during breaks in the legal exchange— such as the fish feeding—she would devise a musical bar and supply notes for phrases she especially liked, such as "concomitant committal," and see where the notes led. She drew in five quarter notes, each rising on the measure, then a couple of half notes, and sounded it out in her mind. She smiled. "Fascination."

Deftly, she drew a musical bar to the tune of "It was fas-cin-A-tion, I know."

Then she penciled in her own version in place of those words:

"Con-com-it-ant com-MIT-tal, I know . . ."

It passed the time and kept Bunny from drowning in nonwords.

Paul had gone into Bobby's outer office to find Bunny. She wasn't at her desk, or whatever secretary's desk it was; he was charmed by the items lined up above the blotter. There was one of those wooden birds with a long beak that kept dipping it into water and went on dipping if you coaxed it with a finger. There was a little ice skater on a pond that moved if wound up with the key at its base. Paul wound it. And there was a ski run (left over from Christmas, perhaps?) down which three tiny skiers sloped, turned, and disappeared.

When Bunny Fogg walked into the office, he had everything spinning, dipping, and rushing downhill. She moved in a flurry of pens, notebooks, and stenographic pads. Paul immediately went to her rescue before the whole lot slid to the floor. He set the notebooks on the desk, moving the bird to one side. It started dipping again.

Bunny looked around. "Dolly's not here?"

Paul looked around with her. "Apparently not."

"Oh. Let me just see if he's free." Her hand went toward the intercom.

"He isn't. At least he's not in. Anyway, it's you I wanted to see. I hope you don't mind," he added, seeing Bunny looking at the moving figures. "I was just killing time, waiting for you."

"For me?" She looked startled as she sat down in her chair.

"You don't work for Bobby full-time as his receptionist, do you?"

"No, that's Dolly. I work for whoever needs me at the moment. I've just been taking dictation at a meeting of lawyers. In Mr. Sprague's office."

Free-floating. Paul smiled, then recalled that he hadn't introduced himself. "Oh, I apologize. I'm Paul Giverney." He held out his hand.

She said as she shook it, "I know who you are, Mr. Giverney, but I'm happy to formally meet you. I love your books; I've read them more than once. What did you want to see me about?"

Bunny could say a lot in little more than one breath, thought Paul. "Thanks," he said as he sat down in a chrome and wood chair that looked and felt uninviting. "Well, there's a project I'm working on." He added hurriedly in case that sounded suspicious, "It's a legitimate job, would take not much of your time, and would pay five thousand dollars."

Perhaps self-possession was born of having to listen to lawyers talking, for Bunny barely blinked an eye, and her mouth, instead of dropping open, opened just a mite. "What in heaven's name is it?"

He leaned back. "Bunny, have you ever read the work of Wilkie Collins? He's often credited with being the first writer of psychological suspense."

While she listened, she thought. Her brow was furrowed beneath that ice-blond hair that Paul couldn't get over. Today, though, she was wearing blue.

Bunny said, as her brow cleared, "*The Moonstone* and all that. Sure." Mackenzie-Haack had recently brought out a new edition of classics. Besides playing the piano, Bunny also liked to read. It was probably working for a publisher and having all of those books around.

"It's the 'all that' I'm interested in." He smiled.

Bunny smiled. Her white teeth were no drawback.

40

That same night, Paul stopped his car at the tall chain-link fence that surrounded Gio's Auto Salvage. But he didn't get out, not wanting to be chased and chewed by a bunch of junkyard dogs. He pictured German shepherds, wolfhounds, and maybe a few pit bulls dotted around. That's what places like Gio's usually had.

The gate opened as if by ghostly hands, and Paul drove his rented Chevy in, but warily. He couldn't recall ever having been in a junkyard and found it an eerie experience, dark and piled high with the carcasses of cars, motorcycles, trucks, and loose parts. There were vertical mounds of tires, narrow and wide, off bikes and eighteen-wheelers; spidery rims off foreign cars; car doors torn off in an accident or a tornado; steering wheels, leather seats.

The place was huge and ill-lit. On either side of the dirt road were several old streetlamps with metal shades. There were also spotlights along his slow way, though they weren't switched on.

Paul loved it; already he was ramping up the engine for a book, the next book after the one he was currently working on.

Farther along the makeshift dirt road appeared a shack. A figure was silhouetted in the doorway, backlit by a couple of naked bulbs. He waved, so it must be Bub.

Paul pulled the car over to one side and braked. At the driver's-side window, Paul saw one old hound. The dog had its nose and paws pressed against the glass. So much, he supposed, for the myth of the junkyard dog. He got out, gave the dog a few pats, then looked at the shack and the figure there. "Bub!"

Bub appeared thrilled to death to have Paul right here at his work-place. "Hi. Come on in."

It was one room, furnished with a table made from orange crates and a wooden plank; a couple of straight-backed chairs and one chair with fancy carved arms. Its upholstery, a kind of orangey damask, was in shreds, as if the chair had been used to train tigers. One wall had been turned into bookshelves, more wooden planks anchored to the wall holding hundreds of paperbacks.

Paul felt right at home. "Reminds me of my own office."

"Oh, come on, man. You work in a shitty little place like this? You 'avin' a larf?" Bub's imitation of Ricky Gervaise.

"Hey, don't call this shitty; you thereby malign my own writing quarters." Paul sat down in the ragged upholstered chair; it was oddly comfortable. "We must have a lot in common. I have a chair that's an offspring of this one, I swear."

Registering utter disbelief, Bub said, "Want a beer?"

"Yes."

"Want a glass?" Bub waved his hand along a collection of jelly glasses and mason jars sitting on a shelf above the rust-stained sink.

"I want the third one over. My mom used to put up peaches in jars like that."

Bub looked as if he questioned that Giverney had a "mom" like other people did. He pulled a quart of Budweiser from the tiny fridge and thumbed the cap off. Then he got down two of the jars and poured. Beer foamed over the rims. Paul and Bub tapped jars in a kind of toast and drank. Bub had pulled around one of the wooden chairs.

"This place," said Paul, "must be knee-deep in memories. I'll bet when no one's around, it wails."

"There's never no one around. It's either me or Gio or one other part-time guy." As if working here were a career for Bub and Gio.

"I think you've found the perfect place to write a book, Bub. It's got it all over a cabin in the woods or a damned chalet in the mountains or something of clay and wattles made."

"Yeats," said Bub. "Innisfree." He seemed proud to have identified the clay and wattles. He frowned and looked through the door to the pile of windshields that reflected the weak light coming from the streetlamp.

"Do you know what stuff is out there?" asked Paul.

"Yeah, some of it. Gio, he knows all of it, every single thing. It all gets logged in, too."

"Yeah. Just look at those cars, Bub. The bare bones of Cadillacs and Lincoln Town Cars, the skeletons of Chevys and Fords."

"That's kind of sentimental, Paul." Bub drank his beer, wiped his mouth on his sleeve. "It's looking at a junkyard as if it's a metaphor for something."

"You think so?" Paul felt deflated. "Maybe I'm just not saying it right." He got up with his mason jar of beer, nearly gone, and went to stand in the doorway. Black heaps of metal as still as glaciers. "How can you take all this literally?"

"Because I work here. I see it come in; I see it go out. It ain't nothing but literal, man. It's a junkyard."

Paul sat down again. "You've written a book called *Robot Redux,* and you're saying you're taking all this literally?"

"You remembered the title?" Bub was clearly flattered.

"I had the impression your robot got put together from car parts."

"But listen. The robot's not a metaphor."

"He—it—isn't?"

"Nah. He's a bot."

"Literally."

"Researchers and NASA, they put robots together."

"Not in junkyards, they don't."

"Look at your Frankenstein's monster; look at your Dracula." Bub balanced a small red rubber ball on his fingertips, then jerked it so it rolled toward his elbow. "What I mean is, those two aren't symbols. They're real, breathing entities."

"Dracula's not made up of bits and pieces. He's not a machine."

"I didn't say he was. I just meant, he's not a symbol. He's a vampire."

Paul wasn't sure what he was hearing. He said, "That benighted monster of Frankenstein, put together with string and sealing wax—that guy is real, as far as you're concerned?"

Bub nodded. "A real monster, yeah. Not a real person."

Paul said, "What about the 'redux' says—I hate to say 'suggests'—this is the second time around for the robot? He's back for further consideration, we could say. Or he's awakened, we could say."

"We could?" Bub was puzzled.

Paul searched through his mental scrap heap, came up with the obvious. "You got your title from Updike, didn't you? Your title sounds satirical. Updike's is *Rabbit Redux.* We first see Rabbit in *Rabbit Run,* okay? We see him as a kind of callow teenager. In the next book, the 'redux,' we see him grown up, more or less."

Bub chewed on the inside of his cheek. "So what you think is I should write the prequel, *Robot Run*? It's a thought. Show him as a—"

"No," said Paul, as fast as he'd ever said no to anything. "No, it isn't a thought. Believe me, I didn't mean that. Any more beer in that bottle?"

"Yeah, sure." Bub took the jars and foamed them up again, handed Paul his. "What I was thinking, Paul, was maybe if you—"

Don't ask me to read it, please don't.

"—if you could maybe get your agent to take a look at it, you know, just to see if he had any ideas about a publisher?"

Paul grinned. "My agent is the guy that's messing with Cindy Sella's mind. And money. My agent's Bass Hess."

Bub put his head in his hands. "Holy shit."

Paul couldn't help but smile as he instructed himself, Do not fall victim to that temptation; do not let Bub be an object of ridicule; do not put *Robot Redux* on the pyre. But wait. What if he, Paul, were to present this manuscript as one ushering in the new Thomas Pynchon or Haruki Murakami? It would be a treat just to listen to L. Bass sucking up to him with phony comments about the manuscript's merits, yet at the same time trying to weasel out of sending it on to a publisher as a Hess Agency— Okay, stop it! he ordered himself. Stop fucking around with other people's lives. That's what Candy and Karl had said to him after the Ned Isaly business.

"That psycho is *your* agent, too?"

"What? Oh yeah. But he's my agent only nominally and for a very short while. The thing is, I'm valuable as a source of a big commission. There'll never be a book contract because I won't agree to the terms. Also, I'm such a valuable client that I can manipulate him to hell and gone."

Bub was chuckling. "I loved the Everglades gig. So what do you want me to do?"

"Hess has been searching for a partial quarter-panel for his Mustang. A '64."

"Guys are always looking for parts for that car. Sometimes I think Ford must only have made ten of them, the way guys come around begging for this part or that. What the hell is it about that car?"

Paul shrugged. "It's a boy toy, a cult car."

"Will the whole project go south if I can't find it?"

"Not at all. It really makes no difference if you find the actual part, as long as you come up with something. All I want to do is to get Hess to the junkyard. Anyway, Gio would know, wouldn't he? You said he logs in everything that comes through the gate."

"You want me to go at this Hess with a tire iron?" Bub seemed happy at the prospect.

"I appreciate your fervor, but no. If we just wanted to break his legs or kill him, no problem. No. What we want is his eternal absence from the city of New York."

"You're trying to scare him off?"

"It's a bit more complicated, but yes, putting a scare in him is necessary. A friend of mine will be out here tomorrow to see you. Her name is Bunny Fogg, and she's a stenographer at Mackenzie-Haack. She'll need to look around. Tomorrow night, what we'll want you to do is take care of the lighting. I'm assuming those old streetlamps can be switched on and off from in here." Paul looked around the shed. "The spots might be a little too bright."

"Sure. Panel's right behind you."

Paul turned to look. "Right. That's what I'll want you to take care of. Bunny can explain more to you. You're on duty tomorrow night?"

"Sure. I'm nine to five A.M."

"Hard shift."

"Not for me. I get a lot of work done." Bub stubbed out his cigarette in a little puddle of beer. "So what's the deal? You'll come out tomorrow night and bring her?"

"No. I'll be bringing Hess, the agent." Paul smiled.

"Hey."

"The idea is just to throw him off balance. This guy is overcontrolled."

"Even after the alligator and the bush on fire?"

"Oh, he'll never regain the control he had before, but he's putting up a fight. He's in denial. Now, is that your boss's log here? Can you see if you've got the part?"

"The log's here." Bub walked over to one of the shelves where a number of thick dark blue binders were shelved. "It's not going to be much help."

Paul frowned. "Why not?"

"The logs aren't made up in categories, which they should be. I mean lists for different types of vehicles and the names of vehicles or the parts applying to those vehicles." He pulled out one of the binders and handed it to Paul. "It's not alphabetical, either. He's keeping records by date: the day such-and-such vehicle or part came in. See here, for instance—2010 January through July." He turned a page that displayed row after row of entries, neatly written down. "See, it's not much help. If you want a part for a particular car, like this Hess does, you'd have to get awful lucky finding it."

"It's relatively useless, then, except to flash at the IRS."

"Not to Gio. He's got a phenomenal memory. If I tell him someone wants a part for an Aston Martin, he'll know if an Aston Martin ever came in, and from there he'll go to the right book and find it, if we have one out there." Bub nodded toward the outside.

Standing in the doorway, Paul leafed through the binder. He looked out at the pyramids of metal and rubber and plastic. He shook his head.

Bub said, "See, Gio says he believes in writing things down as they happen, you know, instead of bringing some artificial order to bear on them."

"Sounds like a writer."

41

"Tell me again," said Bass Hess, shifting down as they followed an articulated van out of the Holland Tunnel, "why we have to do this at night?"

Paul had thought Hess would be more grateful that someone had found his precious '64 partial panel (which Bub hadn't). "Because Bub's there from nine P.M. until early morning, and he's the only one who knows where this part is."

Bass changed lanes. He was such a terrible driver, they could have changed lives and no one the wiser. The Mustang was the perfect color for Bass Hess, a sort of anti-color called (according to Hess) Chantilly Beige. Hess had insisted upon driving the Mustang to make sure the panel fit. Nothing else in the car fit, thought Paul, so what difference did it make?

The car drove smoothly enough around fifty, but get it up to sixty and it rattled. Since no one in New York was going to hang around at anything less than seventy, nor allow any rogue driver to slow them down, the Mustang drilled on the macadam at sixty, lest they be shunted off the road. Paul thought speeding in a cement mixer would be more comfortable, certainly safer. Hess's sudden stops had Paul pressing his foot against the place where a brake would be if the passenger's side had one. The ride was not helped by the fact that it was a convertible and Hess insisted they drive with the top down, "to enjoy the full experience." Paul would have preferred no experience at all, not with Hess driving.

"And then Ford's research person wanted the name Mustang," Bass droned on. He'd been thrilling Paul with a history of the Mustang's advent. "He decided Mustang was a far better name than what Ford wanted."

Another slowdown, another car racing past, another finger poking the air.

"It's not much farther," Paul said, relaxing his foot as if it had been his on the accclerator. "Turn off at exit forty-one."

He could not imagine Bunny Fogg driving out here on her own, but it hadn't bothered her one jot. She had a GPS, she said, then told him for five thousand dollars, she'd drive the highway to hell.

Bub was to watch for headlights and open the gate for them, which he did. Paul liked the creepy effect of the unattended gate slowly moving back, the ghostly invitation.

Bass shifted and drove slowly through the opening into almost total darkness. Bunny had already instructed Bub to leave the lights around the yard off and only the light in the shack burning. The huge stacks of ruined cars and their ruined parts rose upward like Egyptian burial mounds. A few appeared in the dark to form a nearly perfect pyramid.

"This is godawful," said Bass, the car grinding away along the rutted road. "There should be some lights. It's like a cave."

"Oh, your eyes adjust in a minute or two." Paul checked his watch: It would happen any second now, and he wanted to be talking about something boring, like the contract, so he said, "Bobby Mackenzie thinks he can do whatever the hell he—"

Bass yelled, *"What was that?"*

Paul was thrilled by the lightning appearance and disappearance of the white figure flying across the road beyond the shack. It was such a shocking whiteness that it was hard for Paul not to react.

"What's what?"

"You didn't see it? The thing that just crossed the road?"

Paul rose in his seat a little and craned his neck. Then he shook his head. "There's nothing there."

"Not now, there isn't. There isn't now. You must have seen it running!"

"What did it look like?"

"A blaze of white."

"Junkyard dog, maybe."

"Don't be a fool. Did you ever see a white junkyard dog running upright?" Bass was getting out his handkerchief and holding it to his sweaty brow, then, seemingly disturbed by its snowy whiteness, shoving it back in his pocket.

Paul said, "Sorry. I guess I was so wrapped up in wanting to ram a hood ornament up Mackenzie's ass, I wasn't paying—"

"There it is again! *Look!*" Bass was half out of his seat, bent, holding on to the top of the windshield and looking a little like the skipper of a yawl tacking in the face of a gargantuan wind.

Paul opened his door and got out and moved to the front of the car. It was such a wonderful effect: The figure had stopped dead in a circle of misty light thrown by one of the streetlights that Bub had just switched on, good for nothing else but to create a spectral fog. The figure, cloaked in white, raised an arm and pointed directly at the car. Then the light went out and the figure disappeared.

Scratching his head, Paul turned to Bass, said, "I don't see a goddamn thing, Bass. What is it? Where?"

"Don't tell me you didn't see that light!"

Paul climbed back into the car and said it again: "Didn't see a damned thing."

Hess had crumpled into his seat, taken out the handkerchief, mopped his face.

"Listen, Bass, it's just this is a spooky place, I'll grant you that; first time I was here, I thought shadows had substance." (Paul rather liked that and filed it away to use, then decided it was window dressing and yanked it out of the file.) "Christ, the place would make anyone see things that weren't there."

The hand that wasn't holding the handkerchief was frozen on the steering wheel. "Don't you understand? This is the third time. The third instance. You implied 'hallucination.' Is my mind going?"

"That alligator was no hallucination. It was weird, but it was palpable. Look, let's just get out of the damned car and go inside the shack and talk to Bub."

Bub was standing in the doorway with a hatchet—well, it wasn't a hatchet; it was the quarter panel for the Mustang. Or some other car, made no difference.

Paul introduced them and realized he didn't know Bub's last name. In the shape he was in, Hess wouldn't have noticed if the man's name had been Redux.

"Somethin' wrong, man?" Bub was pretending to address both of them, not singling out Hess as the crazy in the crowd.

"No, we're okay," said Paul. "Bass here just had a bit of a fright. Thought he saw something run across the road out there."

"Probably something did." Bub kicked the chair from the table. "Sit down, Bass. Listen, we get all manner of crap running around this yard. We get dogs, wolves, cats, rabbits—" Bub was rattling this off as he got out the jelly glasses and whiskey. (Paul had instructed Bunny to bring a fifth of good stuff.) "A bear once, coyotes, jackals—"

"This wasn't an animal." Bass's voice was tight and whispery, as if his vocal cords were shutting down shop. "And it was white! Really white!"

Bub received this addition to his list of invasive species with equanimity. Brushing his longish hair across his forehead, he suggested, "Something dragging a sheet, most likely." He held out a bag. "Chips?"

"A sheet? A sheet?" Bass said in his new high, thin voice. He sounded like a tenor reaching for an impossible note. "Who would come to a junkyard with a sheet?" He added, "And it was a figure, a human figure. I'm almost certain, at least I think it was . . . yes, it was a woman."

"Oh, why didn't you say?"

"I did. I thought I did." His hands came up to shield his face. "A woman. A woman in white."

Paul savored the sound of Bass Hess saying it and raised his mason jar in a toast to Wilkie Collins and Bunny Fogg.

"Takes all kinds. Now, here's your part for the Mustang."

42

L isten, Bass, forget about the contract for a while."
      With a martyred air, Bass held up his hand, less in a gesture of "no, no," than in one conferring a blessing.

As if L. Bass Hess were sacrificing himself on the altar of Paul's future, when his only interest was in a commission of $450,000. That was the altar Hess dipped his knee to.

They were sitting in the Hess Literary Agency, going over the same shaky ground they had gone over the night before in Libby's all-night diner, where they had sat with cups of cooling coffee for two hours, discussing Bass's incipient madness.

"Don't be absurd," Paul had said the night before. Then added, as if he'd really been thinking about it, "Listen, you're a Roman Catholic, aren't you? I thought so. Do you think Saint Paul was mad? Saint Bernadette? Saint, ah, anyway." He couldn't think offhand of anyone else who'd had visions.

Bass Hess had merely shaken his head wearily.

After the spell in Libby's, they drove back to Manhattan, Bass craning his neck as they crossed the Brooklyn Bridge, as if he'd like to test his implied sainthood by jumping.

They had gone to their separate homes to lie awake staring at the ceiling (Bass Hess) and to sleep the sleep of the just (Paul Giverney).

And then here they were, back in the offices of the Hess Agency, Bass having regained some of his arrogance, still going over the events of last night (and the night before that, and the night in the Everglades). He was telling Paul he didn't need a psychiatrist.

"I never said you did."

Bass rose from his leather chair, his fresh shirt as crisply white as Bunny's dress on the previous night, his three-piece suit making him look like a man who'd never seen a junkyard. He said, "Did you know that Oliver Sacks had a good deal of trouble with his eyes?"

Oliver Sacks? What turned him up?

"I have an appointment with my ophthalmologist this afternoon."

Wanting to distance them from Oliver Sacks, Paul said in an offhand tone, "Maybe it's a spiritual crisis."

This gave Bass pause. "Hmm. Hmm."

As Paul knew it would. Anyone as arrogant as L. Bass Hess would think a spiritual crisis fit him like the pin-striped vest he was presently giving a tug to, just as he thought himself far too good for a mental breakdown.

"Hmm." Hess sat down and steepled his fingers (the image not lost on Paul, who had planted his feet on the coffee table) and repeated the "hmm" several more times before chuckling and saying, "It does occur to me that the burning bush suggested the Damascene."

Paul rolled his eyes. Who but Hess would use the word "Damascene" about personally seeing a burning bush in Central Park? Paul feigned a slight indifference to Saint Paul with a shrug. "I'd say so, yes." He gave a gruff little laugh. "So you're not putting all of this down to a need for new glasses?"

"No, no indeed." Hess picked up the rather worn-out, coffee-smudged, and much-handled contract. "Now, would you agree to the first letter of each chapter printed in the Vijadera font?"

Paul studied the ceiling and wondered how L. Bass would make out in the Hunted Gardens with the Dragonnier.

43

All they'd been able to turn up by way of uniforms were two fluorescent orange vests with horizontal white stripes and BE INC. stamped on the back. They also found a couple of canvas caps with B on the front. That was in a crowded used clothing store on Seventh Avenue.

Not much by way of disguise, but Candy and Arthur didn't want to overdo it. The caps, together with the Ray-Bans, would hide their faces. Arthur was to do the talking in case someone recognized Candy's voice. They would be carrying ropes, electrical cords, and toolboxes.

Only, Candy's toolbox was fitted out for the wet life, lined with a couple of layers of plastic.

They tossed around several words to go with BE on the vests, finally deciding on BIOSPHERE ELECTRONICS. It just sounded more specialized, or high-tech, or something, than the others they'd thought of, like Boone or Buddy's Electric.

The next morning they dressed in black jeans and black turtlenecks. With their orange vests and dark gray caps and Ray-Bans on, they decided they looked official.

With the care of a surgeon proceeding with a heart transplant, Candy dunked a big measuring cup into his fish tank and dipped Oscar out. He then transferred fish and water to a large plastic bag, triple-zipped. He tucked that bag into the plastic-lined toolbox. He was debating punching a couple of airholes into the metal box when Arthur asked him was he nuts? Fish didn't need air. "That's what the water's for, Jacques Cousteau."

"You're nuts. They gotta have oxygen."

"Not air the way we need air. It's completely different."

"Yeah. Like you know." Candy hated closing the toolbox. "Pretty dark in there."

Arthur was adjusting his orange vest. "Candy, what do you suppose the bottom of the sea is like? Do they maybe have strip lighting down there?"

After a little more quarreling, they were ready to go.

They arrived at the Spurling Building at one P.M. Arthur had called ahead and asked to speak with Wally Hale or Rod Reeves and was told they were at lunch. Arthur put on an Academy Award performance of desperation, said he was calling from Hong Kong, and could they tell Arthur at what restaurant the lawyers were lunching so he could call them there? Michael's, said the receptionist, and even gave him the number. Arthur thanked her. "Sweet Jesus, no wonder these guys are having trouble with security."

Michael's was a good fifteen minute ride from the Spurling Building, if the cab sprouted wings and flew over downtown traffic. Arthur said he seriously doubted Wally and Rod would bother with a one-hour lunch. It would take them that long to put away drinks.

Four of the girls in the firm of Snelling, Snelling, Borax, and Snelling were floating about in their designer dresses apparently looking for the runway. The receptionist was motionless, at least for the moment, behind her half-moon marble station.

"Biosphere Electronics, ma'am." Arthur placed one of the business cards they'd had made up, with a Nicholas Ferrari printed on the card as manager. The telephone number, in case anyone wanted to call, was Karl's.

Wide-eyed, she said, "Oh? Is there a problem?"

"You got trouble with your security system/telephone linkup."

"Oh. Someone called AT&T about that."

"We know that, ma'am; the telephone company isn't equipped to handle this job. That's why they notified us. It's complicated. Apparently, the trouble is in a Mr. Hale's office?" Arthur was reading from a small notebook with last year's bets for his bookie.

The receptionist, whose name was Sang-Lu Wong, according to the brass plate on the counter, called over to the tall black-haired assistant, Sigourney (whose name Arthur and Candy didn't believe for a second). Sigourney was dressed in another bloodred outfit and had the advantage (for Candy and Arthur) of being a know-it-all. "Biosphere Electronics?" She glanced at the bogus card. "Oh, yes, I remember, Mr. Hale called. Come this way, please."

With only the silent trudge across the deep carpet and the whisper of silk from dress and hose, Sigourney opened the door and they were in.

Unfortunately, so was Sigourney, who made no move to exit. She stood, arms crossed beneath breasts, as Candy and Arthur set down their toolboxes and looked over the room, concentrating on the ceiling.

Arthur turned, as if a little surprised to see her there. "Oh, that's okay, ma'am. You won't need to walk us through the system. We can tell what the setup is here."

She nodded. "We prefer that someone stay in the office when workmen are around. Just pretend I'm not here."

Fuck-all. Arthur glanced in Candy's direction. Candy made certain he was facing away from Sigourney before he removed his dark glasses and set up his ladder. Arthur shrugged. "As you please, ma'am. Just be careful you stay outside of the five-foot perimeter." Out of his back pocket, he pulled two white masks and tossed one to Candy, who did a brilliant back maneuver to pull the mask out of the air. They should have been in Vegas, helping out at Cirque du Soleil.

Seeing them with masks while she was short of one, Sigourney was looking uncertain. "What's this five-foot perimeter?"

"The radioactive particles, ma'am. Don't have an extra mask, but you'll probably be okay if you keep your distance." He said to Candy, his voice mask-muffled, and with a brief laugh, "Remember that job Dynamics was doing at the Trump? One of the girls broke the barrier and wound up in the ICU at Presbyterian."

Candy whistled. "Not funny, man. That was a close call." He liked the mask; it hid most of his face.

Obviously unnerved but still trying to do her in-charge turn, Sigourney said, "I can't believe what you're doing is that dangerous. If it is, you should alert the people when you're going to do a job."

"We do. Always. Mr. Ferrari takes care of that personal. Since there's usually no one in the room but us, no one can get hurt."

"But us," added Candy.

Arthur turned on his ladder, his hand on the casing of the little red eye and the closed-circuit system. "You want a shock, just try putting your hand on one of these babies."

Sigourney was checking her watchlet, a band of tiny glittering stuff. "Oh, dear, I see it's time for me to make a call to London. Excuse me." She was out the door.

Arthur was off his ladder and around the desk, firing up the computer. He did not sit down. "Come on, come on. Why the hell turn it off in the middle of a workday?"

"You think they work?" said Candy, off his ladder, too, and over at the door, listening.

Arthur tried plugging in two different passwords. Neither worked. He was about to try the third when Candy whispered, "Someone's coming!"

They were both at the bottoms of their ladders when the door opened. Sigourney was there again. "You finished?" She did not set foot inside.

"Nearly. A couple more things to check." Arthur had whipped out a tiny flashlight and was running it over the ceiling.

Sigourney made a disapproving sound and shut the door. They waited. They pulled off their dust masks.

"Hell," said Arthur, "we can't get into the files with her around. God knows who she might send in here to certain death. It's down to Oscar."

"Oscar's backup."

"Yeah, C. That's what we need right now. For Christ's sake, you'll get the fish back." Arthur was back at the computer, switching it off.

"Who knows? Look at the size of some of them." Candy was once again standing before the aquarium.

"There's nothing in that tank bigger than my thumb." He reached for the toolbox. "You want me to do it?"

"What? No. It's my job." Candy opened the box and pulled out the water-filled bag in which Oscar was pumping around and looking dissatisfied; at least that's the way Candy read him.

Arthur said, "Hold on a minute while I get the door, see if anyone's going to butt in." He slid the door open a crack, looked out. "Okay, go ahead."

Candy lowered the bag into the water, opened it, and let that water blend with the water in the tank and Oscar with it. A bright blue fish shimmied up to Oscar, and they swam off together.

"Hey, look at that. He's already making friends."

"He'll do swell in there. Look how clean they keep the tank. That water's clear as crystal. Come on, let's get our gear and get the hell out before Sigourney starts searching her PC for Biosphere."

They folded their ladders, closed their toolboxes, and made their way out, telling Sang-Lu that Mr. Hale would be getting a report.

"He's a hostage to fortune," said Karl, inhaling what felt like the breath of a volcano, "so stop whining. Be proud of him."

"Fuck's sake, Karl, Oscar don't know he's a hostage. What's to be proud of? It's a dirty deal."

"Play the hand you were dealt," said Arthur, eyes closed.

"Since when did you both get so philosophical?" said Candy.

Karl held up one of Lena's cigarettes by way of answer.

Candy grunted. He was on his second cigarette, and it wasn't having the effect he needed.

Lena had come back into the room with a bottle of cognac. "You need something stronger than a cigarette. This is quite a unique cognac and very hard to get." She set out some snifters.

"How's it mix with these?" Karl pointed to his cigarette and smiled.

Lena returned the smile, then said, "Now. Tomorrow we go, or at least I go, to see Wally and Rod. What names. We're short one or two people, aren't we? Are you confident the assistant won't recognize you? You say she was in the office for some moments." She was addressing Arthur as she poured cognac into the snifters.

"People never recognize me. I'm like smoke or mist. And we were dressed in all kinds of crap." Arthur and Candy were still wearing their vests. They'd come to Lena's straight from the Spurling Building. "Anyway, she was thinking more about radioactivity than what the two of us looked like."

Candy had taken first a whiff of and then a drink of Lena's cognac. "Oh, man."

"It's too bad you couldn't get into the files and had to use poor Oscar. But I assume he was easily managed?" said Lena.

Candy laughed. "He'd be real flattered you remembered his name."

"Of course I remember his name. Oscar is a key player."

They all drank their cognac and wondered where their heads were. Except Lena, who knew where hers was.

44

He's trying to rationalize everything. Trying to convince himself it's eye trouble, stuff like that," said Paul.

"How in the hell," asked Clive Esterhaus, "do you make an optical illusion out of an alligator that's pushing you into a boat?" They were gathered again in Bobby Mackenzie's office for an update, smoking and drinking coffee, for once.

"Well, not that," said Paul, dusting one of Bobby's Cuban cigars across the quarter acre of an ashtray.

"This guy," said Bobby, "has got a weird view of reality if he can rationalize all of those episodes, which, by the way, were pretty damned inventive." With the hand holding his own cigar, Bobby gave Paul a thumbs-up.

Paul said, "He just phoned me and told me he's convinced the alligator was sick or too ancient to realize there was a human being on his back."

"Talk about mental," said Karl.

Paul continued, "He's been reading up on alligator behavior on the Internet."

"What the fuck?" said Candy. "This guy thinks he's going to find the answer on Discovery about what happened in the Everglades?"

"What about the burning bush?" asked Karl, trying to blow a smoke ring but ending up with smoke fuzzing his face. "How in hell could he rationalize his way out of that?"

"His ophthalmologist," said Paul. "Dr. See—I didn't make up that name—Dr. See told him that the retina, or some layer of it, was rife with deposits. I can't remember, except it seemed to be the same thing that happens with macular degeneration."

"Oh, please," said Bobby. "Tell me another. Have you ever heard anyone suffering from macular degeneration walk into an eye doctor's office and say, 'I think I'm getting AMD. I saw an alligator'?"

Candy pumped his fist in the air. "But that's an extra, man. Now old Bass has to worry maybe he's going blind."

"He's caught between a rock and a hard place. It's either accepting he's had a heavenly vision or tapping along the pavement with a white cane," said Clive, pouring himself another cup of coffee, adding cream.

"What about the Wilkie Collins Redux?" This was Bobby's personal favorite. "I always knew Bunny had the makings of a Sarah Bernhardt. I wish I'd been there."

Paul smiled. "Yeah. It was some show." As if reminding himself of the view from the office, he wandered over to the enormous window.

"So your overall plan is to have him checking in to Bellevue, but he's balking?" asked Clive.

"No. Hess is already crazy; if we got him installed in a psychiatric facility, he'd be rationalizing that, too. He'd be revamping reality and get out in no time. Nope. This guy needs a whole new way of life." Paul looked around at them. "Oh, don't think he's really convinced himself none of this happened. His mind is like a pinball machine: balls rolling around, falling here, there, Bass in control only insofar as he can pull back the plunger and pray."

"So," said Karl, finally managing a perfect smoke ring, "what you do with a pinball machine is, you tilt it without making the lights go out."

"That metaphor works," said Bobby. "Meaning he needs a good scare."

"What? You think the guy hasn't already had one? That scene in the junkyard, that'd be enough to put my lights out, buddy."

Bobby chortled. He picked up his coffee cup, regarded it as if it were an unfamiliar beverage, and set it down again. "That girl is wasted in this office. She should get a promotion, except I don't know what to promote her to. Why should she spend her precious time taking down what Jack Sprague and those others blather on about. It's like listening to a fucking knitting contest. That's what it's like up there, knitting needles going on, rat tat tat." He did an awfully good imitation of clattering needles. They all laughed, especially Paul, who then said, "Bobby, you're rarely wrong, but in the case of Bunny—"

"I'm never wrong." Which was supposed to come off as a joke.

"In the case of Bunny Fogg, you don't get it. You think she wants to be something else? You think she hates having to listen to Jackson Sprague? She thinks it's fun; she likes hearing their meaningless legal banter. And what would you promote her to? Assistant, associate editor? Oh, that's always fun. Editor? Ask Clive. The only job around here that's not a downer is yours."

"Oh, I dunno," said Bobby. "Don't forget the Good-bye Boys. They've got an even sweeter deal. They're never here."

45

Karl, Lena bint Musah, and Danny Zito walked through the glass and marble lobby of the Spurling Building at ten A.M. the next morning. They went up fifteen floors in the time it would take to zip a body bag and made a smooth exit as the doors whispered open.

Danny was in all black—merino wool jacket, Lauren turtleneck, Boss jeans. In garb very hot for a sunny September day, Danny looked very cool.

Lena was wearing a high-collared black silk dress.

Karl wore a pin-striped suit, pale blue shirt, and abstract-art tie.

To any eye, they were an impressive trio. They were intimidating, chief intimidator being Danny, who, when Sigourney fake-smiled and asked them to "wait here," raised his eyebrows, did not take a seat, suggesting that "wait" was in a language foreign to him. Quickly, Sigourney opened the door to Mr. Hale's office, slipped in and out again.

There had been some anxiety expressed that Danny might be recognized as the author of *Fallguy,* an exposé of the Bransoni family that had sent him into the Witness Protection Program. Danny had scoffed when Karl brought up the fact that Danny's face had been plastered on the back cover of fifty thousand books.

"You don't think these suckers read, do you? Anyway, I look like a couple hundred other guys." Which sounded extremely modest and self-effacing until he rattled off who some of the couple hundred were: Al Pacino, Robert De Niro, Joe Mantegna, and on and on, until he got around to Steve McQueen and Candy had to stop him. McQueen had been tall and blond and blue-eyed; Danny was short and dark, with eyes like marbles.

"I'm a chameleon, a man of many faces."

"One of which is a chameleon."

Danny had haggled over that all the way across midtown, which was such a sea of yellow cabs that they could have been driving through Wordsworth's daffodils.

Wally and Rod jumped up when the three walked in, ignoring Sigourney's announcement. They were into chairs before she finished struggling with the name bint Musah.

Danny molded himself to the white Philippe Starck chair. For purposes of this visit, his name was Zeller.

"Mr. Zeller," Wally said, "may I ask—"

"You may," said Danny, lighting up a Marlboro and dropping his lighter back into his jacket pocket.

"—what your role is here?" Wally smiled. Or smirked.

Danny blew smoke out of his nostrils. "Bluefin Alliance." He blew more smoke, as if his head were full of it.

Wally and Rod regarded each other with something other than admiration for their Armani suits. They looked scared.

Rod said after much throat-clearing, "That's the organization that, uh, oversees the import of exotic fish?"

Danny stubbed out his cigarette and smiled. "Especially the sort that makes the government nervous." From somewhere he'd taken a toothpick, stuck it in the corner of his mouth.

"So, may we ask—"

"We protect the interests of our colleagues, such as Ms. bint Musah."

"Ms. bint Musah feels she's being harassed by the U.S. government," said Wally knowingly. "We need to be apprised of the extent of her involvement in the importation and distribution of illegal species."

Danny took the toothpick out of his mouth. "Who said illegal?"

"You did, didn't—"

Suddenly, there was a commotion in the outer office, raised voices coming nearer and nearer to Wally Hale's office, the door of which opened with a thrust. Although Sigourney (to give her credit) was attempting to block their entrance, a man and a woman shouldered past her, he tall, blond, and dressed in gabardine that had never seen the inside of Façonnable; she, of medium height, fiery hair, dressed in a hot-pink suit and wearing heels so high and thin, they could have impaled a squirrel.

"Wallace Hale?" said Arthur Mordred.

"Roderick Reeves?" said Blaze Pascal.

They spoke simultaneously as they whipped out their government identification.

"U.S. Fish and Wildlife, sir." Arthur spoke softly but assuredly. He pushed back the horn-rimmed glasses he'd bought at CVS.

Danny slid down in his chair. "Not you two."

Arthur's smile was not friendly. "Yes, we two. How have you been, Mr. Zeller?"

Danny didn't reply.

Wally and Rod had stood and were crowding each other toward the corner where the window met the wood filing cabinets.

"What is this?" said Wally, showing some spunk. "How dare you burst into my office? Where's your authority?" He looked at Rod.

Rod picked up some of Wally's leftover spunk. "You can't barge into these offices!"

Arthur shot out his arm, his hand holding the ID. "The U.S. government, gentlemen. That's my authority."

Karl shot from his chair. "Mr. Hale here is within his legal rights to call security."

Arthur faced him nearly nose to nose. "You don't know zilch about what's going on here, buddy. So stow it!" He turned to Blaze Pascal, who had retrieved a net with a collapsible handle from her voluminous bag. She had also taken from it a clear plastic box.

"You're in possession of a peppermint angelfish, Mr. Hale. Where are the papers?"

"Papers? What papers? What fish? What are you talking about?" He nodded toward the aquarium. "I don't know anything about that. Someone else takes care of it."

"Then bring in the someone else."

Rod punched the intercom, told the girl to send in Sigourney. "Now!"

Wally said, "So what's this peppermint, anyway?"

"Peppermint angelfish, Mr. Hale. The ones in captivity you could count on the fingers of one hand. You have to get FWS permission to own one. You, we were told, own one. And we have authority to seize it."

Sigourney came through the door, looking out of character, with stray locks of hair around her ears and streaked mascara.

"Who maintains the fish tank?" said Wally.

"Fish? Fish tank? Why?"

"Never mind why. Who supplies the fish?"

"No one in the office. It's a professional firm. The work is leased—"

"Get the name."

Sigourney nodded, looked over the room's occupants, shook her head, and left on wobbly heels.

Blaze had netted Oscar and was transferring him to his fish hotel. "Got him," she said to Arthur.

"We're confiscating the fish, Mr. Hale. We'll be back with a warrant to search your office."

Wally's voice had gone up a treble note. "I know nothing about this operation."

"Right. You've got Lena bin Musah—"

"Bint," corrected Lena, spearing a black grape from a large platter of fruit on the table with the knife in her brooch.

"You've got Ms. bint Musah and Danny Zeller sitting right across from you, and you're saying you know nothing? Tell me another."

Jesus, thought Karl. "Tell me another!" "Stow it!" Who was writing Arthur's dialogue?

As quickly and obtrusively as they'd arrived, the two of them left.

Or, rather, the three of them, if one counted Oscar.

Wally and Rod seemed completely dazed by the little play that had just unfolded. Danny Zito, however, all but jumped from his chair to go and gaze at the aquarium's contents. "Where in hell did you get a peppermint angelfish? Who's your supplier? It's not Bluefin." Danny straightened up to give them a threatening look.

"We don't have a fucking supplier."

Danny looked at Lena. "It ain't her, is it?"

Wally hit the intercom. "Sigourney? Have those people gone? How did they get past the front desk?"

The voice of Sigourney was anything but composed. "Government agents, what were we—"

"Why didn't you call security? They had no warrant! They seized our property—and where in bloody hell is the company that put these god-damned tanks in?"

Sigourney sounded wounded and weepy. "I've been trying—"

Wally swore for five seconds, shut her off, turned to Rod. "We'll sue."

Lena sighed. She drew out her silver case, plucked a cigarette from it, said, "I told you, didn't I? Now, however"—she leaned toward the lighter in Karl's hand, then back—"now we might be of help."

Rod muscled in. "Help? What are you talking about?"

Lena looked at Karl, who said, "We can make it disappear."

"Or make them disappear." This contribution came from Danny Zito, who seemed enthralled by the fish.

Wally and Rod stared at them and then at each other.

"Don't get carried away, Mr. Zeller." Lena eyed him through tendrils of smoke as she exhaled.

Karl said, leaning forward, "Look, it's a bullshit charge, but they'll make it stick. Probably just a fine, but—"

"A big, big one. And jail time." Danny was back and happy to make a bad situation worse. "You don't know what this world is like, Wally. That little fish they just took outta here? That pep angel we could get forty K for. We got clients"—Danny eased himself to the edge of his chair, closing in on Wally's desk—"clients got tanks like that"—he jerked his thumb over his shoulder toward the office aquarium—"in their living rooms, but that's just a blind. That ain't where the action is, no, the real fish, the fortune in fish, they don't display them in public. What? They'd be nuts. No. Their green arowans, their Clippertons. This is big business, Wally. A lot of this fishing for exotics is in the Philippines because they got next to no regulations there. Aquarium fishermen shooting up the corals with cyanide. Huge business. And these collectors, these people, they got rooms built underground like fucking bomb shelters. Walking into one of those rooms, it's like scuba diving in the Indian Ocean. You can't imagine what they got. Except protection." Danny smiled a shark-like smile.

"That's what the Bluefin Alliance is all about. Not only do we furnish fish like this, we protect our clients. You can't believe what is underground here in the so-called City of Light."

Rod frowned. "That's Paris."

Wally cuffed him.

Karl said, "So what Lena says, it's true. We can make the charge go away. You have a big firm here, Wally. Rod." Karl felt a little sorry for Rod and gave him a nod.

"All right," said Wally. "Do it. We'll owe you." He flashed a smile.

"Not really," said Karl.

Wally raised his eyebrows, surprised there could be a favor that called for no payback. He opened his mouth to say that, but Karl moved in on him. "What I mean is, you won't owe us because you've got something we want, and we'd like it ASAP." Karl smiled.

"What's that?"

"Cindy Sella's file."

Both of them were nonplussed. Rod recovered first. "Why do you want her file?"

Danny Zito said, "Bluefin needs to see what's in that book this woman is writing."

Their perplexity increased. Wally said, "We don't have it." Looking at Karl, he said, "You're the one who told us about it. We had no idea she's working on an exposé of the illegal fish trade. If that's what you're talking about."

"Right. The point being," Danny went on, "I need to have a look at it just in case she splashes stuff around about me and the Alliance."

Wally sat back, looking relieved that he didn't know anything. Rod was puzzled over how to react. He had perched himself on the corner of Wally's desk, arms folded, brow knotted.

"It's called *Fish, Inc.,*" said Karl. "From what I understand, it's real bad news for your illegal importers." He was sorry that Candy wasn't there to tell them just how bad the news was.

Danny had another toothpick in his mouth, moving it around.

Lena was slicing a small black plum.

Rod, somewhat recovered, ate a fig.

"So you've got nothing on Cindy Sella we could use—"

Wally seemed at last to realize that if he had nothing to give them, they would have no reason to take care of the government agents. "Just a minute, just a minute. You're talking attorney-client privilege here." He said it like any lousy-acting TV lawyer would.

Karl nodded. "We understand that. I guess that's it, then. Lena? Danny?"

Lena wiped her knife on the snowy linen napkin, clicked the point back, and reinserted it in the brooch. She smiled at the two lawyers and rose.

Wally's mind was firing, actual currents of thought snapping across synapses, reminding him that the stuff they had on Cindy Sella, someone else also had. It had nothing to do with Bluefin Alliance, but what the hell. It was something to hand over. If the leak came out, the source could be attributed to the two strange men who'd turned up in Hess's office. More confident, Wally said, "You need leverage, is that it? To make her relegate this fish book to the trash?"

Karl nodded. "Right."

Wally snapped his fingers at Rod. "Get what we have on Sella."

Rod pushed away from the desk and went to the cabinets, slid open a drawer, danced his fingers along the tops of the folders, and pulled out one, fairly fat. He handed it to Karl.

Karl opened it, flicked a few pages, and landed on just what they wanted: a memo from L. Bass Hess to Wallace Hale. Subject: C. Sella. "We should speak ASAP regarding the Hess Agency's complaint re: this person." Karl raised his eyes to see Wally eased back in his chair and Rod, one hand in his jacket pocket, lounging against the wooden cabinet like a Hugo Boss ad. They were wearing self-satisfied smirks.

Karl smiled his own self-satisfied smile. "Yeah, this should do it." Assholes. "Shall we go? Lena? Zeller?" He looked around.

Danny Zito was still watching the fish.

"Zeller?"

Danny turned. They all smiled. All of them, including Wally and Rod.

Wally said, "So the little problem goes away, correct?"

"Correct," said Karl. And a bigger one comes back.

Lena bint Musah was as good as her word. The little problem went away.

Wally and Rod, naturally, told each other that FWS could never in a million years have proceeded legally against them, and for the next week, they danced around their offices with synchronized assurance and kept on with their two-hour lunches at Michael's.

Until one day Sigourney walked into Wally's office with an envelope that she said had been messengered over. This was a complaint filed with the Superior Court of the State of New York against defendants Wallace Hale and Roderick Reeves of the firm Snelling, Snelling, Borax, and Snelling, and against L. Bass Hess of the Hess Literary Agency for (to wit, and nineteen pages to get around to it) colluding and conspiring against plaintiff Cindy Sella in the matter of commissions said to be owing to the Hess Agency.

And it went on.

The Richard Geres looked at each other. Grounded.

46

It was as if her life were being lived elsewhere, thought Cindy, not here in her living room with the same page in her old typewriter as had been there yesterday.

Lulu had gone no further than switching off the ignition.

She sat in her car, in the dark.

Cindy had not written a word in her notebook and did not know why she was sitting in front of her typewriter reading the last paragraph of what she had written nearly a week ago. To be honest, she hadn't written about Lulu in *over* a week. Ten days, she bet, maybe even two weeks. She had tried writing around Lulu, which was cribbing from future writing time, she knew, but she wanted to get words down and thought if she just wrote something, she could get Lulu moving again. She hadn't. Stealing from the future.

The trouble was that Lulu had no future. She had only the present dilemma, and it struck Cindy as the most stuck a person could get, worse than being locked in a closet or even bricked up in a wall, like Fortunato in "The Cask of Amontillado." The plight of Fortunato occupied her mind for a horrifying ten seconds, and she decided no, nothing was worse than his fate.

The point was, or the awful irony was, that Lulu had the means to escape right under her hands—the steering wheel of her Honda.

Cindy stalled by going to the kitchen for coffee. She plunked a K-Cup in her single-serving machine. The Mr. Coffee she used only if she knew she'd drink three cups in a row or if she had guests. Guests. There were the two goons; there was Edward; that was about it. When the cup was full, she took it back into the living room, sipping as she went. She stood and watched her clown fish resting on the little leaf hammock.

As if the clown fish had jostled her memory, she picked up *Moby Dick* from the sofa, where she'd left it the night before. Ahab, the deep blue sea, and all that freedom. Fins rising from the waves like "elusive thoughts," fleeting images that one couldn't quite get hold of. For Ahab (or Melville, more likely), the sea was the deep blue soul.

She looked at her clown fish again, both of them bouncing around in the anemone.

Was that why Moby Dick was white? Was he a ghost whale?

After a moment's reflection, she felt more ready to go back to her typewriter, where she watched, in her mind's eye, a fin carving through the deep water. The thought, the words, were beneath it. She could not grasp it with words. Words. The ones that should be hers lay on the ocean floor of her mind where she couldn't get to them, except perhaps in dreams.

Cindy sat with her fingers resting on the keys as Lulu sat with her hands on the steering wheel.

47

To get herself out of her apartment and a slowly settling depression, Cindy had taken her notebook to Ray's coffee shop, thinking that maybe Paul Giverney would be there and she'd have somebody to talk to.

She'd ordered a toasted cheese sandwich, her particular comfort food. Trying to keep her mind occupied with getting Lulu out of the car, she kept her eyes on her sandwich or on her notebook, which had, for that day, one sentence written at the top of the page. She always made sure to do that, write a sentence—practically any sentence—so she wouldn't have to look at a blank page.

So now she was looking at a page with one really bad sentence, and she wondered how much of a prop that was.

It was late in the afternoon, nearly four P.M., so the lunch crowd was long gone and the dinner crowd not yet arrived. There were only a few customers, a few who looked familiar, most who didn't.

One who didn't was a youngish man—well, he could have been anywhere from twenty-five to forty—sitting at the half-moon-shaped counter, having an ice cream soda. Chocolate, it looked like. Never had she seen anyone having an ice cream soda in here; she hadn't even known that Ray had sodas on the menu.

It was hard to take her eyes off him, he was so—she could think of no other word—cute. He looked kind of varsity, as if he had been a college football or baseball player. He was sitting on a counter stool but obviously tall. He had sandy-blond hair. Cindy couldn't see his eyes. She felt as if she'd fallen through a hole in time, back to the forties or fifties, into some old movie filled with college kids and frat houses, parties and football games, a movie in which this fellow starred.

Apparently, he read, for he had placed a book beside him that he occasionally fingered. There was a mirror over the counter, and once in a while he appeared to look into it, though she didn't have the feeling that vanity prompted it. How in God's name would she know? She was making all of this up.

The waitress stopped to ask him something, or just to flirt. She was holding a Pyrex coffeepot and raised it. He shook his head and smiled. The smile was lopsided, one side of his mouth curling up, but the movement pulled the other side up a fraction, too.

If he turned his head ever so slightly, he would see Cindy looking. Just short of a stare. But he was focused on the ice cream soda, the straw, the long spoon. The kind of spoon she had always found comical; she didn't know why.

His back was to the door, which opened occasionally to admit some customer or allow one to leave. Then she realized he was looking into the mirror only when the door opened. He must be waiting for someone. She really hoped it wasn't a girl.

It wasn't.

When the door opened the next time, he smiled and turned on his stool holding his soda glass.

To her astonishment, Candy and Karl, the two goons, walked in and straight over to him. He returned his glass to the counter and shook their hands. All were smiling, Karl laughing and throwing a pretend punch at the cute guy's shoulder; he was carrying a bottle of wine in his other hand. Candy was toting a white pastry box.

What could he be doing with the two goons? He was shoving his arms into a lightweight military-looking field jacket he apparently had been sitting on.

They were on their way to the door when she realized that, after all, this was part of her life, and she could make her presence known. As she was getting out of her booth, the door opened again, and she was further astonished to see Paul Giverney walk in. The tall blond fellow shook his hand enthusiastically, said something, and held out the book he'd brought, along with a pen. Paul laughed, took the proffered pen, and signed it.

Was this a book-signing party? Wine, cake?

Paul's presence gave her even more reason for walking over to them.

And so she did. She hitched her bag up on her shoulder and walked over to the little group, held her hand up in a "hi" sign and said, "Hi." If she'd only washed her hair.

The tall, cute one smiled crookedly, turning on her eyes so deeply blue that all she could think of was the ocean washing up on a beach in Oahu (where she had never been), or Ahab's sea (where she probably had). She stood there, much as she had in middle school, blushing and letting her book bag drag down the sleeve of her shirt as she gazed up at the handsomest boy in the eighth grade.

"Cindy," said Karl.

"Cindy!" said Candy.

"Cindy," said Paul.

"This," said Candy to Cindy, "is Joe Blythe."

"This," said Karl to Joe, "is Cindy Sella."

More astonished than at anything so far, she saw Joe Blythe look at her with real interest. "Really? *You're* Cindy Sella?"

"Well, yes, I am." She smiled, she hoped, brilliantly. Had he read one of her books?

Karl was checking his watch. "Listen, we got to go. We got an appointment." They said good-bye.

Except for Paul, who apparently wasn't included in the appointment. Cindy thought, Good. I can ask him questions. "Who's Joe Blythe? What's he doing with them?"

"Joe? Dunno. I just met him. I don't know anything about him. Want a coffee?"

48

It had taken a lot of talk and a certain level of friendship to drag Joe Blythe away from his pigs and his farm and back to Manhattan. He had forty acres of land, a big farmhouse, a big barn, and ten pigs. Although it was simpler to call it a pig farm, it wasn't, really. Joe didn't raise the pigs for meat but for themselves. He had always loved farmland and pigs. He had been raised on the Great Plains. He liked space.

Although he looked like a college kid, Joe was way past college. He had cultivated the ingenuous look, the blue-eyed gaze, the crooked smile. He figured if he looked innocent enough, the people he had to deal with would think there was no harm in him. He was big but amiable; some had made the mistake of thinking him docile and easily led. They soon found out how wrong they were.

Joe knew Candy and Karl because he was in the same business: He was a contract killer. What made him different was that in his nearly two decades of work, he had killed only one person, a small-timer named Frank Blow. This had happened through a queer confluence of events. A half second after the knife had left his hand, a bullet had come from a doorway—a bullet meant for the same mark—but misguidedly hit the knife so that both bullet and knife had teamed up to get to Frank.

Another knife had left Joe's hand two seconds after the first and pinned the sleeve of the shooter's topcoat to the doorframe. This faceless killer—Joe had no idea who he was—had dropped his gun and yanked free of his coat just before the third knife would have nicked his ear, had the coat still been on his back.

It wasn't that Joe had any particular compunction against killing; he just thought that if you threw knives, you shouldn't have to kill. There was something about coming within an inch of death four times in ten seconds that worked as a marvelous deterrent.

He was a great admirer of Candy and Karl, both for their skill and for their insistence that they would kill only those whom they thought deserved it.

Joe lived a solitary life. He had never married. He said he didn't know why; he must not have found a woman who could stand to live the way he wanted to.

At a party in Manhattan that Candy and Karl had attended years ago, some damned fool was busy with this subject of Joe's solitary life and the possible reasons for it, strongly implying that Joe was gay, perhaps castrated "like that Hemingway guy, what's-his-name." He himself was seated in a thronelike mahogany chair, slipped down on his spine, and with his legs widely spread, meant to display what he clearly took to be the crown jewels. "You should settle down, buddy" was the last thing this man said in Joe's presence.

The knife came out of seeming nowhere. Nobody saw it until the point twanged into the wooden seat, directly where the legs were spread and just missing the jewels by an eighth of an inch.

"Is that settled down enough for you?" said Joe with his crooked smile.

Candy and Karl disliked upstate New York as much as Joe disliked Manhattan. They were hoping that he would see this as a measure of their need.

"I don't do that stuff anymore, you guys."

"You got a target set up on the barn that doesn't speak to that fact," said Karl. "Can we take it that the marks have not been made by a bull?"

Joe laughed.

They were sitting—lounging, more—around his kitchen table, a beautiful piece of wood with acanthus legs he had carved himself. The room was warmed by a flagstone fireplace, made golden by sunlight slanting across the silky rug, and made fragrant by something either in the oven or recently removed from it. It was the perfect storybook kitchen.

Except for the small pig standing by the Viking stove, looking at them and yawning.

Joe turned. "Come on over here, Junior," he said, making what must have been a pig sign with his fingers, for the pig came and sat down like a dog, hindquarters lopsided against the oak floorboards. Joe scratched behind his ears.

"I never knew pigs would come when you called."

"Anything will come when you call if you call right."

"I got a fish. It won't."

"It will. You just haven't figured out the right signal."

"What kind of signal?"

Joe shrugged. "Maybe he likes Jimi Hendrix."

Candy tried to process this advice, squinting at Joe.

Joe looked at the long case clock with the sun and moon on its face. "I've got to feed the pigs. You come, too. Out to the barn. It's relaxing." He looked at their feet. "Those shoes look like they just came off some cobbler's bench. You need some boots. It can get real muddy." Now he was out in the mudroom, tossing things around.

"Have we convinced him?" said Candy.

"Convinced him? Hell, we haven't even told him what it's about."

Thus, for the next half hour, they squelched through mud and manure, watching Joe pour food in the trough and the pigs all lining up in front as if politely. After complimenting Joe on the pigs' good manners, they told him the story of Cindy Sella and L. Bass Hess, told him about Paul Giverney and Danny Zito, Lena bint Musah, the Richard Geres, and everything else pertaining.

Midway, Joe had to put down his bucket to laugh and sit on a bale of hay. "That is absolutely crazy. I love it."

"So you'll help out?"

"Sure. When?"

"You could ride back with us."

Joe shook his head. "Vet's coming this evening. One of the pigs is sick. Tomorrow I can probably make it."

They said great, they'd fix up a meeting with Paul Giverney.

As Karl was revving the engine, Joe butted his head through the driver's window. "Do you think he'd sign my books? I've got all of them. Do you think he'd sign one or two?"

"Man, I think he'd write you a book."

Joe smiled and thumped the hood of the car and watched it bounce down the gravel and dirt driveway.

49

The three of them walked into the Hess Literary Agency with their cannolis and champagne and greeted the receptionist. With a look of deep regret directed mostly at Joe Blythe, as if it wounded her to deny him anything, she said, "I'm sorry, but as you have no appointment—"

"The thing is, Steffie," said Joe, having taken in the brass plaque, "it's a surprise." He opened the white box and took out one of the little paper plates the bakery provided, placed a cannoli on the plate, and set it before her.

"Oh, how delicious!"

Joe handed her a plastic fork. "This is why we didn't make an appointment," he said. "So if Mr. Hess is free—"

"He is, yes." She looked at the pastry with a kind of longing, then rose. "I should let him—"

Joe waved her down. "Surprise, remember?" He smiled again.

Steffie looked as helpless as a kid who couldn't tie her own shoelaces. "Oh, well . . . all right. Just go on in."

Joe said, "Since it's a party, don't be surprised if you hear some noise. But don't worry about it." He winked at her.

She was oozing more than the cannoli.

The three opened the door to Hess's inner sanctum and marched in, shouting, "Surprise!"

L. Bass Hess's head jerked up from the contract he was scribbling on, his mouth agape.

"Hiya, Bass," said Candy, holding up the bottle of champagne.

Joe set the cannoli box on the desk and then sat himself right next to it.

Bass's face turned an unhealthy pink. "Who are you?"

"Joe Blythe." He held out his hand.

Hess looked at it as if it were a cobra. Rage and fear vied for first place in his expression. He tried standing up.

"Oh, sit down, Bass," said Karl. "We just want to have a little talk, a glass of champagne, a pastry."

Joe opened the box, picked up a pastry, a plate, and a fork, and slid it all across the desk. Hess went for the telephone. Joe trapped his hand before it got there. Hess yelled out, "Stephanie!"

Candy and Karl laughed and cheered.

Over their voices, Bass tried again: "Stephanie!"

"Christ's sake, Bass," said Candy as he popped the cork out of the bottle. "Like Joe said, we just want to have a little chat. Got any glasses in here?" The champagne fizzed up and overflowed.

"You two! You were the ones who stole my documents! How dare you march in here?" Again the hand reached for the phone and again missed it when Joe Blythe swept the phone off the desk.

Candy rooted around on one of the shelves, found some plastic glasses, and started pouring. Joe went over to him and leaned against the shelves as Candy handed him a plastic glass of champagne. "Thanks." Joe sipped it and set it on the shelf.

Karl had taken one of the leather chairs and was lighting a cigarette; with the burning match in his fingers, he said, "We didn't exactly steal them, did we? You handed them over. Did you ask us if we were Hale and Reeves? No. But never mind. The point is, you've been feeding information to Cindy Sella's lawyers, which is hardly sporting." He blew out the match.

"That's absurd. Their client is the defendant in a case where I am the plaintiff. I have every right to speak to them. We were discussing settlement." Hess was satisfied enough with his response to offer them his dull blade of a smile. "In any case, you should take that up with her attorneys, not with me." Thinking he'd scored a great point, he crossed his arms and turned the thin smile into a smirk.

"We did." Karl pulled out a folded paper from his inside pocket. He read: "'Your information re: Sella will be used as I see fit.' We got the file, Bass. It doesn't look like your relationship with Wally Hale is all that ethical, does it?" Out of another pocket, Karl pulled the photos. "Cindy Sella and Cindy Sella," he said, tapping one and then the other. "In company with a woman named Rosa Parchment, who's been picked up a couple times for soliciting; and a small-time dealer, a guy named Benny Bennet."

Bass Hess was shaking his head vigorously. "I have nothing to do with that. That's all down to Hale and Reeves."

"Not according to Hale and Reeves. They say it's down to you."

"That's an unmitigated *lie*!" Bass brought his fist down on his desk.

"Thing is," Karl went on as if the man hadn't spoken, "if any of us"—the brief sweep of his hand took in Candy, Joe, and Karl himself—"was to have our picture snapped every time we found ourselves in company with some miscreant, you string those together, you'd have a movie longer than *Gone with the Wind*. So these?"—Karl waved the two photos before he returned them to his pocket—"would be laughed out of court as evidence."

Gaining a measure of confidence, given Joe Blythe's distance from him, Bass said, "Of course they would. I know enough law to know that. And to implicate me in this nonsense, you'd have to prove I had knowledge of those probably bogus pictures." Thinking this a sufficient dodge, he smiled and sat back in his chair.

No one saw a movement; no one saw the knife until it had zipped by L. Bass's ear and buried its point in the wall behind his chair.

"Wrong answer, Bass."

Horrified, L. Bass Hess jumped from his chair, fell over a pile of folders stacked on the floor, and lost the use of his voice except for a sibilant whisper. He wheezed, "You're insane! Get out of here!"

Joe gave him a bland look. "Right answer: You drop this whole complaint against Cindy Sella."

Hess stood, leaning against his desk, pressing his white handkerchief to his cheek. Seeming to gain courage when no one said anything, he said, "This is assault and I am going to prosecute."

Since he was standing, the second knife just missed making a part in his unruly red hair and landed in the wall above the first, where it quivered for a second or two.

Hess shrieked first, then bellowed toward the closed door beyond which Steffi might or might not have been eating her cannoli. "Security! Stephanie!"

"Still not the right answer, Bass," said Joe.

"You're mad, completely mad." He was ghostly pale, snatching up his jacket from the back of the chair, as if holding it in front of his chest would protect him.

In three steps, Joe was at Hess's desk, where he grabbed him by the collar and threw him back in his chair. "You're just wasting time."

Hess wiped the sweat from his brow. "All right. All right. I'll drop the case."

Joe smiled, moved to the wall behind the desk, and retrieved the knives. They went into a pocketed roll; the roll went into Joe's inside pocket.

Candy and Karl rose, leaving their glasses on the table.

"We'd say, you being a man of your word, you'll follow through. Except you're not," said Karl. "So let's just leave it that if you don't drop this complaint against Cindy, we'll be back."

Joe grinned at this, went to the table, and picked up the champagne and an empty glass.

They closed the door on Bass leaning against his desk and mouthing something the shut door muffled.

"Steffie," said Joe, pouring champagne into the glass. "Swell party." He handed her the glass.

She managed an honest-to-God giggle and took the glass. "It sounded awfully happy."

"It was." Joe winked again.

This time Steffie winked back.

The three of them left as they had come.

50

"I'm calling the police," said Bass Hess, the stemmed water glass trembling in his hand. He had called Paul Giverney almost as soon as his visitors had left. "This is insufferable harassment. *Knives,* Paul. He was throwing knives!" He forked up a bite of cod.

Damn! And I missed it! Paul kept his expression concerned and continued stirring his coffee. They were having a very late lunch at Gramercy Tavern, Bass eating broiled fish and white wax beans thin as needles, with a few tiny potatoes rolling around. He had eschewed the warm bread and olive oil, which Paul was eating hand over fist, along with his asparagus risotto. Paul had suggested lunch, seeing how panicky the man was. Which was just how Paul wanted him.

"Hold on, Bass. You've been through a lot lately. Now, you're sure they weren't just kidding around?" Knife throwing, by God! This was Joe Blythe's specialty. How he wished he'd seen it! But he couldn't have been present if he meant to continue as Hess's client and confidant.

Bass looked scandalized, deeply insulted. "*Kidding?* Kidding *around*? That knife nearly took my ear off. Who is this maniac? This degenerate? To say nothing of those two hoods who stole my legal documents. Accusing me of collaborating with Cindy Sella's attorneys. The only way I could get them out of my office was to promise I'd retract the complaint."

The waiter paused by the table and refilled the wineglasses with chardonnay. Bass had made it clear that he did not drink at lunchtime, that he had to keep his mind clear for the afternoon's work. He had made an exception today.

"Will you, then? Drop the whole business?"

"Why should I?" he said, querulous as a five-year-old.

Paul leaned across his folded arms. "Because they'll kill you."

Bass jumped in his chair. The skin beneath his eyes turned to patches of pure white. "You said you thought they were just kidding."

"I don't know. This guy with the knives, he sounds pretty damned convincing."

Picking up his glass of wine, Bass fake-smiled. "At least we agree on that!"

Paul reflected, or gave the appearance of so doing, as his fingers played around the edge of his book. Thomas Mann had become his constant companion, or at least that was the impression Paul wanted to make. "Maybe you should get out of New York for a while. Go home."

"To Connecticut?" He frowned.

"No. I mean Sewickley, PA. That's where you're from, isn't it?"

"Sewickley?" He made it sound as if Sewickley were a supernova a billion light-years from Pennsylvania. "I haven't been back there in years. The old house is rented."

"You should get out of Manhattan, Bass. God knows you need to get away from these lunatics."

"What about the file they said they had?"

Paul shrugged. "Not your problem. It's the lawyers' problem. They could be disbarred. But why in God's name did you get involved with Cindy Sella's legal team?"

"Information. I had to know what she was up to, what she was planning. Moreover, I wanted to know if she'd settle. I fully expected her to settle! Immediately!"

It was hard for Paul not to reach across the table and grab the man's tie and smash his head into his fish and beans.

Hess whined on. "That woman owes me. I saved her career."

Paul unfisted his hand. Instead of choking him with his tie, Paul gave Hess's arm a reassuring pat. "You know what I think? I don't think it's Cindy Sella you're fighting; I think you're fighting yourself." Psychobabble like that always made Paul want to retch.

"What? What do you mean?"

"Look, I'm not a psychologist." He'd been told often enough by Molly and heard it echoed by Hannah. "But I think this Cindy business is a projection of your own—of some deep-rooted issue." He was surprised Hess was attending to this crap. "Just consider the things that've happened: that you were literally—" Saved by an alligator. No, he couldn't say it, so he went to event number two: "You literally saw a burning bush, Bass" (and couldn't that alliteration have been avoided?) "then, in the junkyard, you saw that ghostly figure. Either of those would be traumatic, but both, both . . ." Paul stopped, shook his head, drummed his fingers lightly on *The Magic Mountain*.

"You forgot the alligator."

Paul grabbed his wineglass and poured chardonnay down his throat. Which made him cough rather violently. Was he the one who had written this crazy scenario? Was he, indeed, the one who wanted to go to Pittsburgh?

His idea, the denouement of his plan had not aged quite enough. To give it five seconds to mature, Paul looked down at the Thomas Mann book, thick as a stack of pancakes, picked it up, and put it down on the table. He riffled the pages for a few seconds.

Bass said, "You're reading *The Magic Mountain*."

"This? Yes, for the sixth or seventh time." He hadn't read it for the first time, only a part at the beginning, but he knew there was a notional sanctuary, made concrete, manifested in the hospital for people dying of tuberculosis. "It's the most convincing account of people suffering from spiritual crisis I've ever read."

"It is?"

"You see, the hospital is itself a retreat, isn't it?"

Bass appeared to be hanging on every word. Which was better than Paul was doing, maybe because he was trying to flesh out his idea, but the flesh wouldn't stick to the bones. "The hospital seems to be the mountain itself." Huh. Huh. "Let me tell you." Paul leaned across the table as if in confidence. "I often think of a retreat for myself."

"You? I can't think of anyone less likely to go to a retreat."

Me, neither, thought Paul. The only retreat he needed was his rent-controlled apartment in the East Village. "I'm no stranger to spiritual crisis." Yes, he was. A total stranger. He wouldn't know a spiritual crisis if it fell on him like a safe dropped from a window. How in the hell could a person be a serious writer without a bunch of spiritual crises? "You know, I believe I'll be going to Pittsburgh myself."

"Pittsburgh?"

The place outside of Sewickley, idiot. "I'm from Pittsburgh; I was born there." The plan was growing legs. "You know, I have a friend near Sewickley I haven't seen since school. I can't imagine it, but he's in charge of a monastery." Paul suspected it was more a hotel than a religious retreat. Knowing Johnny.

Bass took a sip of wine. "A monastery? He's an abbot? Good heavens." He cut a tiny new potato in half. It was the only starchy part of his meal. "It must be quite a peaceful existence, quite a relief from the rat race." He ruminated.

Paul hadn't heard that expression in years, but he kept his silence and let Hess ruminate as long as he wanted. He dipped more bread in oil and looked at Bass's lunch. All white, as was Bass himself. Paul thought of Bunny Fogg, the Woman in White . . . He didn't think she'd been close enough for Bass to recognize her if he saw her again. He might well have seen Bunny in the offices at Mackenzie-Haack. Hess was still too ambivalent about his condition. Paul afforded the man a bit of grudging admiration. If someone had been throwing knives at him, he'd sure as hell be on a plane to Pittsburgh. Pittsburgh? Hell, he'd be on Mars with Curiosity.

Paul forked up his risotto for a while as Bass cut his sole into bits. He was trying to recall the name of the woman Karl and Candy so admired. One swell actress she must be.

Lena, that was it. Lena bint Musah. Then there were Monty, Molloy, Graeme, and Bub.

L. Bass Hess needed another step to the edge of the cliff before he dove over it.

51

Pittsburgh?" said Molly. "Why? You usually don't want to go to Pittsburgh. It makes you sad."

"I know. But I have to do some research."

"Why?" said Hannah, who was more and more in the habit of reasking her mother's questions.

"Because I always have to do research. There's a character in my book who lives in Shadyside."

Molly shrugged. "Okay." Then she turned back. "Will your hit men want something to eat?"

"If you're talking about Candy and Karl, I doubt it. We're going to the Clownfish later tonight. Do we have any beer?"

"Yes. But we don't have anything to eat."

"Then I guess we'll just eat beer."

Molly leaned against the doorframe as if it were the most comfortable place in the room and said, "I guess I could go to Dean and Deluca."

Paul smiled at his computer. Molly just needed an excuse to go there. "That would be really nice. A sandwich, maybe. I don't want anything."

"All right. Hannah can go with me." She walked out.

"What are hit men? Is that Candy and Karl?"

"You shouldn't call grown-ups by their first names," he said, ignoring the harder question.

"They told me to." Hannah remained there, a page of her manuscript pressed to her chest. "Do you have to go to Pittsburgh?"

"I'll only be gone a day." He turned back, saying in a comforting voice, "You'll hardly know I'm gone."

"I know I'll hardly know. But can I use your computer?"

"No."

Hannah stalked away, and Paul spun around in his chair to the computer and the Google search box.

"Pittsburgh?" This time it wasn't Molly registering surprise, it was Karl.

In Paul's office, they were eating their Dean and Deluca sandwiches, which Molly had kindly purchased for them.

"Tomorrow. I booked a room at the Renaissance." He had wanted to go to the Hilton, but it was different now; it had been bought up and the name changed. "It's central."

"Central to what? Since you don't know what the fuck you're doing," said Karl.

"I do, too." Paul did not like the note of whine in his voice as he pulled a file card from his desk. "Right here I've got the names of three psychics."

"Psychics? How come?" Candy picked up his bottle of beer, drank some.

"Can't you remember anything for twenty-four hours, guys? S-É-A-N-C-E. Bass Hess has been trying to get in touch with his dad. He's been doing the séance thing for years."

"Okay," said Candy. "But Pittsburgh, it's a fucking obsession with you. You don't have to go to Pittsburgh to have a séance. You could do that in midtown."

"Chelsea, Pier 61." Karl snorted a laugh and chewed a small pickle. "You just want to go to Pittsburgh because you never got to before, when we went."

"Oh, that's ludicrous." Paul drank his beer.

Candy and Karl shook their heads as if both were on the same puppeteer's string.

"No, it ain't. You just want another Pittsburgh."

"I'm *from* Pittsburgh, remember?"

"So what? I'm from Wanker, Wyoming. That don't mean we all have to go there."

"I'd like to go there." Again a voice from the outskirts. Not Molly this time but Hannah, who strode in holding a piece of paper that she dropped on Paul's desk. It was Chapter 117 of *The Hunted Gardens*. She looked at Candy and Karl. "Maybe we could get an apartment in Wanker. Then we could let some poor person have this apartment. It's rent-controlled." She had been talking about this for months, a year, even.

Paul said, "Listen: The school in Wanker has one room, and all the grades go there. Do you think you'd learn much that way?"

"I already know too much. That's what Clarence says."

Paul told them Clarence was the fellow at the desk downstairs. He said to Hannah, "The school doesn't have a printer. You couldn't publish your book."

Hannah thought about this. "Maybe I could send it back here. I'll talk to my teacher."

Hastily, Paul said, "I'd rather you didn't mention Wanker, honey."

"Why not? Is Wanker some kind of secret?"

Another voice: "Is what a secret?" Molly.

"Wanker," said Hannah. "That's where they're from." She pointed out Candy and Karl.

"Why doesn't that surprise me? Come along." She gave all three of them deadly looks as she turned Hannah around and tried to herd her out of the room.

Hannah protested. "But Wanker sounds like it's interesting." She kept on protesting as she walked away. They could hear "Wanker . . . Wanker" coming from the kitchen.

Hannah had found a new word.

52

Cindy Sella was eating spaghetti with white clam sauce and reading *Your Life with an Aquarium* when the six—no, the seven of them trooped into the Clownfish Café that evening. Paul Giverney, the two goons, a tall thin man with light thin hair, and a gorgeous redhead. And Bobby Mackenzie, for heaven's sake.

And Joe Blythe.

Her heart, or her stomach, sank. This time it was she who was sitting on the other side of Frankie's aquarium, nearly invisible to the rest of the dining room unless someone were desperately looking for her through the watery veil of forty fish.

Two tables were shoved together to accommodate them on the other side of the aquarium. She spotted Joe Blythe between two darting star-burst discus fish.

Joe Blythe, friend of the two goons. He couldn't be another hit man, could he? He looked like he'd be much more at home with a football or a power drill or maybe a fast car than with a Uzi or whatever hit men were using these days. He looked like such a regular guy. An extremely cute regular guy.

A whole school of bright blue and yellow tangs whisked by and blotted him out. The view she did get was wavy, disorienting.

And who was that redhead sitting next to him? My God, what fiery orange-gold hair! They were very busy talking, and although she couldn't make out complete sentences, words filtered through as if rising from the water.

What in heaven's name was Bobby Mackenzie doing here? Looking through the tropical backdrop of the tank, she thought the legendary scion of the publishing world was being pretty loud.

She heard Paul's voice but couldn't hear what he was saying. Right next to their table sat a table full of drunks who exploded in laughter. Cindy tried to bump her chair closer to the fish tank but succeeded only in frightening off a cloud of angelfish.

Paul laughed. "The real point of going to Pittsburgh is—"

Cindy heard those words. She wondered what Pittsburgh was all about. She tried to peer through some starbursts heading in the same direction, but all she caught a glimpse of was that redhead leaning toward Joe Blythe. An angelfish fluttered by again, on the trail of the starbursts. Then came a deep blue discus. She was just glad her clown fish were home and out of this war zone.

"Séance—"

Paul again.

Cindy shut her eyes. Séance?

Given his imagination, Paul must be the plotter of some scheme whose purpose she could not discern. She looked past the ghost clown fish she had given Frankie to see the redhead saying something in Joe Blythe's ear. Cindy picked up her wine and finished off half a glass in two gulps.

Damn! She should go home and do some work. Try to get Lulu out of the car. My God! Here was Paul Giverney getting up a plot involving Pittsburgh and a séance, and here she was without the imagination to get her character out of a car.

Cindy threw down her napkin as if it were a glove and she was demanding a duel.

Lulu could not get out of the car because she had no life. That was why she could not pry her fingers from the steering wheel.

Okay, okay, just sit there, Lulu! Cindy could not expect herself to sit with her and suffer whatever wordless trauma Lulu was going through.

Cindy was going to get a life right now, tonight. No more staring with Lulu through the windshield of a car hour after hour, day after day.

She got out her wallet and slapped more than enough money on the table to cover her meal. Then she got up. She intended to walk bravely down the two broad steps to the rest of the dining room and march by their table, perhaps giving them a fluttery wave of her fingers, but not stopping even for a minute to chat.

She was walking so fast she was nearly running to the side door, the door through which L. Bass Hess had made his hurried exit on the night of the Clownfish Café shoot-up.

53

The club was called Grunge, and she'd passed it several times on her way to see her friend Rosa Parchment and her cat. Any time after nightfall—and she imagined it fell early in Grunge—passersby could hear the noise, the dead beat of disco music.

All manner of people went down the steps, mostly girls in skirts that would never cover their ass if they bent over, and guys in leather and bracelets of tattoos.

She walked down the stone steps to the vaultlike door of the entrance, where a thuggish bouncer with empty eyes and a black T-shirt that said *Ratboy* folded his arms against the likes of her.

She had no idea what the Grunge protocol was, so she tried out a lopsided smile and a wink. Then she realized she had put on dark glasses, so the wink hadn't registered. He didn't stand in the way of her yanking open the door except to bark, "Twenty."

Twenty? "Actually, I'm over thirty, though I don't—"

"Twenty bucks, Christ sake." He still wasn't looking at her.

She pulled out her wallet and tried to see the bills in the jittery light filtering out every time the door opened. He waved her in.

Whatever was playing was loud and vicious, but everyone seemed to go with loud and vicious and stoned. She had seen enough TV and film to make it look as if she knew how to dance like this: a lot of hip movement, a lot of arm waving. She needed to build up the nerve to get out there and pretend she was one of them. A drink or two would probably help. On the right side, a bar ran the width of the room, and all of the bartenders, male and female and advertising a lot of hair product, looked like they were in the process of making a Wes Craven film.

She shoved through the crowd at the bar, took a stool that a slick-looking guy was sliding off of, and ordered a bourbon and water. Without acknowledging the order, the bartender expertly unwedged a glass from a rack above the assortment of bottles behind him, dug it into some ice, pulled a bottle from among what looked like a thousand, poured, slapped down a coaster and then the glass, and did it all in six seconds. He was so fast, his hands blurred. When she asked how much, he raised both hands and flicked all ten fingers.

Cindy pulled a twenty out of her wallet and put it down. Apparently, all communication at the bar was semaphoric. She turned on the stool and watched the strobelike colored lights washing in arcs across the ceiling and down the dancers; it made her think of the Clownfish Café, as if this were a huge replica of the brightly colored fish swimming in wine-glasses. The dance floor, surprisingly large for the basement club, was so crowded that she didn't see how she could move her hips and fling her arms properly without hitting someone in the face or bum.

After a second drink, she went for it: She threw her arms up, then down, shoved hair off the nape of her neck. Eyes closed, she could visualize all of it perfectly; it was like watching one of her characters dance. If they ever danced. She only wished she were wearing funkier clothes than the white T-shirt and jeans. Sway hips, grind a little, hips, hips, arms up—

"Whatcha on, babe? I'd like a taste of it."

Who was this idiot? She didn't open her eyes. Fling hair, head back. "I'm on my own self, so leave." Hands slipping down sides, hair tossing.

"Oooo, well, can your own self spare a little self?"

The guy was so close, she was breathing his air. She opened her eyes, took a look at him. He seemed to be of mixed ethnicity. He could have been Latino, Mexican, Native American. Which showed how much she knew. He wasn't bad-looking, just hard to define, part of the scene. He had a day's growth of beard, the stubble beloved by the homeless and the fashion world.

"What's your name, babe?"

"Babe." Cindy waved her arms above her head as the lights roiled around their faces. After all the wine she'd drunk at dinner, the double bourbon wasn't sitting well.

"Babe?" He heh-hehed. "Come on."

She turned her back to him. He put his hands on her hips. She knocked them off. For about ten minutes, his trial-and-error moves went boringly on. Finally, she stopped with the twisting and shaking, said, "I need some air," pushed through the crowd, got mashed and her feet stomped on, but made it to and through the door below the steps.

What an experience! Ratboy was gone, probably to snort some coke. She stood flat against the brick wall, shut her eyes, and took some deep breaths, not many, because here was somebody leaning in to her.

"Hey! What do you think you're doing?"

"What's it look like?" His stubbled face came close to hers. He smelled of sweat and, oddly, tangerines.

Where was the bouncer? Where was Ratboy? She tried moving her head but couldn't get away from his toothy mouth. He was kissing her as if he meant to take it right through the brick. Her eyes squeezed shut, she heard some kind of scuffle, sounds of feet shifting, and when she opened her eyes, he wasn't there. Thinking he must have fainted or had a heart attack from the effort he'd been making to nail her to the wall, she looked around: the stone walk to her right, Ratboy's chair to her left, up, down. There was no one there. Her dancing partner had disappeared.

She walked slowly back to the heavy door. A couple came drunkenly out, groping each other. Through the door, she saw the rave was still raving.

She hurried up the steps, miraculously flagged down the sixth cab that went by, climbed in, fell back against the seat, and almost said "Grub Street" before she remembered that was a fiction, and told him "Grove Street. West Village."

Mickey and his little dog opened the door of the cab for her as if it were a limousine. Mickey bowed and touched his hat.

Here was the dancing master! Cindy lay her hand over her heart, so glad was she that she was home and that nothing had changed.

"Evening, miss. You all right?"

"Fine, Mickey, fine. I've been out dancing."

Mickey raised his eyes either to heaven or the high-rise across the street as he clasped his hands beneath his chin. "Oh, I envy you, indeed I do. Do you know the last time I ever danced was in Prague in the assembly rooms."

"That's been years, Mickey. Do you think you could give me a few lessons? We could go up on the roof sometime."

"Ah. What school of dance were you demonstrating tonight?"

Cindy thought. "It's this sort of free movement where you're not really dancing with someone."

Mickey gave a dismissive wave of his arm. "Those clubs, you mean. That's not dancing, miss. No, the dance requires discipline."

Discipline? He should have been in her head; she'd been dictating the terms of her every movement: hips arms head. If that guy hadn't ruined the evening, she would have ventured to call it a great success.

She bent down to scratch the tiny dog behind the ears. "Good night, Mickey. It's been a tiring evening."

"One of those clubs, I can believe it." He held the door wide and touched his cap again as she passed through.

Cindy felt immensely sad for Mickey, brought from dancing master in Czechoslovakia to doorman in Chelsea.

Her clown fish were lounging on their plastic leaves. Gus was lounging on the bench, waiting for them to make their move.

Cindy undressed and tossed on the old chenille bathrobe and washed her face. Then she padded barefoot to the kitchen and almost got to the Mr. Coffee machine when her door knocker lifted and fell twice. She thought for one awful moment that it must be the guy from Grunge, that he had reappeared and followed her, maybe in his car, maybe in another cab.

She opened a utensil drawer and ran her hand over the big spoons, can openers, looking for a sharp knife, knew none were there, but hell, a knife was a knife. How had he gotten past Mickey? Mickey could be careless, but still.

She went to the door and tried looking through the cracked peephole, which told her nothing. With the chain on, she opened up.

"Cindy." Joe Blythe was standing there.

She dropped the knife on her toe, and as if her fish had been giving her lessons, her mouth opened and closed, opened and closed. No words were at hand.

He was leaning casually against the doorjamb. "What were you doing?"

"Huh?" Her father had loved the word "discombobulated." Right now she knew what it felt like.

"What were you doing at that sorry club?" He was chewing gum, making tiny movements with his jaw in the way few people did, as if indifferent to it.

Cindy blinked. Here she was in her tatty blue robe, face washed to a shine. "What? I mean— How do you know?"

"I followed you from the Clownfish."

Her mouth went back to the fish movement; she felt as if she were underwater. Having come up little by little through the water, she broke its surface and realized she could be seriously indignant: "Followed me? You followed me?" She wanted to say, *The nerve!*

"You should stay away from places like that. That guy was trouble."

Her hands on her hips, she was so busy striking a pose that she overlooked the obvious. A smart retort came to her: "And trouble is your business? Raymond Chandler." The obvious being that someone had dragged the guy away from where he had her pinned to the wall. Her eyes widened. "You . . . you pulled him off me? That was you? I didn't even see you!"

"You had your eyes closed."

She pulled the belt of her robe tighter. "But it happened so fast! You were so *fast*."

"It's a skill."

"When I was dancing, when we were— What were you doing all that time?"

"Having a drink at the bar, watching the people on the dance floor. You call it dancing."

As if he disapproved. Her eyes narrowed. "You were watching me?"

"Sure. You were really into it. It's clear you love to dance." He bit his lip, pulled a pack of cigarettes from his pocket.

She drew closer to the doorjamb, ran her arm up the side, leaned against it, said, "Could I have one of those?"

He shook out another cigarette. "Sorry, I didn't think you smoked."

"Why? You barely know me."

"True." He put her cigarette, together with his, between his lips and lit them with an old Zippo.

"*Now, Voyager,*" she said. Everyone who ever saw it had been enthralled by Paul Henreid. Men were lighting up two cigarettes at a time for years, she guessed.

He smiled and handed her a cigarette. "That was so long ago, I didn't think you'd've seen it and I could take credit for the double-cigarette light-up."

She smiled, too, then coughed when she inhaled, then cleared her throat. "I guess there are some moves one can make that are unforgettable. Does that make them immortal?"

He seemed to be considering this. "Wouldn't that mean a lot of us wouldn't stand a chance of being immortal? Immortality wouldn't be there for the common man. You'd have to leave something behind: a movie, a poem, a painting, a handicap, a strike."

"A strike?"

"I was thinking of Ted Williams."

Cindy was beginning not to know where she was at all when the door to the exit opened and Edward stepped out. Seeing her in her doorway, he did a double take. "Edward!" she shouted as if the three of them had met in Grand Central.

"Evening," said Edward. Looking at his watch, he said, "Or morning."

"This is Joe Blythe. Edward Bishop." She passed the two names between them, adding, "Edward's a poet." She was always pleased to be able to announce that, forgetting that Edward wasn't pleased. "Poet," he once said, was a word that seemed to make everybody anxious, hard to live up to.

It didn't seem to bother Joe Blythe a bit. "I can't imagine anything more difficult."

That irritated her. What about her own writing? Could he imagine it was easy getting Lulu out of the car? She took another drag on the cigarette and said, "Writing fiction isn't a picnic." A picnic. What a cliché.

"I imagine not. It's just that poetry is much denser. Every word takes on more meaning."

"Every word in prose has to count, too." Her tone was a little strident. Joe just looked at her.

"Sorry, sorry. I guess I'm being defensive. Edward! Would you like a drink? I've got the good bourbon."

Edward smiled. "Indeed I would."

"Joe?"

"Okay."

Cindy fairly flew to the kitchen to collect glasses, stopped for a moment to look at the blocked view through her little kitchen window of part of the Seagram Building, and flew back to the living room for the bottle of bourbon. Hurrying, as if the two of them might disappear in her absence, she poured it in unequal measures, then ran back to the doorway with the glasses squeezed in her hands. There she handed them round, found she'd given herself the one with the most, and quickly exchanged hers for Joe's.

They were talking about Robert Frost and not paying attention to her, except to say thanks. Then Edward asked, "Would you have any ice, Cindy?"

"Yes, of course!" Another flying round into the kitchen, yanking the tray from the freezer, slamming it against the counter, ice cubes falling on the floor. She gathered up the ones that fell on the counter and whisked them into a dish and ran back to the doorway.

"Here." She held out the dish. Now they were talking about how long Edward had lived in the building. She dropped two ice cubes into Edward's drink and held it out to Joe, who warded off the ice with an outstretched palm. She set the dish on the floor and once again draped her arm up the doorway. Thinking of her kitchen window and Manhattan put her in mind of Woody Allen's film, and she tried for a Diane Keaton expression but was afraid, putting on the silly smile, she looked more like Woody Allen and stopped doing it.

They didn't notice; they were still talking about the building and, for some reason, looking at the ceiling. She sighed and drank her bourbon.

ANOTHER PITTSBURGH

54

Paul had limited success with the psychics on his list.

Martha Frobish, a pleasant woman with graying hair, asked why he thought she'd agree to help him perpetrate a hoax.

"Because you're a psychic?"

That was just before the door shut in his face on Neville Island. Paul liked the idea of an island just off Pittsburgh's shoreline. He also liked the Neville Island Bridge. He did not like the psychic.

Nor did she like Paul, obviously.

He'd known his answer would close the door, but Martha had been, after all, a tad self-righteous about her God-given gift.

The next stop had taken him through the Golden Triangle out to East Liberty, where he'd knocked on the door of an old, somewhat run-down house, set back off the street and looking squashed on either side by a newish apartment building. This psychic, whose name he had taken down as Elizabeth Gumm, called herself a clairvoyant. Was there any real difference? he wondered as he rang the bell.

The woman in the gray cardigan who answered the door caused him to take a quick step back. Her uncanny resemblance to the actress who'd played the insane wife in *Séance on a Wet Afternoon* was unnerving. Even the little hitch at the corner of her mouth, not a real smile but a mouth thumbing its way to a smile, was spot-on in its resemblance to the actress's. The faux smile, like that of a hitchhiker hoping you'd stop for poor her so she could climb in the car and thrust the knife between your shoulder blades—

"May I help you?"

Darkness behind her in the foyer, no slant of light. He was terribly tempted to ask for Mr. Gumm, to see if she had a husband who looked like Richard Attenborough.

Paul explained that he had found her name on the Internet, on Facebook (not commenting on why a psychic would need Facebook for anything).

With an overly dramatic gesture of the arm, she swept him in.

He followed her through the dark foyer to the dark hall to the dark parlor. This lack of light he forgave her for, as it was probably owing not to her psychic's aura but to the buildings that had been thrown up on either side, shutting out light.

The house revealed its age at every turn, or at least what Paul could see of the turns. Hairline cracks in the gloomy plaster of the ceiling; wallpaper that seemed to be pulling away from the wall from either dried-up glue or distaste; shivery-glassed windows that rattled a little without the help of wind; and the claw-footed, bun-footed, snake-footed furniture. It was in one of these ball-and-claw-footed chairs that she indicated he should sit. Furniture with feet worried him; it looked as though it might beat him to the door if he made a break for it.

The way she looked at him made him wonder if she'd get to the door before either the furniture or him. She sat sturdily on the horsehair love seat opposite, regarding him with a kind of spacey look that people in her line of work perhaps cultivated. She reached up and switched on a lamp, and he wished she hadn't. He had no desire to see the sinister room in bolder relief.

"Now, you say you have need of a psychic. I am, to be a bit more specific, a clairvoyant."

"That's okay," he said, instead of what she probably wanted to hear, something on the order of "Ah! How much better!" Paul merely went on to tell her what he wanted her to do.

"Mr. Giverney—" She pronounced it with a hard G.

And she calls herself a clairvoyant, he thought.

"—you want me to *fake* a séance?" Her look was both disbelieving and condescending.

"Right." He had jettisoned any wish to have her as medium almost from the beginning. He didn't want to sit surrounded by her footed furniture any longer than necessary.

"To *pretend* I'm in touch with a spirit?"

"Uh-huh."

He was not cooperating fully in her supposed outrage. "To *counterfeit, to forge,* to *tamper* with the experience?"

Paul looked quickly at the sofa to see if she had an open thesaurus beside her, but no, just the old horsehair. "All those things, correct." He sat back and relaxed. Too soon.

"How much?"

Paul sat up. "What?"

"How much are you paying for this deceitful display?"

Quickly, Paul ramped down the dollars from five thousand. "A thousand." Then he thought, hell, that was too much for her to turn down. "Naturally, for that, I'd expect you to supply a few players—"

She frowned. "I beg your pardon?"

"I need some extras. Maybe your husband and—?" He was still dying to check out any Richard Attenborough resemblance. "A couple friends? You'd be splitting the money with them."

Ah! That got the required result. Swiftly, she rose.

Out of the corner of his eye, Paul thought he detected a movement of the snake-head stool. He got up. "I take it that's a no?"

"I don't know how you'd have the nerve to present such a plan. What poor soul have you targeted?"

Really. "Maybe the same poor souls you have. Thank you, Mrs. Gumm."

Speedily, Paul made it to the door. All the way down the walk and to his car, he could have sworn he heard the tap, tap, tap not of a cane but of little wooden feet.

He and his car shuddered all the way back to downtown Pittsburgh.

55

He decided to forgo McKees Rocks and the dubious pleasure of meeting with psychic number three. He figured if two hadn't done the trick, three—like a triple dose of Ambien—probably wouldn't get him into dreamland.

Paul checked in to the Renaissance Hotel and thought things over as he changed from a cotton shirt into a flannel one. It was quite cool outside. While he stuffed his shirt into his pants, he stared out of the window at the Allegheny River streaked with September sunlight; the Sixth Street bridge, one of the several that joined the South Side to the North Side; and PNC Park, so perfectly positioned in its basin that it looked done by a master landscaper.

Paul wondered what in hell he'd been thinking, to attempt to hire a "real" medium/psychic/clairvoyant. For one thing, he wouldn't have control over the situation, even if such a person agreed beforehand to do what he wanted.

He had researched Actors' Equity in Pittsburgh and found a couple of out-of-work actors (basically a tautology) to take part in the séance. Their names were in his address book, and he looked up their numbers: Toby Marseille (there was a name for a marquee) and Rebecca Bloom (not much better). He tapped in Toby's number and got him immediately (Toby no doubt waiting right by the phone for his agent's call). Toby was happy to meet Paul for a drink, and yes, he would bring Rebecca along. An hour later, they were in the bar drinking chardonnay (Rebecca) and Level vodka (Paul and Toby).

Toby was fairly tall, very sturdy, and good-looking, with a flinty profile that he liked to present fairly often by looking a quarter turn away as he smoked his cigarette. Rebecca was quite pretty in an insipid way, with a transparency of blond hair and an equal transparency of white blouse.

It was not absolutely necessary to have five participants, but Paul thought it would look more authentic to L. Bass if there were a couple of total strangers in attendance. Toby and Rebecca were two actors "resting between parts," meaning currently out of work. Paul thought offering a thousand to each simply to sit at a table was a profitable way for them to spend an hour or so. Both were happy for the gig and "dying to know" the details.

"Like, what will we be doing, man?" said Toby.

"Nothing," said Paul. "You'll be taking part in a séance."

They looked at each other and laughed. Rebecca said, "You must want us to do something, like pretend we're communicating with spirits, or something, right?"

"Wrong. That's the job of the medium. There'll be only five of us: you two, the medium, me, and one other person."

"So you're stitching somebody up, right? Listen"—Toby leaned across the table, looking with hot eyes at Paul—"I am really good at laying down a scam; I can really—"

"No, you can't. Not this time. I just need two more people at the table. That's you." He looked from one to the other. "That's all."

Said Toby, "I think I do a lot more than fill a chair." He had a helmet of hair falling over his eyes and an untraceable accent (Jersey? London? Brooklyn?). He was wearing jeans and a white T-shirt that put his pecs on display. Maybe he was the new Brando.

Paul said, "Let's be clear: I'm paying you to sit down and shut up." He was not at all bothered by Toby's six feet two or his gym physique. The last time Paul had worked out was when the elevator in his building had a power outage.

Toby leaned back hard, as if offended. "For what you're payin' us—"

"Right. A thousand each. Just to sit there."

Now Rebecca spoke. "It would make me feel, well, guilty."

"No, it wouldn't." Paul lifted his glass. "Cheers."

The Andy Warhol Museum was located just across the Sixth Street Bridge, and that was where Paul went after his meeting with Toby and Rebecca.

Inside, the museum looked as if it were all angles and sharp edges, as if Andy were stiff-arming the patrons. Paul paid the entry fee to a pretty girl at the curving ticket counter and took the elevator to the top floor.

The rooms seemed almost stark in their total absence of furniture; there were no convenient benches placed in the center of the rooms where patrons could sit and muse over the paintings. There were practically no patrons. But it was a weekday in midafternoon, so the lack of customers wasn't all that surprising.

Paul stood looking at one of Warhol's self-portraits. He had always liked Andy Warhol, for some reason, that is, liked him when everyone he knew was dissing him, calling him artificial and superficial. Paul didn't think he was either. Maybe he liked Warhol for the drama, not the personal-life drama but the artistic drama. His technique struck Paul as tantamount to scenery chewing. Indeed, all of Andy seemed made for the stage or Hollywood.

Paul took the stairs down, from gallery to gallery. He stopped in one room where Warhol's "bent line" method was being displayed on video. Although complicated in its execution of transferring images from paper to paper, the bent line was Warhol's slick little way of producing a series of images, all using the same outline of a shoe or a face. Hannah, Paul thought, would like this and would claim to be as good at it as Andy Warhol.

There were no security guards as such, just pretty young women, like the one at the downstairs counter, at the empty doorways, swaying a little, like flowers on stalks.

Perhaps because there were so few people and so much empty space, the place seemed almost forlorn. Forlorn. What a great word, he thought, looking into a room of skulls. Skulls, identical except for variations in color, hung on all four walls. That was the only image.

What interested Paul was that there was an actual sitting place in the middle of the room. He would have thought, had a couple of people not been sitting on it, that the couchlike object was itself an art installation. It was the size of two small sofas, back to back, but lower and longer and covered with parachute material. He went in.

He flopped down on the thing, and it sank beneath him. This was Tempur-Pedic before Tempur-Pedic was invented. Under the parachute silk was nothing but old foam or sponge, a vast sponge. He wanted one for his office. On the other side of the sponge, two people were also lounging. Apparently, he could sit here and enjoy his view of the skulls for as long as he wanted. The girls on stems didn't appear to mind.

Sighing, he got up and, from the doorway, looked at the parachute couch. He wondered how many people could sit on it at the same time. Certainly five. Paul chewed his lip, thinking.

He walked into another room, where one of Warhol's conceptions of Elvis hung. The *Elvis 11 Times*. Elvis as a cowboy with a six-shooter. Paul reckoned (falling into cowboy idiom) there could never be too many Elvis Presleys. In this repetitive image, he wondered what the point was and was sure Andy Warhol would tell him there was no point.

He doubted that and let his eye trail over the eleven slightly different images again. He wondered if, by the time the viewer came to number eleven, Elvis had backfired and left the building.

Paul felt the blow and left, too.

On his walk back to the hotel, he took from his pocket the scrap of paper on which he'd listed the psychics' names and dropped it in a trash can at the end of the bridge. In the middle of the bridge, he stopped and leaned against the railing and thought about hiring another actor to play the role of the psychic. Considering his encounter with Toby and Rebecca, that struck him as tedious. He didn't want to deal with another ego. But he was intrigued with the Warhol Museum, with the sponge couch and the skulls. He did not want to jettison the séance.

In the distance, he could see the Duquesne Incline, the wonderful trolley-like ride up Mount Washington that he had loved as a child, which made him think about his little sister, Jenny, who had died when she was fifteen.

He turned his eyes away from the incline back to the river, streaked with late-afternoon sunlight, and wondered—was this the real reason he was so into the séance thing? Talking to the dead? Had he meant the whole exercise for himself? Was he just looking for another Pittsburgh?

Both disheartened and feeling foolish, Paul pushed away from the rail and continued on his way across the bridge. Back at the hotel, he handed the ticket for his car to an attendant in front and asked that it be brought around or up from whatever urban dungeon cars were kept in.

Inside of ten minutes, he was in the car and on his way to Sewickley.

It had been years—no, decades—since Paul had seen Sewickley (it depressed him to think he was old enough to measure off his life in decades). A wealthy cousin had lived here, and Paul had been invited to visit on summer days and the occasional holiday. The house was big and beautiful, the lawn sparkling green, the massive trees lending shade and filtered light. In his ten-, twelve-, or fifteen-year-old mind, Sewickley had always been a sort of idyll of fireflies in the grass and painted falling leaves.

He drove through the village, which had changed a lot but seemed the same. How would a real estate agent sell you nostalgia? Ah yes— "footprint." ("You can see the footprint hasn't changed at all.") Along the main street, he picked out buildings and businesses, the new from the old. He was guessing, but it made no difference. The footprint was still the same.

Driving on, out the other side, he turned onto a road that led to Sewickley Heights. What he was looking for was a hill, high enough for a vantage point that would allow anyone on top to see the road and the car below. It would also be nice if it were backlit by the sun. Was he driving north? He had no sense of direction. If Odysseus had depended on Paul instead of omens, he'd have been a dead man. Anyway, as far as sunlight went, there would be no way to judge exactly when everybody would converge on the hill he sought.

He consulted the makeshift map beside him, directions he had taken down in a phone conversation with Johnny. The road wound between old stone walls for a couple of miles. Sewickley Heights was not a euphemism, as it usually was for a section of suburbia outside any city. Along this road were clearly pricey houses, some set in acres of woods. The few he could see through a long pathway of trees were white and so distant, they might not have been houses but clouds.

Then he came to it, the perfect hill crowning a big field. The sun was obligingly setting behind it. Paul would have taken this as an omen if he'd believed in omens.

But he was in omen territory: that sunset, those cloud houses, the dark, dense undergrowth. Omen territory. Sewickley Heights, reconstituted by his old childhood friend Johnny del Santos.

Johnny del Santos was of Spanish, Italian, or possibly Mexican descent. It had always been impossible to pin him down, even to the country of his ancestors. When Paul was a teenager in Shadyside (a wonderful appellation for Johnny), Paul had been a freshman and Johnny a junior. Johnny had a Jimmy Stewart way about him, slow-smiling, utterly disarming.

He wasn't the actual star of the high school baseball team because he was too lazy to train. He was an outfielder, and when he was in position, the air grew brittle. Balls didn't want to go through it. They would have dropped at Johnny's feet if he hadn't been there to hold out a mitt and catch them.

Johnny del Santos was the most accomplished scam artist Paul had ever come across. He could even con a baseball. So here he was, running an abbey a few miles outside of Sewickley. No monk would be said to "run" a monastery unless it were Johnny del Santos. "Run," Paul supposed, was exactly what Johnny did.

Paul turned the car around, drove back the way he'd come. He had missed it when he'd driven by, and no wonder. It was up on the right—high up—the undulating building that Paul thought must be the abbey. Imagining Johnny as a man of the cloth made Paul want to weep with laughter.

Then he saw the sign that he had missed because the shaded light fixed to its top had burned out. The sign, creaking (he was sure) in the wind. Sitting on it was an owl.

Montagne Cassino
The Abbey

If there were Johnny del Santos, there had to be a casino.
And that damned owl had to be stuffed.

M ontagne Cassino. Place your bets, folks.

The stone buildings were enclosed by walls of that sun-burned-colored stucco that passed for adobe, with rounded corners and jutting arms and a church tower that resembled the famous church in Taos, New Mexico. Paul had seen pictures of it but couldn't recall its name.

"I've always liked the Southwest," said Johnny.

Paul paused. "What you've always liked doesn't strike me as being the point. This is a 'Benedictine monastery.' Please note the tonal quote marks."

"So? You don't think they have monasteries in New Mexico? I visited one in Pecos."

"Yes, but I'll bet they don't look like the Santa Fe Hilton."

Johnny chortled. "The contractor was from Albuquerque. Hard to restrain."

"You could restrain a mad bull with a red flag, Johnny."

"But look." Johnny pointed up to the church tower and the surrounding roofline. "At least I insisted the roof be tiled."

"Those tiles look Spanish. We're in Pennsylvania. Where in hell did you get the money for all this?"

"Folks like you, Paul." Johnny's smile was a shortstop away from divine.

Johnny del Santos. One great thing about Paul's mission: There would be no hesitancy, no gasping wonder, no door slammed in his face at the idea of doing something off the charts. Would a monk do anything like this? Yes, if the monk were Johnny and the anything were money. There was nothing Johnny would rather do. If it's worth doing, it's worth being paid for—that was Johnny's version of the old saying.

The other thing Paul could depend on was that no matter what amount Paul offered, Johnny would try to up it. As in their conversation when Paul had called him the day before:

"A million bucks for this one small gig, Paul? Must be important." Brief pause. "How about a million two?"

Paul laughed. "I was expecting a million five."

"Nah. We're old friends. What do ya take me for? A two-bit chiseler? You think I'd fleece a buddy?"

"If you didn't have anyone else around to fleece, you bet."

Johnny liked old words like "fleece," "two-bit," and "chiseler." A hustler, a scam artist, a swindler, a con man—Johnny del Santos was an old-time crook, if ever there was one.

Walking through the herb garden, the knot garden, and the rose garden, Paul and Johnny passed the occasional prayerful monk (or "monkish type"), moving with eyes downcast, hands knuckled before waist. Most of the people they walked by appeared to be civilians: i.e., tourists, or "guests," for whom Montagne Cassino was a retreat, a sanctuary.

Paul commented on the number of civilians here in one capacity or another.

"Ah, yes. If you remember Saint Benedict—" said Johnny.

"No, actually, I'd forgotten him."

Johnny smiled. "Saint Benedict believed a monastery should always have guests."

"Are you going to reference the blessed monk for everything?"

"This by way of being a Benedictine monastery . . ."

"'By way of being.' I like that. Aren't these men walking around in black with notched collars monks?"

"Well. Monkish."

Paul rolled his eyes and shook his head. "I love the name, Johnny."

"Montagne Cassino? Monte Cassino was Benedict's first abbey. It's in Italy."

"No, it's in Vegas."

Johnny stopped. He smiled. "Hey. You came to see me, man. Why're you being an asshole?"

"Oh, I'm just jealous. You were always cleverer than me."

"Paul, nobody is cleverer than you."

They were back in Johnny's office. Paul would have said "study" or "den," as it lacked the Spartan simplicity one might have expected in a monastery or abbey. Paul didn't know the difference between the two, but it hardly mattered, given that the place seemed to be neither.

"Just what do you call this place?"

"Call it? It's an abbey, like the sign says."

"That makes you an abbot, right?"

Johnny gave a protracted "umm," a sound that called into question the appellation "abbot," and rocked his hand, a gesture that sent the word even further south.

Paul looked around the office. He saw a lot of zebra wood, oxblood leather, and Oriental carpet. "You've done well for yourself, I'm not surprised to see."

Johnny leaned back in what looked like a task chair designed by Mies van der Rohe, his hands locked behind his head. "Saint Benedict believed in simplicity, not necessarily austerity."

"You're living up to that standard. That liquor cabinet is simplicity itself; you can see right through the etched glass doors." They were drinking Scotch as smooth as the stuff in Bobby Mackenzie's office.

"Explain what you want me to do for this million-plus."

Paul told him the story of Cindy Sella and L. Bass Hess.

"My God, what a creep."

"What I want, obviously, is to get rid of Bass Hess."

Johnny shrugged. "I know some people, but—"

Paul held up his hand, palm out, and shook his head. "I'll bet you do. If that's what I wanted, I wouldn't have left New York. No, what I want is for our friend Bass to—you could say—recuse himself from the New York literary scene permanently."

Johnny met Paul's smile with a slow smile of his own. "So you want him to . . ."

Paul nodded, smile in place. "Right. You do have rules here, don't you? I mean, such as what a monk—or monkish person—has to do, and so forth?" Paul didn't really know what he meant.

"Oh, certainly." Johnny laughed. "What an experiment. How are you going to manage it?"

"Hess has already had one or two, you could say, spiritual experiences." Paul recounted the events in Central Park and the junkyard. "We've got him kind of softened up."

Johnny laughed and shook his head. "Sweet Christ, Paul."

"He's due for another—spiritual experience, I mean—on the way here."

"When will the way here come?"

"In a couple of days. It won't be hard to convince him. The guy's from Sewickley, not that he ever visits."

"I'm looking forward to it." Johnny raised his glass. "Cheers."

"Cheers." Paul lifted his and tilted it in Johnny's direction. "Another thing: There must be stables around here."

"Stables? Racing, you mean? I know a couple of jockeys."

"No, Johnny. Not everything in life involves a bet. Just ordinary horses that people ride."

Johnny looked disappointed. "Sure. About a half mile up the road." He wrote on a slip of paper, handed it to Paul. "Tell them I sent you. You'll get a deal."

"You bet I will. Thanks." Paul laughed, pocketed the notepaper, and said good-bye.

The Duquesne Incline, an inclined railroad similar to a funicular, ferried passengers from the bottom of Mount Washington to the top. Before such inclines—of which only two remained—residents who lived on the top of Coal Hill, as it was called, had been forced to walk.

Paul, who was at the moment walking up the long flight of wooden stairs to the building at the incline's end where passengers boarded, couldn't believe people had walked up to their homes at the top. He remembered how he used to beg his father to take him on this little trip, but he won him over only twice, and probably because Jenny had helped with the begging. Paul had really loved Jenny, who'd been ill for most of her childhood with some form of lymphoma and had lived far beyond the doctors' expectations to the age of fifteen.

A few steps ahead were an elderly woman and a little girl, probably her granddaughter. The woman was dressed in a well-cut suit of gray silk or gabardine that had a sheen to it, something very fine, like the dust on a butterfly's wing. Her white blouse was a frothy material. Her hair was the same gray as her suit and also had a sheen to it. She was quite small, a wisp of a woman, a moth grandmother. She leaned down and said something to the little girl, who was no older than six and probably four. The child shook her head and held up the bear she was carrying, worn but silky, like the old woman.

Paul stayed behind them, moving slowly until they reached the room where tickets were sold. There were a dozen or so customers in the small cramped room from which people boarded the vintage funicular cars. Five of them, including Paul and the old lady and child, lined up to buy tickets.

The ticket seller was a man with a loud voice who was admonishing the couple at the front for not having the correct change; they had to go through pockets and tote bag as if searching for documents to prove their right of passage to border patrol.

Eight or nine passengers were sitting on narrow benches around the room, two middle-aged couples and a young pair who looked left over from London's Goth days, she with a headful of streaked hair, red locks and blue; he with the blackest hair Paul had ever seen and various nose and ear piercings. They sat chewing gum in a desultory way.

After the couple with no change had been shamed into using the change machine on the wall, the old lady and her granddaughter stepped up to the ticket seller. She said in a clear voice that, as she was a senior and her granddaughter only five, they didn't need to pay admission.

That was indeed what the sign said, Paul remembered.

Almost like a carnival barker, the ticket seller said, "Are you a U.S. citizen?"

The woman was taken aback. "I beg your pardon?"

"Are you a U.S. citizen?" he barked.

"What? I don't see what that—"

Paul was—as he'd been informed by Molly—a man of a mercurial temper, to put it nicely. He could gun himself up from zero to sixty in five seconds. Molly had told him (often enough) he should enter himself in the Le Mans Classic. He wouldn't need a car.

As the ticket man stood there looking as if he'd staged a brilliant coup, Paul stepped up and said loudly, *"Que voulez-vous dire? Quelle insulte! Le . . . Le cheval est . . . ah . . . sortie par le porte!"*

The ticket seller took several quick steps back. "What? What? Who are you?" He stepped farther back as Paul got so close, there was barely daylight between them.

"Je suis le consult français!" Paul whirled around to face the astonished but clearly delighted passengers. *"Quel qu'un qui parle français?"* He held out his arms, invitation extended to all French speakers present. *"Parle français?"*

To his surprise, the black-haired fellow got up and came over, grinning. *"Oui?"*

Now there were two of them. The ticket seller looked frantic enough to race for the vintage car, moored at the door.

"Je suis le consult français!" Paul clapped his hand to his chest, then pointed wildly at the ticket seller. *"Dire, dire!"* He got out his cell phone and started tapping in a number.

The fellow said to the ticket seller, "Listen, man, you better just forget askin' folks if they're U.S. citizens. This guy's the new French consul—"

"Oui! Oui!" said Paul.

His black-haired interpreter added (seemingly for good measure), "And he's a good friend of the mayor of Pittsburgh. That's who he's calling."

"What? No! Tell him no no no," said the desperate ticket seller.

The kid turned to Paul and grinned. "No no no."

Paul laughed artificially and spoke into his cell phone to dead air. *"Allo, allo . . . oui . . ."*

The ticket man was waving his arms frantically toward the car at the door. "Everybody can board, go on, board."

The passengers rose with obvious reluctance. They hated to leave the scene. The short-of-change couple wore huge smiles. The grandmother, her hand to her face, was thrilled with this unexpected ally.

Paul continued to spout into his cell phone. *"Que esque ce,* ah, Duquesne Incline." His English pronunciation was remarkably good for one who'd been such a short time in the country.

They all got into the car, the black-haired kid and his girl facing Paul, the old lady and her granddaughter taking seats next to him. The grandmother said, "Thank you."

There was a ripple of applause all around the car.

The boy said, "That was cool, man. Especially that shit about the horse."

"Horse?" said Paul, mystified.

When they left the car and walked out to the street, Paul was surprised to see that it was just a street. What had he expected? Trees and tangled undergrowth? Deer? Bear? A horse? He was even more surprised to see a limousine at the curb, waiting, apparently, for the old lady and the little girl.

She stopped on the pavement ten feet from the car and said to the chauffeur, who had the rear door open, "I'll just be a moment, George." She turned to Paul and put out her gloved hand. "My name is Vera Hudson, and this is Virginia."

"Ginny," said the girl, holding her grandmother's free hand, with her other hand clutching her bear.

"Paul Giverney." He shook the woman's hand.

Vera said, "We want to thank you for the rescue. I was feeling really humiliated. I can't imagine what that man was thinking. I'd say Ginny and I look quite American, don't we?"

The girl tugged at the grandmother's hand. Vera Hudson bent down, and Ginny whispered something in her ear. "Oh. All right." She turned to Paul. "Ginny wishes to tell you something."

Ginny beckoned him down to her level with a small wave. Paul knelt. Quickly, she kissed him on the cheek and then turned just as quickly away before embarrassed giggles overwhelmed her.

"Believe me, that rarely happens."

"Thank you, Ginny." He smiled.

Ginny, having rushed so eagerly toward him, now had to disdain him, lest she be swallowed up. She would not look at him.

"Well, we must go. Thank you again, Mr. Giverney." She paused. "What a lovely name. It's familiar."

"Monet's garden. My name is spelled with an extra E, though."

George held the limousine door, and Ginny climbed in.

Vera Hudson was about to follow, when she stopped and turned, not looking at him as much as the pavement. "Paul Giverney," she said, looked at him briefly, doubted herself, and shook her head. *"Très impossible."* She murmured this more to herself than to him, then got in the car.

George shut the door, went around to the driver's seat, and got in.

Paul watched the limousine pull away with Ginny's face at the rear window and wondered how well Vera Hudson knew French. And him.

It was eight o'clock. They had parted just before dusk; now it was dark as Paul finished his dinner. All of the restaurants at the top of the mountain were positioned to take advantage of the view of the city below.

He was not old enough to remember the Smoky City, though his parents had talked about it often enough, streetlights being on all day because "the smog was so thick, you'd've thought it was bloody London!" East Liberty, where they lived for so long, they had left because it became little better than a slum. That was when they moved to Shadyside.

What the city had given up in industry, it had taken back in beauty. In the early-evening light, it had glowed dimly. In the dark, it was as if that moth in the Lunesta commercial had trailed its silver sweepings along the banks, across the three rivers, outlined the tall buildings and the bowl of PNC Park. The city looked mysteriously, sleepily alight.

About to leave, Paul stood and looked at the scene and bent his forehead toward the glass. He thought of the old Leigh Hunt poem:

> *Jenny kissed me when we met,*
> *Jumping from the chair she sat in.*
> *Time, you thief, who love to get*
> *Sweets into your list, put that in!*

Time, you thief.
That was another Pittsburgh.

B unny Fogg knew just what to do.

Jackson Sprague always left his office at twelve-thirty for lunch at the Four Seasons. His glorified secretary, whose title was "associate" and whom they called the Duchess, left at the same time as her boss, though not for the Four Seasons. She went to Bloomingdale's or Macy's to shop or to get a manicure.

Bunny couldn't understand leaving an office with such reckless abandon, important files that could be plundered so easily, drawers that could be opened, a safe that could (she bet) be cracked, artifacts stolen, computers hacked. (She had a taste for the dramatic.)

Since the job of feeding Jack Sprague's aquarium fish usually fell to Bunny, there would be no reason to question her presence in Jack Sprague's overwrought office. Did he really need to have the hide of a wildebeest layered over a zebra hide, both striking poses over the skin of a cheetah? All on an Oriental rug?

Bunny reached into her white leather tote and brought out Oscar, swimming in a fitted-out little box, a clear square filled with water. She lowered the box into the aquarium and very carefully removed the top. Oscar floated out, unharmed, unbothered by his new environment (if she were any judge of fish). She returned the box to her bag and left Jackson Sprague's office to go to Bobby Mackenzie's.

"Oscar seems to like the big aquarium."

"You think so?" Candy turned in his chair to talk to her. He and Karl were sitting in the same chairs they always sat in, with an air of ownership. (They could have been in directors' chairs with their names splashed across the back.)

Bunny nodded. "Sure. You can tell."

Karl turned. "Oh, come on. How can you tell about a fuc—" He thought better of "fucking fish" and settled for "little fish."

Bunny remained unfazed. "Because you can."

That was what Bobby liked about Bunny. She held her ground. "Come on in, Bunny. Want a Scotch?" He held up his glass. "Gin? Vodka?"

"No, thank you. I just wanted to report on Oscar."

"You think Jackson will notice?"

"No. He pays no attention to the fish. I don't think he'd notice if they all went belly-up and floated on the surface."

The others snorted with laughter. Except for Candy, who looked a little worried.

Bunny said, "Happy to be of service." She half-turned, then turned back. "I just wondered—could I possibly be in the office when you do this? I would so much love to see it."

Clive smiled. "If you can come up with some excuse for being there."

Bunny smiled. "Oh, I imagine I can."

59

The Duchess was sitting at her desk outside of what Bunny (and many others) called the Royal Suite of in-house counsel. The Royal Suite amounted to four rooms, one a conference room, the other three attorneys' offices: Jackson's, Bryce's, and another lawyer's.

Bunny was headed toward Jackson Sprague's office for the second time that afternoon. She had just come from Bobby Mackenzie's office. Oddly, he had wanted to talk to the head of security, and she had found him (Ben Wink), and when she left, Bobby was ushering Ben Wink into his office: "Something I'd like you to do—or, rather, not do," said Bobby as the door closed behind Ben Wink.

The Duchess stopped Bunny with an icy eye and an icier voice. Looking at the secretary's ice-blue dress, Bunny thought she could be watching an ice floe drift by.

"Where are you going?" The Duchess was in the act of dabbing tangerine blush on her cheek. She had a whole flotilla of cosmetics in her desk drawers. Her name was actually Elsie Hoag, which she detested, both first and last, especially last, as most people pronounced it Hog (some deliberately). She could not summarily change the spelling while working for a brace of lawyers, unless she did so legally. So what she did was add an umlaut over the O. That made people puzzle over the pronunciation and not be so quick to say Hog. The barnyard was further invoked by the first name. This the Duchess changed to Elise, explaining that her birth certificate had transposed the I and the S. This change was not onerous to her finicky lawyer-bosses. So the Duchess bore the artful name of Elise Höag.

"Hi, Elsie," said Bunny, not answering the question as to where she was going.

The Duchess snapped, "Will you kindly remember my name, which is Ger—I mean Austrian—Elise?"

Bunny switched her chewing gum from the left to the right side of her mouth. "Sorry." She held up the tin of fish flakes. "Feed the fish."

"Mr. Sprague is busy with a conference call."

No, he wasn't, not if the unlit lights along the bottom of Elsie's phone were testimony. "Okay, I'll wait." Bunny blew a bubble and sat down in a chair, where she hummed and swung her foot. It would irritate Elsie.

"I'll just see if he's still unavailable." Elsie pressed the intercom, got no response. "Well, he must have stepped out."

Bunny checked the wall clock. In ten minutes they'd be here. "Then I'll go in while he's out." She didn't wait for Elsie to reply.

Oscar was swimming in sync with four other fish, all looking as if they meant business, as if they were a gang. Bunny smiled.

In another five minutes, Jackson Sprague swung into his office in the company of Boyd Lloyd, one of his personal attorneys. When Jackson saw her, he frowned. "Was there something, Miss Fogg?"

"I had to feed the fish, and as you weren't here . . ." Her voice trailed off. She had four minutes to kill if she wanted to be present when they came.

"Miss Fogg?" Meaning, "Why are you still here?"

She spent a few seconds pondering, then said, "Oh. You know, I'm a little worried that the blue tang's branchiomycosis might spread to the other fish."

Ordinarily, Jackson Sprague wouldn't bother commenting on Bunny Fogg's comments, but this word was so much like the tongue-twisting opaque terminology of Jackson's chosen profession that he fell for it. "The what?"

"Branchiomycosis." Bunny had looked up fish diseases. "It's gill rot."

Boyd Lloyd took a step back.

Two minutes to go. They could be filled with misinformation so easily that Bunny found it hard not to laugh. "See, it's a disease that could be really devastating or, on the other hand, not all that serious. In the worst-case scenario—"

"Miss Fogg—"

Bunny plowed on: "—the gills dehydrate and slough off." That was probably not the way to use the word "slough." With a look of grave concern, she turned back to the aquarium. "I don't think that's going to happen here."

Voices in the outer office. She'd recognize Joe Blythe's if it came from a space shuttle during liftoff. Her heart did lift off. She had met him just that morning, very briefly. She smiled at Jackson. "So you don't have to worry."

He was leaning on his fists on his desk. "Miss Fogg, would you please—" His head turned toward the door, as did Boyd Lloyd's. "Who's out there?" he demanded.

"Out there" became "in here" with a presence more intimidating than a hundred Jackson Spragues. The door seemed to blow open as three people stormed into the room. Who, wondered Bunny, was person number three? The stunner with the fiery hair? Where had she hooked up with the others?

"Jackson Sprague?" demanded Joe Blythe.

"Who the fuck are you?" yelled Jackson, returning to his King of Prussia roots.

"Joseph Bligh, FWS." He nodded toward his crew. "Agents Morton and Pascoe."

"FWS what?"

"Fish and Wildlife Service. Interior." Joe frowned, as if any fool would know that. They all had their IDs out, small leather wallets holding badges, and all three were shoving them into Jackson's face.

Bunny was thrilled. They all looked so regal, they fairly shone.

Joe went on, "Mr. Sprague, you're in violation of paragraph 119(a) of the Endangered Species Act."

Jackson Sprague was white with fear and red with rage. To Bunny, he looked striped. She thought of all the times she'd seen him humiliate other people, including Elsie Hoag, and she wanted to cheer.

Arthur said, "You're in possession of a *P. boylei*. That's illegal, Mr. Sprague. Blair." He nodded toward the aquarium.

The redhead moved quickly, extracting a small net and a heavy plastic bag from her tote. She snapped the bag open smartly. Her back turned to the lawyers, she winked at Bunny, then asked her to help with the hood of the tank. Together they carefully removed the cover.

Gap-mouthed, Boyd Lloyd was jerking his head from Joe to Arthur to Jackson and back again. "What's a *P. boylei*?"

"Clipperton angelfish. Maybe the rarest exotic fish known, certainly the priciest," said Joe. "You'll come with us, Mr. Sprague." It was not a question.

Jackson blubbered. "This is ridiculous. Those fucking fish aren't mine. I didn't buy them!"

Blaze turned, holding up the plastic bag. "This Clipperton, this fish tank." She hooked her thumb over her shoulder. "In your possession."

Jackson glared at Bunny as if her misdirected presence had caused all of this. "Security! Get them. Where's Miss Höag?" he yelled.

Elsie had already appeared in the doorway. Breathlessly, she said, "Yes, sir?"

"Get security! Immediately!"

She disappeared like vapor.

Boyd Lloyd said, "That tank is maintained by an aquarium service. Probably supplied the fish, too. Mr. Sprague has nothing to do—"

Joe Blythe didn't look at him, only at Jackson. "Does it strike you as likely that an aquarium service that provides these fish would have possession of a Clipperton angelfish, which they would put in *your* tank? Unless your service is linked to Bluefin." His smile was contemptuous. "Will you step around your desk and come with us now?"

"Bluefin? Go with you where?"

"Our office. Downtown."

Downtown. Bunny pressed her hands more tightly against her face. Manhattan. "Downtown." She loved it.

When Jackson stood there, rooted, Joe Blythe reached around under the back of his jacket—

Bunny was twice thrilled to see handcuffs emerge from where they'd been secured at his back by his belt.

Jackson took several steps back, then held up his hands, palms out, warding Joe off.

Elsie was back, just as breathless. "I can't reach them."

"What the hell do you mean, you can't reach them?" Jackson bellowed. "Security is always reachable!"

No answer to that. Elsie vaporized again.

Bunny recalled Bobby speaking to Ben Wink: ". . . something I'd like you to do . . ." Yeah. She smiled.

"This is ridiculous! I'm the chief counsel for D and D. I'm a lawyer, dammit! I know my rights!"

Arthur dropped a paper on the desk.

Jackson, eyes bulging more than any fish's, stared at the paper.

"Warrant. Search and seizure," said Arthur.

This—or, more likely, the handcuffs—brought Jackson out from behind the armor of his desk, objecting. "You can't do this!"

"Yes, we can," said Joe Blythe.

It was almost as wonderful as hearing Barack Obama repeat his political slogan.

As they moved in a wave toward the door of the office, where Elsie had returned, looking dazed, Jackson yelled at Boyd, "Get my lawyer!"

Boyd said, "I *am* your lawyer."

Jackson's voice came from the outer office. "Then get another one, goddammit!"

Bunny rushed to the outer office and looked out the door while Jackson was calling for his legal team all the way down the corridor.

From doors left and right, people were popping out as if on springs.

Bryce Reams, Sprague's associate, lounged in his own doorway, watching Jackson's departure with something less than despair and eating an Eskimo pie.

60

Cindy Sella dropped a few flakes of food into the new aquarium and waited for the two clown fish to corkscrew up and get it. They didn't. They kept touching the anemone, moving up to it and away from it, almost drunkenly.

She had purchased the tank that morning from a little fish-supply store in the East Village, and the owner had helped her carry it to a taxi. The cabdriver had not helped her get it out of the cab, but fortunately, Mickey was on duty and had carried the tank from the sidewalk up to her apartment. It wasn't terribly heavy, just awkward.

Now she was sitting on the bench beside Gus and looking at the clown fish and wondering if they liked their new place and all the extra room. They liked the new pink anemone.

Gus was off the bench and at her feet giving her his castaway look, as if he'd been stranded on a desert island and was waiting for someone to get him food. Anything, anything at all, a nice bit of foie gras, a clown fish, anything you hit upon . . .

He followed her into the kitchen, where she spooned out his favorite food from a new can. She put the dish on the floor. Gus sniffed. Then he thrust his tail in the air as if it were a ladder that she would never be capable of climbing and walked away.

Just be glad Lulu isn't your owner.

She returned to her chair, her notebook, and her computer, neither of which had seen any fresh writing. She wondered if Lulu was indeed her Waterloo and if she would ever finish *You Had Me at Good-bye*. She fiddled with a corner of the notebook page, turning it down and up and down and thinking about Joe Blythe, whom she hadn't heard from since the night he'd saved her. Literally saved her. And then came back here, and they'd had that hall party with Edward stopping by. That didn't mean Joe was interested in her, though. He'd have done the same thing for anyone in such a crisis.

Lulu, for instance.

If Joe Blythe had walked by Lulu's car and seen her sitting there with her head against the steering wheel, he'd have tapped on the window or yanked the door open. He'd have done something.

More, obviously, than Cindy was doing. She poked at a couple of keys on the computer with her index finger and wondered if Joe Blythe had gone, and where he'd gone, and what he did.

She wondered what he was doing right now, right this moment.

61

Jackson Sprague, free of his handcuffs but not of his insufferable in-house-lead-counsel overbearing facade, sat on one side of a plain deal table in a plain office thrown up as fast as a billboard along an L.A. free-way. This was on the first floor of Candy and Karl's converted warehouse on Houston. The floor had not been converted, so they were using it as the "temporary" Manhattan office of the Fish and Wildlife Service investigations team. That was lettered neatly in gold on a new-old door with pebble glass recently inserted into the doorframe. Its temporary furnishings included a large photograph of Barack Obama on one wall, an American flag standing by it; a couple of filing cabinets; a watercooler; and against another wall, a merciless quantity of tape-recording equipment and indications that this equipment had been manned recently by several people who had left personal belongings—scarves, sweaters—draped over chairs before departing.

"I'm lead counsel for New York's biggest publisher! Don't you understand? An attorney! I'm no rube; I'm no mere civilian you can shove around and not expect reprisals! I'll have your jobs!"

All of this was shouted out as if from Shirlee Murphee's manuscript pages, italicized and exclaimed to Joe Blythe, whose cool blue eyes looked at and then slid off the face of Jackson Sprague as if it were the blank wall behind him, the empty air around him.

"Mr. Sprague, sit down." Joe's hand on his shoulder saw to that.

Agents Morton and Pascoe (Arthur Mordred and Blaze Pascal) were sitting opposite Jackson Sprague.

Arthur leaned forward over the table. "The Bluefish Alliance. We've been after them for five years."

Jackson yelled again: "The what?"

Blaze said, "Illegal imports of exotic fish, a huge business. We think you know."

"I don't fucking know what you're talking about. And these are fish! *Fish!* Fucking aquarium fish, for God's sake. Why should you be dragging someone out of his office and down here because of *fish?*"

Arthur looked up at Joe Blythe, still standing, arms folded. Said Arthur, "He can't be that stupid."

Joe Blythe, blue eyes riveting Jackson Sprague to the back of his chair, arms braced on the table as he leaned in to him, said, "Your 'fucking aquarium fish' are as rare as red diamonds. We can put at least twelve fatal shootings in Manhattan down to these fish. So if you've got anything to share with us, do it now, Mr. Sprague, and stop jerking us around."

Jackson, nothing if not noisy, banged his fists on the table and nearly drowned the sound of the knock on the door.

Joe pulled it open and nodded to Graeme, who was wearing a suit for the occasion. "Agent."

Graeme ushered in Lena bint Musah. She stood there in one of her silky crimson dresses with a black stole stashed around her shoulders. Joe thanked her for coming. Jackson Sprague, whose back had been to the door, turned around when it opened, thus presenting his face to Lena.

"Is this him?" Joe asked her.

Lena carefully lit up one of her brown cigarettes, drew in, and blew out a curlicue of designer smoke. "Miles Mutton. Yes."

They all looked at Jackson, whose head swiveled from one to the other. "Who the hell is Miles Mutton?"

Lena exhaled another curl of smoke. "That would be you."

After many and sincere thanks from the Fish and Wildlife Service, Lena left.

If Jackson Sprague had grown any whiter and stiffer, they could have used him for stand-up collars. He was so aghast with disbelief that he was being taken for a trader in illegal fish, and that he was being misidentified as this Miles Mutton, he was, for once in his lawyerly life, speechless.

Boyd Lloyd was not. He demanded that this harassment of his client cease and desist immediately. He was ready to say tons more, except Joe Blythe cut him off with "Okay. He can go."

This left Boyd with unshared legal arguments that he didn't know what to do with.

Joe and Arthur helped the two of them by putting a hand under their elbows and lifting them to their feet.

"Just one thing, Mr. Sprague. You will not leave the country."

Jackson Sprague packed a bag and left the country.

This step was taken against all advice from Boyd Lloyd, who kept insisting that running would only make him appear guilty, and that there was no case against him that made any sense.

"Since when did the law have to make any sense?" After a quick call to Saad bin Saeed, one of the Dubai brothers, Jackson was off through TSA presecurity at JFK and on his Emirates flight to Singapore.

In Dubai, the Good-bye Boys needed someone to handle some off-shore accounts.

Bryce Reams moved into Jackson Sprague's office the same day Jackson took off for Singapore. Jackson didn't technically, physically, *leave* Dubai and Dodge, since he hadn't returned to clear out the office.

Bryce did it for him. One of the first things he did was to put in a call to the Good-bye Boys and, after he'd reached Saad bin Saeed, advised him that D and D drop the Cindy Sella business, as it was a legal quagmire.

Saeed's only comment was "Okay. Who is Cindy Sella?"

The second thing Bryce did was to make sure the fish were all right after their long and toxic exposure to Jackson Sprague. He had the professionals come in and reposition the aquarium on a wall that caught a little sunlight. He asked Bunny Fogg if they really had that weird disease and was happy when she said no.

The third thing he did was to install a small refrigerator with a little freezer, which he stocked with Eskimo pies.

It took him only half a day to do all of this (including the delivery of the fridge), which everybody agreed was a flat-out, all-time, NASCAR track record for a lawyer to take care of anything.

Everyone was happy, including the fish, whose colors brightened in the new sunlight.

62

In the seat beside Paul on the flight from JFK, Hess spent most of the time complaining. It was odd to Paul that such unscrupulous and unconscionable people could be so boring. One would think their lack of moral purchase might make them in some way fascinating. If Paul had to hear one more outcry from Hess that life was being beastly to him, Paul was willing to have Delta Flight #3701 go down in Graeme's fiber-optic flames.

The plane landed without incident at Pittsburgh International Airport, and they headed for the Enterprise desk.

"Why don't we just take a cab?" asked Bass.

"Too undependable. And would you want to stand on a corner hailing a cab after a séance?" Paul gave a dismissive laugh. "I sure wouldn't. Also, there's this four-star restaurant about three miles outside of Sewickley that everybody is raving about. Chef used to own Cecilia's on the Upper East Side. You've been there?"

"No."

Neither had Paul.

"Never heard of it."

Neither had Cecilia.

They dug around in the Enterprise lot and found the car, a standard Toyota Camry, and melted into the early-afternoon traffic, very light, Paul was pleased to note.

He thought it would be wise to get some food into Hess. As they advanced onto Interstate 376, he said, "Tell you what, I'm hungry as hell. You?" He said this to an unreceptive Hess.

There would be no place along the interstate, so Paul took the Moon exit. Five minutes later, as if by magic, right up ahead was a diner rising in its own shimmer of silver and heat. Ah! Diner life! Paul loved diners. They were so wonderfully transitory. Here and gone. Paul pulled in and braked.

Inside, it was no disappointment: booths with dark red Naugahyde, chrome and red vinyl counter stools, a Formica counter curving at both ends.

They took a booth, and the waitress, pleasant and run-down-looking, was there tout suite with menus big enough to hold a Dickens novel.

Paul ordered a double cheeseburger and fries, relishing L. Bass's look of displeasure.

"You'll drown in carbohydrates."

Paul added a side of onion rings.

Bass shivered. The menu held at least ten kinds of fish, all of it fried or otherwise cooked unsuitably. "I would like a piece of flounder, broiled."

The waitress looked squinty. "Boiled?"

"B-R-oiled. If you can't do that, then poached."

"Like an egg, you mean?"

Paul enjoyed this exchange.

Bass ordered boiled potatoes and peas to accompany his fish.

Paul wondered why he didn't carry those foods around with him—a few pounds of flounder, a bag of potatoes, unshucked peas and beans—and hand them over in eateries.

"Are you sure this woman is a bona fide psychic? A responsible medium?"

Responsible medium. Hell, anyone who could see those words in sequence could see the Red Sea parting along the ticker tape in Times Square.

"You bet she is," said Paul. He had already talked about the several times that he himself had made use of this psychic. How, at a séance two years before, he got the entire idea for his novel *Don't Go There*. This was a lie. Paul never got his ideas from anywhere but his own head.

When he told Hess once again what the venue was, the man once again was baffled. "Why would you hold a séance in the Andy Warhol Museum?"

"I wouldn't. She would."

With true diner speed, the waitress brought their orders. The fish had been broiled, and rather nicely.

"Look," said Paul, "you don't have to do this if it makes you uncomfortable."

Quickly, Bass changed his tune. "No, no. I do want to. You've made it sound very compelling."

No, he hadn't, thought Paul as he dug in to his big cheeseburger. He had gotten L. Bass to go along on this harebrained little journey in the same way one often gets people to go along—by telling him he couldn't.

"Sorry, Bass," he had said, "but these séances are limited to the few people who regularly attend them."

"Paul, you could talk her into accepting one more for just a single sitting. With *your* reputation? You must have influence."

"Anyway, you don't want to go to Pittsburgh—"

"For this I would. If this medium is as good as you say she is."

Paul shook his head. After a little more pleading and cajoling, he gave in gracefully.

Now, sitting in the diner, Paul said, "The reason for the Warhol Museum is that this medium, Madame de Museé, she's a huge believer in the power of Warhol to channel, you know, spirits. They channel."

Bass put down his fork full of peas. "They channel? What channels?" He looked full of disbelief.

"The paintings. Madame de Museé's connection to the other world— the spirit world—is channeled through Warhol's paintings. Especially *Double Elvis*. The *Double Elvis*, that's the real game changer." Paul shrugged. "But that's in MoMA. Now, the *Eleven Elvises* is in the Warhol, but for some reason she doesn't find that as, uh, big a draw for the spirits." He could have put it better, but never mind.

Bass flattened his palm against air like a crossing guard, as if rechanneling the two Elvises to another street corner. "You mean to say she holds all of her séances in the Warhol Museum?"

Paul dipped a fry in ketchup. "More or less."

"How in God's name did she get permission?" Bass moved his plate, and the peas rolled around.

Whoever asked for permission? "The museum had an extremely valuable painting stolen years ago. I can't think of the name. Or the painter.

Anyway, it was gone for two years. She found it." Paul chomped down on an onion ring and wished he had a few more artery-hardening dishes to choose from. He was planning on apple pie à la mode for dessert.

Lena bint Musah had found it extremely funny and agreed to play the part. "A masterly stroke," she said, and drank her espresso.

Said Candy, who knew Paul better, "It ain't masterly, Lena. It's motherfuckingly."

They had gathered in Lena's place a few hours after Paul's return from his initial Pittsburgh trip. They were smoking her brown cigarettes and drinking her coffee, which was so strong it could have bowled them down at the end of an alley.

"It means," said Paul, "that we can't do the ectoplasm thing; the girl guards would look on strange rising mists as suspicious. We won't be able to manifest in any way." He took a drag of his cigarette.

Karl left off smoking long enough to object. "Manifest? Manifest what in shit? You don't know what you're talking about, Paulie."

Lena smiled. "Oh, I think he does."

Paul grinned. He hardly ever knew what he was talking about. Maybe that was why his books were popular. There was always that element of surprise.

"I still don't see why you got a fuckin' art gallery," said Candy woozily.

"Because I couldn't get PNC Field. The Pirates have a home game."

The three of them laughed. "So when do we leave?" said Lena.

"Tomorrow," said Paul. "I go with Hess. You go on another flight."

So tomorrow was today.

For the second time, Paul checked in to the Renaissance Hotel. Bass could not stay at what he called the old manse, his childhood home, as it hadn't been lived in for years except by a couple of families who had rented it. He said to Paul it was probably nothing but broken beams and cobwebs. Paul wished he had known before; he bet he could have turned the old manse into a playground for L. Bass's already weakened mental state.

There was a bar on the other side of the lobby, and they headed for it.

It was dry-drunk Hess who did the heading. Paul followed happily along. He would have thought Bass to be just short of a teetotaler, given that the only thing he'd ever seen him drink was the cognac after the burning-bush incident and, yes, the chardonnay at the Gramercy Tavern. Paul was glad to see a limpness in the old Hess collar, but he needed to avoid a complete wilt-down, or even half a one. Paul didn't want L. Bass blaming what was to come on booze, as in: "Oh, no wonder I thought I saw . . . !"

Hess laid claim to a barstool as if it were a parcel of land in the old Cimarron Territory land rush. He ordered a double Hennessy and ate half the nuts in the dish.

Paul asked the bartender for what was on tap and came away with a Blackstrap stout. The wow factor was once again evident. Black as sin and with a head a good two inches thick. "You should try this, Bass."

"I hate beer."

He would.

63

Lena bint Musah was waiting for them in the lobby of the Warhol Museum.

She was wearing a dark gray pin-striped suit that so exactly fit the museum's pale walls and dark leather that the curator might have chosen it. That was the business end of her getup. Beyond that, it was all brass, from the curly wig to enough chunky jewelry to fill one of Ali Baba's urns. Hammered-gold hoop earrings, a couple of necklaces, several bracelets. She also wore large sunglasses. She was a completely different person. Paul wanted to applaud.

There were to be no introductions, Paul pointed out to L. Bass Hess. Madame de Museé had asked expressly that no names be mentioned at the outset. That was usually the case, wasn't it? As if he knew what was usually the case. And he'd forgotten to ask Lena exactly what the case was with séances. Then he remembered that this wasn't a séance and she wasn't a psychic. He glanced at her. She was taking it all with perfect equanimity.

So were Toby and Rebecca, he was pleased to see. They entered the lobby and walked up calmly to the other three and nodded as if silence were their business. Toby had heightened the Brando effect by wearing a worn leather jacket over his white T-shirt. Rebecca was her see-through self in her ethereal dress of scarves that seemed to be moving in different drafts across the lobby.

There were few patrons on the museum's first floor. The five of them filled the small slickly running elevator to the second floor, where there were even fewer people.

Lena bint Musah, or, rather, Madame de Museé, the name chosen by Lena (leading Paul to wonder, wasn't that French for "museum"?), had said nothing so far beyond a murmur to acknowledge the others' presence.

She paused outside the skull room (as Paul had fondly named it) and said to the gathering: "This is my choice for a venue, whenever I can arrange it." The accent was foreign but vaguely so. From a soft leather bag, she withdrew a small bronze sculpture of a pig. Its surface was as worn as Toby's jacket. "If you would be so kind as to hold this for a moment in your hands, each of you."

L. Bass was first. Half closing his eyes, he felt the pig, then passed it along. Oh, this was rich, thought Paul as Rebecca passed the little sculpture to him.

Then Lena nodded toward the white-parachute-silk-covered sofa with a familiarity that implied the odd piece might once have been situated in her own living room. "We will sit there, the five of us. We will not join hands, as it is unnecessary and would be exceedingly awkward." A slightly condescending smile played on her lips.

They trooped into the room. Hess seemed a little overcome by the surround of skulls. The two actors took it in with actorly calm.

"Do not be disturbed by the skulls, please. The art has nothing to do with death. If you know Warhol . . ."

You could've fooled me, Paul thought, looking at Lena with fresh amazement. Just tossing out whatever she felt like. Nor did she complete the "if you know" idea.

Lena had taken in the details of his plan in one long swallow. It was as if she'd been here before, done this before. He began to wonder if she did have psychic powers utterly unknown to the Frobishes and Gumms of the world.

She told each of them to have a seat on the big cloth-covered sponge, which Paul thought was large enough in notion if not in actuality to contain multitudes.

Whoooosh. Everyone sat down, Lena seeing to it that Hess sat near her. In low tones, she directed each of them to try to focus on the skull before him.

That was winging it, Paul thought delightedly. He hadn't specified that as a direction, but he followed it. He thoroughly enjoyed his minutes with the skull on the wall before him. It was a blend of seaweed green, a sort of van Gogh yellow, and a selection of faded reds. He thought at one point that its nonlips moved, but that might have come from spending too much time in the Gumm household.

He turned his head a fraction, enough to see that Hess was collapsed in an ungainly position, though it was hard to sit with dignity on the sponge.

Ten or fifteen seemingly uneventful minutes passed, after which Madame de Museé turned her head and said softly, "That will be all."

There was a general air of bewilderment as they extricated themselves from the sponge, Hess looking more irritated and agitated than bewildered. "That's all? But there was no communication, no message, nothing."

She ignored this comment and said, "One of you feels a grave injustice has been done."

Was she kidding? There were two actors present. Three hands shot up—no, four, when Paul raised his own.

"One of you is a fisherman," she went on, leaving grave injustice behind.

Here, L. Bass's was the single raised hand.

Lena drew him aside and, in a soft yet strangely carrying voice, said, "He sympathizes. What you seek is in the cage." She adjusted her dark glasses and turned away.

Leaving them there openmouthed, including the instigator of the deal, Paul.

"Well, there *is* a story by Henry James," Paul offered, but had to stop on the way out of the museum because Bass had stopped.

"Henry James? Henry *James*? What are you talking about?"

"A short story. 'In the Cage.' It's about—"

Blustering, Bass interrupted. "For God's sake, man, if it was my father she was talking about, he didn't *read*. What did she mean? What?"

"Dunno. Let's walk across the bridge, okay?" Paul hummed. He wished he could just push Hess in the river and take Lena bint Musah to dinner. That had been brilliant, brilliant!

"What could it mean?" Bass struck his balled-up fist into his other hand.

Don't ask me, bud. I've never been to Everglades City. Paul hummed and walked.

64

The five-star restaurant toward which L. Bass thought they were headed was as mythical as Camelot. Paul chewed his lip, wondering why he hadn't thought of working a little of that—King Arthur, Excalibur, the lake, whatever—into the mix.

They were driving along the part of the road where Montagne Cassino sat above them, bathed in moonlit benevolence. Paul wondered how much this effect was owing to expensive exterior lighting.

"Over there," said Paul casually, "is the monastery I told you about. Friend of mine is the abbot." He laughed softly. "Hard to believe, knowing him back in high school."

"The life of an oblat," said Bass Hess, craning his neck to look back at the abbey, "has something going for it. How did this friend of yours happen to wind up doing this?"

"Spiritual awakening. Very sudden. An epiphany, say, like Saint Paul . . . oh, sorry, didn't mean to go there again."

Hess did not respond.

It was country out here, tree-filled, with hills like hammocks. Not another soul, no other cars. The car ticked along with high beams unchallenged, with the occasional lurch over a pothole.

Paul's phone jerked around in his jacket pocket; that would be Molloy calling. This was the signal that the four of them were in place. A hundred feet on, he saw the WORK AHEAD sign beside the road. Paul had asked that a marker be put up in case he didn't recognize the turn before the hill.

In a hazy and uncertain illumination (uncertain because it had been made by Graeme, not God), Paul saw the four horses and four riders in a line atop the craggy hill. Three of the horses were dark, either black or brown; the fourth was dead white, a ghost of a horse.

The four riders wore dark capes with hoods. It was astonishingly dramatic.

"Stop!" yelled Bass.

Paul had all but crawled around the turn and now braked hard, pitching both of them forward. "Something wrong?"

Beside him, Bass Hess nearly went through the top of the car. "What's that?"

The thrust of his pointing finger almost gouged out Paul's eyeball. Paul turned to peer out his window and off to the hill. "What's what?"

Bass grabbed Paul's arm and looked at him in horror. "Horses, four of them. And four horsemen! You must see them!"

Paul squinted toward the hill and shook his head. "Maybe if I get out."

When he opened the door of the car, Bass pulled at him. "No! Don't get out!" The voice was near a shriek. "Don't you see them?"

"Okay, Bass, take it easy." Paul put his hand on the man's shoulder, gently pushing it down. "Head down, deep breaths, come on, now."

When Bass lowered his head between his knees, Paul clicked the high beams to low and back twice. He heard a dry sob coming from Bass.

The horsemen immediately turned their horses and, with a wave in Paul's direction, cantered off. "Nothing out there, absolutely nothing, Bass." He said this to the lowered head. "Look, I'm getting out, I'm climbing up that hill to show you—"

"No!" Bass sat up like a shot and looked past Paul out the driver's-side window. "Where are they? Where did they go?"

"Nowhere. There was nothing there in the first place." Paul had not turned off the engine, in case there was a need to muffle horses' hooves; the car was idling. Paul put it in gear, prepared to turn around. "Listen, I think we should head back. You need a drink. Some rest."

Bass had his fingers to his temples. "I can't believe I imagined that. I didn't *imagine* it. It was too vivid. I can't believe there was nothing there." The small sob suggested he could believe it.

As the car sped away from the site of the apocalypse, Paul said, "This could be another one of your epiphanies, Bass. You'll feel better after a good night's sleep. Then it might be wise for you to think of getting away—I mean, really getting away for a rest. And then, well, maybe talking to someone who can give you spiritual guidance."

Bass got a grip on his arm, almost making Paul lose control. "That monastery! That monastery. Don't monasteries have guest quarters? Guest quarters." Apparently he was going to say everything twice now that his spiritual self was overseeing things. "A retreat, a retreat. You know. Sanctuary. *The Magic Mountain.*" He had Paul's upper arm in a viselike grip.

How nice that he had brought up the monastery as a solution. Paul wrinkled his forehead. "I don't think you can just check in like it's a hotel." The grip on his arm was numbing his hand. Paul drove on.

"You could find out! Look, there it is!"

Damned if it wasn't. Paul smiled in the dark. As if reluctantly, he said, "I guess I could give them a call."

Bass's grip nearly tore his hand from his pocket as Paul tried to get to his cell phone.

"Don't call, don't call! They might say no. Let's just go there. Just drive!" Bass sank back against his seat. His posture said that here was a man who'd run his final mile.

"Okay," said Paul with a shrug.

In under ten minutes, they were pulling into the Montagne Cassino's parking area and getting out, crunching across the gravel to the huge front door. Paul was delighted that the iron door knocker crashed against the wood when he lifted and dropped it. It would wake the dead.

As they stood waiting, Paul said in a small-talkish way, "So you saw three horses and riders? Where do you suppose they were going?" Forgetting they were not supposed to exist, though it made no difference.

Acidly, Bass replied, "The apocalypse, Paul. You're not familiar with the horsemen?"

"Oh? I thought that was four horsemen."

"That's what I *saw*. I told you, *four*."

Paul nodded. "Right." He was glad that Hess retained something of his old condescending tone.

The little wooden door in the big wooden door slid open, revealing a face in a square of light. "Yes? May I help you?"

"Thank you. My name is Paul Giverney. This is Mr. Hess. We'd like a word with"—abbot? Paul couldn't say it—"Father, uh, Brother John? Del Santos? If we may?"

The monk (or kind of monk) opened the door and herded them into a hall that Paul remembered from his first visit. He wouldn't mind spending a few days here himself. It was so cool and so quiet.

"I'm Brother Francis. I'll just go and find the abbot." Brother Francis was off at a good clip, robe swinging behind him.

Paul looked around at the pleasant absence of things, of stuff, of accumulated rubbish, that everyone in Manhattan managed to position around themselves. Life was one big garage sale. There was no furniture here except a long wooden bench against one wall. He thought of his office, its cheaply chosen junk, the chairs and their chic tattiness. He and Molly and Hannah ate their Dean and Deluca dinners on wedding-gift Vilroy and Booth china. He sighed.

It was under two minutes before Johnny del Santos came lumbering down the empty hall, his steps echoing. "Paul Giverney, as I live and breathe!"

"Hello, Johnny." They shook hands. "This is Bass Hess, a friend of mine. Forgive this sudden intrusion."

"Don't mention it. Come on back to my office."

As soon as they sat down, Bass launched into a monologue on spiritual decline and possibly uprising. Johnny leaned across his desk and listened. That earnest look of concern, that empathy, that expression that told the speaker he was the only person on earth Johnny del Santos had any interest in—that was the quality that Paul marveled at.

At the end of this oration, in which Bass had omitted the alligator but made much of the burning bush, Johnny said, "Of course, you're welcome to stay here. But perhaps during the time that you're with us, you might consider becoming a Benedictine oblate."

For Bass, "oblate" was the game changer, the deal-maker, for he was repeating "of course, of course, yes, certainly" as if he wanted to get that understood in case speech deserted him altogether. His head was bobbing up and down like the little wooden bird on Bunny's desk, plucking at a raindrop of water when a finger sets it in motion.

"Wherein you take no vows, and when your time of preparation is through, you may go into the world and practice—you're familiar with the Rule of Benedict?"

Bass looked stupidly at Johnny.

"Never mind. If you choose to do this, you will learn it."

His mouth hanging slightly open, giving him a foolish look, Bass nodded again.

"You would be giving up your current life and attachments. Have you spoken to your family about this?" When Bass said no, Johnny went on. They decided that Bass would stay for an indefinite period but at least five or six months. Bass seemed almost thrilled, relieved beyond measure. He had a suitcase at the hotel which Paul said he would be glad to collect and bring back, but Bass said just to take it to New York.

"Yes," said Johnny, "it's really better to come stripped bare."

Depends if you're Bass Hess or a high-class hooker, thought Paul, studying his cuticles.

"Now, Bass, there are certain rules . . ."

Driving back to the hotel, Paul hummed, all the while thinking of the "rules" that he was sure Johnny had tailor-made for Bass Hess, the chief among them being that Bass would have to wind up business, put whatever was on his mind out of his mind, and generally set such conditions as would make a further assault upon Cindy Sella extremely difficult, if not downright impossible.

The next morning he had time to kill before his flight to New York, so he crossed the bridge again to visit the Warhol Museum. He stood in the doorway of the gallery with the parachute-covered sponge but did not go in. He wandered off to another gallery, a smallish one at the end. Here, beneath the ceiling, floated a mass of silver balloon-like pillows. Two little girls and a teenage boy were busy tapping and thumping the silver pillows up and away. They didn't mind or didn't notice an adult joining in.

This was so Warholian, thought Paul as he hit a silver cloud away from the girls, just as an older brother might do. They put on scowls and ganged up on this intruder, and sent the cloud he was reaching for out of his reach, just as a kid sister would.

———————

Paul stood on the Sixth Street Bridge and looked at the river. He had come down from the high of the previous evening and felt something that wasn't and yet resembled melancholy. Something was going out of his life. It was rather like leaning over the rail of a departing ship as it leaves a harbor, and finding oneself at that distance from shore where the lights of the land are barely distinguishable from the stars. It was the way he felt when he finished writing a book.

YOU HAD ME AT
GOOD-BYE

How long had she been sitting like this, her head bent over her hands on the typewriter? She sat up and looked at the clock. Only ten minutes, but it felt like hours. She was becoming Lulu.

She wondered if she was right about Lulu's seeming inability to feel anything about people or even things until they left her or she left them. That's what it looked like, with Lulu being so standoffish and stiff-arming people—that is, keeping them at arm's length.

Cindy stared at her. That is, stared at the page that Lulu was on. Cindy stared at Lulu's head, resting on her hands, her hands crossed on the steering wheel. Lulu sinking deeper and deeper into immobility.

Cindy felt more and more that she was losing her grip on Lulu.

Was Lulu the way she was because she couldn't stand losing people? No, it was more complicated: Lulu couldn't stand anything changing.

A knock on the door made her jump.

At this hour—ten-thirty, nearly. Edward. She checked to see if the bottle of Old Grand-Dad held enough for a few drinks. Yes.

She looked down at her smock. It was quite ugly; it was stained from the time she'd helped Rosa Parchment paint mirror frames. The last big button was missing. Edward wouldn't care, so she went to the door.

Joe Blythe looked at her smock. "That's attractive, too. Hi, Cindy." He smiled.

She shut her eyes as if that would keep him from seeing her. Then she opened them and said, "No, I've just been painting the bedroom. Hi."

He nodded. "Turquoise. It must be magnificent. Purple trim, maybe? I could use a drink. It's been a hell of an evening."

"Really? A drink? Absolutely. Of course." She was glad she'd checked the liquor level. She hurried to the kitchen, snatched up two glasses, and hurried back to the living room, where she poured a couple of fingers of Old Grand-Dad into each glass. Returning to the doorway, she poked one toward him. "Here."

"Thanks. Where's Edward?"

"Edward? Probably having coffee or something at Ray's."

"That coffee shop where I met you?" Joe leaned back against the wall and sipped his whiskey.

She nodded almost hysterically, as if there were no way she could overconfirm that it was the place where they'd met. She said, "I supposed you'd gone. Home."

"Gone? I wouldn't leave without saying good-bye."

"You wouldn't? Oh, of course you wouldn't." She made it sound quite casual, as if she had nothing invested in the moment. Then she leaned against the opposite wall and sipped her whiskey, too.

Looking down at his glass, he swirled the whiskey and said, "I was wondering—?"

"Oh?" Her voice cracked on the single syllable. She cleared it. "Oh, really?"

"Do you think we could go inside?"

Her eyes widened. My God, she'd done it again: kept him in the hall. "Of course, of course. I'm so sorry." She held out her arm, ushering him in.

"Don't be. I like the hallway."

She was right behind him to close the door to the bedroom so he wouldn't see it was just Calamity White. Joe sank down onto the sofa, and Gus slid from the bench, nosed around his feet, and glared up at him.

"What's your cat's name?"

"Gus." She sat down opposite him.

"Hi, Gus."

Glare.

Cindy got useful and picked up the Old Grand-Dad and poured another inch or so into his glass.

"Thanks. You remembered I don't like ice." He smiled.

She sat down, ran her hand through her hair, and shrugged slightly. "Of course." No, she hadn't. She just hadn't had time to dump out the ice tray. "Cheers." She tried to mirror that one-sided smile of his but imagined she merely looked like one of those crazy ladies in *Grey Gardens*. In this smock of hers. "So," she said, hoping she would be dead drunk in another ten seconds, "you haven't gone home."

"Nope. I wanted to see you."

Three seconds. Her stomach was somewhere around Gus's level, bunched at his feet. "Oh. I'm glad you did. I mean, I was hoping—" God. Listen to her. "How do you know Paul Giverney and the others? Like that redhead?"

Joe seemed to chew the side of his mouth a little bit. "Blaze? I don't know her."

Good. "But you were all at the Clownfish the other night with Candy and Karl and a man I'd never seen."

"Arthur. We were meeting about something."

"You know they're hit men, don't you?"

"Arthur and Blaze?"

Impatiently, she said, "*No.* Candy and Karl. They're contract killers."

"Really. I've known them for a long time. They're pretty nice guys."

"If you like hit men. Are you going back to see my awful ex-agent? If you do, can I go?"

Joe laughed. "He's gone."

She fell back against the soft cushion. "They killed him."

"No. He just left." Joe made a whooshing sound and flew his hand through the air. "Vamoosed. I think to Florida."

"Florida?"

"Um. He has a very rich aunt there. She wanted him to come and stay with her. He's her only heir. You bet he went."

"What about the Hess Agency?"

"I don't know, but I suppose he's turning that over to someone else. Ask Paul." He looked around the room. "This is really nice. You like Manhattan, I guess. Being a writer. I always found it too exotic. Surreal." He slid down in his seat and rested his head against the back of the sofa as if he meant to stay.

Perhaps she could cover him with the wool throw and then he would stay. Before she could do anything or think anything, he'd leaned over and picked up the Gissing book. "I've never read this. What's New Grub Street?"

"A street in London. Or it was in Dr. Johnson's day, in the eighteenth century. Later, it became a street of hack writers. Something to do with the new journalism. That's why Gissing called it *New Grub Street.* It was when writing for the market started, you know, commercializing fiction. It was all a little more complicated than I'm making it sound." She leaned over, as he had, and placed her fingers on the book. "The main character is a writer who can't make himself write for the marketplace. His name is Reardon. Maybe it's sentimental to feel sorry for him, but he's poor; he dies; his wife marries the friend, who's a big commercial writer."

"That's rotten, for sure." Joe leaned back again, sipped his whiskey. "You really love writing, don't you?"

Cindy looked up, astonished; appalled, almost. "No. I hate it. It's too hard."

He laughed. Then he finished off his drink as he rose in one swift motion. "I've got to go, Cindy."

"No!" She was swifter. "Not yet. I don't want you to." She was dangerously close to tears. Her voice was gravelly.

"Cindy—"

She couldn't help it; she threw her arms around him and planted her face against his neck. Just as suddenly, she took her arms away and stepped back. "I could go with you."

"I keep pigs. I throw knives. Do you want that?"

"I like pigs."

"You like knives?"

She tried to make out that it was nothing worthy of consideration. "Oh, come on, you're not always throwing knives."

"Candy and Karl aren't always shooting people, either."

"So now you're telling me you're a hit man?"

"No."

"Ha! I didn't think so. Anyway, I don't care."

He smiled. "Cindy, you don't need me."

How irritating. "Don't you tell me what I need. I hate it when people do that." She was so nervous that she was trying to tie the ends of her smock together. She stuck her thumb through the buttonhole at the bottom. "Don't tell me what I need."

He ignored that. "I don't think you need other people."

"What? I didn't say other people. I said you. I need you. You have the bluest eyes anyone has ever had."

He seemed to be thinking. "What about Steve McQueen?"

She stared. "Steve McQueen?"

"I'm exaggerating. Cindy, you've got what you need. You've got it. Your mind, your writing, your characters—"

Her mouth dropped open. She threw up her hands, or tried to. Her thumb was stuck in the buttonhole, so the smock came up with it. "Oh, now you've done it! Oh, boy, you have really done it now!" She got her hand free and snatched up her notebook. "My characters? Do you think for one bloody minute that this character is company for me?" She shook the notebook in his face. She wanted to throw it against the wall, but with the loose papers in it, she was afraid she'd never get them back in order, so she just slammed it down on the end table. "Lulu? You think Lulu's company?"

"Lulu?"

"Who does nothing but sit, sit, sit in her car! Nothing. Does that sound like company for a person?" She felt either tearing mad or about to dissolve in tears, she wasn't sure which. "Look at me! I'm hopeless. I can't ever plan for anything. I could have worn my red dress, but no, oh, no. I'm in this goddamned smock! And you think this is a life?"

"All right, then." He sat back down. "Get your stuff, and we can drive on up to the farm."

"What?"

"Just pack a bag and we can go."

She half-laughed. "Wait. You mean just like that?"

"Sure."

"Right now? Tonight?"

"Why not?"

"You're being awfully *positive* about it."

"I'm not. You are, though."

And there it was, right there. Right in her hand or right at her feet. The light fandango.

Cartwheels on the floor.

Ceiling flying away.

She stared at Joe.

At last he rose and said, "I didn't think so." Then he leaned down and kissed her, not terribly hard. "Come up to the farm sometime. I'll use you for target practice." He went to the door. "Bye, Cindy."

And he was gone, as if he'd never come.

She looked at the clown fish on their sofa of pink anemone, at Gus on the bench, at the notebook on the table, the pages on the desk, Lulu in the car.

They had her at good-bye.

66

Three months later

We can't exactly bolt him to a chair, Paul."

"I know you can't. I thought he'd last for six months, though. You don't think you can, ah, persuade him?"

Johnny del Santos laughed. "Like with enhanced interrogation? Look, even novitiates who've had serious encounters with the Almighty sometimes pack it in after their year is up, right?"

Paul sat in his office, feet on the desk, staring at the old familiar wallpaper that Molly had sweet-talked the management into letting her hang, promising they would remove it and repaint when they left. How many years ago had that been? Would they ever leave?

"Paul? You there?"

"Sorry. Do you think you could keep him there for, say, another week?"

"Sure. I could concoct all sorts of reasons. I'll tell you something, though. I can understand why you want this jerk out of people's lives. He's a real pain in the ass. I can't find anyone here who doesn't dislike him. Only one of the brothers found something positive in the experience: Brother Walter said that God sent him to test us. 'To test our patience,' he said. 'To test our humility.' God wouldn't be that cruel, I told Brother Walter."

Walter? Somehow that just didn't go with "Brother."

"Brother Walter is without doubt the most humble person in the place, and he said he discovered his own humility was false. False! I said, 'That's impossible, Walt. Of all of us, you're the first out of the gate in humility.' I'd make book on that."

And damned well probably had, thought Paul. Johnny had always been addicted to gambling. Paul smiled. Vegas had been heaven to Johnny del Santos. Probably still was. "Brother Walter sounds like a real Christian."

"Well, this is a monastery, more or less."

"Johnny, 'more or less' just doesn't do it for me. And aren't you supposed to be the model for Brother Walter to follow? Sounds like he's a lot more humble than you."

"Me, the model for behavior? Since when?"

Paul held his phone away from his ear and looked at it: Was he hearing correctly? He brought it back to his ear. "Since you had that place built or restored or whatever the hell you did. You're the leader. Or whatever. You're making me stray from the point. So what's Hess's trouble? What's he complaining about?"

"The food, the menial work he's forced to do, the lack of entertainment. He roared into my office several days ago and said he was the victim of a giant scam, a huge swindle. He swears you tricked him into entering the monastery. I argued that nobody could make him do it against his will, that it had been his decision, the result of the visions he'd had, and blah blah blah, but he kept on about it. Somehow it was *you* who managed to set that bush on fire; *you* engineered that appearance at the junkyard of the woman in white; *you* plotted to get those horses up on that hill." Johnny was laughing. "You never told me about the alligator, Paul. The Everglades gig. Damn, but I wish I'd witnessed that. There's witness worth bearing. How the hell did you manage it?"

"I couldn't have done it without the help of some extremely talented people."

"Plus an alligator." Johnny was laughing again.

The meeting was held once again in Bobby Mackenzie's office. The same people: Candy and Karl, Clive Esterhaus, Bobby and Paul.

The only thing different was the brand of Scotch, a single-malt Benromach, like the Talisker, from the Isle of Islay (pronounced "Eye-la," said Bobby, but nobody believed him).

"So the son of a bitch gets to come back and pick up his life," said Candy testily. He tossed back a large swig of whiskey.

"We got Cindy Sella squared away okay, and that's the main thing," said Karl.

Sad to say, Paul reflected, it wasn't. He'd almost forgotten about Cindy Sella along the way. The purpose of the mission had become the mission itself.

"Hess must have lost his clients when he shut down so suddenly. What's he coming back to?" said Clive.

"Hell, he's an agent, isn't he? He'll find new ones. Even if he has to bottom-feed. Out there"—Bobby swept his arm in the general direction of the window overlooking Madison—"there's some innocent, misguided debut novelist who doesn't know shit about publishing or agents or anything. L. Bass will probably ask for a twenty percent com—"

Bobby Mackenzie suddenly stopped talking and slammed down his tumbler of Benromach. He said, "I've got it! I know what we can do to completely neutralize the bastard!"

"What?" said Paul.

"What?" said Clive.

"What?" said Candy.

"What?" said Karl.

Bobby gulped down his Scotch and looked about to shake hands with himself but only rubbed the hands together gleefully. This pause was not meant to keep them on the edge of their seats but simply owing to his sheer delight in the plan. "The room down the hall."

There was a brief silence into which Clive said, "The library?"

Bobby nodded. "The library."

Everyone looked at everyone else, puzzled.

Paul Giverney started laughing. "Oh, that's great, Bobby. I love it."

Bobby got up, started for the door, and waved them to follow. "Come on, come on."

"We have a week to set this up, Bobby," said Paul, getting up. "That's how long del Santos can stall him at the monastery."

In the outer office, Bobby stopped by Dolly's desk. "He'll be opening up his office, so he'll need a secretary. He fired Stephanie. Dolly—"

Dolly looked at him with round eyes. "What?"

"Go find Bunny Fogg for me."

The five of them continued on their way to the room down the hall.

67

B ass Hess rarely sauntered, preferring a brisker, more no-nonsense gait.

Today, however, he sauntered down Broadway, then continued to saunter along Twenty-third, the way to his old familiar office building where his office was still his office, the rent having been paid until the middle of the present year in exchange for a lower rent. The building's cleaning service wasn't aware that no one was using the office and continued to clean it. Bass chortled at the thought of free cleaning.

Thus, nothing would be changed except the absence of his former receptionist, Stephanie, but he'd never liked her much anyway, had found her to be a silly, self-involved person.

The first thing he saw when he unlocked the door was the poster of Cindy Sella among the blow-ups of his clients.

Cindy Sella. Did she really think she'd get away with it? Did she think he'd dropped the matter? Just wait until the fresh brief landed in her doorway in the hands of a process server. He had spent the last month in the monastery reworking it. Every day he was supposed to be in the monastery garden weeding, hoeing, or plucking up lettuces, he was out there with his notebook and pen.

He looked at the dust-jacket blow-ups of his clients' faces. Some had hired new agents; he hadn't made any attempt to contact them. Now he walked slowly past their photographs and past the shelves of books he'd agented. He looked fondly even at Mia Pennyroyale, ghastly as she and her books were. For the most part, they weren't books he'd want to have to read twice. He hadn't wanted to read Creek Dawson even once. All of that sage and limitless land and horse shit. But he was too eager for their fat commissions to trouble himself about quality.

Indeed, the only books that were worth his time—and how it pained him to say it—were Cindy Sella's. Which only made him want to strangle her all the more. How dare she walk out on him? Who did she think she was to leave the Hess Agency? It was with great effort that he drove her treasonable departure out of his mind.

But the restarting of his life as one of New York's premier agents blotted out the face of Cindy Sella, and he strode to the door of his inner office.

And stopped dead.

Stepped back, then forward again.

What in God's name had happened here?

What had been his walls of books were now walls full of stacks of paper. The hundreds of books that had rested on those shelves! Who had packed them up? Why? And what was that aquarium doing on a shelf between these stacks of paper?

Clearly, someone had come in and leased the space.

In a kind of stupor, he crossed the room, past the leather sofas, the coffee table.

The books that had lined these shelves had been separated and marked by genre, with small brass plates bearing the title "Mystery," "Western," "Science Fiction," and so forth. The stacks of paper (which he was still afraid to look at) were also separated by genre, but there were additions: "Romance," "Teen," "Tween." *Tween,* dear God, what was that? He was sweating profusely. This must be a dream, a nightmare; he must be back in his cell-like room on the narrow bed at the monastery.

To hold some awful reality at bay, he quickly ran to his desk and grabbed the phone. The service hadn't been cut off. He hit the digits for the Big Applebaum Management Company.

"No, sir, no one has been in your office that we know of. No, we didn't sublease the space."

"Where's Applebaum? I insist on speaking to him. He must know something about this mess!"

"I'm sorry, Mr. Hess, but Mr. Applebaum is out of town."

Hess slammed down the receiver.

"I feel like fucking Popeye," said Karl, who'd been leaning against the side of a deli.

Bobby Mackenzie pushed away from the building. "Ratso Rizzo, that's who I feel like, following you around."

Karl was now leaning through the passenger window of the SUV where the others sat. Candy and Paul just looked at him, uncomprehending. "Popeye?"

"*The French Connection,* Gene Hackman and his partner across the street from the hotel." Seeing their expressions, three people acting as if they'd never set foot in a moviehouse, he slapped the car and said, "Fuck, never mind."

Joe Blythe was never-minding behind Leica Duovid binoculars. They had been passing them around since Joe had picked out Hess walking up the street toward his building. They were sitting in Joe's Land Rover, which he said was handy to haul feed for the pigs and other farm stuff.

"He's on the phone," said Joe.

"Who'd he be calling?"

"Cops?" Joe smiled.

"*Publishers Weekly,*" said Karl with a snicker.

"Anyway, he's in his office, so he's seen everything. Let's go."

They all piled out of the Land Rover, except Karl, who was already out. Taking their lives in their hands, they crossed Twenty-third Street as the light turned green and the tsunami of yellow cabs made for them.

68

What he feared was, of course, all too true.

The shelves were full of manuscripts. How in God's name they had gotten there, and what did it mean? It had to be that bastard Paul Giverney! That snake in the grass, that—

L. Bass made a fist of one hand and slammed it into the other, which hurt like hell.

He was about to pick up a manuscript from the top of one stack when he heard voices. He hadn't locked the door behind him, and the owners of the voices were walking through the outer office toward the inner.

Paul Giverney and Bobby Mackenzie walked in, stood, and smiled. "Hello, Bass," said Paul, who was carrying a couple of big brown envelopes.

"You—!" What would have followed was cut off by the entrance of Candy, Karl, and Joe Blythe.

Hess looked as if he'd just been shot but was stubbornly standing.

Joe smiled and took a seat on the corner of the desk. The same corner he'd sat on before.

"Where are my books?" Bass fastened on Paul. He knew the books were the least of his worries. He just wanted to stave off the most.

"Don't worry. They're safely in storage. We made sure the movers were careful."

Karl and Bobby were lounging on the leather love seats.

Candy stood at the aquarium, inspecting the fish. A brilliant yellow tang, some really smashing angelfish—a platinum, a veiled black, one with a tiger design—and a couple of clown fish. "You like your fish, Bass. We figured it would brighten up the place."

"I hate fish." Bass drew himself up as much as he could and said, "I'm calling security." He was reluctant to make a move toward the phone, since Joe Blythe was sitting by it.

"Why bother?" said Paul. "We'll be out of here as soon as we explain things." He went on: "All of these manuscripts. We assume your old clients will have gone looking for a new agent, except maybe that cowboy, what's his name? Creek? That sounds authentic."

"Yeah," said Candy, turning from the aquarium. "We heard even ol' Dwight Staines jumped ship. That must be a hell of a commission lost."

"So you'll be looking for new clients." Paul nodded toward the shelves.

"What? You think I'm going to read these stacks of paper?" Bass's contemptuous tone wasn't convincing. "This *slush*?"

"Ah," said Bobby. "Music to my ears."

"Sure you will," said Paul. "Because there's nothing else to read here." He walked over to the shelf, pulled out a manuscript. "Here's a memoir. *On Your Toes*. Writer used to be a ballerina with the Austin City Ballet. Sounds promising, doesn't it?"

Hess squinted his eyes shut. "You're insane if you think I'm going to waste my time on this fodder."

As if he hadn't spoken at all, Bobby Mackenzie said, "What you'll be looking for is some new writer who might just be the next Salinger or Updike or Thomas Harris."

Bass gave a bark of laughter. "You think in that pile of slush—"

"Ah, but that's the point," said Bobby. "There used to be slush piles; assistants were paid to go through manuscripts, and a writer could actually wrap one up and send it in, unagented. Occasionally, one of the readers would send a manuscript worthy of notice to an editor. It might've turned out to be *The Catcher in the Rye* or *Catch-22* or maybe another *Silence of the Lambs*. That didn't happen often, true, but how often does it have to happen to make it worth your while? Now, with all of the crap that's out there, unstrained and unsieved, you could say; stuff that's never come under the cold eye of an editor or the restraining hand of a publisher, that'll publish for a price; that or some of the self-published swill I see—is there anyone more arrogant than a bad writer?—there'll come a time when, after we've all been forced to read that stuff for so long, we wouldn't know the next Salinger if we fell over him. So go on,

Bass, find him. Find *it*. The next big thing, the next great novel. It's there somewhere." Bobby stopped and lit a cigar.

The face of L. Bass Hess had been flashing pink and going pale like a neon sign. Blood suffused his face and drained away. He was being lectured by one of the most arrogant, amoral, powerful sons of bitches in the industry. "You think I'm going to take orders from you, Mackenzie?"

Bobby shrugged, exhaled a bale of smoke. "From all of us. Yeah, I do."

Bass grunted. Then he picked up his jacket and put it on. To give him credit, he also picked up his briefcase, as one does if one intends to leave the scene. "I'll be going now. Before I go to the police, I suggest you get rid of this pig's breakfast of—"

Wrong word. Wrong, *wrong* word.

There was barely a movement before the air whistled by Hess's ear and the knife landed directly behind him, vibrating where its point had hit the wood shelf.

Bass yelled, jumped back, felt the top of his head. Bloodless.

Joe Blythe smiled pleasantly.

Karl said, "I think maybe what Joe's trying to tell you is your work-day's not over. It's hardly noon, so you might just as well put down the briefcase."

In the midst of this drama, Paul had walked over to the right-hand wall, picked up a random manuscript, leafed through it for five seconds, and said, "This looks promising. *A Lock and a Hard Place*. It's about a safecracker. Don't you just love the punning titles they think up these days?" He dropped it back on the pile. He removed the contents of the brown envelopes and stacked those pages on top of yet another stack. "Clive thought you'd get a kick out of this." He smiled.

Ignoring Clive's offering, Hess said, "How am I supposed to give time to my clients if it's all to be used up in reading this pig"—quickly, he glanced at Joe Blythe—"I mean horse shit?"

"You won't be, will you? I mean, there's just Creek Dawson and that crazy woman, Myra or Mia. You won't be bothering with new clients."

If he could look any more disconcerted, Bass did. "What?" He started to move from behind his desk, saw Joe had returned to sit on it, and stopped moving. "I'm supposed to read this *entire wall* of junk scripts?"

Paul shoved away from the shelves, having positioned *Robot Redux* second down on the second shelf over. Not obviously on top nor deeply buried. "No, we're not unreasonable."

"Ha!" Bass sneered again, as much as a sneer as he could muster with Joe on the corner of his desk, playing with a letter opener.

Bobby ignored the sneer. "Not all of them, Bass. The deal is, after you manage to sell, say, six or seven of these manuscripts to reputable New York publishers like me"—he flashed a grin—"you're off the hook."

Bass sent his arm in such a wide arc that it looked meant to take in the whole wide world. "Are you mad? Sell? *Sell* this tripe! These have already been tossed in the can, and probably more than once."

"No, no. A lot of them have just been passed over. Some have probably never been read. Most have been read by some benighted editorial assistant and then been put on the reject pile. Some might have gotten to an editor and then been rejected. Hell, Bass, in all that slush, there could be the Great American Novel." Bobby relit his cigar.

Before Bass could answer, the door to the outer office opened, and footsteps proceeded to the inner. Bunny Fogg looked in and smiled. "Sorry I'm late."

"Bunny, come in." Bobby said to Hess, "Your new secretary. We know you'll want to send out rejection letters to most of these." He waved his arm at the shelves. "Bunny is very good; she takes dictation at the speed of light. She might even agree to look at some of these manuscripts herself."

Hess was staring at Bunny Fogg. It was the narrowed look of a suspicious man.

Paul had told Bunny to make sure she wore white today. ("Today and every day. White. If you need more white outfits, go to Saks and Bloomingdale's and send me the bill.")

"Don't I know you?" said Bass, narrow-eyed. "You look familiar."

"I've been with Mackenzie-Haack for years. Probably you've seen me there, Mr. Hess."

Bobby said, "Bunny will keep you on your toes. You know, in case you get distracted." His smile was wolfish.

"So she's the watchdog, is that it?"

Bunny's expression was one of innocence; hurt, almost. "Not me, Mr. Hess. But I can probably help you prioritize those manuscripts."

Bass let out a contemptuous sniff.

"You guys ready?" said Bobby.

They all got up.

Except Candy, who was already up, and to whom L. Bass was paying no attention, as he had been simply hanging around the aquarium. He was not engaged in threats or knife-throwing. "Never knew there was so many kinds of angelfish," he said to no one in particular. "You got some nice fish in there, Bass."

Bass threw him a lethal look and said nothing. He had nothing more to say. As they filed out, each gave Bass a smile and a thumbs-up. Candy patted the side of the tank, dribbled his fingers along it in a good-bye wave.

Oscar did not favor him with a good-bye fin.

THE REST IS (ALMOST) SILENCE

One week later

The FWS burst into the paper-strewn offices of the Hess Literary Agency and presented L. Bass with a warrant, claiming he was in possession of the endangered peppermint angelfish.

Agent Pasco (the redhead) deftly removed the so-called peppermint angelfish from the aquarium and deposited him into a cute little fish hotel.

They left with L. Bass Hess in custody.

Hess, without legal counsel, sat in the Fish and Wildlife Service's office on Houston Street with Agents Pasco, Morton, and Graeme, voicing his outrage about the illegality of all of this, claiming the fish had been placed in his office without his knowledge—

Whereupon Agent Pasco gave a snort of derision while she placed the rescued fish in her large tote bag. "They always say that, don't they?"

Within the hour, another FWS agent, Agent Molloy, came to the door and was admitted together with a dark-haired woman in red, who lit up a thin brown cigarette and looked at L. Bass Hess. She nodded. "Yes, this is the one. This is Miles Mutton."

One month later

Clive Esterhaus paid a visit to Simone Simmons and learned that her nephew, L. Bass, had been rushed to the ER to get twenty-five stitches in his hand following Jasper's attack after Bass thrust his hand into the birdcage.

"God knows what the man was doing."

"God knows," said Clive.

Simone was making fresh changes to her will, leaving the bulk of her money to Friends of the Everglades and the Everglades Foundation, and her cottage to her houseboy, Bolly. "I can't trust Bass to take care of anything. He seems completely mad."

As they drove toward Naples and the same little restaurant, Clive told her the disposition of her fortune sounded like an excellent idea, with Clive earnestly hoping he had not walked himself into the sequel of *Some Like It Hot*.

"Incidentally, Simone, just what does that L stand for? What's Bass's first name?"

"His father was a bass fisherman, after all."

Clive waited. Nothing further. "And?" he prompted.

"You mean you haven't worked that out?" She gave a sniffy laugh over the top of her commuter-cup martini.

One year later

1.

Robot Redux was fast-tracked through publication by the venerable house of Swinedale and became a *TBR* instant bestseller. This took the publishing world by storm and left speechless a dozen publishers who had turned down the submission. Sam Driscoll, Swinedale's publicity director, laughed. "This wasn't exactly searching for a bestselling book in a dark alley on a moonless night, was it? I mean, not if you know the market."

"Sure. Everybody knows the market after it happens," said Mackenzie-Haack's publisher, Bobby Mackenzie.

Suzie Moon, Swinedale's executive publisher, was, according to *Publishers Weekly,* "a visionary who predicted the collapse of vampire-themed books and the rise of robots. Said Ms. Moon with a wicked smile, 'Bots are big.'"

Bub Biggins, the author of *Robot Redux,* is at work on the next book in his Robot series and is still employed at Gio's Auto Salvage. He has no plans to quit. According to Gio Beauchamp, owner of the auto salvage yard, his business has quadrupled since the publication of *Robot.* "This is one real guy; Bub ain't changed one friggin' bit in spite of all his success."

2.

L. Bass Hess sued Bub Biggins for the commission he claimed was owing for *Robot Redux*. Biggins's attorneys stated in a countersuit that, since Hess did not agent the book, he would not be entitled to a commission.

Judge Owen Oglethorpe ruled in Biggins's favor.

"I will appeal," said Hess.

3.

Another surprise success, this in the nonfiction field, was the e-book *Silence, All: Where Shakespeare Went Wrong*, by Shirlee Murphee. One of the new Basic Classics line, *Silence* has gained a surprisingly hefty readership among high school students, explaining, as it does, in simple prose exactly how Shakespeare failed to establish the reason for Hamlet's delay. (Ms. Murphee generously acknowledged a debt to T. S. Eliot in this regard. She was also quick to point out "where Eliot went wrong.")

4.

L. Bass Hess sued Shirlee Murphee for a finder's fee for *Silence, All*, claiming that the so-called nonfiction book was a thinly disguised work of fiction by this author originally titled *How (Very) Happy We (Never) Were*, that title having been changed to *The Rest Is (Almost) Silence*. This former fictional treatment had been "found" by the Hess Agency.

Judge Carolee Menekee ruled in favor of Shirlee Murphee, saying that in her judgment, even if the agency were correct, Ms. Murphee had every right to turn her fiction into nonfiction and that, as nonfiction, it was a completely new book with which the Hess Agency had no connection.

5.

The real surprise of the publishing season, hitting stores fast on the heels of *Robbie* (a name affectionately applied to the Bub Biggins bestseller), was The Skunk Ape Trilogy by Donny Thugz. Skunk Ape was published by the new and forward-looking Humpback House publishers, whose innovative CEO took the book on and turned it into three dioramas with more than two hundred moving parts.

The most popular volume of the three-part book is Volume II, which features an alligator cave where the Skunk Ape (as legend has it) likes to rest. The player can move into the cave a number of little cardboard tourists who are searching for the Skunk Ape. Whether the tourists come out of the cave, or in what condition they exit, is up to the player. (To assist the players, extra little tourists are supplied in various stages of dismemberment.)

The Skunk Ape Trilogy has been a complete and utter smash with children of all ages. When Donny Thugz did his book signing at Barnes & Noble, the store was mobbed. All of the bookstores where Donny appeared on his whirlwind tour were bursting at the seams with wildly enthusiastic kids.

For the first time in Barnes & Noble's book-signing history, there were protestors—also children—out on the pavement, most carrying placards put out by the recently formed SKUNKBUNK movement. A number of children were interviewed, both Donny devotees and SKUNKBUNKers. "Terrific," "awesome," "coolest of the cool," "hugs to Thugz," raved Mr. Thugz's fans. "Crap," "derivative," "godawful," "stink-o" were comments coming from the SKUNKBUNKers.

Two of these children were definitely neither fans of the trilogy nor members of the SKUNKBUNK movement. The Hollander-Trump brothers were leaning against the B&N window watching the procedure. Nodding toward the enormous window display, the twelve-year-old said, "Flash in the pan." He added wryly, "Like life." He was carrying a much thumbed and dog-eared copy of DeLillo's *White Noise*.

The younger of the Hollander-Trump brothers claimed to have "read" (air quotes his) this three-part "phenome," or, as he sardonically put it, "Tried passing it off as my one-book-per-week assignment. Three volumes? That should have been good for three weeks. Dad didn't buy it." He rocked his hand by way of illustrating his comment: "But I'll work it, no sweat." Under his arm was *The Art of the Deal*.

6.

The Hess Agency sued Donny Thugz for a discovery fee, claiming that Mr. Hess had spent a great deal of time on The Skunk Ape Trilogy and was himself responsible for it being brought to the attention of Humpback House.

In a surprising move by Judge Owen Oglethorpe, the case was not merely dismissed but banished. Judge Oglethorpe was heard to say in chambers with the plaintiff, "This better be the last ******* time I see you, Hess."

7.

Paul Giverney was sitting rather listlessly in his office when Hannah walked in and placed a document on his desk. She said, "It's still part of *The Hunted Gardens*. It's got a different title because it's a squidway." Hannah walked out.

Paul thought he had misheard. "What in hell's a squidway?" he asked Molly, who had appeared in the doorway in her apron.

"She asked me what you called it when your story went off on another path. I said that's called a 'segue.' Dinner's ready in five minutes." Molly walked off.

Paul picked up the squidway. It was seven pages long. The title page read:

THE RHINESTONE
By Hannah W. Collins
The First Dragon Mystery Ever Written

"You go, girl," said Paul, turning to the first page.

8.

The book that did not make it to the *New York Times* bestseller list was *You Had Me at Good-bye*. The novel was published, however, to great critical acclaim and rave reviews.

Cindy Sella, who had never expected her novel to sell even as well as it did, was perfectly content. Her contentment was owing less to the great reviews than to the miniature pig she had purchased from a sleazy sidewalk pet vendor. She had bought the pig to take to upstate New York but had found it increasingly difficult to part with. She named it Herman and marveled at its ability to use a litter box. Herman sat with Gus on the bench and watched the (still nameless) clown fish lounge on their bed of pink anemone.

Cindy goes often to the Clownfish Café and talks to Frankie and eats the same spaghetti dish she was eating when two hoods came in, hidden in coats, and shot up the aquarium.

She does not need to text or tweet or take pictures.

Cindy remembers.

9.

Candy talks about maybe entering Oscar in a contest.

"Contest? Fuck's sake. What kind of contest is there for fish?"

"There ought to be some endurance contest, something like that. After what he's been through."

Karl shakes his head and tries to snap *Publishers Weekly* to show his impatience. "So you line up a bunch of fish, shoot a gun in the air, and shout, 'Go!'"

"You think you know everything about fish, right? The way of all fish, you think you know all that?"

Karl snaps *Publishers Weekly* again, or tries to. "I just know the way of that fuckin' fish, is all."

Oscar hangs out in his little Hotel W.

Oscar endures.